THE
FALSE
QUEEN

THE FALSE QUEEN

Copyright © 2024 by Meg Humble.

All rights reserved. Printed in the United Kingdom. No part of this book may be used or reproduced in any manner whatsoever without written permission except in the case of brief quotations embodied in critical articles or reviews.

This book is a work of fiction. Names, characters, businesses, organisations, places, events and incidents either are the product of the author's imagination or are used fictitiously. Any resemblance to actual persons, living or dead, events, or locales is entirely coincidental.

For information contact:

meg@meghumbleauthor.co.uk

https://www.meghumbleauthor.co.uk/

Cover design by Wonderporium Ink.

ISBN: 978-1-0687748-0-5

First Edition: October 2024

10 9 8 7 6 5 4 3 2 1

THE FALSE QUEEN

A CURSED QUEEN NOVEL

MEG HUMBLE

For my husband.
Who taught me that happily ever afters don't have to be make believe.

Chapter 1

I SPUN ON MY HEELS, green skirt billowing behind me as I danced around a patch of flat earth between the tall firs of the Iron Woods. My opponent lunged, her sharp sword slicing through the air with vigour, forcing me to block quickly. Arm quivering with impact, I gritted my teeth against the urge to drop my blade.

Drop it and you're dead.

Agnes the Wicked, most powerful witch on the continent, wouldn't hesitate. Her strikes were too powerful. Too sure. It wouldn't matter that I was her daughter. If I failed, it would be because I was not good enough to survive, and that would be my own fault.

'You're not concentrating,' Agnes scolded as she spun away.

I almost sighed with the relief on my tired limbs. We'd been at this for hours. We were *always* at this for hours. I had been perfecting this dance of weapons since I was twelve years old. I had mastered the art, but I would never be as ruthless, as quick, or as brutal as my mother because, unlike her, *I* was human.

Trained to be a weapon, an assassin, a tool in a power struggle with humans, I'd always questioned why I was born different from the rest of my coven. I'd soon become tired of asking questions no one could answer, and tried to accept that my fate was never to possess magic. Instead, I would be the human spy for my mother, to be deployed when needed in order to bring about a time where witches could be free. Free to live amongst humans as they once did – until the humans had gotten greedy and tried to assert their dominance over the witches in the Cursed Wars. After that, the humans became too populous to be overrun, forcing witches into hiding.

I barely had time to breathe before Agnes was on the attack again. Our swords clanged together in a scream of metal on metal, and I bounced out of her way, panting as she circled me.

'Your mind is elsewhere, Blaise. If you do not concentrate on the battle in front of you, you will die.' She followed my gaze as I glanced sideways to where my sisters trained, sparks flying around their half of the training field. Bright and bullish, magic erupted from Marbella's hands towards Ophelia's chest. The latter dove to the floor just in time, muddying her skirts but avoiding serious injury.

'You must learn to defend, Ophelia,' Gaia, my mother's general, scolded as Marbella cast another spell. This one hit Ophelia before she could dart out of the way. She let out a winded moan as she rolled sideways. Marbella's victorious smirk made the hairs on my arms stand to attention, reacting to the danger that lurked in that predatory smile.

'The time for envying your sisters has passed,' Agnes's words cut through my thoughts, drawing my attention back to her. 'We have trained long and hard to make you a weapon in your own right. Magic or not. You will not be powerless without it. I will not allow it.' She sprang at me. My blade bounced off her padded corset before she elbowed me back, lifting her knee, once, twice to my stomach, winding me. I fell backwards and she caught me before I could land on the hardening autumn floor.

'There's no magic that runs through my veins,' I hissed between deep gulps of air, resentment stinging almost as much as the rattle in my lungs. No matter how much I trained, I would never be able to match Agnes for pace. Her limbs were longer than mine, her stamina seemingly infinite. Dropping my sword, I hurled a throwing dagger at Agnes's head. She merely swept it aside with a spell and leapt away, the sharp metal sticking in a tree behind her.

'You do not know what the Mother has in store for you,' she offered, before I could protest at her cheating. 'That is why you have days to study the theory of magic. But today is not one of them. Today you concentrate on your own lesson.' A lesson my sisters would never need to learn because they would always have magic to use in battle.

It would have been one thing for the Mother – the first witch turned goddess, responsible for gifting magic to all enchantresses – to never bestow her magic onto me, but she had also given me no distinguishable traits of beauty that witches beheld, making it clear that I was human from the moment I was born. Something, as far as I had been told, had never happened before.

There was no hiding how I stood out amongst the witches of the Sunseeker coven and, whilst they would never harm me, or face my mother's wrath, they didn't welcome me either. I hadn't even so much as inherited the extra knuckle all witches possessed, making their hands graceful and long, perfect for conducting spells. Nor my mother's golden hair. I was born plain. My hair a dull and lifeless brown, eyes a simple hazel, versus my sisters, who inherited Agnes's golden locks *and* her magic. It wasn't fair. It also wasn't the first time we'd had this conversation.

'Daughter mine,' Agnes began, letting her sword hang by her side, 'there is always a chance you will come into magic. It is not long until your nineteenth birthday. Perhaps you will get to perform the Rite, after all.' I blanched at her words. The Rite was a coming-of-age celebration when a witch came into her full powers, and said witch was required to make a sacrifice.

A *human* sacrifice.

The ceremony demanded that the witch drank the blood of a human. Though some acquired a taste for it, human blood was not a necessary part of a witch's daily diet. As a human, the thought of having to perform the Rite myself made a cold sweat run down my spine.

But I *would* have done it, if it would give me the powers my sisters were about to inherit. Knowing it wouldn't had once made me sob for days as a small child. Agnes had finally sat me down to explain what I had already begun to piece together about how different I was. I'd always known how unlike everyone else I looked, how I couldn't do the things they could. I'd felt both fear, and a quiet sense of understanding, when she'd explained how I was the very thing that I had already been taught to hate from such a young age.

Human.

After that, when my sisters went off into the woods to learn basic spells each day, I begged Agnes to let me train in something else. Finally, when I was big enough to hold one, she pressed a sword into my hand and promised, when the time came, that I would be by her side as we restored the witches' rightful place in the world.

The older I got, the more noticeable my differences became, and I began to wonder what it would have been like to grow up with my own kind. It was often difficult to remember to hate humans when I saw one in the mirror each day.

Tonight, my sisters would go through their Rite, and I would be forced to watch as my own kind was slaughtered in front of me. *You're ready for this. One day you will also slaughter humans,* I reminded myself. I glanced their way again, watching as Ophelia finally managed to block Marbella's spell with one of her own.

The Rite was also when a witch's aging process would slow down. It would be another century before Marbella and Ophelia began to visibly age once more. I tried not to let my obvious envy show on my face.

'You better hope I don't,' I finally quipped, responding to Agnes's pondering about my own powers, or lack thereof. Retrieving my dropped sword, I attacked again. 'That would ruin your plans entirely.'

The whole reason Agnes bothered to train me at all – and hadn't abandoned me at birth when she realised what I was – was because of her plan to use my humanity to her advantage. She was only waiting for me to come of age before she sent me off to a faraway kingdom to bring her plan to life.

Agnes grunted in acknowledgement, and defended against my quick assaults with minimal effort, barely even looking at me. My frustration turned into a growl, and I lunged too quickly, tripping on my skirts as I fell forwards. Agnes lifted her sword out of the way before I impaled myself on it. She extended a hand to help me to my feet. Brushing her off, I pushed off the ground, using the force to lunge into what should have been a fierce blow.

I met nothing but air, my mother's apparition disappearing as I rammed my sword through it. Nothing but an illusion. I whirled on her, furious. Her throaty laugh made my spine stiffen.

'Very good, sweet daughter. You almost had me there.'

'You cheated,' I panted.

'You're right. I have relied on magic for too long,' she smirked, no more breathless than if she had been sitting all afternoon. 'That's enough, for today, daughter mine. We are needed elsewhere. We must begin preparations for this afternoon.'

For me, preparing for the Rite meant helping my sisters bathe and dress, a task none of us were overjoyed with.

'Ouch! Be careful!' Marbella hissed. I had tugged too tightly on her soft, golden hair as I braided it.

'Sorry,' I muttered, picking up more berries to intertwine in the braid that I was looping across the top of her head to form a natural crown.

'You're not doing it right!' she whined. 'Get Sapphire, she does it better!'

I rolled my eyes. 'Sapphire is busy. You'll have to make do.'

My mother's second hadn't yet returned from a scouting mission in the skies, where she'd been looking for threats from humans getting too close to the coven. She had left the night before last, and it was unusual for scouting to take so long. My stomach dived at the thought of anything happening to her. Sapphire would never miss my sisters' Rite if she could help it.

'Make do? *Make do?*' Marbella's voice rose an octave. 'This is the most important day of my life! Start over.' I let her golden curls fall from my hand, watching with envy as they bounced around her face and shone in the light.

Witches have only three hair colours: resplendent golds, moon-kissed silvers, or glowing whites. They also have three common eye colours: black as dark as coal, shining quicksilver, and a violet so bright, it is said the night sky itself was jealous. My own eyes were a colour so uninteresting, nobody bothered to describe it at all. Second to the lack of magic, lacking the ethereal beauty was what really made me stand out from the coven.

'Now, do it properly!' Marbella huffed, inspecting her nails. I picked up her beautiful strands of hair and tugged a little tighter than strictly necessary as I began again.

Two hours later, both Marbella and Ophelia's hair was braided to their standards. Their makeup was striking, and the white dresses they wore looked otherworldly against their impeccable skin.

'You both look beautiful!' I gasped, squeezing their hands. They must have been nervous, because they allowed the touch and did not push me away. Ophelia even held on a little longer, her palm slick with sweat.

'You know what you need to do, girls?' Gaia asked, and the pair of them nodded.

'Your chosen sacrifices were brought in moments ago. Your mother awaits you on stage.' I felt the colour drain from my face, and Ophelia's gaze lingered on me at the mention of the sacrifices as she worried her lip between her teeth.

Gaia walked to each of them, pressing gentle kisses to their foreheads. 'Good luck. When we next speak, you will have power flowing through your veins. Witchlings no more.' Then, she ushered me out of the tent with her.

The whole coven had gathered in a large clearing between trees, and my knees clacked together as I shivered – not from the cool afternoon air, but through fear. I looked out over a sea of beautiful witches, young witchlings, and old crones, who eagerly awaited the sacrifice, and I wondered how many of them wished it were me.

The Iron Woods we called home, were full of dense forestation, and home to all manner of creatures – Ophelia had sworn she'd seen a gnome once. Every few miles, there was a break in the trees, opening to delicate meadows that blossomed beautifully in the spring. It was in these clearings that we pitched the tents we slept in, celebrated every occasion, and trained. It was where we gathered now, for the Rite.

Agnes stood before the block where the sacrifices would be made, making a speech that I could not hear through the buzzing in my ears. It was stupid to feel this way. I owed the humans no loyalty. Just because I *was* one, didn't mean I didn't want them punished for what they did to witches. Hell, I had been trained to butcher them! But something about the sacrifices in the Rite felt different to coming up against a human in battle. *Not that I'd ever done that, either.*

When my sisters stepped onto the stage, the crowd gasped at their beauty. Marbella held her head high and confident. She would go first, being the first born. Ophelia looked less sure as she hesitated a few steps behind.

'Bring the sacrifices!' Agnes bellowed, and the crowd cheered as the two human men were hauled onto the stage. They were both naked, their hands bound behind their backs with rope, a hessian sack over each of their heads. I swallowed hard as the sacks were removed, and the men stared out at the gathering of witches, pure terror in their eyes, sweat pouring from their temples. One man caught sight of Marbella and snarled.

'You witch!' he cried. 'You betrayed me.'

The crowd hissed and jeered at the man as Marbella circled him, a predator's gleam in her eyes. When she spat at the man's feet, the crowd laughed and applauded her.

How many times had she wanted to spit at me?

'Ophelia, is that you? Who are these people? Help me, please!' the other man begged. The crowd laughed once more at the pitiful words, at the snot that leaked from the man's nose, at the sobs that heaved through his body. Ophelia said nothing.

'Let the sacrifice begin!' Agnes boomed, and the crowd erupted.

Marbella's sacrifice was hauled to the wooden block, which was discoloured from all the blood that had seeped into it over the years. The man dug his heels in and fought against the two witches pushing his head towards the cool surface. In the end, there was nothing he could do as his head met the wood, and Marbella was handed a sharp dagger.

Agnes's eyes shone with pride as she recited an incantation I would never need to learn, and Marbella slit the man's throat in one smooth movement. My nails left crescent moons in my palms as I squeezed my hands into fists, trying to distract myself from the barbaric sacrifice that was supposed to please the Mother. The drinking of the blood, which started as purely ceremonial, was now believed by many to make a witch's new powers more potent. Either way, it made my skin crawl.

You hate them, too. I reminded myself, though I could barely watch as the blood pooled on the wood, before running down the specially-designed block and into the vial Marbella now held at its base.

Gaia's steadying hand found my back as my knees wobbled, and the crowd cheered as Marbella lifted the vial to her mouth, knocking back the man's blood. Killed for that tiny amount? It didn't seem worth it, to me.

'He beat his wife and children,' Gaia whispered into my ear. 'Marbella bewitched his wife and left her a small sum of gold to cover his disappearance. She will believe he died in an accident.' My mouth hung open, but it quickly turned to a wince as Marbella grinned, the man's blood staining her teeth red. The witches whooped and cheered.

Agnes began another spell, and Marbella's eyes closed. Silver light began to shine all around her as the Mother, goddess of magic both divine and dark, gifted Marbella her full powers. A proper witch at last. When the silver light faded, my sister looked more beautiful than ever, skin glowing with the power that now ran through her.

Agnes took Marbella's hand and led her to a silver throne fixed to the stage. My sister waved out to the crowd before taking a seat. The witches around me curtsied as one, and Gaia shoved my shoulder down, forcing me into a curtsy of my own.

I could barely breathe as the next man was hauled forwards, sobbing and crying out for Ophelia to spare him. Agnes began her incantations again and Ophelia was handed her own blade. I closed my eyes this time as the man's cries were cut off, turning to gurgles as Ophelia sliced his throat. The dripping of his blood echoed in my head.

'That one murdered his elder brother so he could inherit the family fortune,' Gaia whispered, and my eyes shot open again in time to see Ophelia drain the vial of blood she had collected.

'Why are you telling me this?' I whispered back.

'Your sisters deliberately looked for humans who had done wrong. They did not want to murder just any man.' *Murder*, not sacrifice. 'They made sure the man they chose would deserve it.'

I breathed in deeply as it was Ophelia's turn to shine and glow. It was not a requirement of the sacrifice for the men to deserve their fate. In fact, most of the witches chose men they admired, believing the Mother would appreciate the sacrifice more and grant them extra powers. Sometimes, they chose men they wished to bed before they were killed. My sisters hadn't given that a thought, instead choosing men who had done evil. A small part of me hoped it was because of their human sister that they did not simply revel in spilling human blood.

As if she heard the thought, Ophelia, still glowing, looked to me and nodded, before allowing Agnes to lead her to the throne beside Marbella. This time, when the witches curtsied, I mustered up the strength to dip low with them.

'Today, as the sun shines down on us, we have seen two beautiful witches earn their power. And my own two daughters, no less!' Agnes shouted across the crowd. 'We are blessed by the Mother!'

The witches whooped and cheered; the forest alive with noise. But even that didn't drown out the sound of brooms crashing to the ground in the clearing beside us. Sapphire and her scouting unit had returned, stricken looks on their faces. Agnes moved towards Sapphire with purpose.

'What news, sister?' Sapphire shook her head, as though she was unable to talk. 'Come.' My mother took Sapphire's elbow and led her from the crowd, Gaia and my sisters following immediately. I fell into step behind them, unsure of my place.

One by one, we pushed back the heavy flaps of the war tent and filed in, taking places around a long table used mainly for war strategy. It hadn't seen much action in my lifetime, but certainly in Agnes's. My mother was just a witchling in the Witch Wars – when covens tore each other apart for power – but she had fought shoulder-to-shoulder with those same covens when the first battles amongst humans and witches were fought. Agnes didn't look a day over thirty, but she had centuries of history. Whilst witches didn't have the immortality of other fae folk like the elves, they outlived humans tenfold, and held a grudge for eternity.

Beside me, Marbella and Ophelia stood together, arms linked. Truly identical, they still glowed with untapped power. For an outsider, the only way to tell them apart from looks alone was by the colour of their eyes – Ophelia's violet iris compared to Marbella's stony black. Their golden hair was of equal length, each with gorgeous curls that caressed their backsides and framed their impeccable faces. But I could tell them apart by each minute difference in their face. Marbella's had a hard edge, compared to the softer set of Ophelia's jaw. Phe had a clever gaze, Marbella a cold one.

Opposite me, Gaia looked wary. The most battle-hardened amongst us – having fought in the Witch Wars three centuries ago, and an experienced soldier by the Cursed Wars – Gaia's youth had long left her. That wasn't to say she wasn't still beautiful. Though wrinkles adorned her dark face and hands, her quicksilver eyes shone bright with life and wisdom, and her face was kind and welcoming, despite the battles she'd seen.

Beside my mother stood Sapphire, who was younger than Gaia, but had around fifty years on my mother. A grim look on her youthful face. Her beautiful silver hair was tied back, her pointed ears peeking through the windswept strands that stuck out.

'What did the skies reveal, Sapphire?' my mother pressed. I held my breath, having never seen Sapphire look so forlorn, almost frightened.

'Our sisters in the Moonkeeper coven were attacked,' Sapphire finally spoke, her tone caught somewhere between bereft and venomous.

Four covens were spread throughout the continent of Esiks, and whilst the covens kept to themselves, they were sisters, all children of the Mother. To the west, in the kingdom of Harensarra were the Starchasers, and furthest away, due north, in the kingdom of the Vale, were the Stormbreakers. The Moonkeepers were our closest neighbours and were also located in the kingdom of Starterra like us, the Sunseekers.

Sapphire didn't need to explain who had attacked the Moonkeepers. There was only one kind that would hunt and murder witches. An inexplicable guilt churned in my gut.

'How did they find them?' I barely whispered, unsure if I'd even spoken aloud. Unlike our coven, which was hidden from outsiders by a powerful glamour, the Moonkeeper coven lived atop the tallest mountain in Starterra, which should have been protection enough.

'They were betrayed!' Sapphire hissed. 'One of their own misplaced her affections with a human, and an army of Reili's finest waltzed right in, led by their bastard general no doubt.' She held out a piece of royal-blue and gold material, and it took me a moment to realise it was a crest – Reili's emblem of a rising phoenix surrounded by the sun.

Past Harensarra, so far west you almost fell off the continent, lay Reili. A kingdom famed for its many wars with Starterra, Reili had eradicated any covens that once called it home. The queen's adopted son was the youngest general in Reili's history and had a hand in forcing the witches out of their kingdom. My mother had told me stories about his famous witch hunts. My blood boiled inside my quickening heart at the thought of such a threat descending on the Moonkeeper coven.

'Did any escape?' Ophelia's lip quivered.

'They burned them all while they slept!' Sapphire choked on a sob. 'Not even the witchlings were spared.'

Tears pricked at my eyes. A whole coven gone. Just like that.

'I will not stand by and let this go unpunished!' Agnes slammed a pale fist on the table, making me jump. Her silver eyes gleamed with wicked intent as they landed on me.

I knew what was coming before her mouth opened again, and my heart beat so fast it hurt. Truthfully, I'd known it the moment Sapphire had explained what had become of the Moonkeepers.

It was time for me to play my role in this war.

Fear speared through me as Agnes said, 'Blaise, your time has come. You must go to the kingdom of Reili to join Queen Lizabeta's court. There, you will become my spy. You will help us to infiltrate the kingdom and get revenge for our fallen sisters. This will be *your* sacrifice, Blaise. This will be *your* Rite.'

Chapter 2

'YOU HAVE TRAINED FOR THIS moment,' Agnes continued, oblivious to the panic taking root inside me, my heart pumping faster and faster until I thought it would tear through my chest. I tried to swallow, and my breath lodged in my throat, forcing a warped garble to escape my lips.

Every head in the tent swivelled to look at me. Sapphire's eyes softened with pity where Gaia's filled with concern. Agnes was right, I *had* been trained for this moment. I just never thought it would actually arrive. And I didn't think I would feel so alone when it did. Agnes didn't look at me with pity or concern, if anything, her features had hardened at my display of weakness.

'You know your cover story, don't you?'

I'd had it memorised since I was fourteen. 'I am Blaise Vermont. The estranged grandchild of Lord Vermont.'

The real Lord Vermont was Reili's emissary to Starterra. He had no living family, and my mother had long possessed papers that had been glamoured to look legitimate, stating that everything he'd owned – including his titles – had been left to me. Agnes had planned my entire future, down to the moment I would stand by her side as I betrayed the people I was to now meet and send to their deaths. A chill ran down my spine, and I forced myself to continue.

'My father, Peter Remington, died in Reili's defeat over Starterra. I was raised solely by my mother, Evangaline Vermont, until she passed from the Pox when I was sixteen, leaving me in the employ of House Lovett, where I waited on the lady of the house, Maria.' All of these people were not so real, though Agnes had left a long trail of evidence that they were, should anyone want to investigate. 'I was unaware of my grandfather and his position with the crown until recently. Now I know, I wish to do my grandfather proud and serve the queen, the crown, and the country of my ancestors.'

I took a deep breath. There was an obvious problem with this plan. 'But mother mine,' I wrung my hands as her storm-filled gaze narrowed on me. 'Lord Vermont isn't dead.' The last I heard, my *grandfather* was very much alive.

Agnes laughed. A short and bitter cackle. Then, she turned to Gaia, who nodded once and left the tent. I heard the whoosh of her broom as she took to the skies. 'Convenient then, that he only has hours left to live.'

I gulped. They didn't call her Agnes the Wicked for nothing.

'You were born for this, Blaise. To help us overcome our enemies.' I met Agnes's feverish gaze. 'It is sooner than we planned for, but it does not matter. You *are* ready.'

'I don't feel ready, Mamma,' I squeaked. 'Shouldn't we just leave them alone? Stay in peace?' The words were a mistake. Another moment of weakness. One I regretted instantly. *Craven.* I scolded myself.

My mother's eyes turned to molten rage.

'You expect me to do *nothing*, while the ashes of our sisters float on the wind?' She stormed around the table towards me as she spoke, catching my chin between her long fingers, her blood-red nails digging into my cheeks. This was the Agnes that the world feared, that witches bowed before and humans fled from. I tried to keep my eyes from watering as she continued squeezing. 'You wish for us to live in hiding forever, while their prince picks us off, one coven at a time?'

'No, Mamma,' I breathed, eyes watering with pain.

'Good!' Her eyes glowed with the flicker of something maleficent. 'Because I have a new idea. One that is sure not to fail should you suddenly find yourself too weak to hurt them, as you seem now.' Shame washed over me like oil, thick and slimy.

'Surely you cannot change the plan now, Agnes?' Sapphire questioned, but shut her mouth when my mother glared at her.

Still gripping my face, her focus was drawn back to me. 'Sweet daughter. Daughter mine. Your new role will be to seduce the queen's precious prince. You're beautiful enough to do it, by their standards anyway.' It was hard to take the rare compliment when her nails were still embedded in my face.

The plan had always been for me to find a place in the queen's court, befriending her inner circle. I was to spy, taking down any immediate threats, and playing the long game until I could bring the witches inside the palace and force the humans out. It had never involved putting myself in *direct contact* with the continent's most renowned witch-hunter!

'Once he has fallen for you, he will make you his queen,' Agnes continued. 'Then, you will convince him to allow us into his kingdom. Allow us our freedom. If you cannot convince him . . . well . . . by then, you'll be in the perfect position to kill him while he sleeps!' She laughed, the noise a horrid sound, and pressed a kiss to my cheek. When she released my chin from her grip, I could already feel the bruising there.

Resisting the urge to rub the sore spots she had left behind, I asked, 'How am I to seduce him? You've spent my life teaching me the exact spot to stick a knife to kill a man. You've never taught me how to *flirt*. I've never even *spoken* to a man before!'

'You've read books, haven't you?' Agnes smirked, and my face flushed. She knew about the romance novels I'd asked Sapphire to smuggle me back each time she ventured to new towns on scouting missions.

A giggle full of malice snapped my attention to Marbella, who seemed to be finding my embarrassment highly amusing. I snarled and, instinctively, my hand reached for the sword usually strapped down my spine. Grasping at empty air, I remembered that I'd removed it for the ceremony. Marbella noted the threat, pushing Ophelia behind her slightly, as if an attack on Marbella was an attack on Ophelia, too. Her favouritism felt like being doused in ice water.

I am your sister, too.

I focused on Agnes again. 'What if I get caught? Will they not suspect me a witch? Will I not burn?' Just because I was *not* a witch, didn't mean that burning at the stake would not be my death sentence, too.

Agnes's nostrils flared, eyes once more swirling like lava. 'Do. *Not.* Get. Caught,' were the only words of advice she offered. She released my hand and pushed past me; my stomach full of angry bees as I watched her depart. Sapphire placed a comforting hand on my shoulder and that was all it took for the tears to fall.

CHAPTER 3

DESPITE THE HORRIFIC NEWS Sapphire had brought, Agnes refused to cancel the celebrations, and so, as the sun dipped beneath the trees, I found myself wedged between my two sisters at one of the several long tables that had been laid out. Their glow was blinding, and they would continue to shine until they burnt through some of their new power.

At the head of the table, Agnes had ditched her ceremonial robes, now wearing an incandescent gown of pure silver, with a glow that rivalled that of my sisters' skin. She stood, and the chatter among the witches died, all attention shifting to her.

'It is always a special day when a witchling receives her full powers and becomes a true witch,' Agnes began, the crowd nodding their approval, for it *was* a wonderous occasion when a witch made it to adulthood.

Witchlings were rare. Though witches lived for much longer than a normal human lifespan, they were not blessed with the human's nature to reproduce so fruitfully. Which is why many witches chose to copulate with humans – rather than other creatures like Fae and Mer – to try and increase their chances of children.

Being so rare to conceive, it was all the more special when Agnes confirmed she was carrying *multiple* children. Twins sometimes occurred when a witch was blessed, but triplets were almost unheard of. Yet, I often wondered if the other witches even considered us triplets, given that I was not a witch, and that it had taken two extra months for me to be born after my sisters – something about humans needing longer to develop in the womb.

It was even rarer that, once conceived, a witch-babe would survive. Labour is a difficult time for any witch. Her power flares during it, and is often uncontrollable. More often than not, the witch can accidentally harm her own child in delivery.

Should the witchling survive the difficult birth, there is then the obstacle of living with the gift of magic. Teaching a baby to walk and talk is one thing. Teaching her how to control her magic, when she can barely understand those things, is another. So, for a witchling to become a fully-fledged witch was special, indeed.

'Today, Sapphire brought awful news from the skies,' Agnes spoke again, and the coven fell silent, listening with intent. Sapphire's eyes welled with tears. 'Our sisters, in the Moonkeeper coven, were slaughtered.' Anger boiled up from the crowd, shouts and cries of anguish bouncing around the forest.

'With this attack happening in our own kingdom, the humans are getting too close for us to sit by and do nothing! We mourn the loss of the Moonkeepers, but we will not sit idly by in sorrow, we *will* have our revenge!' Her expression shifted, and the coven murmured their agreement. 'My daughter, Blaise, is almost grown, and it is time she put the skills we have taught her to good use. *She* will be our key to retribution!' The witches eyed me suspiciously. 'But, for now, we celebrate the gift the Mother has bestowed upon us!' Agnes boomed.

She clicked her fingers once, and the tables filled with food and drink. Plates full of roast chickens, mountains of sausages, steaming potatoes, baked tarts and pumpkin pies, and gallons of wine.

All around me, the Sunseeker witches were dressed in their finest gowns, and they loaded food onto their plates. Chatter filled the air.

Some whispered, intensely discussing what had happened to the Moonkeepers. Others paid compliments to Agnes's spread. My sisters floated wine and tarts towards themselves, trying to burn through some of the raw magic now coursing through their veins.

I couldn't understand how any of them could eat at a time like this; carrying on like nothing had happened. But witches didn't feel emotions like humans. Sure, they *felt* emotions, but without a human heart, they were not as intense.

Agnes sat back in her chair with a goblet of wine in hand, content to watch as her underlings helped themselves to her feast. She caught my eye and smiled. The wine that stained her lips and teeth reminded me too much of the blood that had stained Marbella's teeth only an hour ago. Agnes's eyes narrowed but, before she could say anything, I picked up a chicken leg and forced myself to swallow a bite, tasting nothing but ash.

'I tried to choose someone that deserved it. I know it was hard for you to watch,' Ophelia whispered from beside me. Marbella cast us a cautious glance before distracting our mother with conversation as I stared at Ophelia; eyes wide, unsure what to say. Neither of my sisters had ever shown me much kindness. They had never been particularly hateful, either. They simply chose to avoid me most of the time.

Ophelia winced. 'Your thoughts are . . . loud,' she shrugged, and I blinked twice.

'You can hear what I'm thinking?' I choked.

'It's not just you. Since The Rite, I can hear everyone's thoughts. But yours are . . .' she trailed off and I waited. 'You sound like you're screaming.'

My jaw dropped open. Mind reading was a powerful gift, even for a witch. When the Mother walked the earth, bringing with her the magic of the witches, it is said that she harnessed incredible powers, from mind reading, to teleporting, to turning invisible.

Over the centuries, particularly as witches mated with humans, magic dwindled, with only some witches gaining extra gifts. The divide in power was what ultimately led to the Witch Wars, and wiped elemental witch covens, like the Earthraisers and the Airbenders, off the map.

The covens on our continent are known as empyrean witches.

Pulling their magic from the skies, their power can be enhanced at certain times of the day. As Sunseekers, my coven is most powerful when the sun shines. The sun wouldn't give them extra powers, but would fill them with extra energy, allowing them to boost their magic.

Every so often, a witch would be born who seemed a law unto herself, with no one really knowing the full extent of her power. Agnes was one of those few. And while mind-reading would set her apart, Ophelia's gift wasn't as rare as that unbound power.

'I'll try and be quiet,' I grimaced, and Ophelia's lips twitched upwards in a half smile. 'Have you told Mother?'

She glanced over my shoulder to Agnes, who was still in deep conversation with Marbella. Ophelia shook her head. 'I can hear her thoughts, too, and before she finds out, I need to tell you something. Mother, she —'

Ophelia stopped mid-sentence; eyes wide with terror as Agnes's head snapped in our direction. My sister's sweaty hand found mine under the table and she squeezed hard.

'Blaise, you should go to bed.' Agnes's voice was cold.

'Why?' I asked, the confusion in my voice genuine. She had forced me to be at this celebration. Why was she suddenly sending me away?

'You leave tomorrow for Reili. The journey is two months on foot and horseback, and you shall need rest.' Agnes eyed me, taking another sip of wine, daring me to question her.

I stood, not wishing to defy her in front of this many witches whose attentions were all now on us. 'Where do you think you're going?' Agnes asked Ophelia, who had risen with me, still clinging to my hand.

'I . . . I thought I might retire with my sister. It has been a long day, after all,' she stammered.

'I also would like to get some rest and say goodbye to our sister.' Marbella threw her napkin onto her still-full plate, rising with us.

'You will do no such thing!' Agnes barked. 'Our sisters are gathered here for *you*. To celebrate *you*. You shall not disrespect them by leaving early. And you shall not pretend it is for Blaise's benefit — a sister you have shown no interest in before this evening! Now. Sit. Down.'

The two of them sat so sharply, Ophelia's hand ripping from mine, I knew that they had been given no choice but to obey. Agnes had used magic to force them back into their seats.

'Go,' my mother jerked her head at me. 'I shall see you in the morning.'

Trying to make sense of Agnes's reaction to my sisters actually giving a shit about me for a moment of their lives, I scrambled away from the party and left them all behind.

CHAPTER 4

AS I LOOKED AROUND THE bare canvas walls of the tent I had been ordered to return to, a boiling rage roiled within me. In a fit of fury, I swept my arm across the dresser, knocking its contents to the floor. Then, I kicked over the stack of books next to my single bed and tossed each item from my wooden clothes rail to the rug-covered floor.

Snatching a thick, feathered pillow from my bed, I sat cross-legged on the floor and screamed as hard as I could into the cushion. When my voice was hoarse, I chucked the pillow onto the pile of destruction I had caused, and let the rage slowly ebb out of me in deep, panting breaths.

With a groan, I began to put everything I had upturned back into its rightful place. I couldn't pinpoint what had caused the snap inside me. Whether it was Agnes banishing me from the party, when I finally felt like I was getting closer to Ophelia, or whether it was because the plan had changed last minute to involve something I had never trained for, throwing me completely off-kilter.

When everything was back in its place, I picked up my sword from where it rested against the tent's bottle-green canvas. Tipping it in my hands, I felt the balance, running my fingers along the smooth edges. I would be leaving this behind, of course, like so many other things, but I thought I might miss the security this sword gave me the most.

Here, in the Iron Woods, I had always felt like an outsider. But, from the moment I learned to use a sword, I hadn't felt quite so *useless*. Nor had I felt like prey anymore. This sword had given me protection, and a purpose, and now I would be walking into a viper's den without it, having to rely on my wit and wiles to protect me instead.

Knowing how to fight wasn't going to help me win over the prince. *A witch-hunting prince at that.* I shook my head and took up a fighting stance, raising my sword and keeping it flat. Did I even *want* to win him over? *Since when has what you wanted counted for anything?*

Since I was born, I'd never had a say in what happened to me. Not when the covens met and fretted about what to do with a human baby in their midst. Not when Agnes replaced my dolls with daggers, and first told me about her plan to send me away. And certainly not now.

I arced the sword and sliced it down, twisting my way through one of my many training routines, careful to avoid slashing the canvas of my tent. As I moved, I thought about everything that had led to this point. It was hard to be bitter about my fate, when the witches had far more to be angry about. With that thought, the last of my remaining anger slipped free.

I placed the sword down, not knowing when I would hold it again, and got changed into a night gown for bed. As I slipped under the covers, Agnes pushed into my tent. I hated how I tensed at her presence.

'Daughter mine,' she said sweetly, coming to perch on the edge of the bed next to me. 'I am sorry for snapping earlier. It's been a hard day, and perhaps I am not handling it as well as I thought.'

She grimaced, and my heart softened. Of course she was having a hard time. It was supposed to have been a great day for her, what with my sisters coming into their full powers, but that had been overshadowed with the news of the Moonkeepers' murders. No wonder she was a little tetchy. I'm sure she had friends in that coven, and she was grieving.

'No, Mamma, *I* am the one who's sorry. I've been making this all about me. But it's not. It's about getting revenge for our fallen sisters everywhere. About allowing the witches to live freely.'

She nodded and, in the candle-lit dusk of the tent, I couldn't be sure, but it looked as though her eyes might have welled up. She reached out to stroke my hair, and I leaned into her touch, yawning.

'Will you tell me a story, Mamma?' I asked, allowing myself to feel small and childlike, for one more night, before I had to leave everything I knew.

'How about I tell you the full story of your birth?' Agnes's smile made me uneasy, and not just because of the way her elongated canines still gleamed blood-red where they were stained with wine. A cold shiver ran the length of my body, and I eased myself into a sitting position as she began.

'Your father was leading a human army through Starterra during the war,' she sighed, giving me time to recall details I already knew about the war she spoke of. It was a war Starterra lost, and the king upped his people's taxes to pay the substantial debt he owed to the kingdom of Reili for the price of losing.

Agnes continued. 'The army began to stray too close to the coven. So close, I wondered whether we had been betrayed. And so, I glamoured myself to look human, and went to investigate. It didn't take more than a few flirtatious looks and comments to get past your father's guards to speak to him – a king ought to have been better protected. But he was young, and trusting, and led me right into his tent,' Agnes smirked.

'My father, was the *king of Reili?*' I exclaimed, shock like an icy bath roiling across my body. *How had she never told me this?* I couldn't help but wonder if my sisters knew, or whether this secret had been kept from them too. Had this been what Ophelia was trying to tell me? Surely Agnes wouldn't have reacted in such a way if she planned to tell me anyway? Which meant there were more secrets. I suppressed a shudder.

Agnes gave one nod of her head. 'He was beautiful, as humans go. One of the most beautiful men I had ever seen. You look like him,' she added softly, and my heart did a little flutter. As she'd pointed out earlier, I was not considered attractive compared with the beauty of the witches, but perhaps, amongst my own kind, I would be. Maybe I had more chance courting the prince than I realised.

'We talked, and he invited me to stay in his tent for the evening. He told me I was the most beautiful woman he'd ever laid eyes on.'

'I can believe it,' I whispered. Even glamoured to look human, I could bet that Agnes was still the most beautiful amongst us.

She let out a low chuckle and readjusted herself on my bed. 'I stayed for a few days – I needed an heir after all,' she winked, and my neck flushed. 'It wasn't long before the king needed to move on. He asked me to come with him but, of course, I could not leave the coven for long. After a month, he returned to me, when the war with Starterra was won. I already knew I was with child by that time. However, it was only once I told him the news, did he tell *me* that he already had a queen. Back in Reili,' Agnes spat, her rage rising.

'He told me he loved me, and that he would have his little queen removed from the throne. *I* would be his queen, and *my* children his heirs. But, I would not leave. I would not pretend to be human for the rest of my life, nor would I force my children to do the same. And I would *never* have subjected my children to the danger of a scorned queen.

'When I told him I would not go with him, he threatened to return and take my child to his kingdom, to be raised by him and his *queen*. Naturally, I had to kill him,' she sounded almost rueful.

'What I *do* regret, is not taking more time to plan his death. In my anger, I lashed out, killing him with a spell that snapped his neck in front of his guardsmen. The moment I exposed myself, I returned to the coven to hide, for I could not kill them all.' I held my breath, scared that, if I made a sound, she would stop telling me the things she had kept hidden before.

'I went months without hearing anything, until I discovered that *she* had sent armies after me. The news sent me into labour. Your sister, Marbella arrived first. So silent, was she, that the midwife feared she was stillborn, until she looked into the infant's eyes and saw a gaze so steely it was clear she was my child, already plotting from her first moments in this world.' She sounded proud of Marbella's devious nature.

'Ophelia was born next. She came out kicking and squalling, letting the whole world know she had arrived,' Agnes smiled a toothy grin that died quickly when she continued. 'After two hours, you were yet to appear, and the midwife advised me that you had likely died in the womb, asking permission to open my stomach and remove you.'

Her hands gripped my bedsheets so tightly that her knuckles turned white. 'Of course, I demanded a new midwife was found. One that would not threaten to cut me open and steal my unborn child.

'Yet, there were none. So, I turned to a Seer instead. She advised me that you lived, but that your future was murky, and she could not make it out. For another two months and six days you grew inside me. I could feel you getting stronger. It was most unusual. No one had ever heard of triplets not being born together before. Finally, you were ready, and when you arrived you were so . . . different. I knew you were special. That the Mother had a plan for you.' Her eyes were far away as she relived the moment she'd been handed her human daughter for the first time.

'What happened to the armies?' I asked. 'The ones that were after you.'

'They never found me, of course, so they turned back to their homeland to find a new king. But their queen was young, and hot-headed like her husband, thinking she could rule by herself. For years, her counsel tried to get her to remarry, bringing in suitor after suitor for her to choose from, but she refused them all. She claimed it was devotion to her husband, but of course, she knew the moment she remarried, she would be ruler no longer. She would once more become the pretty face in the shadows of a king.

'She did have the problem of an heir, however. Without a man to produce a child with, she had no one to succeed her. This made her appear weak, and others tried to take her throne by force once she refused their hand in marriage. Yet still, she held on by the skin of her teeth.' I leaned closer to her, desperate not to miss a single whisper of her story.

'Needing to secure her future, the queen formed a plan. The war had made many children orphans, so she planned to adopt such a babe, and claim him as her heir. Noble families were asked to present their orphaned nephews and grandsons to Her Majesty, but she soon realised that choosing a noble child would mean there would always be a distant relative who felt they had claim to the throne. Instead, she demanded the common folk present their children, orphaned or not, and she would take her pick from them.' I gasped, stomach churning wildly at my mother's words, but she continued without hearing me, lost in her tale.

'She chose a boy of three. Some say he had a princely look about him, others say he was weak, *sickly*, and the queen knew she could manipulate him. More say he looked strong for his age, and the queen knew he would grow up to protect her. Though accounts differ in why she chose the boy, they all agree that she wrenched him from his mother's arms before ordering the woman killed in the street.' I clenched my fists tightly, a strange anger coursing through my veins.

'The queen stripped the boy of his birth name, and named him Prince Kaspian, her heir and successor. With age, the boy forgot all about his past life, and stepped into his new role as his new mother's protector. Thus becoming the youngest general in Reili's history, and one of the continent's most feared witch-hunters – though, there are still families who feel they have more claim to Reili's throne than the boy and the queen together. Some women claim they are mother to the murdered king's bastard son, and that *their* child is the rightful heir.' She lifted my chin gently with her long fingers until our eyes met.

'But you see, sweet daughter, *you* are the king's human child, and *you* are the rightful heir to Reili's throne. Your sisters too, have a claim, but the Mother has other plans for them. As my human child, the heritage is yours.' She sighed, squeezing my chin slightly too hard, pressing on the bruises she had already left there. 'If I thought the humans would accept your claim, we wouldn't need to involve the hunter at all. I would storm the palace and place the crown upon your pretty head myself. But, alas, we must take another route to get you what is yours by birthright. Once you succeed, you will forbid the humans from burning and maiming witches, and we will finally be free to live as we please without hiding in the shadows. We will thrive! We will have a kingdom to call home,' Agnes finished, definite tears gleaming in her silver eyes at the possibility of a new life.

I swallowed hard.

I wanted my family to be free. To live without the fear of burning at the stake because they possessed magic in their veins – *beautiful* magic, that could do so much good for the world! Magic that could heal wounds, and build things, growing crops faster and more nutritious. Magic that, if given the right freedom, could transform the world into something better. But the crown being *my* birthright? I shuddered. What did *I* know about ruling a kingdom?

'What was his name?' I asked, surprising myself. 'My father. What was his name?'

'Kaspian,' my mother breathed. 'She named the boy after him.'

Chapter 5

AFTER A FITFUL SLEEP, I waited for Gaia and Sapphire on the outskirts of my usual training ring, shifting my pack nervously. I'd packed all that I could, leaving my sword behind, and I felt naked without the familiar weight of it resting against my spine. Agnes made her way towards me. She was dressed for a long journey, in warm leggings, a thick cloak, and sturdy boots.

'You're coming with us?' I asked.

'For the first couple of days. I cannot leave the coven unprotected for too long, but I would like to spend some time with you before I release you into the queen's clutches.' The way she spat the last two words made me nervous.

'Will Ophelia and Marbella see us off?' I hoped.

'No. They were up late celebrating, and are likely still asleep, or too hungover to rise,' Agnes offered coolly.

My stomach twisted, remembering that Ophelia had been trying to tell me something last night. Before I could dwell on it further,

Gaia approached. I stared at her, wondering what she had done to dispose of Lord Vermont so quickly. Was his blood on her hands? Or had she ordered someone else to dispatch him?

'Come on, let's get this over with. I'll never get used to this.'

Agnes's returning grin was one of wicked delight. 'Oh, come now, Gaia. When have I ever made you look anything less than handsome?'

'It's not my looks I'm worried about. It's pissing standing up that I can't get used to!'

I laughed, despite my worries. Agnes was to glamour Gaia and Sapphire to appear as Starterrian soldiers, under the guise of delivering me to the queen of Reili as her emissary's next of kin. It would look less suspicious travelling in a group with men than it would as all women. The human world believed women had no place travelling by themselves. Doing so would mark us as a target.

The witches were more than capable of glamouring themselves, but it was not a simple magic. All glamoured individuals were ringed with a blurriness that was visible in broad daylight but barely at all in the dark. It was a tiny wave that moved behind them, a fraction slower than they were, as if the magic couldn't keep up. Almost all humans never noticed it and, if they did, they blamed their own poor eyesight. Many witches could also never get the shade of glamoured eye colour exactly the same every time, but again, most humans passed it off as a trick of the light. Agnes's extra powers allowed the glamours to hold for longer, and be almost unrecognisable, providing a much stronger cover for Gaia and Sapphire.

'Humans don't *want* to think they are being tricked,' Agnes told me once. 'They don't know what to look for, but even if their tiny brains noticed something was amiss, they would rather blame poor eyesight than admit they'd been duped by a witch.'

Now, Agnes's wicked grin only spread at Gaia's complaining. 'Quit whining or I'll give you a small one. *Or* one so large, you'll have to tie it in a bow to stop it falling out from the bottom of your trousers.'

Gaia actually blushed at that, the apples of her dark cheeks turning rosy. 'I don't understand why we have to be quite so thorough, Agnes. Surely the face and body would be enough?'

'What if we're in a tavern, and you go to the privy? Do you want to get caught with your trousers around your ankles and no wand to wave about? Our cover would be blown! Now, no more complaints, or I'll put a wart on the end of it! Tell me, was big or small the decision?'

'If we're choosing sizes. I'll take a big one, please,' Sapphire winked, sidling up to us with swagger.

'Oh aye, and what will you be doing with *that*?' my mother cackled, the genuine laugh so uncommon that I drank in the sound.

'What I do in my own time is no concern of yours,' Sapphire laughed, and Gaia rolled her eyes.

'Stand still then,' Agnes rolled up her sleeves, concentrating.

Before my eyes, both Gaia and Sapphire's features began to shift. Their long hair became shorn, transforming from their vibrant colours to a dull brown like mine. Gaia sprouted rough hairs from her chin, her eyes taking on a bright blue hue. Sapphire grew a foot taller, her jaw now chiselled, with a feather-dusting of stubble completing the look. Their pointed ears became curved, their arms, legs and torsos packed with rippling muscle. They were both handsome, as promised, and the faint blur around them was almost unnoticeable to my human eyes.

Sapphire pulled the waist of her trousers, having worn a larger size to accommodate for her new appearance, away from her body and peered down. 'It will do,' she stated, her voice considerably lower than before. I couldn't help but laugh with them.

When I looked back to Agnes, she had transformed, too. Her golden hair was now dulled to a soft blonde, eyes a subtle hazel to match mine, ears curved rather than pointed. Even with her beauty dimmed down to pass as human, Agnes was still striking.

'Your father looked at me like that, too. Pick up your jaw, darling,' Agnes winked, tugging my pack over my shoulder. I grunted at the heavy weight as we headed away from the coven.

It took half a day to get free of the Iron Woods, the tall firs that penned in the Sunseeker coven finally giving way to smaller trees, then clearing altogether into luscious fields of green. Not one night away, and my heart already pined for the familiar scents and sights of the forest. The Iron Woods had been my home since I was born, and the smell of grass and dirt, the sound of babbling brooks, and the din of chattering birds, were all I'd ever known. When the fields gave way to cobbled streets, I caught sight of the first town we were to stay in.

'The humans were this close all along?' I asked no one in particular. Sapphire nodded. 'We were all surprised you never went looking.'

What would I have gained by sneaking off to be amongst my own kind when I'd been raised to hate them? I knew all the sensitive parts of their flesh that I could drive a knife through, and which poisons would kill them without them tasting it in a drink. I didn't know anything about how they actually *lived*. Panic flared, and I suddenly realised how little of my training had prepared me for the part where I had to live amongst them before I stabbed them in the back.

By sunset, we made it to rows of brick houses lining cobbled roads – a world away from even the most luxurious tents the coven lived in. The buildings looked warm and cosy, but devoid of nature, and I'd bet their residents didn't ever wake up with toads in their beds, or foxes trying to nibble their toes.

'I'll find us rooms,' Gaia dipped under a tavern doorway.

'Take a good look around, sweetheart,' Agnes whispered low in my ear. 'These are your people.'

I did, greedily drinking in the faces around me. They looked like me, with their natural eye colours, dull shades of hair, and their rounded ears. But they couldn't have been more different to me. I stared in awe at the way they laughed freely at the children getting under their mother's feet as they swatted at them with towels to shoo them out of the way. I watched as men stumbled out of taverns, supporting their inebriated friends, singing in gaudy voices. I noted the smell of smoke, and different foods, cooking on hearths, and I breathed in the scent of ale, basking in the wall of warmth that hit me every time someone opened a tavern door.

Before I could wander off and explore the town, Gaia emerged. 'We have two rooms, and the cook has some rabbit stew I'm sure he's overcharged me for. Four coppers a bowl. Ridiculous.'

'It's a good job those coppers will turn into leaves by the time we're gone then, isn't it,' Sapphire laughed, as she pushed her way into the tavern, bumping her head and yelping as she forgot the extra height she had gained under the glamour.

I followed, gaping at the scene before me. All around, tables were filled with men and women eating, drinking, laughing, and playing cards. Seeing this many humans in one place was . . . overwhelming.

I hadn't expected to *want* to spend time amongst the humans but *Gods*, everything here felt so new and exciting. The people looked like they could really take the time to have fun. At the coven, everything was for a purpose. Though we celebrated events like the Rite, most of the time was spent training. The witches honed their powers, whilst I trained in combat. When that was over, there were the witchlings to look after, the camp to run. There were rarely moments of downtime like these people were enjoying and, when there were, I was often by myself, reading one of the books Sapphire smuggled me, never part of the coven proper.

'Gentlemen, the keys to your room,' a serving lady stared at us, expression puzzled as Sapphire elbowed Gaia to get her to react to the term 'gentlemen'.

'Oh, yes! Thank you,' Gaia recovered, ushering us into an empty booth.

'I'll be along with your dinner in a moment,' the lady smiled, gaze lingering on Sapphire for a while before she spun on her heel and danced through the tables of other patrons.

'I appear to have made you too handsome. I bet she's already whispering about you to the barmaid,' Agnes muttered, settling herself next to me. Sapphire flashed a crooked grin.

The stew that arrived at our table moments later was warm and tasty. Nothing compared to the food created with the help of magic, but still pleasant. Once our bowls were cleared, a group of men approached our booth, and I stiffened instinctively, but the others seemed relaxed.

'Care for a game?' A tall man, with a round belly and hands the size of dinner plates asked, while shuffling cards with a nimbleness I would have thought impossible given the size of his sausage fingers.

'Oh aye,' Sapphire nodded. 'If you came out tonight to lose all of your money, we'll be happy to play.' The men tittered, pulling up some stools and settling at the end of our booth.

'That good, are you?' A second man, with dark black hair and toned arms asked, rolling up his sleeves and placing his muscled forearms on the table while the first man continued to shuffle the deck.

Sapphire grinned. 'Not me, sir, but our lady friend here, who you haven't taken your eyes off since we walked in. *She's* a master of cards.' Sapphire nodded towards Agnes.

The man bristled, but still didn't take his eyes off my mother. 'Is that right? Lucky in cards, unlucky in love, the saying goes, doesn't it?'

Agnes's eyes flashed with something like pain, but she picked up the hand that Sausage Fingers had dealt. 'If you believe in luck, yes. I think cards is a game of skill.'

'Care to put your money where your mouth is?' A third man, with long red hair and a small scar above his right eye, interjected, placing a small pile of silvers and coppers on the table.

'It would be my pleasure to teach you gentlemen a thing or two,' Agnes winked.

A fourth man, with short brown curls, muddy-brown eyes, and a bushy beard, gestured for the barmaid to place a pitcher of ale on our table. I watched, transfixed, as Agnes and all the men, including Gaia and Sapphire, picked up their cards and began to play.

———— · ✦ · ————

Several games – and several pitchers of ale – later, Agnes had a small mountain of coins in front of her, and the black-haired man had thrown his cards down on the table to fold once more.

'Perhaps if you spent more time looking at your cards, instead of my face, you may win a round,' Agnes laughed, pulling more silvers towards her ever-growing pile.

'If I stare at your pretty face long enough, I might figure out your tell,' the man grinned, taking a long swig of ale.

'You can try, but it doesn't seem to have worked thus far and, by all accounts, you haven't taken your eyes off of me.'

'It's a good job! Because, if I had, I would've been convinced you were cheating!'

I covered my laugh with a cough, because Agnes *was* cheating. She had glamoured the cards almost every time to ensure she had the winning hand, only giving up the win a handful of times to make it believable. Twice to Sapphire, once to Gaia, once to Sausage Fingers, and once to the man with the scar.

'I don't think cards is your game, sir. Why, I think even my ward here could beat you, and she's never played in her life.' I flinched, not liking how everyone's attention landed on me, but I'd been watching the games eagerly, and I now understood the rules and how to play.

'Shall we say . . . double or nothing?' the man asked, grin relaxed and easy as he swallowed another mouthful of ale.

'Deal.' Agnes extended a hand for the man to shake. Sausage Fingers began dealing again, and I picked up my cards, gulping down a few swigs from my own tankard to disguise the glee at my hand.

I was surprised that Agnes let me play without cheating. She watched me, never once interfering with the cards, and a sense of pride filled me when I laid my hand down on the table and announced, 'straight flush.'

The man cursed, and Gaia covered my ears, pretending to keep my delicate lady's disposition protected from such vulgarity. I laughed, deep and genuine. My cheeks were flushed, and the ale was keeping my belly and skin warm. It felt *good* to be at ease among the humans.

He pushed his last remaining silver towards me and clapped me on the back with a firm hand. 'Beginner's luck,' he boomed, voice having grown louder the more he drank. 'The next round is on you,' he laughed, as the barmaid placed more jugs of ale onto the table.

'Afraid not, gentlemen,' Gaia cut in. 'We have an early start. It's already way past time we retired.' She pushed me towards the stairway.

'Of course, of course! Bleed me dry and then leave! I think I've been hustled, lads!' he guffawed, slapping Gaia on the back. 'The next time you're passing through, I'd like the chance to win back my silver?'

'I know where to find you,' Agnes smiled, flipping him a silver coin for his next round of drinks. The man bowed deeply to Agnes before returning to his friends.

———·✦·———

Agnes and I shared a room, whilst Gaia and Sapphire bunked together next door. The only bed was a double, and Agnes pulled me in tightly.

'You did well tonight,' she planted a kiss on the top of my head.

'You blended in seamlessly. It was like you had been around humans your whole life. And it *is* important for you to fit in with them. If this plan is to work, the prince *must* trust you completely.'

I nodded against her chest, eyes already heavy with sleep.

'When Gaia and Sapphire present you to the queen, it may not be plain sailing. If rumours are to be believed, she did not care for Lord Vermont all that much. Whilst the name we have chosen for you will give you some power in the situation, and she won't disregard you entirely, you will still need to prove useful to her, so that you can worm your way into her inner circle.' Agnes spoke like it was easy, yet something told me it wouldn't be quite so straightforward.

'You will never defend yourself in front of others unless your life depends on it. If anyone sees, tell them your mother trained you to defend yourself before she died, but you feel it unladylike, so you would always prefer a gentleman protect you unless strictly necessary. The men are proud enough to believe it, and lies are more convincing when they are filled with half-truths. Tell the truth, when it doesn't give your identity away.'

I nodded against her once more, and tried not to worry about how often my mother dealt in half truths.

'Your goal is to get close enough to the queen's heir that he trusts you and feeds you secrets.'

I gulped. Before tonight, I had never had so much as a conversation with a man, let alone tried to seduce one, and I opened my mouth to ask how I was supposed to get close to the prince, but instead a yawn slipped free. Agnes chuckled, breath warm against the top of my head.

'Sleep tight, Blaise.'

CHAPTER 6

MY HEAD WAS POUNDING, but that didn't matter to Gaia as she dragged me up from the bed, shoved me into some warm clothes, placed my bag on my shoulder, and practically kicked me out of the tavern door.

'We need to make the next town by nightfall, and you've already overslept. Get a move on!' she hissed.

'Okay, please just stop yelling,' I winced, clutching at my temples. Whilst the ale had gone down smoothly last night, I was paying the price now. I nearly walked straight past Sapphire waiting outside, having forgotten overnight what her glamour looked like.

'Over here,' she waved me down. 'All that silver you won us last night has acquired us these,' she gestured to the three horses standing patiently behind her.

'Good. That will make up for our late start,' Gaia huffed.

'Late? The sun isn't even up yet,' I yawned, petting one of the horses on her large neck. Agnes arrived before Gaia could argue further.

'Let's move,' my mother hoisted me up onto the back of one of the horses, settling herself in the saddle behind me, and I breathed in her scent, acutely aware that today would be our last day together until I completed my mission. *If* I completed my mission.

We made it to the next town over by early evening, having only stopped to allow the horses a moment's rest and some water, while we ate a small meal of bread and hard cheeses.

This town was quieter than the last. The roads were filled with dust and were virtually empty. The people we *did* come across, scuttled by with their heads down, rather than engaging in conversation like in the town we had just come from.

'Where is everybody?' I asked, frowning.

Agnes's body tensed behind mine, Sapphire merely shrugged, and Gaia concentrated on locating a tavern for us to stay in as we continued through the barren streets, the eerie silence feeling more and more uncomfortable.

'I'll ask in here,' Gaia jumped down from her horse, passing the reins up for me to hold onto. She disappeared, only to return a matter of moments later shaking her head. 'We're going to find it hard to find somewhere that will rent a room to outsiders tonight,' she swallowed. 'There's to be a burning.'

Sapphire stiffened. 'Should we ride right through?'

'No,' Agnes seethed. 'Blaise needs to see what these people are really like. It will remind her that, whilst they can be polite and friendly, they are killers at heart.' My ears were ringing, pulse beating against my skull.

A burning.

These people were going to *burn* a witch – and Agnes was going to make me watch.

'We'll try the rougher parts of town, they won't turn down the silver,' my mother said, and she was right. The taverns in that part of the neighbourhood were happy to accept our coin, strangers or not. The seedy bar we ended up in smelled of dust and moths, the carpets had holes, and the sheets looked less than clean, but it was still better than sleeping on the ground. Plus, they had stables for the horses.

'I can hear them,' Gaia muttered, staring out of the shattered window, face paler than usual.

I listened, feeling my own face drain of colour as a roaring crowd began to scream and jeer. Agnes dragged us outside into the now-moonlit street, following the noises of the crowd. We met them on the road, joining the back of the angry mob who waved flaming torches and pelted rotten fruit. I eyed the flames warily, careful not to get too close to those brandishing them around and, as we rounded a corner, my heart sped at the sight of the pyre built a story high.

The crowd surged with fury, their roars growing louder as they neared the pyre. A female's screams echoed, and the crowd swelled with anger once more, as the culprit was dragged towards the unlit bonfire. Digging in her heels, the girl cried out to anyone that would listen.

'Please!' she cried. '*Please*! I am not a witch! I am *not a witch*!'

'Liar!' the crowd bellowed back, and several men spat at the girl, who could not have been older than sixteen.

A group of men forced the girl's back against the pyre, fastening her hands to the wood above her. She tried to wriggle free, kicking one of her attackers in the stomach, but the others grabbed her kicking legs and tied them down, too, putting an end to her struggles. Sweat laced my palms and trickled down my back.

'Look closely,' Agnes whispered. Every inch of me wanted to turn and run, but I eyed the girl, watching for any sign of a glamour that did not come.

'She's not... she's not even a witch,' I stammered, low enough that the people surrounding me couldn't hear. Agnes shook her head. 'We need to help her!' I pleaded, my knees threatening to give out beneath me.

'We cannot. Or we will all burn with her,' Agnes whispered.

'Please! Please! I beg you!' A woman with greying hair fell to her knees in front of the men, and I could only assume she was the girl's mother. 'She is no witch! She's just *a girl*!' the woman begged. Rotten fruit was hurled at the mother, though the girl's captors simply ignored her.

'Light it!' one man bellowed above the crowd, and the captors obeyed.

The kindling quickly caught flame, the girl still pleading innocence until the fire began to lick up her legs, her pleas twisting into cries of agony. I tried to turn away, tears threatening to spill over, but Agnes held my head, forcing me to watch as the flames climbed higher up the girl's body, forcing me to stare as she writhed against the ropes tying her down.

'These humans might appear friendly on the surface, you may even like some of them,' Agnes murmured low in my ear. And I *had*. I'd liked the men we had drunk and played cards with last night.

'But they are all the same,' Agnes continued. 'They *all* want to see us suffer. Their hatred runs so deep, that they are blind. That girl is no witch. She probably just showed an interest in herbs, or writes with her left hand, and that is enough for them to accuse her. To burn her alive.'

The girl's screams rose to a fever pitch, and the woman on her knees wailed loud enough to rival them. My nose burned from the smell of scorched flesh.

'Even if she *were* a witch, would she deserve this? What would a witch do here if left to live peacefully among them? Bring healing magic and herbs to this shithole of a village?' Agnes spat. 'These people will *never* accept you if they learn who you are, who your family is. In Reili, it would not just be this girl they burned. It would be her mother, too, and any other females in her family, so as not to risk that any of them also possess magic. Remember this day, sweet daughter, remember this girl's screams, and let it drive you to bring them all down.'

She let go of my head and I doubled over, retching on the floor. When I closed my eyes to compose myself, the image of the girl as the flames engulfed her, mouth set wide in one last awful scream, skin sluicing off her neck in melted chunks, was ingrained into the back of my eyelids. I retched again, as Gaia and Sapphire each grabbed hold of my arms and dragged me away from the crowd.

Chapter 7

EACH TIME I'D CLOSED MY eyes that night, I'd been unable to shift the image of the girl as she burned, and I'd cried until tears seared my cheeks. Eventually, Agnes took pity on me, using magic to soothe me to sleep in her arms as she gently stroked my hair.

Yet she could do nothing to ease the hateful dreams that frequently tore me from my slumber. In one dream, men hauled my sisters to burn, at a pyre made from the strong trees set deep in the Iron Woods. Ophelia begged me to save her, Marbella's eyes full of hurt and rage, as I stood by with the humans and watched them burn, jeering and hurling rotten tomatoes with the rest of the crowd.

In another, it was me that was the witch, with golden hair and silver eyes like my mother's, casting spells that burned villages to the ground. Sparks flew from my long fingers, and my pointed ears heard screams clearer and louder than I would've as a human. And I relished in their pain and suffering, until I was sat on a throne, Agnes placing a golden crown atop my head as I looked out across a sea of dead humans.

The most frequent terror, was the human girl's face as the flames swallowed her whole, her mother weeping at the base of the fire as it turned her into nothing but ash, floating away on the wind as she desperately tried to catch every piece drifting into the air, scorching her hands on the burnt remains of her daughter.

Each time I woke breathless, a cold sweat running down my back, my hair plastered to my damp forehead, Agnes had been there to calm me. But, when I woke from the latest torment, desperate for my mother's soothing magic, she was gone. Panic flooded my veins as I scrambled out of bed, my eyes taking a minute to adjust to the poor light as I fumbled towards the door. In the hallway, I heard voices and, recognising them as Gaia's and Sapphire's, I started down the hall, stopping outside of their room.

'Will the glamour hold, with you being so far away?' Gaia asked, an unusual amount of worry edging her tone.

'I have no way of knowing,' Agnes responded, and I breathed more easily knowing she hadn't left in the middle of the night to return to the coven. 'I haven't been this far from one of my spells before. You shall have to top it up with your own magic if you begin to notice any cracks.'

A long pause followed, and my eyes began to close in the silence. Knowing my mother was safe, my exhausted body wanted to return to the warmth of my bed, and I began to creep back to my bedroom, until Sapphire asked a question that made me stop dead.

'You're sure we shouldn't tell her? You saw how she handled today. Should we not at least *try* and give her every defence possible?'

'If you tell her, you shall ruin everything!' Agnes snarled, in a tone I had never heard her use with Sapphire before. 'Stick to the plan,' she growled, her footsteps heading towards the door. I ran the remainder of the corridor and darted back into bed, flinging the covers over my head, heart pounding. *Could whatever Sapphire wanted me to know, be the same thing Ophelia had tried to tell me?* The door swung open, and I tried to calm my breathing, to dull the pulse ringing in my ears as Agnes stalked toward our shared bed.

'You're awake.' It wasn't a question.

I twisted into a sitting position. 'I had another bad dream, and I came looking for you,' I offered, hating how shaky my voice was.

'How much did you hear?' she asked.

'Nothing,' I lied.

In a flash, Agnes dropped her glamour, her familiar silver eyes swirling with rage. Her long fingers curled into fists, and her golden hair billowed behind her as she moved towards me. My heart hammered in my chest, and I cowered backwards as she cupped my face in her hands, eyes shining with a predator's glaze.

'Do not lie to me! I will not tolerate being lied to!' she growled.

'I was scared. I thought something had happened to you!'

I hated how my lip trembled, not from the terror of something happening to her, like I pretended, but at the fury on her face now. The display made her eyes soften, though, and her glamour shifted back into place. I couldn't hide how much calmer I instantly became when she looked human once more. Her eyes narrowed, displeased.

'Do not be scared, sweet daughter. You have been raised to be strong. You are one of only four I have ever loved, and *you* may be my greatest love of all.'

Curiosity dampened my fear, and I raised an eyebrow. Ignoring my unspoken question around her fourth love, Agnes continued, with a determined look in her now-hazel eyes that were a slightly greener shade than last time.

'You know now, what has to be done. *You* are the rightful heir to Reili's throne, Blaise! Your sisters are relying on you to restore us to the power that the Mother intended for our kind.' The desire in her eyes was overwhelming, and panic spread through me with the possibility that I would not be able to achieve her goals. Agnes sniffed the air.

'Do not fear, daughter mine. You shall be our salvation! You will end the suffering we have endured for a millennium. Never again will a witch know what it is like to fear a fiery death. We shall thrive, as we always *should* have. And it will be you, sweet daughter, that makes it happen!'

'I don't know that I'm strong enough, Mamma.' I hated the tremble in my voice, hated how I felt so small and insignificant after a mere few days in the human's world. This wasn't how I had been trained to be.

'There is a reason we have been forced to live in fear, darling. Humans are not as weak as they look. *You* are not as weak as you fear. You must harness your human attributes as strengths, for you are the only one who can succeed.'

'What aren't you telling me?' The words slipped out before I could clamp my jaw shut around them. 'I did hear you before.' *Gods, I sounded like a child.*

Her eyes darkened, threatening to turn once more into silver storm clouds. But her words were soft. 'There are things you do not need to know, child. Things that will only hurt you to know.'

I stared deep into her eyes and saw no hint of lies. I had to let it go. She knew better than me. She had trained me my entire life to be strong and brutal. Why would she fail me now? I needed to trust her.

'I must leave,' her shoulders drooped in a rare display of sorrow. 'The coven needs me. Your sisters will be missing me. But I want you to have this.' She pressed a gleaming silver dagger into my hand. A large ruby adorned the pommel, with smaller rubies framing the surrounding edges. The grip was decorated with delicate flowers, all made from a light steel that didn't upset the balance of the blade. I gasped as the cool metal met my skin.

'Did you really think I would let you walk amongst them unarmed?' She cradled my face as I stared at the blade in awe. 'I had it made for you, at the same time your sisters' blades were crafted for their Rite. It is enchanted with my own blood, and it will never miss its target.' I gripped the knife, feeling safer for the first time since I had left my sword behind. Meeting my mother's eyes, I could have sworn I saw the beginning of tears, but she blinked them away. 'When we meet again, you will have changed the world, sweet daughter.'

She embraced me in a tight hug, planting a gentle kiss on my forehead as I took a deep breath in, swallowing her familiar scent of bark and pine, my own eyes burning as tears threatened to fall.

'Sleep now, child. I must speak with Gaia and Sapphire before I leave.' I could feel her magic working its way along my skin, forcing my eyelids to close, and my breathing to soften, rocking me into a gentle slumber.

When I awoke after another nightmare, dawn had broken, and Agnes was gone.

CHAPTER 8

I MUST HAVE FALLEN BACK asleep in the early hours, because I was roughly awoken by a man ripping the blanket from me. I flinched, and instinctively brought my arms across my chest to shield the bare skin from the cool air. Still caught somewhere between nightmare and reality, I struggled, immediately believing this man had come to accuse me of being a witch. I glanced to Agnes's enchanted dagger, where it lay out of reach on the nightstand. The man followed my gaze, and a familiar, cackling laugh escaped his lips.

Gaia, I realised, breathing a sigh of relief.

'Come, Blaise. There is much of the world for you to see. Let's not waste time sleeping,' she winked at me, mischief shining through the unfamiliar human eyes she currently possessed, before tossing the blanket back over my head and leaving me to get dressed.

I smiled sheepishly to myself. Gaia was right, there *was* so much of the world I hadn't seen. It couldn't *all* be fire and death, otherwise she wouldn't have sounded excited to show it to me. Unlike Agnes, Gaia did not relish in the pain of the world. As my mother's general, she had seen enough pain and suffering to last a lifetime. Several human lifetimes, in fact.

Even so, as I dressed in thick wool leggings and a warm cloak that would be comfortable for a day of riding, I strapped the dagger to my thigh, finding comfort in the cold metal. Each slight prick on my skin as I walked, reminded me that my enemies could bleed, too. For they *were* my enemies, the humans. Though they were like me in many ways, I would never be like *them*. The witches were my family, and I would guarantee them a safe future, even if it limited mine.

·✦·

I was pleased to see that awful village disappear behind us. One of the horses had been exchanged for a tent and some bed rolls, which we would sleep in until we reached the next planned stop in a few days. Being a horse down, Sapphire sat behind me on one, and Gaia walked ahead on the other.

'Why couldn't you magic up a tent and keep the horse?' I asked, yawning.

'We'll be using magic as little as possible on this trip,' Sapphire whispered. 'We're too exposed, and it's not worth the risk. Plus, you don't know how to ride, so we don't need the extra horse.'

I frowned. Though I was comfortable around horses, Sapphire was right. I couldn't ride them, and that could be a problem. 'Do noble women know how to ride?'

'Mostly,' she shrugged behind me, her strange male limbs flush against my back.

I pondered if the reason I had never been taught was due to a lack of planning on Agnes's part, or because she hadn't wanted to give me a way out of the Iron Woods. I would've had no room to learn in the dense forest, requiring a venture into human territory. Had she been trying to protect me, or trap me?

'I need to learn,' I resolved. 'I know our lie will account for why I'm unable to ride, but what if the prince asks me to accompany him riding and I cannot? That will put me at a disadvantage against other suitors, will it not? You must teach me before we reach Reili,' I commanded.

'Oh, you are your mother's daughter,' Sapphire laughed, kissing the top of my head. I tensed at her words, though I couldn't put my finger on why they made me uncomfortable.

'Confident you will win over the prince enough that he wants you to ride with him?' Gaia winked.

'Is that not the idea?' I smirked, though I *wasn't* confident. At all.

'Very well, you shall learn as we go. Here, take the reins,' Sapphire handed them to me, the worn leather fitting perfectly into my rough hands, callused from years of sword play. The beautiful creature below me didn't seem to notice as my nervous hands took over from Sapphire's steady ones, and I gave her large grey neck a pat.

'You steer with these,' Sapphire guided. 'Be gentle. She knows what she's doing, she just needs you to guide her into which way she's going. Don't tug her head this way and the other, you'll only piss her off, and she'll dump us both on our arses.'

I gave the gentlest tug with my right hand and, below me, the horse veered to the right. I did the same with my left hand, and she came back to the centre of the road.

'Good,' I could hear the grin in Sapphire's voice as Gaia dropped back to ride alongside us, nodding her approval, too.

'You'll need to know how to stop. Pull back on the reins, but never pull too hard or she'll rear up and dump us on our arses.'

'I'm sensing a pattern here,' I muttered.

'Understand this – she doesn't want us on her back. She's tolerating us. Any opportunity she gets to –'

'Dump us on our arses?' I interrupted.

Sapphire laughed, nodding. 'She will.' The horse huffed out of her nose as if in agreement.

'I get it,' I patted her neck again. 'I'll try not to piss you off too much, girl. Bear with me, though, I'm learning.' She huffed again, her tail swishing behind us, but when I pulled lightly on the reins, she stopped like I asked her to. 'How do I make her go faster?' I grinned and Gaia laughed, shaking her head.

'You haven't even learnt how to make her go *at all* yet,' Sapphire laughed, too. 'That will be tomorrow's lesson,' she took back the reins, flicking my nose when I crossed my arms and pouted.

'There is plenty of time before we get to Reili. I promise you will be an expert before we get there,' she vowed. 'For now, we have ground to cover.'

She kicked her legs, pushing the horse into a gallop, and I squealed as the air caught in my lungs with the sudden speed increase. Before I knew it, Sapphire and Gaia were racing the horses against one another, with me clinging on to the saddle for dear life. When we stopped to give the horses a drink, my jaw ached with laughter, the feeling very welcome after the anguish of the day before.

CHAPTER 9

I SLEPT WELL – BEING EXHAUSTED from the lack of sleep the night before – but not comfortably. Gaia hadn't been kidding when she said they wouldn't risk using magic. Even in my tent in the Iron Woods I'd enjoyed the comfort of a feather bed, but the thin bedroll we'd slept on last night had barely offered even the slightest cushioning between the hard floor and my back, which now ached terribly. Each step the horse took sent pain through my spine. I grumbled constantly until Sapphire kicked me in the back of the leg.

'Stop your griping! We have a long way to go, and it won't always be taverns and inns. You best get used to sleeping on the floor. Here, take the reins, it's time for your next lesson.' Sighing, I accepted the leather straps, welcoming any distraction from the backache. Patiently, Sapphire taught me how to squeeze the horse's sides in order to make her move.

'Give her a little tap with your feet. Harder than that! Let her know you're in charge! Good, now you're getting it.'

By the time we stopped to give the horses some water by a shallow stream, I was smiling to myself. I had controlled the horse, giving her commands that she had obeyed. It wasn't much, but *I* had done it. It was something *I* learned for myself, and, for the first time, it was something I didn't wish I had magic for, something magic wouldn't make any easier.

'Good girl,' I ran a hand through my mare's mane as she drank. I should have given her a name, but I didn't want to get too attached.

A small gust of wind caught in the trees nearby and the smell of pine wafted towards me. If I closed my eyes, I could picture Agnes. Golden hair blowing in the wind, silver eyes full of life, the breeze rippling her familiar red cloak. My stomach twisted into tight knots. I missed her terribly.

'I'm sure she misses you, too, darling,' Gaia said, as though she could read my expression.

My thoughts turned to Ophelia, and how she could read minds. Had she told Agnes yet? Or would Agnes have figured it out on her own? Perhaps *Agnes* could read minds. She *did* always seem to know what was going to happen before it did.

'Do you know of any witches that can read minds?' I blurted out.

Sapphire shook her head. 'It's a rare trait. A powerful one, that hasn't been seen in our coven for a few generations.'

'I know of a handful of witches in the Stormbreaker coven who have the gift. One of the Moonkeeper witches, also, before . . .' Gaia trailed off and we all swallowed, blinking back tears. 'Amongst our own, the Mother has not blessed us with the gift for a long time. Why do you ask?'

I wasn't sure if I should be the one to give away Ophelia's secret, but something niggled at me. Something told me she would need support, and that Gaia and Sapphire would willingly give it.

'Ophelia,' I started, biting my lip nervously, 'she received the gift during her Rite.'

Gaia and Sapphire exchanged a wordless glance, so fast I couldn't pin the emotion in their eyes. Was it pity? Awe? Perhaps worry? Maybe a little fear?

'She tried to tell me something,' I was once more reminded of Ophelia's thwarted warning. 'Something she heard in Agnes's thoughts. But Agnes sent me away before Ophelia could tell me, and she wouldn't even let us say goodbye.'

I cried then. Not because I was ever close with my sisters. In truth, I hadn't expected them to even *want* to say goodbye to me. But, in those moments during the Rite, when Gaia had explained why they had chosen those particular men, it became clear they understood me more than I had given them credit for.

Gaia's strong arms found my shoulders, pulling me in tight against her hard chest as I sobbed. Sapphire knelt before me, my hands gripped in hers, but I couldn't seek the comfort that I needed in their faces. Their glamours made it impossible to see *them* underneath, to understand what they were truly feeling.

'Everything Agnes does is for a reason,' Gaia offered, wiping the tears from my cheeks. 'Everything she does is to protect you and your sisters. To protect the coven.'

'The other night, at the inn,' I continued, wondering if they knew Agnes's reasoning behind keeping more secrets from me. 'You asked whether you should tell me something. I overheard you talking. She's hiding things from me! Things even *you* think I should know. Is that to protect me, too?'

Gaia's hands went still on my face, and Sapphire's eyes widened in alarm, mouth opening and closing as if she couldn't find the right words. Her panicked gaze met Gaia's, and I flicked my eyes between them.

Gaia couldn't look at me, mouth mimicking Sapphire's, the only sound coming out a tiny whimper so at odds with the situation that I examined her for signs of pain. A bead of sweat trailed from her temple, running into the beard that lined her chin. I looked to Sapphire for an explanation, but her hand was clamped over her mouth.

'Can't,' she squeaked around her fingers, and my stomach sunk as realisation smacked me in the face.

Agnes had put a spell on them.

They physically *couldn't* tell me her secret, even if they wanted to. Both fought against the magic that prevented them from speaking. Sweat still ran across Gaia's forehead, and Sapphire tried desperately to pry her fingers away from her mouth.

'Stop! Stop it!' I yelled at the magic. 'I don't need to know! Let them go!' It wasn't until I stormed away that the spell dropped, and Sapphire slumped to the ground, a small sob escaping her lips. Rubbing her chest, Gaia bent to pick Sapphire up, pulling her into a tight hug.

I turned away, horrified at the lengths Agnes would go to, to keep me in the dark.

CHAPTER 10

'SQUEEZE YOUR LEGS INTO HER side to make her go faster, and snap the reins a little,' Sapphire commanded from behind me, as I tried to make the horse gallop to keep up with Gaia.

It had rained consistently for almost a week, and sleeping outside had been miserable. Gaia felt we would reach the next village – and be out of the downpour – by sundown, if we moved fast. So, what better time to teach me how to gallop? My riding had improved dramatically, in spite of the flaring tempers of the horses with the ever-worsening weather, and I could now trot confidently without aid.

The horses weren't the only ones getting increasingly wound up. I was bored of always wearing wet socks, my feet were in a permanent state of pruning, and my hair was always plastered to my head in such an unruly fashion that I'd stopped even attempting to brush it. It was the only time I'd been jealous of Gaia and Sapphire's cropped trims that had come with their glamoured appearance.

Gaia grew ever grumblier with each raindrop, and Sapphire had taken to napping on the back of the horse when I had the reins, as she said it was drier than the ground. She'd barely slept at night thanks to Gaia's snoring.

It was no surprise *they* were struggling with the weather. They were Sunseekers after all, which meant the witches pulled their power from the sun. Whilst the Stormbreaker coven would be perfectly at home – stronger, even – in the downpour, the Sunseekers were strongest when the sun was highest in the sky. Just as the Starchaser coven thrived on a cloudless night when the stars were most clear, and the Moonkeepers were – *would* have been – most powerful on a night with a full moon. It was another reason they had chosen the tallest mountain in Starterra as their home, in order to be closer to the sky. It was said that some nights, the moon was so large, and appeared so close, it was as though you could reach out from the top of the peaks and touch it.

I tightened my grip on the reins and geed the horse below me to move faster. Thinking of the Moonkeepers, and how Queen Lizabeta and Prince Kaspian had ordered their destruction, filled me with renewed determination. I would never allow that to happen to another coven, especially not my own. For, though I was not a witch, I was still a Sunseeker. By name, and by birthright.

'Look!' I cried out, relief audible in my voice as I pointed to the buildings now visible only a few miles away.

'I can almost feel the warmth,' Sapphire smiled.

'I can almost taste the rum,' Gaia winked. 'Last one there's a goblin!'

She took off with a cackle, horse thundering beneath her. Behind me, Sapphire snatched the reins, and forced our horse into a desperate run that had me clinging to the saddle for dear life. But, whilst I struggled to keep a hold of my seat, laughter tumbled from me with an easiness I hadn't felt in days.

'Barkeep!' Sapphire hollered, as we tumbled through the door of the nearest tavern, still laughing. 'A round of rum for everyone! Including your good self!' The full bar cheered.

'Oh aye, what's the occasion?' the barkeep asked.

'I've just had a good win,' she winked at Gaia, who rolled her eyes. 'Feeling generous.' Of course, it helped that it wasn't real money she was paying with. I swiped a glass of rum and left them to it at the bar, searching for a quieter spot to rest my legs.

Despite its worn fabric chairs and damaged tables, the tavern was clearly a popular establishment, and I had to walk right to the back of the room before finding an empty booth to slide into. With the chatter around me providing white noise, I felt content enough to let my eyes fall closed.

'Well, aren't you a pretty thing.'

I was pulled from my moment alone, to see that a small man, with thinning hair and a bulbous nose, had sidled up to my booth, and was leering at me with beady black eyes in a way that made my hands tighten into fists. I glanced around to find Gaia and Sapphire making friends at the bar. There were a lot of bodies between us and them, and I wouldn't be able to get their attention. Even if I yelled, I wouldn't be heard over the rowdy patrons.

'I'm trying to enjoy a drink in peace, if you don't mind,' I scowled, gesturing with the rum in my hand, causing some liquid to slop over the rim.

'Where's the fun in drinking alone, when you could have a drinking partner?' he licked his thin lips and edged closer.

'My friends will be back in a moment. I will ask you again to leave, sir.' I tried to find a way out of the booth, but he blocked the only exit, and the table leg below was made of thick wood that stretched the entire way across the booth, making crawling underneath impossible.

'I'm sure they won't mind me keeping you company while you wait for them,' he grinned, showing his missing teeth and blackened gums as he slid into the booth next to me. I backed away into the far corner, squishing myself against the wall.

'Now, now, I'm only being friendly,' he sneered, putting a cold hand on my knee. I tried to jerk away, but I was already backed as far into the corner as I could get.

'Sir, I heard the woman ask you to leave. Are you deaf? Or just plain stupid?'

I looked up, to find an impossibly beautiful man stood at the end of the table, hand casually resting on the pommel of the sword strapped to his side. He didn't look much older than me. His dark brown hair curled across his brow, a few errant strands – that, for some reason, I desperately wanted to run my hands through – drooped into eyes that were the deepest shade of blue.

My uninvited visitor whipped his head around but left his hand on my knee. He took in the man's large frame and sword but didn't back down. 'What you doin' bothering me when I'm with my girl?'

'Oh, *your girl*, is she? Funny, because I saw her arrive with the gentlemen over there,' he nodded to Gaia and Sapphire's glamoured forms, 'and I definitely heard her tell you to leave. Several times.'

'What's it to you?' the man still had his hand on my knee, and it was taking all of my restraint not to bend his fingers backwards so hard that they broke. That would bring unwanted attention, though. I might have been trained to handle danger, but here, I had to play *the lady*. I scowled, hating that I knew how to defend myself and yet this stranger, albeit a handsome one, was having to do it for me.

'I'm not in the business of letting handsy pricks have their way with women who quite clearly have no interest.'

My jaw hung open a little, as another, even taller gentleman arrived, standing at the handsome stranger's back. His shaved hair made his angular face appear somewhat menacing, but his grey eyes, that were currently fixed in a sharp scowl, were even more threatening. 'Is there a problem here?'

The man gripping my knee blanched slightly, finally withdrawing his hand as he turned to face them properly. 'Not a problem. Your friend just seems to be very concerned about the girl's wellbeing.'

'Should he be?' I watched the grey-eyed man's hand slip to his own sword, and the man beside me gulped.

'Not at all! I merely wanted some fun with the thing. She's hardly worth all the fuss!' He stood to leave. The other pair stood firm, blocking his exit.

'Charming,' I muttered under my breath.

Blue Eyes heard and smirked. My eyes fixated on the way it made a small dimple appear in his left cheek, the slight imperfection somehow made perfect on his otherwise flawless face. After another beat, he finally stepped sideways, letting the creep pass. All three of us watched as he disappeared into the crowd.

'Are you okay?' Blue Eyes asked.

'Perfectly. I had it covered. I didn't need your help,' I snapped, and then inwardly grimaced. That was *not* a very ladylike reaction.

Blue Eyes let out a low chuckle. 'You know, most people would say thank you.'

'Well, I'm not most people.' *I couldn't help myself, could I?*

'I can tell. What's your name?'

'So, you fend off one creep, just to have a go yourself? Nice move. Bet that works for all your damsels in distress.'

Oh wow, Blaise, if this is how you talk to men, you really need to sort your shit out before you meet the prince!

Grey Eyes looked aghast, and made to step between us. I found the movement highly comical, given his friend thought *I* needed protecting, and yet this other man seemed to think I needed to be protected *from*. Blue Eyes merely laughed again, the sound like music. Damn, everything about him was irritatingly flawless.

'Asking for your name is hardly making a move,' he smirked again, that infuriatingly perfect dimple making another appearance. 'I just wanted to know the name of the damsel I rescued.' He'd said it to anger me. I knew it, and the ever-growing smirk on his face said he knew that I knew it. And Mother above, it worked.

'I am not a *damsel*! And I didn't need your rescue!' I pushed past him, letting my shoulder barge his, and feeling satisfied when he wobbled into Grey Eyes slightly.

I stormed up to Gaia and Sapphire. 'We're leaving.'

'We just got here,' Sapphire whined. 'I was getting us rooms for the night.'

'I'd rather sleep in the rain,' I snapped, fully aware of the pair of penetrating blue eyes bearing into the back of my head.

'Uh-oh,' Sapphire glanced behind me. 'Made a friend, did we?'

'Can we leave or not?' I hissed.

'Sure m'lady,' Gaia's sympathetic gaze infuriated me further, so I spun on my heel and stormed out of the tavern, never once looking back at the handsome stranger that had come to my *rescue*.

CHAPTER 11

'WE'RE GOING TO STORMHOLD,' SAPPHIRE announced, when we finally made it to Starterra's capital, Windmere. I had questioned why the pair had suddenly changed into Starterrian soldier uniforms. Though it was part of the plan, they had yet to wear them thus far.

'The palace?' I squawked.

'How many other Stormholds do you know of? Yes, the palace. We've been invited to a ball.'

'A ball?' I questioned. This really did not feel like the time to be partying, especially amongst so many humans.

'It's been planned since we left the Iron Woods,' Sapphire's grin was devious. 'There's a familiar face there I would like to see, and it gives you the opportunity to try and blend in with nobility before we throw you in at the deep end.'

'We know you've been worried about how well you'll mix in when it's not all taverns and card playing,' Gaia winked. 'And now we'll know for sure if you have it in you, or whether we should just turn around and tell Agnes you failed.'

I felt my skin pale. Failing Agnes utterly *terrified* me. It wasn't an option.

'Plus, you packed all those fancy dresses Agnes had made for you. The poor horses have been carrying them for weeks, and we've not gotten to see you in any of them,' Sapphire pouted. I rolled my eyes. After so long in comfortable leggings and a warm cloak, the thought of having to wear a tight corset and layers of skirts wasn't a pleasant one.

'And there will be men.' Gaia looked down at herself and added, 'real ones!'

That was even less appealing than the skirts. If my last encounter with a man was anything to go off, this would be a disaster.

───・✦・───

The sight of Stormhold greeted us from miles away. A strategic location for battle, Stormhold bordered Harensarra. The palace offered a formidable view that made enemies cautious of crossing the border. Its great turrets were so high that the tops were lost amongst the clouds, and the outer walls were a splendid dark brick, streaked with flashes of strong white marble. The overall look was one of a stormy night, giving the palace its name.

All Starterrians, witch or human, knew the story. Long before the palace was built, a violent storm destroyed almost all the buildings in Windmere – Starterra's capital – killing thousands. Rumours would lead one to believe the Stombreaker coven was responsible, but they had never accepted responsibility for the act. Despite the tragedy all around them, one small hut – made from mud and straw, and owned by one of the poorest families in the capital – stood untouched, the family unscathed.

When the storm passed, the then-king of Starterra demanded his new palace be built on the land where the hut stood, believing it to be blessed by the Gods, and protected against storms from the skies, as well as the storms of war.

By means of thanks for the blessed land, the king moved the family who owned the hut into the old palace. Though half of it was in ruins, it was still better than the mud hut they were used to, and they gave their gratitude to the king. A year later, another storm struck, destroying the other half of the old palace and killing the family inside. Stormhold, on the other hand, had never fallen foul to another storm – or to its enemies – ever again.

We were greeted at the palace's grand gates by a footman who showed us to a guest suite. One look at Gaia and Sapphire's uniforms had people answering to *their* command, not the other way around. Nobody questioned soldiers of the Starterra army. Starterra's soldiers were always held in the highest regard, even after losing the war nineteen years ago. According to Sapphire and Gaia, many considered Starterra the real victors. Though Starterra's king was the one to surrender and pay great penalties to Reili, their king was also the one to survive the war. Reili's king – *my father* – never returned home, courtesy of Agnes.

Gaia and Sapphire used the room to change into stiff suits, with little tails that trailed past their bottoms, and high collars that forced their chins into the air. Meanwhile, I squeezed my curves into a tight ivory corset that pushed my bust up under my arms. A blush-pink gown, with cream detailing and layers upon layers of skirts, slid over the top. Underneath hid matching pink slippers, as well as Agnes's dagger that I had strapped to my thigh.

Sapphire braided my hair, like she had many times before, into a twisted crown atop my head, and I squeezed my eyes shut against the memory of myself braiding Marbella's hair before her Rite. Despite her constant scolding, I desperately missed my sister. Sapphire painted rouge on my cheeks and lined my eyes with kohl before staining my lips with red berries.

'You're almost a woman now,' she told me. 'It's time you looked the part.'

Catching my reflection in a tall mirror, I could have almost described myself as beautiful.

———✦———

The ballroom was magnificent, with a speckled marble floor that had been polished until it sparkled. One wall was lined with art and flowers, and another with large windows that looked out across the palace's rose gardens. The setting sun washed everything in a subtle orange glow.

At one end of the room, tables were lined with rows of champagne flutes that bubbled invitingly, and canapés that were never touched. At the opposite end, the king of Starterra perched upon a golden throne. His golden crown slipped over his dark brow as he accepted another glass of champagne, slumping back against the hard metal.

Despite all of the stories, the king didn't look like a man to surrender. His large frame was packed with muscle, his shoulders broad and chest puffed out. His brown eyes darted around the room as though waiting for the next attack, and the only sign that gave away his age, was how his dark hair was receding, exposing a large forehead etched with frown lines that never smoothed.

Beside him, as slender as he was broad, sat his queen. Her bony face was only made sharper by the way her lips pursed in a state of constant irritation. Wearing a fuchsia dress that clashed daringly with her orange hair, her high cheekbones were dusted with so much powder that every time she moved her head, she left a cloud in her wake, like an imprint in time.

To the side of the queen, at the bottom of a small staircase, stood a row of the king's consorts. The six beautiful women were, no doubt, the reason the queen looked so irritated. I scanned the line, and my eyes kept darting back to a particular woman with long blonde hair and striking blue eyes. Her youthful skin glowed, and her pure white smile never faltered, but something was . . . odd . . . about her. I couldn't pinpoint what until we made our way closer. Edging around the dancefloor, I noticed the slight blur around her outline, and my jaw almost hit the floor.

I tugged Sapphire closer by her sleeve. 'That one, is she a – OW!'

I squeaked as Sapphire pinched the skin above my elbow hard, interrupting my question. My squeal caught the attention of the witch posing as the king's consort and she whispered into the ear of the girl next to her before making a beeline right for us.

'James. Bill,' the woman stopped before us and curtsied with a knowing smile. Using the fake names we had given Sapphire and Gaia, she extended a gloved hand for the pair of them to kiss in turn. Sapphire's lips lingered, and it became clear how the pair knew each other.

'Crystelle,' Sapphire finally released her hand. 'It's been too long.'

'You know you're always welcome to visit. If you can shake the ball and chain.' Her voice turned sour, and my neck prickled, realising she was referring to Agnes. I coughed, a scowl already locked in place for when Crystelle dragged her eyes from Sapphire to me.

'And little Blaise,' Crystelle cooed. 'The last time I saw you, you were just a baby, and the covens had gathered to decide what to do with you. Don't worry, I was firmly on the side of *not* eating you,' she added in hushed tones with a wink.

My chest and neck warmed, as both embarrassment and anger washed over me. I knew there were witches that had wanted Agnes to drown me as a babe, ridding herself of the human child she'd created. But to hear that *eating me* had been an option . . . I shuddered.

'Crystelle is a Starchaser,' Gaia spoke in a low voice that only the four of us could hear. 'She's been infiltrating the king's network here for years.'

Years.

I felt the colour drain from my face. I should have guessed that more than one of us had been tasked with infiltrating kingdoms to offer some semblance of freedom to the witches, but to hear that Crystelle had been doing this for *years*. . .

Had I expected to be done in a matter of weeks? Months, maybe? That I could be reunited with my family as soon as *that*? It seemed foolish now, that I hadn't thought about the road ahead, and how hard I would have to work to get *near* the prince, let alone to make him trust me. To confide in me enough that I could leak secrets back to Agnes.

'I have already passed word to my sisters that you will be passing through Harensarra. You'll be welcome to stay before you move on to Reili,' Crystelle whispered to Gaia and Sapphire. They muttered their appreciation as Crystelle led us closer to the dancefloor.

'Now then, Blaise, I hear you need some practice amongst royalty? Come,' Crystelle grabbed my hand and dragged me onto the dancefloor. 'Prince Adelaide!' she called, hauling me through twirling bodies, 'you simply *must* meet Lady Blaise Vermont!'

I dipped into a low curtsey as I stopped in front of a prince with a hairline like his father's, only his was golden blonde, rather than brown. He offered me a bow and took my hand. 'Care to dance, Lady Vermont?'

'I'd love to,' I offered him my most winning smile and let him lead us into a fast waltz.

Learning to dance had come with learning swordplay. *The faster you can spin, the lighter you are on your feet, and the faster you'll be able to slice a man in two*, I remembered Agnes saying and thus, had commenced dance lessons. I'd loved it when Sapphire started travelling throughout the continent for scouting missions, returning with knowledge of the latest dances across the kingdoms. Practicing with her was far different to dancing with an actual man, though, as I was quickly finding out now. The men were far clumsier.

The king of Starterra had seven children, all boys, with Prince Adelaide being the second eldest. Prince Jacob, one of the middle boys, swept in after Adelaide to ask me for a dance. His hair was dark like his father's, but his eyes were sky-blue, and his cocky grin was somehow endearing.

Prince Elijah – another middle child, who had spent most of the evening by the champagne table – dragged himself away to step in when Jacob grew bored of me, leading me into a quickstep before disappearing quickly to empty the contents of his stomach.

Prince Benjamin, the eldest of the brothers, only stepped in to see what his younger brothers were finding so fascinating. He looked very similar to his mother. Though his orange hair was not quite as vibrant as hers, his bony face was even pointier.

Prince Maverick, a fair-haired boy who could be no older than sixteen, towered head and shoulders above his brothers, and had a gentle touch as he spun me around the dancefloor.

Prince Billiam got red-faced and angry when I called him William – because, honestly, what sort of name is *Billiam*? – and had to be ushered off by the gentle-handed Maverick to calm down.

Prince Titus then bowled over, bowing so low he almost kissed the marble floor, and flicking his sweeping dark hair out of his eyes – causing several girls around us to swoon – before asking me to join him for a dance.

Finally, Prince Ivan strolled over as I had been about to rest my feet, offering me a glass of champagne, and allowing me to catch my breath before instantly stealing it again. He kissed my hand, never taking his rich brown eyes from mine, and told me I had saved the best until last before sweeping me around the dancefloor.

Gaia watched carefully, untouched glass of champagne in hand, as the prince twirled me dizzy with the speed of the song. Sapphire whizzed passed me several times with Crystelle in her arms.

'Lady Vermont,' Ivan started, 'how is it that I have never seen you at court before? A woman as beautiful as yourself should not have been kept from me.'

I blushed. I would never get used to being called beautiful, though the compliment had been thrown at me by all his brothers – except the insulted Billiam – this evening.

'I have only recently discovered I am of noble heritage. My grandfather, he was Lord Vermont, Reili's emissary, perhaps you've heard of him?' Ivan's scowl told me he didn't think much of the man. 'He died recently, and his lands and titles have been passed to me as his only living family member,' I offered, the rehearsed lie sweet on my tongue.

'I am travelling to Reili, to find out what the queen wants to do with me. I do hope I can continue my grandfather's work as emissary. Perhaps then I could see more of you,' I lied.

Ivan's shoulders straightened, his chin tilting at the not-so-subtle flattery, tongue darting out to flick across his bottom lip. 'I do hope so, Lady Vermont. I would love to keep a fine thing like you within arm's reach.'

His entitlement made my skin prickle, and I refrained from letting my hand drift to my dagger. This was a tiny fragment of the rage I would feel when faced with Prince Kaspian, who had sent an army to murder the Moonkeeper coven whilst they slept, so I swallowed it down and smiled sweetly.

'For now, Your Highness, I must bid you goodnight and farewell. I have a long journey ahead of me.' I slipped free of his grasp, excusing myself from the dancefloor. Grabbing a glass of champagne, I swallowed it in one before spinning to leave, instead colliding with an incredibly firm body.

'Apologies m'lady, wasn't looking where I was going.'

That voice.

I looked up, craning my neck to see the face of the body I had crashed into. Piercing blue eyes landed on mine.

Shit.

'What are *you* doing here?' I blurted, cringing almost instantly because, whilst I recognised *him* – with my hair done, my face full of cosmetics and a pretty gown on, I looked very different to the last time he had seen *me*. I might have been able to get away without him recognising me. But, the moment those words left my lips, those deep irises sparked with recognition. Before he could speak, his grey-eyed sidekick stepped in.

'That's no way to speak to the future king of Reili.'

Did he say . . .

I could have vomited. I was sure my eyes almost bulged from my head as I stared at the man in front of me, who was still impossibly handsome, but wearing much more formal dress than the last time I had seen him. And now I looked closely, I noted the royal blue emblem with the golden rising phoenix embroidered over his chest. Shock and anger rippled through me. My fingers twitched towards my dagger.

'Oh, calm down, Cole,' the prince clapped, what I now assumed was his royal guard's shoulder, and some of the tension left the man's face. 'It's a perfectly reasonable question. It's not everyday that Reili's heir is seen in his enemy's homeland.'

My heart raced even as I stood perfectly still. I had two options: introduce myself to him now as Lady Blaise Vermont and begin the lie we had set out to tell. Or figure out a way to excuse myself from the conversation that would be enough for him to forget all about me when he next saw me in Reili trying to worm my way into his mother's circle. The latter felt impossible, but the former meant going with him now and being split from Gaia and Sapphire. It was childish, but I wasn't ready to say goodbye to them just yet.

Unable to make myself choose a course of action, I simply stared up at him. This devastatingly handsome man was responsible for wiping a whole coven off the map. I didn't know why, but I'd expected him to be . . . uglier.

'I'm here on official business,' the prince continued, oblivious to my inner turmoil about why people who did ugly things weren't punished with an equally-ugly appearance. 'It's the fifteen-year anniversary of our countries' peace agreement and, every five years, one of us is required to visit the other's homeland to ensure that the agreement is being upheld.'

Peace agreement? No one had ever mentioned a peace agreement between Starterra and Reili in my history lessons.

'Oh.' Apparently, my brain couldn't come up with anything better to say that wasn't a string of curses ending with me stabbing him on this very dance floor. I pulled my hand away from my thigh to stop myself ripping my dagger free from its hold and acting on that impulse.

'How about you, my lady? Need rescuing this evening?' his eyes sparkled with amusement, and Cole did a double take as he put together what his prince already had.

'Only from this conversation.'

Mother above, why did I say that?

Several people turned their heads in our direction as the prince tipped his head back and laughed. I ignored the way the sound made a shiver run the length of my spine. He had murdered so many witches, what right did he have to be so happy?

'How about a dance? Or perhaps a drink?' he nodded at the empty glass I still held.

'No,' I spat in disgust. 'Thanks,' I added, as an afterthought.

He smirked. That dimple had no right to be as attractive as it was. 'Another time then.'

Over my cold, dead body.

He brushed past me, his guard on his heels, and I took a deep breath, steadying my nerves as I finally made my legs walk me from the room. Gaia fell into step behind me.

'Do you know who that was?' I hissed, and she nodded in the corner of my eye. Face calm. Ever the war general. Never betraying her true feelings which must have been as vengeful as mine. 'Do you think he'll recognise me when I get to Reili?'

She shook her head. 'You better hope if he does, he believes whatever reason you come up with for not telling him who you are supposed to be.'

'Can't you just cast a memory spell, or something?'

'Too many people,' she hissed. 'Too risky.'

Panic sat like a heavy weight on my chest. I couldn't think of any reason he would believe. I just had to hope that he wouldn't remember my face. Even though he'd already recognised me once . . .

'Forget him.' *As if I could.* 'You had six princes practically *falling* at your feet tonight!' Gaia teased.

I couldn't help but grin wickedly back at her. I *had* done that, and it had felt incredibly powerful to have the heirs to the throne of Starterra falling over themselves for a chance to dance with me. Until Prince Kaspian had come along to ruin my evening. My grin faltered.

'Where's Sapphire?' I asked, trying to distract myself.

'Oh, I believe she and Crystelle are getting reacquainted somewhere,' Gaia laughed. I didn't know how she *could* laugh when our enemy was sleeping in the same halls as us tonight.

'Won't the king mind one of his consorts running off to bed the nearest soldier?'

'He's got five more to occupy himself with, I doubt he'll notice.'

'He's not noticed that he's let a witch into his harem, so I suppose you're right,' I muttered, as Gaia shut the door to my suite behind us. Not as luxurious as the main palace rooms, it was still grand, with ivory-painted walls, and a hearth burning in one section. To one side stood a large, four-poster bed with an adjoining bathing chamber.

'Crystelle doesn't have a very good opinion of my mother,' I frowned, remembering Crystelle's words about Agnes.

'Your mother is a strong witch, Blaise. Not everyone always agrees with her actions.'

'Do you?'

Gaia hesitated, searching my face for whether I could bear the truth. 'Not always.'

Before I could ask what Gaia disagreed with, Sapphire and Crystelle burst into the room giggling between embraces.

'I like this body. Can you keep it?' Crystelle stroked down Sapphire's broad chest.

'I could ask you the same thing,' Sapphire cupped Crystelle's round backside.

'Mother above! We're not listening to you two all night! Find somewhere else to appreciate those new bodies for the evening,' Gaia rolled her eyes. In a flash, Crystelle grabbed Sapphire's hand and led her back the way they came in. Gaia slammed the door shut behind them, twisting the key in the lock.

'She looks happy,' I smiled at the door. I hadn't seen Sapphire this carefree since before we left the coven. At least the prince hadn't ruined *her* evening.

'She does, doesn't she,' Gaia replied. Before I could ask more about Crystelle and Sapphire and their no doubt sordid history, Gaia slipped out of the room to stand guard by my door.

'Goodnight, Blaise,' she whispered.

CHAPTER 12

WE CROSSED INTO HARENSARRA a day after the ball. It would take a couple of weeks to travel through and across Reili's borders, and a further few days to travel into Reili's capital, Broozh, where the queen's palace was situated.

Harensarra was a sparse nation, with few towns and even fewer people. When I asked about the empty buildings and ashen faces of the people we did come across, Gaia told me how the kingdom had fallen foul to a Pox a few decades previous, which had led to mountains of bodies piled up in the street. Those who did survive were largely traumatised from the sights and smells they had endured.

Of course, the Starchaser witches could have healed the pox – and *had* cured any of their own that had been stricken – but humans would rather die than accept that a witch's powers could be used for good.

'Some did seek the witches out,' Gaia told me. 'Those that had heard rumours of healers made the trek up the Rocky Mountains to ask the Starchasers to cure them or their children. Some witches took pity on the families who had lost everything and offered their healing powers at no price other than secrecy.'

'But the humans couldn't even offer them *that*. Once cured, they immediately spread news to others in the village, and many of the witches were found and burned,' Sapphire spat.

'Since then, the Starchasers have tripled their enchantments to hide their coven, and forbidden witches from using their powers to help the humans. After that, all the humans that got sick died,' Gaia finished, face sombre.

The foolishness of my own kind never ceased to amaze me. So frightened of things they did not understand, that they would rather wipe out two thirds of a kingdom than let magic be their saviour.

'How will we find them, the Starchasers?' I asked.

'They will likely find us,' Gaia promised.

A week into our journey, we reached the fated Rocky Mountains where the Starchasers dwelled. Not as high as the mountains in Starterra where the Moonkeepers had spent their nights close to the moon, but more treacherous. With no trees to block the view, just endless rocks, shallow streams and dusty paths, there was an uninterrupted view of the stars each night, which was why the Starchasers felt so at home.

The horses, on the other hand, were struggling to see the appeal, and I couldn't help but agree with them. I missed the smells and noises of the Iron Woods. The Rocky Mountains were nothing but rock and more rock. The forest was dense greenery, with wildflowers bridging the gaps between trees and it was always *alive*, with the sounds of birds, frogs, bugs, and bees.

The only animals I had seen on the mountains were snakes that snapped at the horses' ankles as they climbed ever higher, or tiny flying bugs that tried their hardest to bite my skin and take my blood. And, despite the beauty of the stars at night, the day bore never-ending rocks that were dull to look at, even irritating at times.

And the heat! Oh, the heat was the worst of all. Though I had never seen the mountains in Starterra, I knew them to be covered in snowy points, with a chill in the air that Sapphire said turned her nipples into glass cutters.

These mountains were nothing like that. The humid air was likely the reason nothing ever grew here, the paths dusty from the dry earth. A constant sweat ran dampened my brow and my back, causing my clothes to stick and irritate my skin. I removed my cloak, rolled my leggings up to my knees and kept my blouse buttoned down low, and still the pools of sweat didn't cease.

The horses struggled even more so. Their tails constantly batted away the flies that surrounded us and our stinking bodies, and they stopped every few meters to drink from the shallow stream that flowed through the rock formations, though I was sure they inhaled more dust than actual water. I felt sorry for the beasts, and regularly rewarded them by petting their large necks and treating them to my lumps of hard cheese.

When I was about to scream that I couldn't spend another minute in the bastard heat, a small woman, with wispy grey hair and a hooked nose, appeared from behind a large boulder. Dressed in all-black robes that looked far too stifling for the weather, wrinkled skin sagged around her sunken blue eyes.

'Come,' she beckoned with a pointed finger, 'we've been expecting you.'

I twisted in the saddle to look questioningly at Sapphire, who smiled without a word and handed me the reins. We followed the woman higher up the perilous rock side until the horses panted with the lack of oxygen. I was about to ask when this nightmare journey would be over, when we passed through an invisible barrier and the mountains came alive with movement.

Witchlings ran between large homes made from giant boulders, scattered around the mountain, and huge golden telescopes were dotted everywhere, pointing towards the sky. The dusty floor of the mountain had become lush green grass, and the sound of gently running water echoed over the babble of witches.

Mother above! Magic was beautiful.

The woman's appearance also changed once we crossed the barrier. Her sagging skin became youthful, strands of grey hair turned silky white, and her blue eyes turned violet. Her hooked nose was now upturned in a delicate point, and her fingers extended to make way for her extra knuckles. Her robes fell away to become cool, billowing linens. I raised an eyebrow at her, and she smiled, flashing brilliant white teeth.

'Humans sometimes come up here expecting to find a witch, I give them what they want to see. I can't bring myself to add a wart to my nose, though,' the witch cackled, and I laughed, too, despite the nagging question of what happened to those humans that came looking.

I looked to Gaia and found her already staring at me, holding her breath. When she caught me looking, she jumped down from the horse and pulled the woman into a tight hug.

'Helena, my old friend,' she smiled, silver eyes crinkling.

I gasped, realizing at once that Gaia's glamour had disappeared. I twisted atop the horse to look at Sapphire, whose features had also returned to the face I knew and loved so well. I almost sobbed to see them again.

'You passed through an enchantment wall,' Helena told me, helping me down from the horse, as she saw me staring at the pair of them. 'As soon as you pass back through, their glamours will fall back into place. They can be themselves here,' she smiled before adding, 'welcome to our home, Blaise. We are so *pleased* to have you.'

Something about the way she lingered on the word *pleased* sent a chill down my spine, but she squeezed my hand, and I returned her smile before she spun, white hair billowing behind her, and pulled Gaia back into her arms.

'It has been a lifetime, Gaia. Come, old woman, you must be tired,' Helena jested.

'Call me old again, Helena, and I will have to show your coven just how past her prime their leader is.'

'Aye, I'm sure they will believe you without a demonstration. It has been several years since I've had to wield a defence spell.' Helena led us into the heart of the village they had made within the mountains, but I couldn't take in many of the surrounding sights, as my gaze lingered on Gaia and Sapphire.

'I've missed seeing you with my own eyes, Blaise,' Sapphire told me, after catching me staring for the umpteenth time. 'But, Mother above, now I've got my full sight back, I can see how much you need a bath!' I elbowed her in the ribs as she cackled, trying to dance out of my reach.

'Thistle, Sybil,' Helena called, and two small witchlings came running. 'Take Blaise, and show her where she can wash, will you. Then tell Theodora our guests have arrived, and to set the table for dinner.'

The girls nodded in sync, each taking one of my hands and leading me away. They took me to a rock pool filled with steaming water that looked clean and inviting. A waterfall poured down from rocks above, and I couldn't wait to dunk my head under it. The witchlings showed me where I could leave my clothes, and handed me a bar of sweet-smelling soap before I climbed into the pool. The water hissed and spat as I lowered myself in, and the warmth felt refreshing against my clammy, sticky skin.

I soaked my hair under the waterfall, feeling mild embarrassment as dust and dirt clouded around me as I scrubbed at my body with the soap. Once the water began to run clear again, the grime washed away by the flowing waterfall, I took the soap and scrubbed at the dirt that had bedded itself under my nails.

As I washed, Thistle and Sybil stole giggling glances at me. I tried not to feel self-conscious and reminded myself they had likely never seen a human before, especially not this close, and there were many differences between my human body and theirs. As I climbed back out of the pool, trying to keep as much dignity as possible, the girls handed me my clothes and I put them on over my wet skin, sure the heat would dry me soon enough. My hair dripped onto the hot ground as they led me back to the rest of the coven.

'Much better,' Sapphire nodded her approval and, with a click of her fingers, my hair dried instantly. I marvelled at even the tiniest bit of magic she had spent over a month holding back.

'Come sit, Blaise. You arrived just in time to appreciate Theodora's cooking.' Helena's smile didn't meet her narrowed eyes. I had thought I would feel more at home surrounded by witches once more, but something about Helena made me hesitant.

When we were all seated, a plump witch, with golden hair and contrasting silver eyes – who I assumed was Theodora – clapped her hands, and our plates filled with slabs of cooked meats, mounds of potatoes and lashings of gravy. Most humans would assume that all witches dined on flesh and blood every night, yet their staple diet was the same. The only difference being that the witches' food was prepared with the help of magic and, for that reason, was infinitely tastier.

Hesitations forgotten at the sight of the food, I tucked in, groaning as the delicious flavours exploded around my taste buds. Theodora beamed at me and, once satisfied her guests were all enjoying the meal, helped herself to mountainous portions.

'So, Blaise,' Helena started, pushing potatoes around her plate. 'You are to be our saviour, is that right?' Her smirk betrayed her true feelings towards my mother's plan, and I clenched my fist around my cutlery.

'I will try to bring about peace for the witches, yes. A place where you can live freely, without enchantment walls and hidden covens,' I stated, carefully.

'You have no sympathy for your own kind?' she asked, finally spearing a potato with her fork.

'Blaise is more like us than her appearance would lead you to believe,' Gaia spoke freely.

'Alas, she looks distinctly human to me,' Helena shrugged, eyes never leaving mine.

'I have only ever known life in the coven. My loyalty lies with my sisters across all the kingdoms. I wish to end their suffering.' I swallowed hard.

'*Sisters*.' Helena repeated the word. '*My* sisters and I have been betrayed by humans before. We showed kindness and trust, and the favour was returned by those same humans marching on our coven with torches of fire.'

I tried not to recoil from the venom in Helena's voice and the hurt in her eyes.

'Forgive me, if I will never call a human my *sister*,' she continued.

'Helena,' Sapphire warned.

Helena's violet eyes turned to Sapphire. 'I must speak true, sister. She must know the wrath she seeks to invoke should she betray us.'

Sapphire opened her mouth to defend me, but I spoke for myself instead. 'If I ever betrayed you, Agnes would crucify me before you even made it down from your mountains.' Gaia's dark skin paled at the thought.

Helena let out a bitter laugh, raising her glass in mock cheers towards me. 'You are wise to be scared of her. At least that will motivate you to succeed.' She turned to Gaia, 'You may stay as long as necessary to prepare Blaise for her success. I will keep out of your way, if you don't mind.'

'Don't worry, we'll be out of your hair come morning,' Gaia bristled. I expected she'd planned to stay longer, but Helena had not been as welcoming as Crystelle had painted when she said we would have a place to stay in Harensarra. Helena gave a curt nod before rising from the table, food uneaten, much to Theodora's evident dismay.

'Blaise, I look forward to seeing you succeed,' she announced, before turning on her heel and leaving the meal to continue in strained silence. The delicious food that Theodora had worked so hard on turned to sawdust in my mouth, and I let my cutlery fall to my plate with a crash, before storming away to check on the horses.

CHAPTER 13

WE LEFT THE STARCHASER COVEN at first light, heading back down the Rocky Mountains. I studied Gaia and Sapphire's faces before we passed back through the enchantment wall and their glamours slipped seamlessly back into place, knowing it may be the last time I would see their true forms before we reached Reili.

'Helena was welcoming,' I glared at Gaia.

'I'm sorry, Blaise. I should have expected it. We can't expect her to forget or forgive what the humans did to her. Her wife was one of the healers they burned,' she explained. I sighed, deep understanding settling in my heart. Sapphire squeezed my shoulder tightly and I gripped the reins and urged the horse on faster.

'Let's get out of these blasted mountains.'

———— . ✦ . ————

A fortnight later, we left Harensarra's hellish humidity behind, welcoming Reili's late autumn breeze. As much as I wanted to be relieved, a sinking dread took root in my gut. There wasn't much time until I would be left alone in Reili with an impossible mission.

Reili's towns were heaving with endless flows of people bustling through, all of whom looked happy and content, even though their threads of clothing told me they didn't have much spare coin. The buildings were crammed into neat rows and the streets lined with stalls. Chatter flowed freely between vendors and their customers, taverns were full of singing patrons, and children played happily in the streets.

At every smiling face, bile filled my throat at how I was to end life as these people knew it, bringing witches into their homes. Maybe Helena had been right to question me. Despite the hatred I felt for the royal family and the soldiers, at what they had done to the Moonkeeper coven and thousands of witches before them, the common folk were largely innocent.

As if she could see the panic on my face, Sapphire muttered, 'remember who was cheering for that young girl's burning. They were not royalty. They were small folk. They are all as bad as each other.'

Her words did little to comfort me. I was to live among these people, and I was always going to be one badly told lie away from burning on a pyre. I gulped back my fears and rode on.

The deeper into Reili we rode, the more people noticed the Starterra uniforms that Gaia and Sapphire wore. Many people lifted their noses as we passed, as though they had smelled something awful. Others spat at our feet, and some outspoken people called out names and vile slurs. Through it all, Gaia and Sapphire rode with their heads held high. They were not *truly* Starterra soldiers, after all. They held no loyalty to the colours they wore, and so they did not bite at the curses or sneers.

They brandished the name 'Vermont' like a weapon, using it to gain access to inns and taverns that would have otherwise turned them away. The innkeepers would eye me suspiciously, having never heard about the old Vermont lord having a family in Starterra, but the gold I handed over kept them quiet – real coin, this time, so as not to raise suspicion when their earnings were suddenly down at the end of the night.

'We can send for Reili soldiers my lady,' one barkeep had told me.

'You're now *our* banner woman, after all.'

'That's very kind, sir, but these soldiers have been given the job to see me turned over to the queen. My grandfather was very clear in his instructions,' I'd lied. He'd looked like he might not let it go, but had shown us to clean rooms and left, though I was sure our arrival would no longer be a surprise to the queen.

——— ✦ ———

'I've been thinking,' I began one night, as we sat alone and undisturbed at a bar, even the pleasure girls giving us a wide berth. 'How am I supposed to write home, if my entire family is supposed to be dead? Who do I claim to be writing to?'

Gaia cupped my face, as she had a thousand times throughout my childhood, and I pressed my cheek into her palm. 'You tell them you are writing to your friends, sweet child.'

Her eyes brimmed with tears, and, for a moment, I thought I saw *her*, and not the glamoured appearance I had become so used to. I closed my own eyes before emotion could overwhelm me. Today was my last day with them. Tomorrow was my nineteenth birthday, and the day we would reach the palace and say our goodbyes.

'You are strong, Blaise. Stronger than any of us,' Sapphire began, and I scoffed loudly. 'You *are*,' she insisted. 'What you do, you do with love. For your family, and for all the witches you have yet to meet. You defy every instinct of your human body to provide us with a shot at peace. Do not, for a second, think we believe this is easy for you. You risk more than any of us. You always have,' she cleared her throat.

I could feel my own airways constricting, great sobs threatening to spill out through my clenched teeth.

'Whatever happens, Blaise, we love you, and will always love you. You are not just Agnes's child, but all of ours,' Gaia added. 'From the moment you were born, we swore to protect you, no matter how funny you looked, and how strangely human you were,' she smiled nodding at my rounded ears. I looked at hers as if I could see the points underneath the glamour.

'We will never stop protecting you,' Sapphire finished.

I swallowed hard as a hot tear ran down my cheek. 'I'll see you again, this won't be goodbye.' I laid my hands palm up on the table and each of them grabbed one, gripping tightly.

'The next time will not be in a shitty tavern. You will be sat on a golden throne, a crown atop your head,' Gaia beamed as if she could see it clearly, but no such vision found me. I squeezed their hands tight and savoured the comfort their calluses brought me.

———·✦·———

The palace was even grander than Stormhold, the walls lined in a gold that gleamed in the sunlight. Turrets towered high into the sky, with rows of iron bars that stopped birds from perching on them and soiling the walls with droppings that could never be reached to be cleaned.

The magnificent solid-oak drawbridge had Reili's crest carved into its front, and when it lowered to let us inside, a golden statue depicting the same image sat in the courtyard. Streams of Reili soldiers stood at every doorway, dressed in royal blue, golden crests over their hearts. Their appearance was immaculate, without even a speck of lint, nor hair out of place. They let us enter without argument, but an escort stayed close at all times. I had been right, word had travelled, they knew who I claimed to be, and they did not hide their dislike of the situation.

Inside the palace, thick stone pillars reached stories high, to ceilings that homed splendid chandeliers dripping in rubies and other fine gems. There wasn't a cobweb in sight, and how they got up there to polish them was anyone's guess. It was a different world compared to our tents in the Iron Woods, or even the streets we had passed through to get here.

Portraits lined the walls, and the white marble floors were clean enough to see your own reflection. Even Gaia raised an impressed eyebrow at the glittering candelabras lighting the way through room after room. It made a nice change from the worried looks she had been exchanging with Sapphire all day.

The pair of them had become fussing mother hens, checking me all day for any sign that I was going to faint or vomit. If they weren't fretting over me, they were staring at me from a distance, examining me from head to toe. For *what*, I couldn't tell. When they weren't doing either of *those* things, they were exchanging wordless glances with each other that did little to ease my nerves.

'The queen is hosting a ball tonight. You will wait here until I receive word that she will allow you to attend. Get dressed suitably,' our escort informed us, before closing the doors behind us. I took in the small room that housed a dressing table, a lone stool, and a dirt-flecked mirror, wondering what this room was used for. A key turned in the lock. We would not be leaving any time soon.

'What if she throws me straight in the dungeons?' I asked with a shudder.

'The Vermont family was once one of the wealthiest families in Reili, and the queen will know the value that name holds. She won't want to send you out of her sight with the family's money and name in your pocket,' Gaia placed a steady hand on my shoulder.

I took a deep breath.

'It's now or never, Blaise,' Sapphire shrugged. 'Are you ready to make an impression?'

I nodded slowly, and Sapphire squealed with delight as she pulled out one of my finest ball gowns from the pack we had been allowed to bring inside.

'This is going to be fun!' she cooed.

I wished I could share her enthusiasm, and that my stomach wasn't turning over violently as each moment passed. Yet, despite my roiling insides, I sat down on the stool and let Sapphire transform me into a woman fit for court.

Chapter 14

EVEN I COULD TELL I looked resplendent. My white ballgown dazzled in the lights from the chandeliers, the lace skirts flowed behind me. The corset sucked in my waist to appear tiny, whilst the beaded top drew attention to the curves of my breasts.

My brown hair was half-braided into a coronet atop my head, the other half allowed to curl freely past my shoulders. My eyes were lined with heavy kohl, the lids painted with various gold powders. My lips were stained with deep-red berries, and my cheeks dabbed with rouge.

The queen had agreed to allow me to be presented to her. It was now up to me to prove my worth.

Gaia and Sapphire walked stoically beside me, not letting any tension show on their faces, as we were led to a grand staircase that, from the sounds of music, glasses clinking, and endless chatter, led to the ballroom.

'Lady Blaise Vermont!' a herald shouted from the doorway, before ushering me into the light of the ballroom, whispers and titters beginning the moment I entered. I held my chin high and paraded through the room, thankful that my white slippers had barely a heel. Sapphire and Gaia remained close behind me as we stalked through the crowd, towards the golden throne. The queen eyed their Starterra uniforms with suspicion as we approached.

Queen Lizabeta had a look about her that indicated she had once been beautiful. But that time had passed. Her auburn locks were pinned into a giant tower atop her head that threatened to topple her should she ever lean forward, and her crystal-blue eyes were edged with deep frown lines and purple shadows, making her look perpetually tired.

Her skin, though largely covered in a satin beige gown with a high ruffled collar and long sleeves, was milky white, as though she had not seen the sun for years. She gripped the golden throne with such vigour, as though she expected someone to rip it from beneath her at any second. Her eyes met mine from across the room, and any colour she'd had swiftly drained from her face.

You look just like him.

My mother's words rung in my ears, and I panicked the game was up before it began.

That worry was quickly eclipsed by another, as I caught sight of the prince sitting next to the queen, on a throne that matched hers. He slouched slightly, hair a mess of waves, the thin band of a golden crown perched crookedly atop his head, like he hadn't cared enough to put it on properly. He absentmindedly fiddled with the pommel of his sword, looking almost bored, until he caught my eye and recognition flared.

I was done for.

We stopped before the raised dais, Gaia and Sapphire dipping at the waist into deep bows as I dropped into a low curtsey. The room was quiet, holding its breath to see what their queen would do with the unknown child who came brandishing the name of their dead emissary.

'What is the meaning of this?' the queen asked, eyes darting between the three of us. 'I wasn't aware Lord Vermont had a family. I was already choosing his replacement after his death. His heart attack was inconvenient to say the least.'

I tried not to snap my head to Gaia, who'd likely had my

grandfather poisoned to look like a heart attack.

'*Then*, I hear that a girl, claiming to be his granddaughter, was making her way to me.' The queen's voice was shrill but strong, commanding authority.

'Apologies, Your Highness. We were told riders would be sent ahead to inform you. It appears they never made it,' Gaia answered, laying on a thick Starterrian accent. 'I have all the papers, left in Lord Vermont's will and testimony, which stipulate that the girl would receive his titles and his wealth upon his passing.'

She extended the paperwork, and an advisor snatched it instantly. After a moment's reading, he bent to speak into the queen's ear, likely confirming the papers were in order. She waved him away like he was an irritating fly buzzing around.

The prince watched me with interest. I tried to only look at his mother, avoiding the intensity of his ocean blue gaze.

'I shouldn't be surprised Lord Vermont had a bastard somewhere,' the queen spat. 'Even Starterrian riffraff wouldn't have wanted the world to know she'd lain with such a spineless, insufferable . . .' she trailed off, the advisor stooping to her ear again.

'What is it you expect me to do with her?' the queen asked, though it wasn't clear who the question was directed towards.

'Mother, if I may?'

Every head in the room, including mine, swivelled to look at the prince, and the queen's nostrils flared, but she waved a hand at him to continue. I held my breath, certain he would have something to say about meeting me twice on the road, neither place somewhere I probably *should* have been, and neither time introducing myself.

'The lady Blaise is from a great Reili family, is she not? Should she not be welcomed with open arms into our kingdom, and treated with the respect her grandfather, Gods protect his soul, was always granted?'

I choked, and the queen's head spun towards me as the prince raised an eyebrow. I had no idea why he was defending me, but I picked up on his cues.

'I don't know much about my lord grandfather, and I know even less about his duties as emissary, but I do know how to serve a noble household. Of course, not one as important as this,' I added hastily when her nostrils flared again. The prince had thrown me a boon, perhaps without knowing it, so I made it count.

'If Your Grace would have me, I would offer my services as one of your ladies-in-waiting. It would be an honour to learn about my heritage, and this great kingdom, from you, Your Majesty. I would, of course, also offer my grandfather's wealth in support of the crown and its royal armies.' The queen sniffed once, and I took a deep breath as the prince seemed to lean forward on the edge of his seat.

'Let me have a closer look at you, girl.'

Sapphire shoved me forward, and I made my way up the steps towards the throne, trying not to show how my hands and knees trembled. The queen's eyes widened as she took me in.

'Very well. You'll stay at the palace with my other ladies. But, mark my words, if I do not like how you attend me, you will be stripped of your grandfather's *honour*,' she spat the word, 'quicker than you can say Starterrian scum.' She raised her eyes over my head and out at the crowd, as if she couldn't bear to look at me any longer, and I barely managed to curtsy before her royal guard escorted me back down the steps as quickly as I had come up them. I heaved a sigh of relief as I slipped back amongst the crowd who had returned to their chatter, disappointed with the lack of blood spilled.

'You're not out of the woods yet,' Gaia nodded to where the queen moved in our direction, and then slunk off into the crowd, leaving me to fend for myself. Apparently, Her Majesty had not wanted an audience for this conversation, and she glided towards me, thick skirts trailing behind her as her eyes locked onto mine.

'Your Grace,' I curtsied, 'I am most grateful you have granted me a place at court.'

As if I hadn't spoken, she said, 'you do not look like him, your grandfather,' she glanced upwards, and I followed her gaze to a painting of the former king – her former husband, and my *father* – that hung on the wall.

I almost gasped at the resemblance. He had my eyes, and my hair was precisely his shade. I quickly swallowed my shock, blinking back surprised tears. I wouldn't allow myself to wonder about this man who had sired me. I knew all I needed to from Agnes.

'I am pleased, Your Grace,' I replied, 'people tell me that Lord

Vermont was an unsightly creature.'

The queen grunted in agreement, eyeing me up and down once more, before catching a glass of champagne from a floating tray as a serving boy made his way through the room. She gulped down the glass in one and sidled back to her throne without a backwards glance.

'What did you do to drive my mother to drink?' A deep, familiar voice behind me made me jump. I spun, finding myself face-to-face with the crown prince.

Chapter 15

PRINCE KASPIAN SMIRKED; AN IRRITATINGLY handsome tug of his generous lips that revealed the infuriating dimple in his perfectly symmetrical face.

In the few weeks since I had last seen him, his chiselled jaw had become layered in a thin coat of stubble that, though scruffy, looked striking against his tan skin. This close to him, I noted how his long eyelashes could be the envy of every woman in the room. His dark brows were raised, waiting for me to say something.

'I'm quite sure I had nothing to do with that,' I choked as I looked behind him, desperately trying to find Gaia or Sapphire in the crowd to rescue me.

'Nonsense. I'd say a Starterrian girl inheriting the richest family in Reili's wealth when the queen was ready to claim it for herself, might have something to do with it.' I sputtered again and he let out a low laugh. 'It seems I have finally learnt your name, Blaise.'

The sound of my name on his lips was something I thought I would quite like to hear again. The thought sent a jolt through my body, and I dipped into another curtsey, staring at his feet rather than his face. 'Your Highness, I can explain.'

'Please, Kaspian is fine,' he reached out a hand, taking mine to lift me from my curtsey.

'Very well, *Your Kaspian*, I can explain,' I smirked, not able to help myself.

The prince snorted. 'I like you already, Blaise. There's no explanation needed. You didn't know who I was when we first met, and I didn't ask who you were the second time. I'd learned my lesson after you cut so viciously at my ego at our first meeting,' he winked. 'Perhaps I'll get that dance later. That would really ruffle some feathers.' He disappeared into the crowd, leaving me standing alone. I blinked. None of my encounters with the prince had been anything like I'd expected.

Anyone would have expected him to love his role as a prince – with him being taken from lowly beginnings to become the heir of Reili – but he had brushed off his title as though it pained him to hear it. He wore his crown in such a manor it was almost disrespectful, and he didn't seem to care that I hadn't told him who I was. He was arrogant, certainly. Infuriating, most definitely. But he didn't at all seem like the monster I had been told about.

Shaking my head of the thought, I banked what I had learnt about him for later. Right now, I had to find Sapphire and Gaia. Sneaking away from the ballroom under the guise of needing some air, I found the two of them outside by the stables.

'You goblins! You left me!' I called out.

'You seemed to be doing just fine,' Sapphire sneered, and I elbowed her hard in the ribs.

'You're going to fly home, aren't you?' I asked, my mood turning sour. 'What will happen to them?' I nodded towards the horses.

'They're yours.' Gaia patted the horses on their firm sides.

'Mine?' I squeaked.

'Happy birthday, Blaise,' they said in unison. With everything going on, I had forgotten that today was my birthday. I laughed and pulled them both into a tight embrace that soon turned my laughter to tears.

'If we leave now, we can be in the skies as night falls to its deepest, and we'll be back in the Iron Woods the morning after next.' Sapphire's voice was muffled as she hugged me back.

I sighed. The journey that had taken us so long by horseback, was going to take them a matter of days by broom. Glamoured from sight, and magicked to be small enough to fit in their bags, the brooms had made the journey with us. Soon, Gaia and Sapphire would be home, surrounded by familiar faces. And I would be *here*. Alone.

'Look after Ophelia,' I reminded them. They exchanged meaningful glances and nodded.

'Look after yourself, Blaise. Be safe,' Sapphire squeezed my shoulder.

I forced a smile, though thick tears now ran freely down my cheeks.

Gaia cupped my cheek, brushing tears away with her thumb. 'We'll pass your love to Agnes.' At the sound of my mother's name, my body went rigid. I couldn't let Agnes down. I couldn't let *any* of them down. They were relying on me.

I swallowed and wiped the last of my tears, before turning and walking away from Gaia and Sapphire, back towards the ballroom before I could change my mind and run back to them, begging them to take me with them. To take me home.

When I reached the doors and looked back, they were gone.

'You and those soldiers look close,' Prince Kaspian's voice startled me from the shadows.

'Would you stop doing that!' I snapped, storming inside.

'Doing what?' he asked, innocently.

'Creeping up on me and making me jump!'

His head tilted to one side, like an animal. 'Creeping implies I'm not supposed to be here and, as *I* can go where I please, it implies that *you're* the one up to no good.'

I rolled my eyes at the arrogance dripping from every word. 'I'm not sure I understand your logic.'

'Why were you crying? Seems strange you were so sad saying goodbye to two soldiers.' Blue eyes bore into mine, searching for lies, and I reminded myself that he wasn't just a pretty face. He was the youngest general in history. An infamous witch hunter. I had to be careful around him.

'They are the only people I knew from home. The only comfort I had here, and now they have to leave.' Not a lie.

Better to deal in truths where possible, Agnes had told me.

'Soldiers or not, they have become my friends on the road. They want the best for me, but now they get to return home, and I am surrounded by strangers.' I gave him a pointed look.

'We've met several times now, I'm hardly a stranger.' A grin spread across his face.

Mother above, he was annoying. 'Semantics.'

'I'm sure I could make you feel more at home here. How about that dance?' he offered, holding out a hand, the irritating dimple making its return.

'I'm afraid my dance card is full,' I snapped.

The glint in his eyes dulled and I sighed inwardly. I knew I should say yes. My goal here *was* to seduce him, after all. But I needed a moment alone. Trying to claw back my damage I added, 'I'm sorry. It's been a long journey, and I am quite weary. I would prefer if you could show me to where I will be staying?'

'An invitation to your room already? I thought you were a lady, Blaise!' I rolled my eyes hard enough I could almost see the inside of my skull, and his smile fell away. I internally scolded myself for wounding his very large ego, yet again.

'Very well,' he continued. 'I'll have Cole show you to your chambers. As much as I'd love to show you myself, I'll be missed if I'm gone for too long.'

He hurried off before I could respond, leaving me with a narrow-eyed Cole, who seemed to have appeared from nowhere. Evidently, he'd been guarding his prince's back without my notice, and he looked far less eager to forget the fact we had met before. Obeying orders, he didn't comment, only eyed me with suspicion as he showed me to my new rooms.

CHAPTER 16

AFTER MONTHS ON THE ROAD, my chambers were a welcome sight. Not as well kept – the thick, grey stone walls were decorated with several bright paintings that needed a good dusting – or as grand as the main areas of the palace, but luxurious all the same.

The living area contained a pastel-pink chaise lounge seat, as well as two matching armchairs. It wasn't to *my* taste, but I wasn't in a position to start complaining about the décor – I didn't even have *walls* to decorate back home, just plain tent flaps.

Leading from the living quarters was a spacious bedroom that housed a creaky four-poster bed lined with a thick mattress, thin quilt, and feather cushions. A dressing cabinet with an oval mirror was pushed against the wall, next to a large oak armoire that would house my clothes. Through the bedroom was a bathing area, with a large claw-foot tub, a deep wash basin, and something else I didn't recognise.

'What's that?' I asked Cole, as he showed me where my bags had already been placed.

'That's a toilet, m'lady,' Cole blinked.

'A . . . *toilet?*' I asked, unsure I had pronounced the word correctly.

'It's for you to do your . . . business,' he coughed, and a gentle flush appeared on his cheeks.

'How does it work?'

Cole coughed uncomfortably again, but entered the bathroom all the same. 'They're a fairly new design. Kas . . . I mean *His Highness* . . . helped develop it. They are quite expensive, but he wants to replumb the whole of Broozh, and eventually the whole of Reili, to house them.' I noted the pride in his voice, and I couldn't mask my surprise that Prince Kaspian had been involved in inventing something. 'You simply do your . . . business . . . in there, and then pull this chain and it is taken away.' Cole demonstrated, pulling the long chain, and I marvelled as the water that filled the bowl began to swirl and drain.

'Where does it go?' I asked, curious.

'Into the plumbing, m'lady. I take it you did at least have running water in Starterra?' Cole gestured to the taps and faucets that would fill the basin and the bathtub.

'Of course!' I snapped, though the truth was that the first time I had seen a tap was on our travels through Starterra. There was no need for running water in the Iron Woods when the witches could fill buckets with a click of their fingers.

'If that's all then, miss?'

'Yes, thank you.' I waved Cole out, watching as he had to duck through the doorway before shutting the door behind himself. Mother above, he was tall, and practically as wide as he was giant. And yet, his flushing embarrassment made him appear somewhat less threatening than I had first thought.

I pulled the chain on the toilet once more, and wondered again at how the water swirled and drained. Moving to the wash basin, I splashed my face with the cool water. Finally, I wriggled out of the horribly tight dress and into a soft nightgown. It was a struggle, trying to loosen the ribbon on the corset by myself, but I didn't have anyone to ask for help, and I certainly wasn't going to ask Cole, who I was certain stood guard outside my room. I slipped my dagger under my pillow and sunk into the mattress, breathing a sigh of relief.

My first day of pretence was over and, though both Prince Kaspian and Cole were certainly suspicious, no one had foiled my ruse yet. It was the first hurdle of many I would face, but I found, as I nestled amongst the puffed pillows and warm quilt, that I could stop caring about what was to come for a moment and simply sleep.

I woke to a gentle tap on the door to my bedroom and, a moment later, a sheepish Cole let himself into the room.

'Excuse me, Lady Vermont,' he began, eyes widening before he averted his gaze entirely.

I looked down. I must've kicked the sheet off in the night, and my nightgown had ridden up, exposing an indecent amount of thigh. Indecent for a *lady,* anyway, witches were far more liberal with these kinds of things. I made the perfect show of clutching the covers back up to my chest in horror at how much flesh a man had seen. And not just any man – a man of the royal guard, no less!

'My apologies, m'lady, I didn't mean to intrude.' Cole stammered, his pale cheeks and neck flushed with violent pink. His embarrassment was so at odds with his tough exterior, I had to stifle a giggle.

Muscle was packed tightly into his uniform, thinning it in certain areas, the material being tested to its limits trying to contain him. His hair was cropped close to his head, likely to keep it out of his eyes should he suddenly have to defend a member of the royal family. He was clean-shaven, and pristine in every way, from the neat lapels on his royal blue jacket, to the perfectly aligned medals on his chest that glistened in the light. His grey eyes were always darting about, taking in every detail, every potential threat. If I was going to dupe the prince, I would have to make sure that Cole was equally duped, because *I* was the threat he was trained to find.

'What is it, Cole?' I asked, sweetly. His eyes narrowed in suspicion, as I remembered that he had met me before, and on none of those occasions had I been sweet.

'The queen has requested that you join her and the other ladies for breakfast. I am to escort you to her gardens once you are dressed.'

My stomach flipped in anticipation, but I made myself say, 'I can't believe she wants me to join her! This is such an honour!' Cole stood silently by the door, giving away no hint as to whether he believed my words or not.

'Cole, unless you would like me to meet Her Royal Highness in my nightgown, I need you to leave, so that I can dress.'

'Oh, of course! Apologies, m'lady,' he stammered, and backed out of the door to wait in my living quarters.

I quickly freshened up, pulling on a light dress that was appropriate for breakfast in the gardens, but warm enough to keep out the autumn chill that had settled over the kingdom. I donned light slippers to match, quickly arranged my hair into twisted braids atop my head, and applied a thin layer of pink powder to my cheeks. Finally, I snatched my dagger from under my pillow and fastened it to my thigh.

Despite the obvious seating in the living space, Cole stood to attention by the door. When I emerged, he wordlessly examined my appearance – likely checking I wasn't going to offend his queen in some way – before leading the way into the hallways beyond my room.

'Will the prince be at breakfast?' I questioned, hoping I sounded like a coy girl who was interested in pursuing a romance, and not a spy trying to gather knowledge on the prince's whereabouts.

'I should think not,' Cole scoffed, as though he knew something I didn't. 'It is a breakfast for *ladies*,' he added, side-eyeing me as I pouted in mock dismay.

'If you see him, please do extend my apologies for being unable to dance with him last night,' I said. 'I was extremely fatigued after my time on the road, and needed a good night's rest. It would be an honour to dance with him at any future ball.'

Cole eyed me warily. Maybe I was laying it on a little thick. I needed to find a way back from the rude girl he had met before, but do so without rousing his suspicions. I looked away, pretending to marvel at the marble statues that lined the palace corridors, and we walked the rest of the way in uncomfortable silence.

Once deep within the gardens, I spied the table laid out for breakfast. Decorated with stunning lace cloths and polished finery, the table was adorned with pastries and fresh fruits. My mind wandered back to the people I had seen on streets of Broozh. This spread alone would be more than any of those citizens could afford in a year.

Six other ladies of the court were already seated at the table, gossiping behind large handheld fans. In the centre, was the queen. Her auburn hair was still upright in a tall beehive, as it had been the night previous, and she wore a thick, ruched dress that seemed far too high-fashion for a simple breakfast in the gardens. She paused her conversation with the lady to her right as we approached.

'Your Grace,' Cole bowed. 'Lady Blaise Vermont.'

The queen looked at me expectantly, as did all the ladies at the table. It took for Cole to elbow me subtly in the side for me to realise she expected me to curtsey.

All this damn curtseying! How did they ever get anything done?

I placed one leg in front of the other and dipped. 'Your Majesty, it is an honour to be invited to break my fast with you.' The queen sniffed once, before returning to her conversation.

Well, that went well.

Cole ushered me into a seat at the far end of the table, and stooped low to whisper into my ear that he would return for me later. I wanted to bark at him that I didn't need a keeper, but instead I smiled sweetly. As he left, he gave me a look that told me to behave myself, and that he didn't trust me in the slightest. I frowned. I was going to have to try much harder to get him on side.

The woman next to me slid a bowl of fruit towards me, and I picked it up but, as I turned to thank her, I nearly dropped the bowl in shock. Barely older than me, the girl's platinum hair met her shoulders in a straight cut that complemented her round face and made it appear sharper. Her pale skin was dotted in honey-coloured freckles, and her large green eyes were fixed on me. But, it wasn't her appearance that startled me. It was the subtle blur around her body.

This girl was a witch.

I fumbled with the bowl I had almost dropped, and tried to recover quickly, as the girl reached a hand up to her face, as though checking her glamour was in place after my startled reaction.

'Sorry!' I grimaced. 'I'm no good in the mornings! Until I've had caffeine, I'm useless.'

The girl laughed and slid a pot of ground coffee towards me. 'I'm the same, though I can't promise this is any good. It's much weaker than the stuff at home.'

'You're from Starterra?' The accent was undeniable.

She nodded, 'I was watching last night. I'm pleased the queen let you stay. It will be nice to have someone from home around.'

She had seen me at the ball. Had she seen me with Gaia and Sapphire? Had she noticed their glamours? Did she know who I was? Did she know that I would know she was a witch? How had she gotten into the queen's court?

I put the coffee down to hide my shaking hands, taking a deep, grounding breath. As far as I knew, this girl wasn't from the Sunseeker coven, and there was only one other witch coven in Starterra. Which meant . . . she was the last remaining witch from the Moonkeeper coven.

Did she know what had become of her sisters? Was that why she was here? Or had she been sent on a mission to infiltrate the queen's court long before her coven was slaughtered? Agnes hadn't mentioned anything about another witch being here. Did she even know? This could ruin everything.

I needed to talk to the witch alone. But with five other ladies at the table, not to mention the queen, that would be impossible. I took a large gulp of the coffee and forced it down. The witch was right, it was awful. Whether it was truly any worse than Starterra's coffee, I had no idea. I had never tried it before. We drunk herbal teas at home, but never coffee. The lie that I drank it had tumbled easily from my lips, something I had overheard someone say on our travels. Now, I regretted it as I forced another gulp down, shuddering.

The witch laughed again, her loose-fitted sage green dress rippling with the movement. 'I told you so. Blaise, isn't it? I'm Luna.'

Luna. *Definitely a Moonkeeper.* I forced back tears and plastered a smile onto my face. 'It's a pleasure to meet you, Luna.'

Chapter 17

BREAKFAST WAS TEDIOUS AND LONGWINDED. The queen did not directly speak to me, but I didn't care. In fact, I was relieved, as it offered me no chance to slip up. All I wanted, was for the blasted meal to end so I could catch a moment alone with Luna, who was trying to fill the hours by whispering stories about the other ladies at the table into my ear.

Lady Marie Druskell – married to Lord Alabaster Druskell, who apparently only had one arm, the other lost in a fight with a Starterra boy-soldier or bitten off by a shark, depending on whose stories you listened to. Marie was a pompous lady, whose face looked like all the features had been squished into the centre, leaving mountains of forehead and acres of chin, framing shrew-like eyes and a turned-up nose that, though she was five foot nothing, she managed to always look down at you from.

Duchess Hyacinth Caerphilly was the widow of an old uncle of the queen, who had become a duke after the king's passing, but found himself following suit not a year after. The official story was that he choked on a boiled sweet, though many believed he had been poisoned after Hyacinth caught him mid-affair with a scullery maid. Many gossiped that it had been the queen, herself, who had slipped him the poison, wanting no male relatives who could pose a threat to her rule. It was treason to say so, of course.

The duchess was a pruned old thing, with blue-washed grey curls pinned with an unnatural neatness into a bun. Partially deaf in one ear, she spent a lot of the time demanding people repeat themselves, and then asking them not to shout.

Lady Aleera Cresthorn sat closest to the queen, and was the only person Her Majesty had any interest in speaking with. Aleera was the picture of perfect. Porcelain skin, pretty blue eyes, streams of yellow-blonde hair, blushed cheeks, and a laugh so shrill it went right through you. Lady Aleera was the queen's personal choice for Prince Kaspian's bride. Though, according to Luna, the prince had shown little to no interest in the match. A fact that left me feeling undeservedly smug.

To the queen's right was Lady Natalia Marshore. A middle-aged lady, and the only daughter of an old lord, Natalia had no husband, and dedicated her life to the queen, ensuring the Marshore name would die with her. The woman was slender, with dark hair, and dark eyes that lit up with glee every time someone took an interest in her or offered her a pastry. She was the only person who didn't have to address Her Majesty by any royal titles, or even her full name. Natalia simply called her 'Lizzie', to which the queen always responded with a soft smile that perhaps others would give a puppy returning a stick that had been thrown.

Quietly squeezed between Luna and Natalia, was Daisy Hearthorn. Daisy's family was distantly related to the Cresthorns but, where Aleera's skin was pale, her eyes blue and hair golden, Daisy had a deep-golden tan, hazel eyes similar to my own, and brown curls that stopped at her shoulder. Where Aleera was confident and shrill, Daisy was coy and softly spoken, and was on the queen's radar for all the wrong reasons.

Rumour had it, the king had tangled with Daisy's mother as he rode through Reili on his way to war with Starterra. The queen chose to shake off the rumour by inviting Daisy to court, though many believe it was to keep an eye on the young lady, to see whether she bore any resemblance to her former husband.

With hair and eyes like mine, it was easy to believe King Kaspian could have sired Daisy. What would Agnes make of another potential claim to the throne? Not that Daisy showed any interest in anything royal. Luna informed me that her mother, Lady Rose Hearthorn, had gone missing shortly after Daisy was brought to court seven years ago, and that Daisy had been trying to stay out of the queen's way ever since.

Once the tea was cleared away, the ladies stood and curtsied as Her Majesty made her way from the gardens, escorted by no less than twelve members of the royal guard. Clearly the queen took no precautions, even in her own gardens. How did she live with such paranoia? Although, I was a potential assassin plotting her demise from the inside, and there was at least one other witch on palace grounds, so perhaps she was right to be cautious.

I saw Cole making a beeline towards me, and I tried desperately to think of an excuse that would allow me to get rid of him so that I could speak to Luna alone. I needn't have panicked. As soon as Luna saw Cole aiming for me, she sprang into action, and Cole stumbled at the sight of her, fumbling with his belt as though *she* made *him* nervous.

'Cole! I simply *must* take Blaise on a full tour of the palace! She's only seen the ballroom and her chambers, and she hasn't even seen the most spectacular part of the gardens yet! You don't mind if I borrow her, do you?'

'I have orders from Kas – His Royal Highness – that Blaise is to be brought straight to him after breakfast. He would like to take the lady riding,' Cole argued.

'Oh, I'm sure His Highness won't mind if you tell him that it was *me* who kidnapped her. I promise I'll deliver her myself in exactly one hour,' Luna winked, and a blush began creeping its way up Cole's neck.

'Very well. But if she's not at the stables in one hour, I will come looking for her, Luna,' Cole started, but Luna had already looped her arm through my elbow and begun leading me away.

'You *have* to show me how you did that,' I hissed.

'Oh, it's easy! Cole might look like a brute, but he's easily embarrassed, especially when it comes to women. A few wily winks, or a flash of your ankles, and he'll do whatever you ask just so you start acting more appropriately,' she smirked.

'He saw more than my ankles this morning! I thought a vein might burst in his forehead,' I smirked.

Luna laughed, 'I want to hear more about *that* later.'

She led us deeper into the gardens, eyes darting around nervously, ensuring we weren't being followed before pulling me behind a brick wall that was lined with delicate pink roses. The flowers climbed well over the top of the wall, hiding us from view.

'You're Agnes's daughter, aren't you?' Luna whispered, hurriedly. 'The human girl! I saw you with those glamoured Starterrian soldiers last night. I assume it was Gaia and Sapphire? There's no one else Agnes would trust with her own blood. But what are you *doing* here?'

'The same thing you are, I'd imagine. Spying,' I breathed.

'But why you? No offence, but you're *human*. Surely, she could have sent any witch? A witch would at least be able to defend herself should things go wrong!'

'I know how to defend myself, thank you,' I snapped, flashing her a look at the dagger strapped to my thigh. 'And I can do it *without* magic giving us away. There's no danger of a glamour slipping, or a spontaneous spell to cast suspicion. And . . . well . . . there's more, but first I need to know when *you* arrived here? Who are you really?'

'My name *is* Luna, I'm the daughter of Esmeray Moonkeeper, and I was sent to Reili a year ago to pose as a lady and get close to the queen. A few months ago, I lost contact with my coven. At first, I thought someone was intercepting my return mail, but no one has cast any suspicion on who I am. Did you visit them on your journey here? Are they okay?'

My heart dropped into my stomach. Luna was the daughter of the Moonkeeper's coven leader, and now I had to tell her that her mother and entire coven had been killed. Murdered by the very people she had been sent to get close to.

'Luna,' I started, my voice small and brimmed with tears. I cleared my throat and tried again. 'Luna, they're gone. The prince sent a group of soldiers to Starterra, and one of the girls from your coven got involved with one of them. She made the mistake of leading him to your home. No one escaped. I'm so sorry.'

Luna sat down hard on a carved bench, her eyes glassy, hands curling into fists. 'How? How did they do this without me knowing? I should have gotten word of the prince's plans. I should have warned them!' Tears fell from her bright green eyes, leaving wet stains on her satin dress. I sat, gently curling an arm around her.

'You weren't to know what would happen. Even if you *had* known about the army, you could never have predicted this! It's why Agnes sent me. She wants revenge for your coven, and she wants to make sure this can never happen ever again.'

'How?' Luna asked, both doubt and anger fighting to set the tone of her voice.

'By making *me* queen,' I gulped, and Luna's eyes widened. Before I could think better of it, I told Luna everything. Who my father was, my plan to seduce Prince Kaspian, Agnes's plan for peace. I wasn't sure at what point in my tale Luna stopped crying but, when I finished, she gripped my hands tightly, determination in her eyes.

'I will help you. Whatever it takes, I will help you! I will avenge my sisters and my mother,' her eyes shuttered. 'And I will ensure the Moonkeeper coven lives on.' I hugged her tight, wiping the fallen tears from her cheeks. 'Come on,' she tugged me to my feet. 'Let's get you to the prince. I'll tell you everything I already know.'

Chapter 18

LUNA WAS THOROUGH IN HER tour, showing me a dozen entrances to the palace, including through the barracks, where the royal guard slept when not on duty. She also showed me the aviary, which was full of exotic birds, and even dared to take me as far as the queen's chambers, where we ran off giggling when the guards there yelled at us to clear off.

As we walked, Luna had told me about her time at the palace, and all she had learned. I stored useful details, about the queen's love of parties, about the members of the guard and their dwindling numbers, and about Prince Kaspian's routine as general of the queen's armies, involving lengthy training sessions outside of the palace in an undisclosed location.

She led me to the stairs leading up to the prince's chambers – notably *not* guarded – but with our hour running out, we didn't dare explore them further. She finished by showing me the kitchens, where the cheery chefs gave us each a jam tart, before finally leading me out into the large open corridors that backed onto the gardens, our tour ending at the stables. As we rounded the corner, we came face-to-face with a pursed-lipped Aleera Cresthorn.

'Lady Cresthorn,' Luna dipped her head in a polite nod. Aleera wrinkled her nose as though she could smell something awful, completely ignoring Luna to look me up and down instead. Luna ploughed on undeterred. 'Allow me to properly introduce, Lady Blaise –'

'I know who she is,' Aleera interrupted, sniffing once in my direction. 'Just what this court needed. Another Starterrian castoff. A nobody in her own kingdom, so she must plague someone else's.'

I choked on a surprised laugh. Aleera hadn't said much at breakfast, but I had gotten the impression she looked down on most of the others. No wonder the Queen doted on her.

'And . . . you are?' I asked, knowing precisely who she was and, similarly, knowing exactly how to wound this snake's ego.

'I am your future queen. Lady Aleera Cresthorn! You shall treat me with respect, and you shall stay out of my way!'

'My apologies, Your Grace! I wasn't aware the prince had already chosen a bride. I would've brought an engagement present, had I known.'

'He hasn't . . . we aren't . . .' she stammered, red-faced. 'The queen! *She* has selected me herself!'

'But not the prince?' I asked.

She stared, wide-eyed and open-mouthed, back at me.

'Ah, I see. Then not a Grace at all. Just a mere hopeful, like the rest of us,' I flashed my teeth. 'I'll make sure I pass on your regards to the prince. I'm off to meet him now, as it happens. He requested I ride with him today.'

'He *what?*' Aleera looked aghast.

'Yes, I was shocked too! A poor Starterrian outcast like myself? I couldn't have hoped for such a request. However, what the prince wants, the prince gets, I suppose. Tata now, Aleera.' I waved and strode past her, smiling at the sound of her foot stomping on the floor in disgust.

Luna's hurried footsteps caught up with me. 'Well,' she cooed, 'you didn't come to play, did you.'

I winked. 'I shouldn't have done that, she's too close to the queen.

But, Mother above, that felt good!'

Luna's answering laugh echoed all the way out to the stables.

———·✦·———

'Blowing me off is becoming a bit of a habit for you, Lady Vermont,' Prince Kaspian drawled, a soft grin tugging one corner of his mouth upwards as I sidled up to the stables. I hated that grin. It made him look boyish and innocent, when I knew he was anything but. He was a murderer. Slaughterer.

The feel of my dagger pressed against my thigh grounded me, as anger bubbled up inside me at the pain he had caused. How Luna could even *face* him right now, after finding out he had ordered the massacre of her family, was a mystery to me.

'My fault, Your Highness,' Luna batted her eyelashes. 'I was so pleased to meet another lady from home that I wanted to keep her to myself for a little while.'

'I dread to think the trouble you two will get into together,' the prince sighed, his dark curls flopping further into his eyes as he shook his head in amusement.

'Reili won't know what's hit it, Your Highness.' Luna winked at me; lips curled back in a feral grin that was positively non-human, despite her glamour.

'I don't doubt it,' Kaspian responded, oblivious to the glint in Luna's eye that promised destruction, not just trouble.

'Now, if you don't mind, Luna, I'd like to take our new lady-in-waiting riding for a while, to see if I can truly get to know her.'

Luna gave my hand a gentle squeeze before curtsying low to the prince and turning on her heels to leave.

'As much of an honour as it is to be invited to ride with you, Your Highness, do you not have better things to do with your time than entertain ladies?'

'My mother would say there is no better use of my time,' he muttered, dark eyebrows pulling together in a frown. 'But, I have to admit, you intrigue me, Blaise. Any lady that sends my mother into such a tizzy seems worthy of an hour of my time.'

There he goes again, openly criticizing the queen.

'If that was a tizzy, I would hate to see her bored,' I shrugged.

'You were looking in the wrong places. If she has a drink in her hand, or if her skirts sway at a rate that generates its own wind, she is positively ruffled.'

I held in a startled laugh, instead taking the chance to reprimand him. 'You shouldn't say such things about your queen.'

'My *queen* has had far worse said about her, I'm sure.' He saddled a horse as he spoke.

'Don't you have servants to do that for you?' I asked, instantly regretting it. I should have used that moment to ask what other people were saying about the queen, but I was so shocked to see the prince saddling his own horse that the words tumbled out.

'I'm sure someone would, if I asked, but what an awful waste of their time it would be, when I am perfectly capable of doing it myself. Would you like me to saddle one for you, or should I ask a *servant* to drop what they are doing to assist?'

Scowling, I took a saddle off the wall and made my way through the stables, to the horses that Sapphire and Gaia had gifted me. I began saddling the mare that Sapphire and I had always ridden, and now it was the prince's turn to look at *me* with surprise, one eyebrow raised as he watched me secure the bridle and saddle. I petted the horse fondly on the neck.

'You forget, I have not always been a lady. Before I inherited my grandfather's titles, I aided my mother, serving wealthy households. *He* hadn't even tried to provide for us, despite apparently knowing of our existence. He was too embarrassed, I suppose, to have bedded someone so beneath him.' I began spinning my story, using my annoyance from our interaction to fill my words with venom. 'So, I know how to take care of myself. It is breakfasts, luncheons, and the life of a proper lady that I am less used to.'

Filling lies with truths.

We led the horses from the stables together. 'I assure you, I am no more used to this life,' Kaspian sounded solemn. 'Though I have long forgotten the appearance of most of the family I left behind, I have not forgotten our struggle. All of this seems as unnatural now as it did all those years ago. To suddenly have more than enough food to eat, and to eat from silver spoons rather than with my hands. I struggle asking for help, especially from those I still see myself as being more similar to, than those I am supposed to be like.'

I blinked, not having expected such sad truths from him, but quickly recovered. 'Forgive me, Your Highness, if I feel little sympathy for you and your sudden blessings. Perhaps you should learn to appreciate the life you were given.'

'Of course,' he stammered, and I felt a rush of delight at how I had made him trip over his words. 'I didn't mean to sound ungrateful when many have it worse than you or I could imagine. I just wanted you to understand why I do not have servants at my beck and call.'

'Oh, I understand, Your Highness.'

He winced. *'Please*, call me Kaspian.'

I mounted my horse and waited as Kaspian climbed onto his large red mount, with a glossy coat and shiny mane. A moment later, Cole rode up beside us on a giant brown mare.

'No servants?' I asked, eyeing Cole.

'Cole is not a servant.' The prince sounded more annoyed than I had heard him, and I had to respect his fierce devotion to his guard. 'He is a friend. And protection,' he added, as Cole's chest puffed with pride.

'I'm pleased you see me as such a threat, Your Highness,' I smirked.

'It's Kaspian,' he corrected again, 'and you can never be too careful. There are many venomous ladies in these parts.' I followed his gaze to spy Aleera watching from the open corridors we had left her in. Her fury was visible in the form of a pulsing vein in her forehead. I bit my lip to contain my glee.

Waiting for Kaspian to lead the way, I urged my horse to follow on, Cole a few paces behind remaining silent and watchful. I could sense Kaspian staring at me, and I turned to face him, head tilted and questioning.

'You don't ride like a girl,' he commented.

'Oh?'

'Most women ride side-saddle. You do not, despite your dress.'

I glanced down to make sure my dress covered as much of my legs as possible, whilst still giving me enough room to move comfortably on the horse. The truth was, Sapphire had tried to teach me to ride side-saddle, and I couldn't get on with it. It felt stifling, like holding back from how a horse should be ridden. She'd said it wouldn't matter. Mostly, only the upper-class rode side-saddle, and it would fit in with the narrative that I hadn't been raised highborn.

'You'll find there are many things I don't do like a proper lady, Your Highness,' I winked, as Cole spluttered and choked behind me. 'Because where would be the fun in *that?*' I spurred the horse into a gallop and sped away, and Kaspian howled with laughter. Urging his own horse to speed after me, we raced past Aleera, and several other preening ladies dotted around the grounds.

By the time we returned to the stables, I was out of breath, my hair a wind-torn, tangled mess, and the hem of my dress coated in speckles of mud that had been flicked up from the horse's hooves as we had raced the entirety of the palace grounds.

'I'd say you need some practice. Are you not a war general? You should feel ashamed, losing to a *girl*.' I flashed him my most victorious grin.

'There is no shame in that, my lady, especially not in losing to one that cheats.'

'Cheats! Tell me where I cheated?' I protested.

'That last bend. You cut through the hedges, and you know it. The gardeners are going to be pruning those bushes for a week thanks to the mess you made.' He jumped from his horse, and I allowed him to help me down from my own, the touch of his skin on mine sending a violent jolt through my body.

With his other hand, he reached up and pulled a bramble from my hair. 'Here is the evidence,' he smiled, white teeth glistening and obnoxious dimple returning. I tugged my hand from his grip, all too aware of how close he was.

'Can you honestly tell me you've never fought dirty in order to win, Your Highness?'

'Kaspian,' he corrected once more. 'I can neither confirm, nor deny. Perhaps our soldiers should heed a lesson from you. Cheaters do prosper, it seems.'

We returned our horses to the stable, Cole trailing behind. He had not been pleased as we'd raced around the grounds, I could tell by his red face and stern expression. Kaspian clapped him on the back and offered him a cup of water, as I fed both the horses an apple as a reward for their hard race. I also slipped mine a sugar cube that I had taken from breakfast.

'What's her name? Your mare?' Kaspian asked.

I frowned. 'I haven't given her one,' I confessed.

'How about Lady? Because, like you, she seems to be anything but.'

I grinned a wicked smirk. 'How about it, girl? Are you a Lady?' I asked, patting her rump. The horse whinnied as if in agreement.

'Very well, Lady it is.'

'Well, I hope you and Lady will give Ginger and I a rematch some time?' he asked, sounding hopeful.

'I would like that.' I was surprised that the words didn't sound like a lie. Maybe I was better at this pretence than I thought. He smiled that irritatingly handsome smile.

'Well then, I bid you good day for now. Cole, see that Blaise finds her way to dinner.'

As I watched him leave, I abhorred the fact that this had been the most fun I'd had since I arrived. I certainly refused to acknowledge the excitement I felt at the prospect of doing it again.

CHAPTER 19

I MADE TO START TOWARDS THE dining hall, Luna's tour fresh in my mind, when Cole asked, 'Where are you going?'

'Did the prince not just say to make sure I get to dinner?'

'You can't go like that!' he looked aghast.

I looked down at myself. At the mud on the hem of my dress, and the slippers that were certainly less white than they had been at the start of the day.

'No, I guess you're right,' I frowned.

I wasn't used to all this propriety. Whilst Agnes always looked immaculate, it was never expected at the coven. We lived in the middle of the woods. Dirt happened; it was inevitable. Not to mention the witches could simply magic it away with the flick of a wrist. Bathing in the frigid springs was hardly something one wanted to do very often, and there was never a need to change outfit for every occasion. I sighed. Playing pretend already felt stifling.

I felt trapped beneath skirts, longing for a comfortable pair of leggings and a breezy tunic that didn't bruise my hips and chest the way a corset did. How long would it be until the parts of me that loved the outdoors – the way the trees smelled, the way the dirt beneath my fingernails felt natural, and the way the wind ripped through my hair – were stripped from me and labelled as improper?

It was a small price to pay, I reminded myself, for the freedom of my sisters. For the chance at witches living in peace without the constant threat of being hunted. For them, I would sacrifice this, and more.

But I didn't have to like it.

Cole fell into step behind me as I changed direction and headed for my chambers. Once inside, I filled the tub, the warm, running water a luxury I wasn't sure I would get used to.

I soaked in the lemongrass-scented water until it could no longer be considered warm, doing my best to wash all the mud from my ankles and shins, and the thorns and brambles from my tangled hair.

It was only when I was drying, and staring at my dresses, that I realised the ones which were appropriate for dining in a room of nobles and royalty, were those with ribboned corsets that I would need someone else to tie me into.

I knew Cole would be standing guard in the corridor, but would he leave me alone to go and find someone else to help me? Would he trust me enough to leave? I didn't think I had done anything to cause him to doubt me, and I had no other choice.

Or did I? An idea formed.

I picked a fancy gown of dusky lilac with pearl beading and stepped into it with ease. Holding it over my breasts with one hand and picking up the skirts with the other, I shuffled to the door and knocked on the inside with my elbow.

Cole's confused expression as he opened the door turned quickly into one of horror when he took in what I was half-wearing. That now-familiar beetroot shade he often turned began climbing from his wide neck to his pale cheeks.

'I need some assistance. Could you tie the ribbons for me?' I asked, fluttering my lashes.

'I . . . I should get a serving girl or s-someone else,' Cole stammered, face impossibly redder.

'It will only take a moment, and won't everyone already be helping with dinner?' I had dragged out my bath, so it *was* plausible. 'Please, Cole. I can't go like this.' He hesitated for a moment longer and then ushered us back into my chambers, hurriedly closing the door behind us. He took a deep breath before turning to face me.

I carefully spun, twisting my hair over my shoulder and away from the ribbons he would need to tie, whilst exposing as much flesh as possible without him truly seeing anything indecent. I didn't want to give the poor boy heart failure. We locked eyes in the mirror I had turned to face, and his face flushed so red it looked as though it might explode. I just wanted to loosen his inhibitions a little. If he were a little flustered, he may say something he otherwise wouldn't.

'What do I need to do?'

'You need to hook the ribbons through the holes and tie it tightly once you get to the top. Whatever you think tight is, make it even tighter than that,' I ordered. He took another deep breath before stepping towards me. It was another moment after that before he fully closed the gap between us.

He picked up the ribbons, gently dusting the bare skin on my arms with his large hands – which were clammy, though they didn't tremble, which I had almost expected. I wondered if he had ever been so close to a woman. I certainly hadn't been this close to a man.

I was pleased Cole was concentrating on the task, and not meeting my gaze in the mirror because it was *my* turn to blush. Every tiny brush of his hands on my skin sent goose pimples crawling over my flesh, as he began threading the ribbon with ease, large fingers surprisingly nimble. He tugged lightly as each ribbon was looped.

'Tighter,' I commanded.

'Doesn't it hurt?' Genuine concern filled his voice.

'It's supposed to. Apparently, we should suffer for fashion.'

'That seems impractical. And a little barbaric.'

'I won't disagree, but if I am to impress His Royal Highness, it will need to be tighter.' I let out a small oomph as he obeyed, squashing my insides together.

'Pretty dresses won't impress Kas.' He didn't correct his slip up as he had done previously.

Interesting.

Kaspian had insisted I didn't call him by any titles, but it seemed improper that a member of the Royal Guard would not refer to him as 'Prince Kaspian,' if not 'His Royal Highness,' around others, especially ladies-in-waiting. 'And since when were you interested in impressing him? You were nothing but rude to him before.'

I was wondering when this would come up.

'I didn't know who he *was* when I first met him. I'd just been leered over by some creep, and I didn't know he was any better, despite rescuing me from the situation. I was shaken.'

Cole's voice softened slightly, 'Understandable.'

'At Stormhold, I was shocked to see him, and to find out who he was. I shouldn't have acted that way, but I'd only just found out about my grandfather. I knew I would be leaving my home soon. Whilst I'm grateful to be here now, at the time, I was apprehensive. When I found out who he was, it was a reminder of that.'

Lies with truths.

'Well, I'm pleased you've seen the error in your behaviour. Though, Kas has been intrigued by it, to say the least.' I beamed, pleased that Cole didn't see the danger in that grin.

'You know him well?' I asked smoothly, not having to feign interest.

'I knew him before,' Cole trailed off.

'Before?' I pressed.

'Before he was . . . Prince Kaspian,' he tugged tightly and I jerked, letting out another deep 'harrumph'. 'Sorry,' he mumbled.

'Don't be. That's when you know it's right. What was he called before?' I tried to sound casual, but curiosity got the better of me and the words were eager, though I wasn't sure why it mattered.

'It is treason to speak his birth name. I shouldn't have mentioned it,' Cole's voice turned panicked, hands suddenly stumbling over the ribbon.

'Forgive me, I shouldn't have asked. I didn't mean to pry, it's just that his story fascinates me,' I soothed, glancing over my shoulder. 'How did you know him before?'

'We grew up together,' Cole's voice warmed with fondness. 'My mother was friends with . . .' he paused. It was also treason to say that the queen was not Kaspian's real mother, despite the whole kingdom knowing it.

'I understand. So, you played together as children?'

He shot me a grateful glance in the mirror and nodded. 'Even when Kas came to the palace, he would sneak past his guards and come to play with me. Kas begged the queen to let me stay here. When she refused, he ordered his own guards to have my belongings moved to a spare room.'

'That was kind of him.' I tried not to sound too surprised that the prince was capable of kindness. He *had* tried to save me from that oaf in the bar, after all. I knew there had to be a decent bone in him. Just not when it came to witches. 'Does he show any kindness on the battlefield?'

'That's a strange thing to ask,' Cole's voice shifted, apprehension weighting his tone. It occurred to me then that Cole had been trained to dispatch the very threat I had been trained to be . . . maybe his panicked appearance was as much an act as mine. He finished the last loop on my dress and tied the remaining ribbon in a neat bow. 'You're all done.' I turned slowly to face him, casting my eyes downwards, trying to appear coy.

'Thank you. You have been such a hero this evening, Cole. I don't know what I would have done if you weren't here.' I patted him gently on his sizeable bicep, feeling relieved when his eyes almost bulged out of his head, and he mumbled something incoherent. I had successfully distracted him from my misstep. I ran a brush through my hair and adorned some satin lilac slippers whilst he regained his composure. Once I was ready, he opened the door for me, like a true gentleman.

As we made our way to the dining hall, Cole cleared his throat, 'If you want to impress him, you should stop calling him His Highness.'

'I know,' I nodded, 'but it's fun watching him squirm.' Perhaps I had let an ounce too much venom slip into my tone, because Cole looked utterly scandalized. I tipped my head back and laughed.

———— ✦ ————

The dinner hall was as grand as everything else in the palace, with a raised top table that accommodated the queen, Lady Natalia, the Duchess Hyacinth, and Prince Kaspian, allowing them to look down on everybody else.

Noticing my arrival, the prince tipped his glass in my direction, and I inclined my head, before catching sight of Luna and rushing to join her. At the sight of her, Cole cleared his throat and slipped off to the side with the other guards to stand watch, keeping a careful eye on me.

'How did it go?' Luna asked, tipping meat and vegetables from the huge banquet onto my empty plate. I barely looked at what she chose for me, keeping one eye on the queen.

'I think I got his attention,' I murmured back.

'He brushed off Aleera entirely when she entered, and he usually entertains polite conversation, at least. I'd say you definitely have his attention!' Luna grinned. Sure enough, when my eyes found Aleera among the sea of people, she was shooting daggers in my direction.

'I seem to be making enemies already.'

'Then it is good you are not here to make friends,' Luna winked. 'Eat. The food is better than the coffee, I promise,' she urged, passing my now-full plate to me. Before I could take a bite, a guard approached.

'Lady Blaise Vermont, Her Majesty has requested an audience.'

I looked to Luna. If she was worried, she didn't let it show. Instead, she nodded and pushed me forwards. The guard escorted me up the steps before the queen. I could feel the eyes of the entire hall on my back as I curtsied, once to the queen, and then to Prince Kaspian. *Again with the curtsying!* It would be a miracle if my knees made it through my stint here without incurring irreparable damage.

'I see you have become fast companions with Lady Luna,' the queen sneered. 'Another Starterrian. I know you have spent your life in Starterra, but do not forget your family belongs to Reili's banners. If I have reason to doubt your loyalty to this crown, and this kingdom, I will not hesitate to strike.'

So threatened was this queen that I, barely more than a girl, worried her by simply *talking* to someone from my own kingdom. I did not know whether she deserved punishment, or pity.

'What say you?' she barked. 'Are you still loyal to Starterra?' Chatter amongst the tables had stopped completely, waiting for my response.

'I am loyal to no place.' It was easy to say, since it was true. My loyalty had never been about a place or kingdom. My loyalty was to the witches. To my family and friends. 'I am loyal to people. Luna has made me feel welcome, showing me the grounds and helping me settle into life here. I did not mean to offend you, with my chosen friends, Your Grace.'

The queen's face filled with rage. She had clearly believed I would appear more guilty of betrayal than I did. Picking up a cup, she lifted it for a serving boy to fill with wine, and I risked a glance at the prince, whose eyes danced with amusement. I had once again driven his mother to drink. I bit my lip to suppress my own laughter.

The queen waved me away without another word, and I curtsied once more to the royal family before descending the steps to rejoin Luna. I took a large gulp of my own wine, which Luna had filled for me, and began to eat, not letting my nerves show. It had been bold of me to answer back. I should be pandering to the queen's every need, not offending her. But I couldn't seem to stomach it. Luna raised an eyebrow at me.

'Like you said, I'm not here to make friends.' I held Kaspian's amused gaze as I took another gulp of wine.

CHAPTER 20

'IT SEEMS YOU HAVE QUITE the talent for getting under my mother's skin. One I thought only I possessed,' Prince Kaspian approached me at the stables the next morning. It was barely dawn, and I hadn't expected to see anyone else here.

After dinner last night, I had made myself scarce, having Cole escort me back to my rooms before I could offend any more of the royal family. I had found my own way out of the dress – using a wire hanger, and almost dislocating my shoulders to try and bend to the right angles – but it was less awkward than watching Cole squirm had I asked him to help me out of it.

'Is that why she has one of her royal guards following my every move?' I nodded to Cole, who quickly pretended he hadn't been watching me like a hawk from several paces behind Kaspian.

It was a question I had thought about in bed last night. No one other than the queen had guards in tow, and Luna hadn't mentioned being given the same treatment when she'd first arrived here. If the queen already suspected I was not who I claimed to be, I needed to rethink my plan, and do some serious arse-kissing. I suppressed a shudder.

Prince Kaspian smirked. 'I think she feels a trifle threatened by you. Your appearance is somewhat . . . familiar . . . to her.'

I was careful not to react. 'Oh?' I turned away, hiding my face behind Lady's large neck.

'We've all seen the portraits. You have a striking resemblance to the late King Kaspian.' The words hung between us.

'She believes I am one of her husband's bastard children?' I schooled my features into a look of dismay.

'One of?' Kaspian's eyebrow raised.

'There are rumours. Daisy Hearthorn–'

'I would be careful not to give rumours credit, if I were you,' the prince interrupted.

I nodded. 'So, she is keeping a careful eye on me in case I what? Try and lay claim to her throne?' I scoffed, the idea truly sounding ridiculous out loud, despite it being exactly what I had come here to do.

'Something like that,' Kaspian helped me finish saddling Lady.

'Will you ride with me?' I asked.

'Ginger is currently out of action. She's having her hooves reshoed. Yesterday's race reminded me that she needed them doing.' A small smile tugged at the edge of his lips.

'I have a spare horse. Or perhaps we could ride . . . together . . . on Lady?' I did my best to look hopeful, and not unnerved, at the prospect of being so close to a killer.

'Very well, it's probably too early for us to tear through the fields. We would wake half the palace. Let's ride together.'

I allowed him to mount the horse first, and he offered me a hand, helping me up to settle in front of him. I tried to keep my back straight, not allowing myself to sink into the fine contours of his chest, but I was still keenly aware of how close we sat. His thighs pressed firmly against mine, and the gentle caress of his breath tickled the back of my neck sending shivers down my spine. His scent of sugar, mixed with freshly cut grass, washed over me. No one so evil should smell so . . . *divine*. He should smell of ash on the wind and the iron of blood, from all the witches he had butchered.

As I gripped the reins and urged Lady into a slow walk, Kaspian placed a hand against my waist to keep himself steady. I tensed at the touch, resisting the urge to slap his hand away, but the prince had already noted my sudden stillness.

'Apologies, my lady,' he made to pull his hand away, but I pinned it in place with my own, despite the aggressive butterflies in my stomach, and ignored the urge to recoil as far away from him as possible.

'Not at all, Your Highness.'

'Kaspian,' he corrected.

'How long will your mother have me followed?' Even now I could hear the footsteps of another horse behind us.

'Likely until she can find some way to prove you are who you say you are and not her husband's daughter. Why? Does being followed make you uncomfortable, my lady?'

'Not when my guard is as handsome as Cole.' Cole spluttered, attempting to disguise the noise with a cough, and Kaspian's huffed laughter tickled my ear. 'But it does make me feel a little unwelcome.'

'I am sorry for that. I shall try to make it up to you. Though, I ask you to be gentle with my mother, seeing the resemblance of his face on another is a reminder of what she lost.'

'She gained a kingdom.'

'She lost a husband.' Kaspian's voice was soft.

'She truly loved him, then?'

'I pray that I someday love someone the way she loved him,' his words surprised me by all accounts. Firstly, that the queen loved the king so – despite his betrayals with Agnes and, if the rumours were to be believed, a handful of other women.

Secondly, that the prince cared so much for love. He struck me as a practical man. A man that understood the benefits to be gained from marrying for power. This new information could work in my favour. Now all I had to do was make the prince fall for me. I almost laughed.

'She still mourns the king. Is that why she will not remarry?' I pried.

'Partly, I believe, yes. Though it has certainly become about more than that. She seeks revenge.'

'On Starterra? But why? Starterra lost the war,' I peeked over my shoulder as I steered Lady around the grounds.

Prince Kaspian shook his head. 'Not on Starterra. On the witch that killed the king.'

I stilled, though my heart pounded hard in my chest. 'A witch?' I tried to pour disbelief into my words.

'Do they not teach you the story in Starterra?'

'My mother didn't have time for stories.'

Kaspian cleared his throat. 'The war was almost lost. The Reili forces were depleted, and many needed to see their king if they were to find the strength to continue the fight.

'So, King Kaspian crossed the border into enemy lands and rallied what was left of his troops. On the road, he met a temptress who took him to bed and had her way with him. Though the king always had a wandering eye, many say this was different. That the king appeared enchanted, *envigored*, in this woman's presence.

'His soldiers practically had to drag him away to participate in the war they had come to fight. Once away from the woman, the king talked of nothing else, according to his soldiers. Many feared all hope lost, for King Kaspian was distracted, consumed by thoughts of this beautiful woman.' I resisted the urge to smile at the mention of my mother's beauty.

'But the king led his army into battle and, in the jaws of defeat, Reili's army managed to push back hard enough that Starterra's king surrendered.

'The war over, King Kaspian immediately took the chance to return to the beautiful stranger he had met on the road. The woman was waiting, her belly swollen with child, despite only weeks having passed. The temptress tried to claim that King Kaspian was the babe's father, but the soldiers could not understand how that could be true, and the king's advisors told him he should have the woman beheaded for a liar.'

I tightened the grip on the reins and Lady faltered a step. The prince seemed not to notice, continuing his story in the same breath. 'King Kaspian swore he loved the woman, and would return to Reili with her and their child in tow. Upon hearing his declaration of love, the woman revealed herself as what she truly was – a witch. She lifted the spell she had placed on the king, and he was horrified at what he'd done.

"'I could never love a witch!' his guards said he told the sorceress. "I love my darling Lizabeta! She is my queen! You and your babe will burn tonight!"

'The witch thought he truly loved her, beyond her spells, and that she could rule alongside the king. But once the king discovered the truth, and ordered her burned, she lashed out with her magic, snapping his neck and killing him in an instant. The king's guards tried to chase after her, but she vanished into thin air.

'They brought his broken body, and the tales of what they had seen, back to the queen. From that day forth, Lizabeta swore she would tear the world apart until she found the witch that murdered her husband.'

The prince finished his tale, and I sat in stunned silence. Much of the story I knew to be true, but in Agnes's version, she had never loved the king. She had simply used him for an heir . . . hadn't she?

In Agnes's version, the king *had* loved her. She had never used potions or enchantments to trap him. He had fallen for her, and promised she would be his queen, but *she* had turned *him* down to protect her daughters. She had only killed him when he threatened to steal her unborn child from her.

I shook my head to clear the hum of thoughts. Agnes hadn't been the woman scorned. This tale was a lie, concocted by the queen and her advisors to keep her on the throne. This way, no one could dispute that King Kaspian had loved her, and that she had no right to wear the crown.

'You tell a good story,' I turned Lady back towards the stables. I was ready for this ride to be over, and for the prince's strong hands to be away from my body. For his warm breath to no longer caress my neck. For a moment alone with my thoughts.

'You think the tale is a lie designed for Lizabeta to keep the throne?'

Had I been so obvious?

'What need had the witch for power? Did she not already have it in the form of her magic?' I had to be careful, I was treading on dangerous ground. 'Your mother has used this *story* as justification for snatching you from your *real* mother's arms, and using you to murder women and children in the name of justice. If I were you, I wouldn't be so quick to forget that the only person who knows the truth in this, is dead.' I jumped down from Lady's back as the stables came into view, and the prince jumped down behind me, catching my wrist and forcing me to face him.

'My mother is a lot of things,' he started, deep blue eyes narrowing, 'but she is not a fool! Do not let her hear you speak of such things. I like you, Blaise, I would not like to see you punished for talking of things you do not understand.'

I snatched my wrist back, the circle his fingers had formed around it burning. 'There are a lot of things *you* do not understand, Your Grace.'

'I do not doubt it. But I *do* understand this. Whether the story is a lie or not, Lizabeta holds the throne and, while she sits upon it, people will suffer until she gets her revenge. Try not to get caught in the crossfire.'

I flinched, picturing the Moonkeeper coven burning, now knowing that this story was the cause for so many lost lives. It was the reason Kaspian had been trained to hunt them down. But the way he'd said it . . . did he regret his part in this?

'You do not agree with how she rules?' I hedged.

'I remember where I came from, Blaise. It is *my* people that fight in her wars. It is *my* people that lose their lives to her revenge. It's never the nobility that send their sons to battles they didn't choose to fight in. It's the sons of bakers, of butchers, of bricklayers, carpenters, blacksmiths, and medics who are selected and sent for slaughter. It is why I trained hard to become a general. To go with them. To fight *for* them. Because who else does?' A fevered glint entered his midnight eyes, and his voice shook with emotion, hands clenching and unclenching into balls of fury.

'Why have you never walked away from the title? If you despise it so much.'

Kaspian turned, leading Lady back to the stables and removing her saddle. His voice was softer when he spoke again, and I too found I was able to gain some composure when his eyes weren't on mine. 'It's a long game, Blaise. One I'm not sure I have any hope at winning. But, if I'm patient, I can bring about change. Lizabeta trusts me. She truly dotes on me as if I am her son. And some part of me loves her, too. She gave me a life I could have never dreamed of,' his eyes squeezed shut and, when they opened once more, they were glassy.

'But, when I go to sleep at night, I see the face of my real mother. I've never forgotten the sound of her scream when they tore me from her arms, or the sound of the arrow piercing her heart . . . the way her body crumpled to the floor,' his eyes shuttered, and I unwittingly took a step towards him.

'I have never liked the idea of ruling,' he admitted. 'But, when *I* take the throne, I could bring about real change, Blaise. For the people who were born with nothing but the love in their hearts. It is for them, that I must sit patiently by and continue to earn Lizabeta's trust. Tell me you understand?'

He reached for my hand, his eyes piercing into mine, and I took another step towards him. Because I *did* understand. Wasn't change what I was hoping for, too? Change for the witches. For our people to live in harmony. An understanding, that magic was not something to be feared, but something that could help life to thrive. Could he truly regret his part to play in hunting witches?

For the first time since I arrived, and our plan was set into motion, guilt gnawed at my insides. Kaspian wasn't what I expected. He did not appear to be the force of evil Agnes had painted him to be. On the surface, he came across as kind, compassionate, charming, understanding, free-thinking . . . and irritatingly handsome.

But, despite not coming across as a monster, I *knew* what he had done to the Moonkeeper coven. Even if he wanted to see change for his own people, it didn't mean he would include mine in his new world. The way he had told the king's story told me enough.

He was still my enemy.

He had trusted me with this information about his intentions and, despite how much I agreed with him, I was going to have to betray that trust to liberate my own family. I snatched my hand away from his gentle grip, knowing what I was about to say was too bold, too risky, but I couldn't hold it in.

'You may be able to be patient whilst you enjoy your silver spoons and luxury chambers, but how much patience will your people have when they go to war, or when you use them as pawns in some wild witch hunt? Soon they may require more action from you. Are you willing to do what needs to be done to free them from their shackles? Or will you stand by and watch their suffering in the name of the *long game?*'

His brows furrowed, dragging his curled locks down over them, as his eyes weighed all I had said to him. Before he could answer, I turned and stalked away. Turning my back on a prince, after giving him a lecture, was probably some form of treason, but he didn't protest.

Cole followed me out with heavy footsteps that portrayed his disapproval, but I tried to remind myself that I didn't care what he thought, as I marched to my chambers with my head held high.

Chapter 21

'YOU SAID *WHAT* TO THE prince?' Luna screeched. 'You do remember you're trying to seduce him, don't you? Not to tell him to stick a knife in his mother's back to save you a job!'

I rolled my eyes. 'I'm not going to fawn all over him, Luna, I can't do it! Not knowing what he's done to your family. What he would do to *us*, and our sisters, if he knew what we – what *you* – are.'

Her green eyes flashed with sorrow. 'If *I* can still look at him without tearing the flesh from his body and letting his insides be mopped from the damn marble floors, you can do what it is you came here to do!' she scolded. 'You have a job to do! *We* have a job to do! When the time for revenge comes against Kaspian, and that bitch queen, we will get it. Until then, you stick to the plan Agnes gave you. He must fall for you!'

'He didn't have me beheaded. That's a good sign.'

'Blaise, this is serious!'

'I *am* being serious,' I protested. 'Whatever I'm doing is having *some* effect on him. It's gotten me further than Aleera, at any rate, and

I'm sure she giggles and compliments him at every opportunity she gets. Just like every other woman he meets, and he hasn't shown any interest in them.' Luna considered, pacing back and forth in circles around my living chamber. I sat on the stiff, pink chaise and waited.

'Okay, maybe you're right,' she conceded, and I began to grin. 'But,' she added, and I poked my tongue out at her, 'you need to pull back slightly. If you carry on exactly how you are, he's going to become suspicious. I mean, for Mother's sake, you have directly questioned the witch hunts! You need to learn to flirt, as well as challenge him.'

I made a gagging noise, and she huffed a laugh. 'Blaise Sunseeker,' she whispered, stopping her pacing to crouch directly in front of me. 'You've never flirted with a boy before, have you?'

The deep heat that flushed my face was answer enough for Luna, who cackled. It wasn't as if I didn't know pleasure. Despite never laying with a man, I knew the workings. I had even elicited my own pleasure on more than one occasion. But *that* didn't scare me so much as attempting to flirt with someone.

'Oh, and you have?' I bit out.

'Oh, sweet baby Blaise, I have done a whole lot *more* than flirt,' she flashed me her brilliant white teeth, and then cackled again when the heat crawling up my cheeks intensified.

'I don't want to know,' I stuck my fingers in my ears as she opened her mouth to talk again, and she laughed as she pulled my fingers free.

'You're going to listen! You need to learn how to make a man want you,' she winked, and I wrinkled my nose in disgust.

'We're going to start with *mouth techniques*,' she drawled, in a low, suggestive tone.

'Oh, Mother above! Nope! *Nope*! *La la la la la*,' I sang, shoving my fingers back in my ears as I ran through my chambers and shut myself in the bathroom.

When Luna finally stopped laughing at my embarrassment, she managed to convince me to come out of the bathroom and taught me what she called 'the four Ls of flirting' – looks, lips, lashes, and laughter.

'You *look* into his eyes, and then to his lips. This lets him know that you're thinking about kissing him.' Heat crept up my neck. The last thing I wanted to do was *kiss* the prince.

'You lick your *lips*. Or pout them. Just do *something* with them to make him notice your lips and start thinking about kissing *you*.' The flush spread to my cheeks as my brain conjured an image of Kaspian leaning in to kiss me. I shuddered.

'You flutter your *lashes* at every opportunity.' I tried to practice this, but stopped immediately when Luna snorted.

'And you *laugh* at whatever he says that is even remotely funny. And try and make it a seductive laugh. There's really nothing to it.'

'How exactly does one laugh seductively?' I questioned.

'You know, like low and sweet,' she emphasised with her own giggle.

I had tried, and failed, to replicate it several times before Luna gave up, deciding any laugh would work well enough, and moved on to practicing the other Ls.

'Why have you gone cross-eyed?' She looked at me like I was insane.

'I'm trying to look at my lips.'

She looked up to the skies in exasperation. 'Mother, help me! You're supposed to look at *his* lips, not your own!'

'Well then, what's the *lip* one again?'

'This is going to be more work than I thought,' Luna huffed.

———·✦·———

After a further afternoon of practice, Luna declared that I was as ready as I would ever be and, armed with the four Ls and a lavish royal blue gown that captured Reili's colours, I was pushed through the doors of the dining hall and into the lion's den.

'Cole,' Luna waved a stern-looking Cole over to our bench. 'Won't you join us for dinner tonight?'

'I'm on duty,' Cole tapped the sword at his side.

'Oh, pity. I know it's not proper for you to be in our chambers, but we missed you this afternoon.' She pouted, and I watched as Cole's grey eyes softened and darted to her lips.

'I was just telling Blaise how lucky she is to have the strongest, most handsome member of the Guard as her regular companion,' she fluttered her long eyelashes, and I bit back a laugh when Cole's cheeks turned a fetching shade of crimson as he stuttered out a denial.

'Oh stop,' she leaned closer towards him, sharp green eyes darting from his eyes to his lips as she tucked a strand of white-blonde hair behind her ear. 'Don't be modest, Cole. There's a reason the prince trusts you so.'

'I'd like to think that has everything to do with my ability and nothing to do with my looks.'

She laughed a deep, throaty giggle in response and placed a hand on his arm. I noticed how he leaned into her touch. 'Oh, you *are* funny, Cole! Well, it's a shame you can't join us. Just know that you're always welcome to seek our company, even when not obligated to do so.' Luna removed her hand from Cole's arm, and he blushed, muttered something indecipherable, and returned to his post.

She turned to me. 'I hope you were paying close attention.'

'How did you *do* that?'

'Oh, let's not pretend it isn't easy to fluster poor Cole,' she grinned.

'I'm never going to be able to do this! Even *I* believed you wanted him.'

Luna looked over her shoulder and shot Cole a small smile. He smiled back and then averted his gaze. 'Who said I don't?' she winked. 'Now it's your turn.'

I turned in time to see the prince enter the hall, arm in arm with his mother. The diners rose from their seats as the queen made her way past the rows of banquet tables, adorned with silk tablecloths and silverware, to the raised plinth that housed her throne and the large dining table that she, and her selected few, would eat at.

Prince Kaspian held her arm and aided her up the stairs, clutching her hand as she lowered herself into her seat. When he had taken his place beside her, Queen Lizabeta said 'sit', and the whole room sat once more.

I peered up at Kaspian as the crackling boar and creamy potatoes were served. Perhaps feeling my gaze upon him, his eyes landed on me in the crowded hall, and he excused himself from his mother's table, the queen watching with pursed lips as he made his way towards our bench.

'May I?' he asked, gesturing to the spot next to me. I nodded, as those surrounding us were quick to dip their heads in a sign of respect to their prince.

Servers darted to our table to ensure that the prince had a goblet full of wine and a plate full of food. He thanked them, and made a show of tasting the food so that others around us began eating. I suspected, for all his talk of being one of the people, he rarely dined amongst them.

The accusation must have been written on my face because he leaned in close to whisper, 'these are not my people, they are *hers*. Those in my army who are allowed to dine in here, feel so duty bound to protect me that they cannot relax when I am among them. I prefer to keep out of their way at mealtimes to allow them some time to unwind.'

'I didn't ask,' I snapped, and Luna kicked my shin under the table. 'I mean, how thoughtful of you,' I stammered, trying to flutter my eyelashes at him.

'Is there something in your eye?' he asked. Luna rocked with silent laughter beside me.

'Oh, yes, there's so much dust in the air! Stuffy halls.' I gestured around me, cringing when the staff tensed at the unintended insult. In the corner of my eye, Luna sunk her head into her hands. This was going even worse than expected. I tried again, 'What brings you to our table this evening, Your Highness?'

'I've been thinking about what you said,' he started, and I glanced to his lips. They were full, and soft-looking against the coat of stubble that peppered his strong chin. What would they feel like to kiss? *Shit.* I wasn't supposed to *actually* think that! I forced my gaze back up to his rich blue eyes. 'You were right.'

'I-I was?' I stammered, taken aback. I had been expecting to be rebuked for the way I had spoken to him.

'I need to do more. I cannot wait for the crown to sit atop my head before I enact change. For all my mother's faults, I love the woman. I want her to live a long and happy life. But I don't want that to be at the expense of my people.' He leaned closer still, his whispers tickling my ear, and I sucked in a tight breath.

'I held a private meeting with her today, to try and gain funds for rebuilds in some of Reili's poorest villages. I have also requested that the laws are changed, to ensure noble households must also contribute to my armies. Their second-born sons will be required to join the ranks at the age of eighteen. This will allow for the townsfolk to also send only one male from their family to the ranks, as opposed to requiring a minimum servitude of ten years from all males born into the family, as the current law demands.'

He pulled back to study my face as I snapped my gaping mouth shut. 'I am impressed, Your Grace. How did Her Majesty take the request?'

'About as well as you would imagine. She's already on her second glass of wine.' He nodded to the throne, where the queen did indeed seem to be gulping back a large glass of dark red liquid.

I chuckled and, remembering Luna's four Ls, tried hard to turn the sound into a low and sultry giggle as she had demonstrated. The noise sounded strangled, and both Luna and the prince looked at me in alarm.

'Are you quite well, my lady?' the prince asked.

'Yes. Fine. Thank you,' I squeaked, biting my lip.

He eyed me carefully, glancing from my eyes to the lip pinned beneath my teeth. I released it, and he held my gaze once more, whispering, 'she agreed to consider both requests before the year is out. Although, she made it clear that she would be more inclined to agree with my arguments if I were to choose a wife.'

'That's a very roundabout way of asking me to marry you, Your Highness. I'm afraid if I am to say yes, I'll require a more elaborate proposal.' I kept my face deadpan.

Prince Kaspian choked, before a deep and musical laugh escaped him. 'I'll bear that in mind, Blaise.' With that, he rose from the bench, still laughing, and made his way back to his mother's side as she took another deep gulp of wine.

'Well?' I asked Luna.

'I think he played you at your own game,' she grinned.

CHAPTER 22

THE NEXT MORNING, COLE ESCORTED me to the stables, where I brushed Lady and saddled my second mare for a morning ride around the grounds.

'Would you like me to accompany you?' Cole asked, gesturing to a second saddle he could use for Lady.

'Do I have a choice? Isn't your current task to follow me everywhere?' Cole cringed, and I felt a tiny amount of guilt.

'Of course you have a choice. I can either ride behind you and you can pretend I am not there, or we can ride together and enjoy the scenery. Perhaps we may even talk a little?' Cole offered, extending an olive branch.

'You want to talk to me?' I was surprised.

'Yes, m'lady. I would very much like to get to know you.'

'Personally? Or as a spy for His Highness?'

The audacity of me.

Cole flushed. 'Personally, of course, miss. Kas – His Highness – has shown a lot of interest in you, and that undoubtedly means we will be spending a lot of time together, even when I am not duty bound to shadow your movements. I should like to have a friendship of our own. If you would like one?'

I had told Luna that I wasn't here to make friends, and I certainly shouldn't trust *this* man. Not when he was a member of the Guard, was likely involved in the witch hunts, and had already appeared suspicious of me. But, something about the hopeful way Cole looked at me, and the pinkish colour still staining his cheeks, was endearing. I'd never had a human friend before. I hadn't even really had *any* friends . . . until Luna, of course. What would it be like to talk to someone without needing to feel ashamed of my humanness? Without feeling like I was lacking?

'I think I would like that very much,' I told him earnestly, handing him the second saddle. He beamed and began fastening it with ease.

———— · ✦ · ————

We rode through the grounds until the sun was high in the sky and the horses were exhausted, the morning flying by without so much as a dip in conversation as Cole told me more about his childhood. I learned more about how Kaspian had protected Cole in his youth, moving him into the palace when his mother and father died.

'I thought the queen would punish him,' he told me, 'but she was proud. "Princes do not ask, they command. What a fine young prince you will be," I remember her saying. I've never heard him give another order within these walls since.'

He also told me how Kaspian had gotten Cole lessons with his own tutors, and even went so far as to secure him a spot on the Royal Guard.

'It sounds like you have been through a lot, Cole,' I told him. 'Yet you still stand strong and proud. Don't give all the credit to His Highness, I'm sure your tenacity had something to do with it, too.' I smiled as his cheeks stained a familiar beetroot again. 'I can't imagine the others in this palace made it easy for you, despite the prince's favour.'

'His faith in me did not count for much when we were small. I will admit there were those that said I did not belong. I like to think I have proved them wrong, though. That I earned my place among the Guard and wasn't simply handed it.' My heart squeezed painfully in my chest. Cole and I weren't all that dissimilar. We had both grown up the odd one out.

'I'm sure you have, and I'm sure you've had to work twice as hard for it.'

There was something about Cole that made me want to open up. But what could I tell him? All my stories of childhood involved witches and magic. I didn't feel like lying to him about it, so instead I said, 'you always make Kas sound so kind, but he leads armies.'

The topic was dangerously close to what had made him suspicious before, but this time he answered quickly. 'The soldiers respect him. You do not have to be cruel to earn respect.' I thought of Agnes, and how cruel she could be. Yet the witches obeyed and respected her. Were fear and respect the same thing?

Cole filled the ensuing silence with more stories from his past. In our time together, I discovered that his husky laugh was rare yet contagious, and I found myself joining in. His presence had become familiar and welcome, even steadying, when earlier that morning it had felt an inconvenience. He drifted close to my side now, instead of hovering a few steps behind me, which made his company much more enjoyable and less formal. It had been a pleasant morning, and I couldn't help the sudden lightness in my step as we led the horses back to the stables on foot.

As we entered, we found the prince making conversation with the stable boy, who had returned Ginger from being reshoed. Cole took the horses' reins and led them to their stools, allowing us a private moment, though I knew he was still within earshot.

'Your Highness,' I curtsied.

'Kaspian,' he corrected, as the stable boy hurried off.

'Why do you hate your title?' I blurted out before I could think better of it. A morning of casual conversation with Cole had perhaps loosened my tongue a little too much.

'I do not hate it,' he answered, surprising me. 'I fear it.' I hadn't been expecting that, and I tilted my head in surprise, inviting him to say more.

'The great king Kaspian is someone everybody in this country adored. He is the king that united the people. Every home, from the tiniest of village shacks to the richest of manor houses, has a portrait of their fallen king hung somewhere on the walls. He was loved by all. "He was going to change the world" they tell me.' Kas shook his head, a sadness looming over him.

'Having been given his name, the whole of Reili looks at me with the same expectations. There's a lot of pressure that comes with that, and I'm scared to let them down. What if I am not the king they want me to be?'

I pushed down my own revulsion that the man who had sired me and threatened to steal me from my mother, had led armies into Starterra and butchered thousands, was considered a good man. Instead, I asked, 'what if you could be even better?'

He scanned my face, for *what* I wasn't sure. After a moment, he loosed a shaky breath and continued on a different path. 'I am pleased I caught you this morning, Blaise. I will be gone for the next couple of days, and I'm relieved I had the opportunity to tell you to behave while I'm gone.'

Gone.

A surge of disappointment rattled through me. Telling myself it was just due to not being able to progress with the mission, I kept my tone casual as I asked, 'where will you be going?'

'Not that it's any of your business,' he flicked me gently on the nose and I swatted his hand away as he smiled, infuriating dimple returning, 'but there's been some trouble on the border I need to attend to.'

'Witches?' I breathed.

'What? No,' his eyebrows pulled into a frown. 'Just some Harensarra soldiers trying to start trouble.' I puffed a sigh of relief, which he took as concern for him, his frown softening. 'I shall be back in a few days. Try to stay out of my mother's way until then. Cole will remain with you.' Cole, having approached once finished with the horses, gave a tense nod.

'When I return, I would like to take you for dinner,' Kaspian made it sound like I had a choice in the matter.

'I can't say no to a prince, Your Highness.'

'Please,' he begged, 'it's just Kaspian.'

'I know.'

'You're maddening.'

'I know.'

He grinned a beautiful smile. All white teeth and sparkling blue eyes and, damn me, my heart skipped a beat.

'Look after her,' Kaspian clasped hands with a frowning Cole.

'Something tells me she can look after herself.'

Kaspian laughed, deep and wicked. 'I think you might be right, old friend.' Then, he left, and *Mother damn me* once again, because I was sorry to see him go.

Chapter 23

'I HAVE A SURPRISE FOR you,' Cole told me as we walked back to my chambers.

I raised an eyebrow, interest peaked. 'What kind of surprise?'

'Wait and see,' he smiled, a lopsided grin that made him look younger and incredibly handsome. I almost blushed. As we rounded the corridor towards my chambers, I noticed another door open, with members of the Guard moving belongings inside. I looked at Cole questioningly, who nodded his head once, urging me forwards.

'No, no, *no*! The drawers must go on the *left* side, and the wardrobe on the *right*! Otherwise, the balance will be all wrong!' Luna stood in the centre of the room, orchestrating the layout.

'Luna, what are you doing here?'

'Hey, neighbour! I'm moving in! Cole might have mentioned something about tricky dresses, and seeing an indecent amount of flesh that he really didn't want to repeat. So, I'm moving in here to save him from the horrors of your naked body!' I whacked her arm, and she squealed as she spun away, rubbing the spot I'd caught.

'I'm sorry my shoulders offended you, Cole,' I shot a pointed glare at him. A blush had already begun creeping up his neck, staining his ears.

'I didn't say it was a horror! I . . . you have very pretty shoulders. It's just, I thought you would prefer . . .' he stumbled over his words, getting redder by the second.

I laughed. 'Cole, I'm joking. Thank you! This was really kind of you.' I pulled him into a sincere hug, his eyes bulging out of his beetroot face. He tensed for a second, before his arms relaxed and he hugged me back, his smell of shoe polish and hay enveloping me.

'Look!' Luna exclaimed as I released Cole and turned back to her. 'Our rooms join through this door.' Sure enough, when Luna opened the door, it led straight into the living area of my chambers.

'How did I not notice this door before?' I wondered aloud.

'It was behind that awful painting of the fruit bowl. I had Jon here take it down.' Jon, less than impressed at having to move the cabinet for what I guessed was the third or fourth time, let out a small grunt of acknowledgment.

I paused, looking to Luna, wondering if any of the other paintings in my room were hiding doorways. Luna gave the tiniest of nods, barely noticeable and I knew she had mentioned it deliberately to lead me to this knowledge. *Interesting.* That would be something to investigate later.

'Well boys, I'll leave you to finish this while I help Blaise here get dressed for her luncheon with the queen.'

'My *what?*' I spluttered, as Luna ushered me into my room and shut the door behind us.

'She's requested a private lunch with you. It will just be you and her. Well, and Lady Natalia, but that's to be expected.'

Mother above.

'Why? Does she do this with everyone?' Panic swelled thick and fast.

'I don't know, and no. And before you ask, no I don't know if she suspects anything. But why should she?'

Shit.

So much for avoiding her while Kaspian was gone. I slumped into a chair.

'There's no time for that. Up! Bath! Now! Be quick about it. I'll pick you out a gown.' Luna pulled me from the chair and shoved me towards the bathroom.

I bathed quickly, my heartbeat seemingly pulsing against my temple, not leaving room for anything but pure panic. But really, what could the queen know? If she *did* know that I wasn't who I claimed to be, she wouldn't be inviting me for lunch, she would be organising my beheading.

I forced myself to take some deep breaths as I emerged into the dressing area. Luna had laid out a delicate white gown with ruched sleeves and purple ribbon detailing, and she helped me step into the dress, tying the ribbon neatly at the back. Thankfully, there was no corset to be secured into, I wasn't sure I would have been able to breathe.

'Sit,' she barked, and I obeyed.

Delicate fingers wove through my hair, plaiting the strands before fastening the neat braids into a bun at the nape of my neck. My heart tugged at the memory of Sapphire's countless hours doing my hair. Not just on the journey here, but throughout my childhood. Luna added powder to my face, and stained my lips a gentle pink colour, nodding in approval before adding some to her own lips. Finally, she brushed a line of kohl under my eyes.

'There,' she gave my shoulders a squeeze. 'You look beautiful.'

'Fit to be presented to the queen?' I gulped.

'Take a look for yourself,' she spun me around to face the mirror above the dresser.

I gasped.

Agnes stared back at me.

Her golden hair was tied back like mine, but it was *her* silver eyes that watched me.

'What is it?' Luna asked. 'Don't you like it? I can choose a different colour?'

I blinked, and when I looked again, it was my own reflection staring back at me once more. 'No, it's nothing. I love it! I thought I saw . . . I think I'm going mad.'

Luna frowned. 'Thought you saw what?'

'I thought I saw my mother. I think I need some more sleep.'

Luna's brow furrowed together even further. 'Well, sleep is going to have to wait. You need to go!'

She pushed me out of the door, where Cole was waiting to escort me. 'You look lovely.' He sounded sincere, the tips of his ears a delicate, shining pink.

'Yeah, yeah, we haven't got time for you to blush, let's get this over with.' I tried to smirk, but it felt wobbly as I linked my arm through his and let him lead me down the hall towards the queen's chambers.

———·✦·———

Cole nodded to the guards at the entrance to the queen's suite and left me at the door. I slipped in quickly, hoping the sooner I went in, the sooner this would be over with.

Everything about the room was excessive. Chiming in the corner was a huge grandfather clock made from stained oak, and finished with golden leaf patterns that I didn't doubt were made from real gold. Lining the fuchsia walls were dozens of paintings, many of them portraits of the queen. A cream chaise, with thick arms and oak feet that matched the clock, sat in the middle of the room surrounded by several high-backed leather armchairs. My eyes lingered for a moment on a grand table with a plethora of pastries and sandwiches laid out upon it, several chairs vacant around it.

Despite the multitude of seating arrangements, the queen – and Natalia Marshore – were propped up on an assortment of colourful pillows on the floor. To my surprise, Aleera joined them, her spine perfectly rigid, scowl locked in place like she'd been practicing it all her life. Hadn't Luna said this would be a private luncheon? Ignoring Aleera, I dipped into the lowest curtsey I could.

'Your Majesty.'

'Lady Vermont, please take a seat.'

I sat across from her on one of the small round pillows strewn across the floor. 'Please, call me Blaise.'

'You sound like my son. However, I must insist on formal titles, as I urge him to do.' I tried not to smirk, knowing the prince was ignoring that advice.

'Thank you for inviting me for lunch, Your Majesty. It was quite a surprise.'

'Yes, I imagine it was.' An awkward silence followed. It felt rude to ask *why* she'd summoned me, and she didn't seem to want to elaborate.

'Natalia dear, do pass Lady Vermont the sandwiches.' Were the lack of proper titles for Natalia a familiarity, or a snub? Natalia obeyed, slender hand reaching out to offer me a platter of tiny sandwiches with the crusts cut off. I helped myself to two cucumber sandwiches, and two cheese and onion chutney ones, leaving the salmon and cress untouched. They were small enough to eat in one bite, but that seemed improper, so I nibbled at the edges.

Queen Lizabeta and the other two ladies both had sandwiches on their plates that remained untouched, and I had the sudden panic that perhaps they were trying to poison me. Taking a subtle sniff, I didn't detect any, but set my half-eaten sandwich down anyway, hoping that, if it *was* laced, I hadn't eaten nearly enough for it to kill me.

'I hear you have been riding with my son.' The queen began, face void of anything other than mild irritation. Aleera, on the other hand, looked positively ruffled.

'I have. If we caused any damage, Your Majesty, I am happy to pay for it.'

She smirked. 'For someone who has not yet received the wealth of their grandfather's estate, you are very keen to be rid of it. That's twice you have offered me your money now.'

'My apologies, Your Grace. I did not mean to offend.'

With a flare of her nostrils, she flicked her wrist lazily, and a serving boy poured a cup of tea from an ornate china pot. 'No, it is not about that, girl. I am keen to know why he has shown such an interest in you. He has not expressed any desire for any of the ladies I have presented him with, like darling Lady Cresthorn here, and you . . . you are so *plain*. I had hoped for better for him, truth be told.'

Ouch.

I didn't dare glance at Aleera's smug face, and bit back the several responses I wanted to snap at her. Lines including: 'if I'm plain, it's because I inherited it from your husband,' and, 'I had also hoped for a better potential mother-in-law, but here we are.' Instead, I opted for stunned silence.

'Oh, I don't know, Lizzie, she's got quite pretty ears,' Natalia murmured, twirling a strand of dark hair around her finger. Aleera snorted, and her blonde strands swayed with movement as she hid her giggles behind her hand.

Nice *ears*.

Mother above! If that's all I had going for me, I had no hope in wooing the prince. *Lizzie shot Natalia a glare that would have sent many a man to their knees, but Natalia either didn't care, or was too simple to notice.*

'Be that as it may, it takes more than *nice ears* to become a princess. Is that what you're after, Lady Vermont? To become a princess?'

Try a queen, you old hag.

'It would be an honour if the prince were to choose me to be his bride,' I said instead of the barb. 'But I haven't been trying to pursue him.' *Much.* 'I have just been myself.' *In no shape or form.*

'And that is what worries me,' her words were clipped. 'Because what you *are*, is a bastard-born child of meagre stock, related to a man that was more insufferable than any I have ever come across. You are a common serving girl, who has lucked out in ways she cannot even begin to comprehend. You could have wound up a whore, and yet you try your luck at becoming a princess. Why does my son seek to consort with a would-be whore, when I have presented him with fine ladies like our Aleera? Does he mean to upset me?'

My spine went rigid. Even having grown up away from human prejudices, I knew an insult when I heard one. Resisting the urge to reach for the dagger under my skirts and put years of training to good use, I instead tried to soothe the rotten woman's ego.

'I'm sure he does not mean to hurt you. He loves you dearly, he has told me as much himself. Perhaps he simply wishes for a friend? He has not made any advances towards me, and I am not sure he sees me as a princess. I think he finds me fun to ride with, because I don't do it as a lady should.' I kept my eyes on the floor, hoping it gave the appearance of shame, as well as hiding the murderous glint in my eye.

'Another thing to add to your list of faults,' Aleera spoke for the first time, and the queen hummed in agreement.

Mother above! These people were intolerable.

'I agree. But perhaps, Your Grace, you could use my friendship with the prince to your advantage?' I dared to meet her eyes and found rage simmering there, boiling over into curiosity.

'Go on.'

'The more time I spend with His Highness, the more I can encourage him to spend time with the ladies *you* choose for him,' I proposed, though I had absolutely no intention of doing anything of the sort. 'I can point out all of their attractive qualities. Perhaps open his eyes to what he has been ignoring,' I gestured to Aleera, and if looks could kill . . .

'Oh, what a wonderful idea, Lizzie!' Natalia cooed, clapping her hands together in delight. The queen ignored her as she eyeballed me, her pale, cold eyes stripping me bare as she looked for any hint of deceit.

'Very well,' she nodded, lips pursed as she contemplated. 'See that he dances with Lady Cresthorn at my next ball.'

I nodded. 'Yes, Your Majesty.'

'You may leave us now.' Aleera's glare turned into a smirk at the queen's dismissal.

She didn't have to ask me twice. I stood, dipped into a quick curtsey, nearly tripping over my skirts in my hurry to get out of there, and found Cole waiting for me in the hall. Seeing the look on my face, he didn't dare ask, instead taking me back to my chambers, where I immediately shut him out and used the connecting door to slip into Luna's rooms.

They were empty.

Emerging back into the hallway, I asked Cole, 'do you know where Luna is?'

He shrugged. 'Perhaps the gardens?' After searching the entire palace, a worried Cole on my heels, it was clear that Luna wasn't there.

'She may have gone into the city proper. Perhaps she had some errands to run?' Cole suggested. I nodded, trying not to worry that anything had happened to her. *No one has discovered who she is. Cole would know if they had.*

It wasn't until dusk when I heard Luna's door shut and her bed springs creak. I slipped into her room, and she jumped when the door creaked open. 'Mother above! Don't frighten me like that!' she clutched her chest.

'Where have you been?' I asked.

'I went into the city. The queen had given me some errands to run for her.' Strange that she hadn't mentioned it before, when I'd been on my way to meet the queen. But the task was not unusual. We *were* her ladies-in-waiting, after all. 'Have you eaten?' Luna asked.

I shook my head. 'Not unless you count those tiny finger sandwiches.'

'I don't,' she beamed, a wicked glint in her eye. 'Come on, let's get you some real food.' At that, I pushed my concerns aside, and let her lead me towards the smell of cooked meat coming from the kitchens.

Chapter 24

AFTER WE HAD EATEN A dinner of roasted turkey legs with rosemary and thyme seasoning, a baked potato topped with grated cheese, and a side of honeyed carrots, Luna and I made our way back to my chambers.

'I'm stuffed,' I moaned, clutching my stomach as I fell into a soft chair.

Luna laughed, the sound melodic, her blunt, platinum hair dancing with the movement. 'Lucky for you, we don't have to wear a corset tonight.' I'd been relieved to find out that we wouldn't be expected to dine in the hall every night, so I could eat my fill without worrying about breathing.

'What are we doing tonight, then?' I asked, suppressing a burp.

'We could figure out where some of these hidden doorways go? There must be a reason they're blocked off with paintings.' Luna eyed the walls suspiciously, as if she could see through them if she tried hard enough.

'How many do you think there are?' I glanced between the dozens of paintings on the wall. Some of them were tiny, and I couldn't imagine they hid anything. Others were large enough that, even with our combined strength, there was a risk we could drop them.

'There's no way to know without removing them all. My last room had two. One led to an adjoining room, like mine does to yours now, and the other led into a dingy hallway that came out at the kitchens. Handy for a late-night snack but not much else.'

'Maybe the paintings are only for privacy?' I suggested. 'Like the one between our rooms? To prevent unwanted visitors crossing between them?'

'Perhaps.' Luna shrugged once more, her green eyes – which looked more emerald today – narrowing. 'Or . . . perhaps they're hiding things.'

·✦·

'Do you have your end?' I hissed through gritted teeth, struggling to lift the giant golden frame from the wall. Luna grunted under the weight of the frame in response.

'Three, two, one, lift!'

The painting tore away from the brackets on the wall, and together, we eased it onto the ground. We'd been at this for an hour. Removing each painting – big or small – from the walls of my chamber, looking for discreet doorways. One painting of a sour-faced old lady had concealed a bricked-up window but, other than that, nothing. There was only this one frame left, the painting a hefty depiction of a majestic black horse, and I held my breath as we faced the papered wall it had occupied.

Luna let out a sigh of disappointment. There was no obvious door, like the one that adjoined mine to hers, but that didn't mean someone hadn't taken the time to hide it beyond just the painting. I ran a hand over the wall, tapping as I went, until my heart lurched. There! Right in the middle of the wall, the sound of my knocking changed.

'Listen,' I whispered, tapping again.

Luna's eyes lit up with excitement, and she dragged her hand over the wall. Her fingernails caught on what must have been a gap in the door, pushing through the wallpaper covering the area. Feverishly, she

THE FALSE QUEEN

began to rip and tear the paper from the wall.

'What are you doing?' I exclaimed in horror. 'How are we going to hide this?'

'We can cover it back up with the painting! And we'll just hide the torn paper, or throw it out somewhere, I don't know! Just help me find this door!'

We ripped at the wallpaper, tiny scraps coming loose at first, until larger strips began to tear free. We panted as the last piece fell to the floor, fingers sore and nails broken, as we faced an old wooden door with a rusted handle. We stared at it, then at each other, then back to the door.

'Now what?' Luna whispered, a tiny sliver of fear shaking her voice.

'We open it, I guess.' My own voice wasn't as steady as I'd hoped.

'You first,' she nudged me forward.

'*Me?* You're the one with magic! You go first!' I argued in hushed tones, pushing her in front of me.

'It's your room!'

'It was *your* idea!'

'It's your–'

'Oh, Mother above! We could do this all day!' I interrupted, wrenching the door open before I could think better of it.

The door creaked on its old hinges, swinging open to reveal a hallway. Fixtures, that had once housed lanterns that had long burned out, ran along the walls. The brick smelled damp, the air stale and dusty, and it stretched further than the light from my room illuminated.

'How old is this corridor?' I asked aloud, not expecting Luna to have an answer. 'The brickwork doesn't match the rest of the palace.' I took a tentative step into the dingy hallway, running a hand along the large stone bricks that had none of the grandeur of the rest of the building's stonework.

'Is it even safe?' Luna cringed, as pieces of stone crumbled where my hand trailed.

'There's only one way to find out.' Making sure the doors to both of our chambers were locked, I grabbed a candle from my room. It wouldn't make the best light, but it was better than nothing and, at the very least, the smell of spiced rhubarb was mildly comforting. I headed into the corridor and, a few paces in, Luna latched onto my arm.

'Well, aren't you the big brave witch,' I murmured, resulting in a bony elbow being dug hard into my side.

'If anything attacks you, even if it's a sodding spider, you're on your own,' she shot back, and I huffed out a laugh.

The candle was halfway dwindled, hot wax running down the sides and collecting in the rounded holder, and still the tunnel went on and on. The corridor so winding and uneven, I couldn't even begin to place where we were in the palace.

'This has been even less useful than my old passageway that led to the kitchens,' Luna yawned. 'At least that ended with a snack.' She'd stopped clinging to my arm after a while, her usual blasé attitude returning the more time we spent in the corridor without being attacked. A moment from suggesting we turn around and go back before Cole came looking for us, something caught my eye.

'What's that?' I whispered, making my way closer to the warm yellow glow of a lantern emitting from beneath an otherwise-hidden door. Voices sounded from inside, and I pressed a finger to my lips, signalling for Luna to be quiet. She rolled her eyes and mouthed the words, 'I'm not stupid'. I shot her an apologetic grimace while tiptoeing closer.

'I hope this is important, Mother. I should be well on the road by now.'

I almost tripped into the door at my rush to get closer upon hearing Kaspian's voice inside.

'You're leaving?'

I laid myself flat on the ground, peering through the tiny crack between the door and the floor that, from the other side, would barely have been noticeable. Luna reflected my position across from me, our heads almost touching.

The queen sat stiff-backed on her chaise longue, it was the first time I had seen her hair loose, the edges were frayed and wispy. She wore a thin gown, her bare arms pale, almost pallid. The cosmetics she usually wore had been rubbed off, leaving dark circles under her eyes. The prince stood before her, shifting from foot to foot. He wore a dark tunic and trousers, a pack already slung on his back, like she had truly caught him as he was about to leave.

'Yes, Mother. I have duties I need to attend to. One of them being to ensure our borders are well protected.'

'Harensarra again?' The queen's face went sickly pale as Kaspian sat beside her, wrapping an arm around her bony shoulder.

'Yes. But nothing I can't handle.' He gave her a gentle squeeze, face softening at her evident fear.

'These skirmishes with them distract you from your real duty,' the queen's face drew into a frown.

Kaspian stood, and walked towards where we were concealed behind the hidden door. He could have been playing with a trinket over the fireplace but, from this angle, I couldn't quite make it out. Luna slapped a hand over her mouth to stop herself breathing so loudly, but I felt like I couldn't draw breath at all.

'We've talked about this. The witch hunts are no longer fruitful. We've caught a few trying to hide in plain sight, but never *her*,' Kaspian put the trinket down a little heavily and turned back towards the queen. Luna went rigid beside me, and I felt like my heart would fall out of my chest. *Did he just say . . .*

'Well, you know how I feel about that,' her pale eyebrows drew even further together, 'but that's not what I meant. I meant your duty of choosing a bride.'

The prince groaned and ran his large hands down his face. 'We have had this conversation a hundred times. I will not wed for the sake of it. And I do not need a bride!'

'You need an *heir*,' the queen countered. 'Do not make the same mistakes as me.'

Kaspian's eyes shuttered, and I wondered if her words had wounded him. Whether he thought himself one of her *mistakes*, but his voice didn't falter as he said, 'I am not even king. I have time for those things. Time to find someone I love.' His eyes filled with a hope that made my stomach churn and I looked away, finding it difficult to look at him.

'Do not be a fool, my son.'

Kaspian bristled. 'You do not want me to experience what you did? You do not want me to find love?' I found myself drawn back to staring at him, my heart still hammering.

The queen's expression sharpened. 'I couldn't think of anything more dangerous for you. Love is for fools, not kings.'

'But, Mother–' he tried to protest but she wouldn't listen.

'No, Kaspian! I will not hear it! You *will* choose a bride before the year is out! That isn't a request. It is a command. Queen to subject, commander-in-chief to general, mother to son.' She used a bony hand to wipe tears from under her eyes.

'I don't understand why this is so important to you. Our kingdom is in disarray, and our coffers are empty thanks to your *obsession* with that witch. We can barely afford a royal wedding! Harensarra breathes down our necks! War is imminent! There are hundreds of things more important than *this*!' he brandished a hand in frustration. 'In fact, I should be dealing with one of those issues right now!' The prince turned to leave.

'She's coming for me, Kaspian!' The queen shrieked, and Kaspian's hand stilled on the door handle.

'What did you say?' he turned slowly.

'The witch who slayed my husband. She is coming. For *me*!' I wasn't sure I was breathing, and Luna let out a barely audible gasp. 'She's been taunting me. Sending me letters!' The queen stood, rifling through her drawers and pulling out a wad of parchment. From where I lay, I couldn't make out the handwriting.

Kaspian closed the gap between them and snatched the letters from her hand, scanning them. 'This is madness! Why would she write you after so many years? It has to be a hoax.'

'I hope for all our sakes it is. But if it isn't, Kaspian, these letters say she is coming for me. I'll be dead before the year is out!' I covered my mouth with one hand to stop the cry from escaping. Luna grabbed my other hand in hers. Both our palms were slick with sweat as she squeezed.

'If this is true,' Kaspian was saying, 'I won't let her get to you.'

'You won't be able to stop her.' The queen's eyes were feverish, glistening with tears. 'It's why I have been so suspicious of this *Vermont* girl. Appearing out of nowhere, claiming to be some bastard.

They can disguise themselves, you know. What if it's *her*?'

Kaspian walked away, creating a gap between them once more. 'Blaise? She has nothing to do with this. She's harmless.' Luna breathed a sigh of relief in my ear, but I didn't share her reassurance. Had Agnes really been writing to the queen? Taunting her? She could have risked everything!

'You've gone soft, my boy,' tears dripped from Lizabeta's pointy nose as she dipped her head in disappointment. 'Do you forget that *you* are the man who drove witches out of this kingdom?'

'Of course not! Why do you think I'm so sure that Blaise *isn't* one?' I felt my own surge of disappointment. He really had done it, then. I didn't know when I had started hoping he wasn't responsible for so many witches being forced into hiding. Or burned. 'Do you really believe she would come here, knowing what I'm capable of?'

Luna's grip tightened on mine, and I knew she was imagining her coven burning, just like I was.

'The ones you have found of late, they return because they are no longer threatened by you! Perhaps she too has heard the rumours that you've not killed one of them yourself!' the queen screamed, and Kaspian recoiled a few steps, eyes wide with shock. I exhaled a shaky breath as the prince mumbled something I couldn't make out. Whatever he said, Lizabeta snapped in response.

'It doesn't matter! *She* believes that she can come here and finish me off, just like she did your king! Should she succeed, you must be prepared to fight back! And you must give this kingdom its strongest chance of survival. You *must* choose a bride!' Kaspian's head hung in shame as she closed the gap between them, forcing his face upwards to look at her. 'Promise me.'

He hesitated, and then extracted himself from her grip, backing towards the door. 'I promise to choose. I don't promise you'll approve.' The queen frowned but, before she could argue, Kaspian fled the room, dropping the letters in his haste.

Luna and I remained silent where we were. Finally, the queen wiped her tears away, straightened her rumpled clothing, and slipped from one chamber to the next. Quickly, we picked ourselves up off the dusty floor and made our way back down the forgotten corridor. Slamming the door shut behind us, we returned the painting to its rightful place on the wall.

Chapter 25

THERE WAS NO SOUND BUT that of our rapid breathing. I could barely think, brain whirring with everything we had overheard, not being able to make sense of any of it. Why would Agnes risk our plan by taunting the queen with letters? Was Kaspian really a witch-killer or was there a softer side to him that hadn't been able to go through with it? If there was . . . maybe I could manipulate that.

'Do you think he did it?' Luna's question made me jump, and I spun to her, startled. 'Do you think he killed my family?'

'Does it matter whether he did it, or if he told someone else to light the match? He's still guilty.' My voice wobbled on the word *guilty*, making it sound like a question.

She nodded, her dark eyebrows drawn into a crumpled line across her forehead. 'Why would Agnes be taunting the queen?'

'That's exactly what I intend to find out,' I sighed. 'Go to bed Luna, I have a letter to write.'

The letter had taken me most of the night to compose, and I restarted several times over, burning the unfinished versions – along with the wallpaper we had stripped from my walls – leaving no evidence behind.

Using enchanted parchment, that would only reveal its true message to Agnes, I wrote a decoy, mundane message which chased news on my *grandfather's* estate. Beneath it, the hidden message gave Agnes a brief report on what I had found out, including details on the conflict with Harensarra. I also asked her to warn the Starchasers to remain well hidden while Kaspian was on their border.

Other than that titbit, I barely offered her anything of note, childishly wanting to retain my information until I had answers to my own questions. I detailed the conversation I had overheard, leaving out the implication that the prince hadn't been the one killing witches after all, focusing instead on what the queen had claimed. I wanted to know why Agnes had risked making the queen suspicious of me and nearly blown everything. At the other end of a letter, I felt brave enough to do what I wouldn't have done in person – question Agnes's decisions.

———— ⋅ ✦ ⋅ ————

'Are you even listening to me?' I questioned Cole.

'Hmm?' he responded, giving me my answer.

We had been in the stables for the last hour, as I groomed Lady and my other gifted mare, much to the stable boy's disapproval, who had muttered multiple times about it not being a woman's place. I had been asking Cole his opinion on a name for my other steed but, after receiving no response to my choice of Queenie, it was clear that Cole had stopped paying attention.

'You're worried about him, aren't you?' I surmised, noting the worry lines etched on Cole's face were nothing to do with me or my name suggestions, inappropriate as they may be.

Cole's pale grey eyes finally focused on me. 'I'm his guard. I should be with him.'

'He's a big boy, I'm sure he can look after himself,' I continued, brushing Queenie's dark mane – yes, the name had to be Queenie.

Cole's stare turned wide-eyed, and I frowned. 'You don't think he can take care of himself?'

'It's not that. It's just . . . I thought I saw . . .' he trailed off, shaking his head.

'What? Do I have something on my face?' I reached up self-consciously, rubbing at places potential dirt could have ended up.

'No, it's nothing. Your hair looked a different colour. Must have been a trick of the light,' he rubbed at his eyes.

I reached up, pulling a lock of hair in front of my eyes. 'Still brown. Are you getting enough sleep?'

'Four hours a night, since I was fourteen.'

'Four! That's not nearly enough, Cole! No wonder you're seeing things!' I scolded.

'Four is plenty. I have things I need to be awake for.'

'Trailing me doesn't seem all that meaningful a task,' my top lip tugged up in a slight snicker.

'Usually, I'm watching Kas's back. That takes a great deal more concentration, I'll be honest,' Cole grimaced, and I couldn't help but chuckle.

'I imagine he's quite the handful,' I coaxed.

'There was one time, we were barely sixteen. I'd just been given my position in the Guard, and Kas was already on his way to becoming general.' Cole's eyes lit up with pride when he spoke about the prince, and his lips twitched with amusement. I paused my brushing, wanting to listen fully.

'We were on the edge of Harensarra, dealing with some border trouble, when Kas thought it would be a brilliant idea to go for an ale in one of the local taprooms. I warned him that a soldier in Reili uniform would likely not be well received, but he is my prince as well as my commanding officer and, unfortunately, he always gets the final say,' he rolled his eyes, laughter dancing in them.

'Well, I was right, obviously. The barkeep let him get well and truly pissed – charging double the going rate of a standard pint, I might add, making a small fortune from him – and then allowed a local band of rogues to have their go at us.'

'But you were there to rescue him, like a damsel in distress?' I guessed.

'Not exactly. He'd commanded me to have a few pints myself, and I couldn't exactly go against my prince's orders now, could I?' he grinned, and I found myself mirroring him.

'Of course not.'

'Both of us were half-drunk, and had to fight our way out and back to the border where the rest of the escort waited. Even drunk, the pair of us managed to take down a dozen men and make it out relatively unscathed.'

'Relatively?' I raised an eyebrow.

'Once we got out, I remember Kas saying, "I really need a piss. Do you think the barkeep would let me use his privy?" and, before I could stop him, he'd sauntered back in and asked him,' Cole laughed, shaking his head at the memory. 'Well, the fellow threw a glass at his head, and I can't say I blame him. We'd destroyed his bar, and knocked out half of his favourite clientele, I'd wager. Kas ducked, but when the glass hit the wall and shattered, a piece of it lodged in his shoulder. He still has the scar to this day. It's shaped like a crescent moon.

'We ran back to camp, Kas making such a racket I think our escort believed he'd lost an arm. The healer took one look at it, and said that he didn't care if it was classed as treason, but the prince was a big baby. Then, he dropped the tiniest piece of glass you've ever seen into Kas's palm. Kas framed it, it's hung on a wall in his quarters,' Cole guffawed with laughter, the sound a contagious delight.

I couldn't help it, I laughed so hard I snorted, which made Cole laugh even more. Then we both laughed until tears streamed down our cheeks.

When I could catch my breath, I said, 'no wonder you're worried about him.'

Cole sobered a little, and I was sorry to hear his laughter come to an end. 'We were young then. He's done many a reckless and stupid thing since, don't get me wrong, but all of them were to protect his people. He's had worse injuries, and he's barely even flinched. Kas is prone to throwing himself into situations that someone far less important could handle and, when I'm not there, I worry about who will have his back.'

'He has a whole army to defend him, Cole. All of them have sworn to protect him as you did,' I offered, hoping it was a comfort.

'But when it comes to it, will they give their lives to save his? Will they be quick enough? Strong enough? Will they *care* enough?' Cole's eyes squeezed closed, and I could see how much it pained him not to be at his prince's – his *friend's* – side.

'From what His Highness told me, it's only a small bit of trouble. Nothing he can't handle. He'll be back tomorrow, and you can stop fretting, I'm sure. But, if you really question their loyalty to him, perhaps you should ask yourself this instead, would he give his life to save theirs? Because, from what he's told me, that answer is yes. And I fail to believe that any prince that offers *that* level of loyalty to his soldiers, wouldn't incite that same loyalty in return. He is loved by the people *because* he loves the people,' I wasn't sure where the words came from, and I told myself they were just to comfort Cole. My insides twisted.

Cole smiled, some of the tension leaving his face.

'Come on, let's go inside, Queenie has had enough of my time for the day,' I laid down the brush and patted the large mare on her smooth neck.

'Queenie?' Cole raised an eyebrow.

'It was that or Lizzie. You missed your chance to vote when you were being a worrywart,' I winked.

Cole shot me an exasperated look but didn't comment, simply offering me his arm and escorting me from the stables.

CHAPTER 26

'LADY VERMONT,' PRINCE KASPIAN SAID with a mocking bow. He had returned a few days prior, much to Cole's relief, but this was the first time I had run into him since his return. And I had, quite literally, run headfirst into him in my rushed attempt to get to the dinner hall, famished after yet another day of finger sandwiches and idle chitchat with the other ladies of the court.

'Just Blaise,' I corrected, and the prince's eyes sparked with amusement as an arrogant smirk formed.

'Of course, *Just Blaise*. I believe I promised you dinner. Would you care to join me for a trip into Broozh?' Despite the fact that I desperately wanted to see more of the city, I wanted to see the smirk wiped from his face more.

'I'm sorry, I have reservations for this evening,' I slipped past him.

'In the dining hall?' he raised a dark eyebrow, smirk slipping slightly.

'Yes, I'm afraid so. The food's okay, but the company is better,' I slipped the tiniest splash of venom into my voice, and his eyes turned a shade darker, tinged with disappointment.

'I see.'

Perhaps I'd taken our game too far. I needed him to *want* to play.

'Tomorrow?' I suggested, plastering a delicate smile onto my face.

His eyes lightened a fraction. 'I'll swing by your quarters at six?'

'I do hope you'll actually buy me dinner first, before you expect me to let you inside.' Cole choked behind me, but both the prince, and I, ignored him.

Kaspian's eyes darkened once more, this time with pure heat, and I resisted the urge to shiver under his burning gaze. I waited for a response but, instead of rising to my bait, he simply said, 'goodnight, *Just Blaise*,' and spun on his heel to leave.

'Goodnight, *Your Highness*,' I countered, noting the gentle bob of his shoulders as he laughed before I disappeared into the dining hall, not sure which of us had won that round.

Luna hadn't been at dinner and, when I let myself into her suite to tell her about the dinner date with Kaspian the next day, she was nowhere to be found. *Strange.* It wasn't like there was a curfew, but Luna didn't have many other friends in the palace, so I couldn't work out where she would have gone off to.

Before, Cole had explained it away by saying she was running errands for the queen. But it was dark out now. What kind of responsibilities would she be seeing to at this time? Something felt off, and I couldn't help but worry about her. Luna was a witch, living in plain sight amongst her enemies. She shouldn't be wandering off on her own. *She was alone before you got here*, I reminded myself.

I slipped back into my own rooms and drew myself a bath, but even when I eased my body into the hot water, my mind whirred. Just like everyone else in my life who kept secrets, there was something Luna wasn't telling me.

'Would you sit *still*,' Luna hissed. She had at least returned in time to help me prepare for my date with the prince, and her gentle fingers now ran through my hair as she braided it. To finish off the look, she lined it with sharp pins that ended in delicate white flowers.

'I can't help it!' My worries about what Luna was hiding were gone for the moment, as I sat before my dressing table, fidgeting with the hem of my dress, my knees bouncing up and down with restless energy. 'I'm nervous.'

'It's not a real date, Blaise,' Luna scolded, sticking a pin roughly through my hair.

'Ouch! Fake or not, it's still my first ever date! Besides, for *him* it's real,' I murmured. 'What do you even talk about on a first date?'

Luna met my eyes in the mirror and flashed me an exasperated look. 'Usually, people talk about their favourite foods, or places they have always wanted to visit. But if you could get him to open up about his war plans, that would be ideal.'

I rolled my eyes but couldn't stop my grin. 'Seriously, this is a bad idea, isn't it? I should cancel.' Luna twisted me to face her, gripping my shoulders tight before crouching to whisper to me at eye-level.

'Blaise Sunseeker. You are the daughter of Agnes the Wicked. You were raised by witches. Not to be a quitter, but to be fearless. You have already ridden with the prince, given as good as you got to the queen, and have Cole eating out of your hand most days. You are going to be queen of our joined people someday. You cannot possibly tell me that a simple dinner with a *boy* is what turns you chicken!'

I cringed for a multitude of reasons – no less Agnes's nickname, or the mention of me being queen – but I knew Luna was right. I had to do this.

A knock at the door put an end to any further hesitation. It was too late to back out now. I drew in a few deep, steadying breaths, pressed a hand to the comforting weight of Agnes's blade strapped to my thigh, and opened the door.

Immediately, I sucked in a sharp breath at the sight of the prince. His dark hair dropped over one eyebrow as always, though he had at least run a comb through it. His blue irises were somehow made brighter by the black tunic and dark trousers he wore, and the collar of his shirt which was embroidered with gold. The arrogant smirk he usually sported was replaced with a coy, endearing smile, and he hummed with the same nervous energy I was trying to stifle.

'You look beautiful,' he said, by way of greeting, and I glanced down at my own cream gown, dotted with tiny pink and yellow flowers all along the flowing skirts, feeling underdressed. I said as much.

'Nonsense,' the prince replied. 'Corsets are a fainting hazard. I'd much rather you were able to breathe.' I shot a glance at Cole, who stood behind His Highness pointedly avoiding my gaze, his soft expression focused on Luna instead. 'Plus, where we're going, you're going to want room for seconds.' Kaspian's smile was pure and genuine, and, for some reason, I no longer felt self-conscious. It was hard to, when he looked at me like I was a freshly baked pastry, and he a starving child.

'Shall we?' He offered me his arm, and I looped my own through it.

'Have fun,' Luna called from behind me. And perhaps, for one night, I could manage that.

Chapter 27

I EXPECTED US TO TAKE a carriage from the palace into the city, but the prince preferred to walk, so we made our way through the cobbled streets on foot. Cole walked a few paces behind us, politely out of earshot, but close enough to intervene should anything go sideways – which was highly unlikely, given the reception the prince received in every street. Though the nobles who lived in large manors outside of the palace grounds stiffly bowed and curtsied as we passed, it was in the city proper that the people came alive when they saw their future king.

The courtiers had cast me sceptical and stunned glances, whispering their shock at seeing me with the prince but, past the luxurious manors and towering town houses, the townsfolk beamed at us both. As we wandered through the busy cobbled streets, moving amongst the rows of little houses with thatched roofs, the people waved feverishly as we passed. But nothing surprised me more than the way the prince transformed in their presence.

He shook hands with men lining the streets and called them by their first names, asked how their wives were, and if their little ones had recovered from the bout of Whooping Cough that had been tearing through the city. Women handed him slices of freshly baked bread and he tasted every one, telling each of them how divine it tasted, and requesting they double the orders he had already placed to feed his army. Children ran up to him and clung to his legs, giggling as he walked with them still hanging to him.

Cole seemed at ease with each new face approaching, like this truly *was* how the townsfolk greeted Kaspian each time he wandered amongst them. He had no reason to be on guard here, like he was in the viper's nest that was the palace. I stared in disbelief as the prince bent to speak to each of the children in turn, asking them about their schooling, and even placing a tiny young girl, who had approached him in tears, atop his shoulders until he located her frantic mother in the crowd. Upon returning her, he made the girl swear not to run off from her mother again.

'Thank you! Thank you!' the mother cried, squeezing Kaspian's hand and pressing the young girl tight to her chest. 'How can I repay you for finding her?'

'You don't need to repay me, Rosalie, but I wouldn't turn down one of your roses for my lady here,' he nodded at me with a gentle smile.

'Of course!' Rosalie nodded, dipping into a basket at her feet. 'Red is traditional, but white will match the pins in your hair, my lady.' She handed me a stunning white rose, that was trimmed for thorns, and so pure I almost didn't want to touch it for fear I would make it imperfect.

'It's the most beautiful rose I have ever seen,' I accepted the flower and Rosalie beamed at me, cheeks flushing pink with the compliment.

'I like her, Your Grace,' Rosalie nodded at me, and it was my turn to blush.

'She's alright,' Kaspian winked playfully, but the smile on his face was sincere.

'Now, Ruthie, remember what I said. Don't go running off. Your mother will worry.' He flicked the young girl's nose with a gentleness that belied his strength, making her giggle. 'Excuse us, Rosalie, we have reservations at Otto's.'

He took my arm once more, leading us through the busy streets until we reached a single-story, slightly lopsided building with flecked, white-painted brickwork. A sign that hung from the thatched roof proclaimed the inn THE ONE-EYED THIEF. I raised a questioning eyebrow at the dubious-sounding name and Kaspian grinned in return.

'You can judge after you've tasted Otto's food, and not a minute before.'

I held my hands up in mock-defence. 'I didn't say a word.'

'You didn't have to, your face said it all,' he hit back, still smiling.

'After you,' he swung the door open for me, Cole taking up guard beside it.

'You're not coming in with us?' I asked, nerves pooling in the pit of my stomach once more. Cole had been a steadying presence for the journey here. Without him a few feet away, I would be truly alone with the prince, and I didn't like the way that made my stomach twist.

Cole shook his head. 'Bring me out some roast lamb when you're done. Otto will put it in a box to take away.' I nodded once, stepping past His Highness and into the crowded inn. Perhaps I wouldn't be *completely* alone with the prince, after all.

'Kaspian!' A large man with a round belly, twirling moustache, and salt-and-pepper hair came out from the kitchens to greet us after we were shown to a table in the quietest part of the tiny inn. He wiped his large hand on his white apron, leaving smudges of varying colours along it, before reaching out to shake the prince's hand. It didn't slip my notice that he hadn't used any formal titles.

'Otto, my old friend!' Kaspian took the man's large hand and shook it enthusiastically.

'And who is this?' Otto looked to me. He spoke with a thick accent I couldn't place.

'Otto, this is Lady Vermont. Lady Vermont, Otto.'

'Please, call me Blaise,' I interjected, before Otto could say anything. He shot Kaspian a knowing look, a smile dancing on his lips.

'Mademoiselle,' he took my hand and kissed it, his whiskers tickling my knuckles. 'Such a pretty name, Blaise. It sounds like fire. I will cook you something special, will you try?'

'I would love to, everything smells delicious!' It wasn't a lie. I could barely stop myself from drooling at the delicious aromas filling the rundown but packed dining room. Otto beamed at the compliment.

'Garcon!' Otto called to a waiting boy nearby. 'Fetch the finest bottle of red we have! You know the one! It will go perfectly with the duck!' The boy ran off to fetch the wine as my stomach growled in anticipation. I had never tasted duck before. Otto shook the prince's hand once more, before kissing my knuckles again.

'Enjoy your evening,' he bowed at the waist before disappearing through the sea of diners and back into the kitchen.

'Otto's from Versaille,' Kaspian said without me asking, and my eyes widened. Versaille was in the Vale, which was such a long way away. 'I do not know the story of how he came to be here. I asked once, but he looked so sad that I couldn't bear to ask again.' It was hard to imagine Otto sad, and I didn't blame Kaspian for not wanting to see it, or be the one to cause it.

'What did you think of the city?' he asked, eyes hopeful. I could see how much he loved it, and how the people adored him in return. Yet, I struggled to comprehend how the Kaspian that was so gentle with the townsfolk, could be the same general that had burned a coven to the ground without an ounce of remorse. Not even for the witchlings who would have been barely older than little Ruthie who he had shown such kindness to. It didn't seem like the man in front of me could be capable of such a callous act, and yet, perhaps he did not think it callous if they were not human.

I toyed with the stem of the white rose I had placed on the table in front of me, answering his question about the city. 'Is it strange to say I prefer it to the palace? I fear the palace corridors will feel vast and empty compared to the buzz of these streets. And the faces will be far less friendly.'

The prince's eyes gleamed with satisfaction, his whole face lighting up with the smile. 'That's exactly how I feel! It might be smaller, but everything is more beautiful, more exciting, more *freeing*, here!' My words had been carefully chosen to incite this reaction from him, but it didn't make them any less true. I agreed with every word.

'The people love you.'

'I'm one of them.' He smiled, but his eyes were sad.

'You really think so? After all this time behind the palace walls? You still feel more like one of them?' My tone was softer than my words.

He held a hand over his chest where his heart would sit. 'In here, nothing changes. I will always be one of them.'

Like I would always be one of the coven. Despite looking so different. Despite possessing no power. Despite how I was starting to fit in amongst my own kind.

'I remember what it's like to always be hungry,' he continued, 'to never have quite enough, but to make do. To share with those who have even less. To be happy.' His eyes shuttered against the word.

'You're not happy now?' I asked.

'Mostly. Don't think of me as ungrateful, Blaise. I know I've been blessed. But I want to make changes! I don't want to sit idly by, locked behind marble walls, drinking the finest wines from golden goblets, and throwing away more food than most of these people eat in a week! I want more for them. For Reili. For the world.'

A spark shimmered in his ocean eyes. One I was sure was reflected in mine. Because wasn't that what I wanted, too? Yet, I didn't dare hope that I could align our views to include *my* people. The witches. Before I could think of a way to respond, the serving boy returned with a bottle of wine, pouring the dark red liquid into polished glasses. He waited for Kaspian to sniff deeply and take a large gulp, assuring him it was perfect, before he disappeared again.

I looked at him dubiously. 'You have no idea what that's supposed to taste like, do you?'

'Am I that obvious?' His lip tugged upwards in half a smile.

'I'm afraid so,' I returned his lazy grin, before taking a swig from the glass. It was rich and smooth, like nothing I had ever tasted before, and I quickly took another gulp.

'I heard my mother invited you to lunch.'

I winced, not liking the switch in conversation. 'Did she tell you what it was about?' He shook his head as he took another sip of wine, mild irritation crossing his features.

I sighed, not having to force myself to look put-out as I explained. 'She doesn't think I'm good enough to spend time with you. In fact, I can't believe you asked nothing more than a *whore* to dinner. Your poor mother must be heartbroken.' Kaspian choked on his wine, and I bit my lip to stop from smirking as droplets of red spilled down his chin.

'She didn't! She didn't call you *that*, did she?' I nodded. 'I'm sorry, Blaise. I'll speak to her.'

'Don't!' I snapped, and he flinched. 'It doesn't matter to me what she thinks. Only what you think,' I recovered, and he relaxed, eyes warming.

'Well, nevertheless, I *am* sorry. That was an appalling thing for her to say.'

'Not as appalling as what I promised in order to appease her,' I confessed.

'Why do I feel like I'm not going to like this?' A small crease appeared between his brows as they furrowed together. I had the sudden urge to soothe it.

'I promised that you'd dance with Aleera Cresthorn at the next ball,' I grimaced, not able to read how he would react.

He laughed, a low chuckle that spread into a deep chortle, but when I didn't laugh with him his eyes bulged. 'Oh Gods! You're serious, aren't you!'

'Oh yes! I've promised to be quite the matchmaker,' I let a sad smile dance across my lips.

Kaspian shuddered and put his head in his hands. 'It couldn't have been anyone else?' His voice was muffled behind his fingers.

'Unfortunately, Lady Caerphilly was unavailable,' I smothered a laugh.

'It's not funny.'

'Then why are you laughing?' Because I *could* hear the laughter on his lips, despite his head in his hands.

'Honestly, I would rather risk being poisoned by Hyacinth than spend a minute alone with Aleera.' He dropped his hands from his face and his eyes met mine.

'Now, now. What have you told me about rumours?' I reminded him. He bit his lip to hold in a laugh, and a strange heat pooled in the very core of me at the sight of it. Dark hair flopped over eyes that sparkled with amusement, and his full lips were pinned beneath a white tooth. His knuckles were clenched tight around his wine glass, his bicep curled and pressed against the loose-fitting tunic. I had to shake my head to stop from staring.

'For you, I'll do it. If it keeps my mother off your back. Though just know I would rather dance with a witch than with Aleera Cresthorn.'

'Perhaps that can be arranged,' I muttered, raising my glass in mock cheers, the heat that had been pooling low in my stomach doused by his mention of witches.

He laughed, thinking it nothing more than a joke. At that moment, our food arrived, saving me from any more polite conversation. Two steaming plates were placed before us, filled with roasted duck in smoky plum sauce, dauphinoise potatoes, and a medley of seasoned vegetables. My mouth watered at the sight alone, not to mention the *smell*.

The taste was a palate-altering experience. The duck was crispy on the outside but smooth as silk in the middle, the potatoes melted like butter in my mouth, and the vegetables were seasoned to perfection. I didn't speak again until I cleared my entire plate.

'I've never eaten food like that!' I sat back, clutching my full stomach. Even made with magic, no food I had ever eaten at home in the Iron Woods had tasted like *that*. It was so good, that it was hard to believe magic *wasn't* involved.

'Wait until you try his chocolate gateaux,' Kaspian smiled, his plate also clean.

'There's dessert?' I almost squealed, and Kaspian's eyes filled with wild delight.

'The best you'll ever try.'

He was right, of course. It felt like a sin to eat the delightfully rich and indulgent chocolate cake. The light frosting against the bitterness of dark chocolate complimented the sweet taste of cherries, and I couldn't help but shovel forkful after forkful in until that plate was clean, too.

The prince left half of his own, claiming to be full, but when I asked if I could have his, he pushed it towards me with such genuine glee I could have sworn he'd saved it just for me. When I finished his cake, too, I resisted the unladylike action of licking the plate clean.

When Otto came to personally check we had enjoyed our meal,

and deliver a box full of lamb for Cole, Kaspian whispered something in his ear. The large man beamed and disappeared, before returning with the remainder of the gateaux – approximately three quarters of a large silver platter that was now boxed and tied with a ribbon – and handed it to me with a smile.

'For you, mademoiselle,' he bowed.

'Your other customers, won't they want some?' I asked, hoping he wouldn't change his mind.

'None of my other customers are as important.' I looked sheepishly to Kaspian. 'No, mademoiselle, not him. You! You have made a chef very happy! No one has ever managed more than one slice of my gateaux before. You deserve it all!' I beamed back at him, already salivating at the mere thought of another slice.

Kaspian tried to press gold coins into the man's large hand, but Otto waved him away. 'Your money is no good here! Just bring this one again. She eats more than Cole!' His laugh boomed. 'It makes me very happy. A real woman knows her food.' It was *definitely* unladylike to eat more than an adult male – and a member of the Guard, no less – but when Otto said it, it sounded like a compliment.

Kaspian shook Otto's hand and, when we made to leave, I noticed he dropped five gold coins into the man's apron. I couldn't help but smile. Cole waited by the door, eyes lighting up when he saw the huge box of lamb Kaspian carried.

'Enjoy yourselves?'

'Yes, thank you,' I grimaced internally, realising I'd enjoyed it far more than I ought to.

With the sun almost set, the streets were clearer as we headed back to the palace. The first bite of winter fuelled the autumn wind, the coolness not unpleasant on my skin, which was flushed from the wine. My head spun a little, and the smell of the cake, mixed with Kaspian's sugar-and-grass scent, formed a sickly-sweet aroma that encircled me entirely.

We walked in comfortable silence until Kaspian asked, 'How's Lady?'

'She's well. Ready to race,' I peered up at him through my eyelashes to find him smiling.

'I've been practicing with Ginger. I'm not sure you'll get one up on us this time.'

'Perhaps I'll take Queenie for a spin instead.'

'Queenie?' he raised an eyebrow, humour written in the upturn of his lips and the glint in his eye.

'Your mother is an inspiring woman, Your Highness.'

He rolled his eyes, but the grin remained. 'No wonder she dislikes you. She's found out you've named a bloody horse after her.'

'The queen should be flattered. She's a very pretty horse.'

Kaspian's laugh filled the street around us and it sent a thrill through me that I wouldn't care to admit. *He's a murderer,* I reminded myself, picturing Luna's tear-streaked face when she found out what had become of her kin. The butterflies in my stomach died a violent death, and I forced myself to keep the conversation flowing. 'I never asked, how was the trouble on the border? Did the great Prince Kaspian resolve it?'

His face hardened, and I regretted being the one to quash his laughter. 'It's not something I enjoy dealing with, but we must keep the peace. Harensarra are interested in war, they have made that clear these past months.'

'How so?' I pried, trying to keep my voice casual.

'They've been sending people across the border into towns and villages, slaughtering children in their beds,' his voice was cold. Full of hate and anger.

I couldn't blame him, but his words pricked at old wounds and before I could stop them, the words came tumbling out, 'like you and your soldiers did to a village in Starterra?'

He stared at me dumbfounded. 'What?'

It was knowledge I shouldn't have, I realised, in the aftermath. I might have exposed everything. Because it wasn't a village. It was a *coven*. I shouldn't know about it, and even if I *did*, it shouldn't matter. Because they were witches. But the wine had loosened my tongue and there was no undoing it.

I stormed away from him down a near-empty side street, disguising my panic with horror, but he caught my arm and pulled me back to him, his face unreadable. My skin burned where he held it. 'Blaise, wait! What are you talking about?'

'Don't pretend! Your army burned a village to the ground! Women and children with it!' Real tears blurred my vision, but I could still see the shock on his face.

'Who told you this?'

'All of Starterra knows it.'

'Blaise, listen to me. We did not attack a village in Starterra. Our armies have not been across the border in fifteen years! It's a clause in the peace treaty we signed.'

The one he had been in Starterra to ensure was being upheld.

'You're lying!' He had to be. The alternative didn't make sense. 'You told me . . . you told me the queen would tear the world apart until she found the witch that murdered her husband. Did you think the witch lived among those villagers?' I suggested, hoping he would tell me the truth if I got close enough to it.

'Blaise, no! We can get away with the odd spy. Assassins, even, if we really want to, but no Reili army can cross the border. Why do you think she's never been able to find the witch? She can't send an army to hunt her down!' His eyes were full of sorrow as his callused fingers wiped away the tears running down my cheeks.

'But she can send you.'

My words were an accusation. He was a witch-hunter. A villain. Surely, he didn't need an army to carry out his dirty work for him. At least . . . that wasn't what the stories that spread through the continent suggested. Unless what the queen had said was true.

I didn't dare hope.

'To uphold the peace, Blaise!' he protested, eyes filled with a desperate plea to believe him. 'I promise you, we did not do this! *I* did not do this!' He held my face, cupping each cheek so gently, yet forcing me to face his stricken expression, swaying my confidence in what I was accusing him of.

Something he saw in my gaze must have given away my inner turmoil, so he pressed. 'It's important I know where this story came from, Blaise. Whoever spun the tale is doing so to have reason to start a war with us. I need to know. Did you hear the story when you were in Starterra? Or when you travelled through Harensarra?'

I stared at him, unable to talk, mind reeling. It couldn't be true. He *had* to be lying! Because if he wasn't . . . it meant that Agnes had lied to get me here. But she couldn't . . . she couldn't have hurt the

Moonkeepers herself. *Could she?*

No. She couldn't.

She *wouldn't*.

She had simply been mistaken. Someone else had been responsible for their deaths.

But Sapphire had found the Bordeaux crest at the burned coven. *Hadn't she?*

I couldn't breathe.

'Blaise?' Kaspian called my name, but he sounded far away. I couldn't make my eyes focus on him. My vision was rimmed with black.

I couldn't breathe.

I was vaguely aware of my fingers releasing their hold on the perfect white rose.

'Blaise, I need you to tell me where you heard this. Blaise?'

I couldn't breathe.

I was falling.

I felt a strong pair of hands catch me, and then everything went black.

CHAPTER 28

FLUFFY PILLOWS PROPPED UP MY head as I woke, but a thick quilt constricted my movements. My eyes fluttered open the tiniest slit, feeling too puffy and sore to pry open any further. Luna sat beside my bed on a chair she had dragged to my side, my hand grasped in hers, her face pale and uncharacteristically solemn.

Cole stood behind her, guarding the door, genuine worry written in the lines across his forehead. His eyes were rimmed with dark purple circles. When had he last slept? Movement caught my eye, and I forced my heavy head to turn a fraction, my heart pounding so loudly against my ribs it felt miraculous that Luna didn't cover her ears against the sound.

Kaspian paced back and forth, looking glum.

The prince! In *my* bedroom!

'Would you stop that? You're going to wear a hole into the floor!' Luna snapped, in a tone that made me wince. Cole looked at Luna like she was out of her mind, but Kaspian stopped, slumping onto the edge of my bed. I snapped my eyes shut.

'I'm sorry. I know I'm not helping. I only wish I *could* help. I mean, it's been two days! Why doesn't she wake?' the prince asked.

Two days?

I had blacked out for two days! I was pretty sure that's what happened. I had collapsed. Memories of that night clawed their way to the front of my mind. The wine. Talking to the townsfolk. The chocolate cake. The white rose. Otto's moustache. The conversation with Kaspian. Strong hands catching me. Agnes.

Agnes was a liar.

I shot bolt upright, a scream on my lips.

Kaspian was there at once, a hand on my shoulder, easing me back down onto the soft pillows. Luna squeezed my hand tightly, shock in her eyes. Cole scanned the room for signs of a threat.

'Blaise, Blaise! Listen to me! It's me, it's Kaspian. You're okay. *You're okay!*' I couldn't tell whether he was trying to convince me, or himself. My breathing was fast and shallow, and I couldn't seem to make the oxygen stay in my body long enough to do anything useful. 'Blaise, look at me. Look at *me*!'

My eyes snapped to his. So deep. So captivating, and filled to the brim with worry and relief, as well as another emotion I couldn't place.

'Breathe,' he ordered. So, I did. A deep breath that filled my lungs to the brim. 'Again.' I did as he asked. My eyes locked on his, the pools of his eyes as soothing as the breaths I took. 'Good girl,' he released my shoulders, and I instantly missed the steadying weight his hands provided.

'Are you okay?' Luna asked, and I reluctantly tore my eyes from Kaspian's to look at her. I nodded the tiniest fraction and realised that it was a lie, so I shook my head, tears clouding my vision.

'Okay, everybody out!' she ushered the two men to the door.

'But–' Kaspian began to protest.

'Out!' Luna snarled, and he nodded, letting Cole drag him through the door with a fleeting look back at me. Luna slammed the door behind them and was beside me in a second. Her arms wrapped around me, and I couldn't hold back the tears anymore. Each drop stung my already-swollen eyes, and uncomfortable sobs shook my body. Luna held me to her, not saying a word, stroking my hair. The motion made me think of Agnes, and then I couldn't breathe all over again.

I was terrified of the questions I knew were coming. More scared still of the answers I would have to give. The answers could unravel Luna. They had already broken *me* into tiny little pieces. She eased me out of the hug, still gripping my shoulders, and it took every ounce of my self-control not to cling to her and bury my face in her chest so I would never have to face her. Never have to answer the question I could see forming on her lips.

'What happened?'

I opened my mouth. Closed it again. Took a deep breath in. Closed my eyes.

'It was all a lie.'

I counted the seconds. Luna was silent. Until she realised that I couldn't – *wouldn't* – expand.

'What was?'

'Agnes. Reili. Reili didn't . . . Kaspian . . . he didn't,' the words were lodged in my throat, hurdles tripping me at the start of every sentence. Luna waited. She didn't push, staying still until I opened my eyes to meet hers, her brows furrowed in confusion as I recounted the details of what Kaspian had told me about the peace agreement.

'He said it wasn't them. So, it must have been . . .' I trailed off, unable to say it aloud, not wanting to truly believe it. Luna looked more confused than before, her green eyes scanned me, no doubt searching for signs of a head injury.

'Blaise, what in the name of the Mother are you talking about?' Before I could answer, more questions were fired at me. 'How on earth did you even bring this up with him? Who else could it have been? Did you just come out and ask him? Are you stupid?'

The last answer was probably 'yes,' but I chose to ignore it. I sighed, and decided to start at the beginning, telling her in as much detail as I could remember, her eyes growing wider with each revelation.

'He promised me it wasn't him,' I finished, as she gaped at me open-mouthed.

'And you believe him?'

'Yes.' I didn't even hesitate.

'But you asked him if he burned a village, not a coven,' she said, simply.

'He would have corrected me. Told me it was 'just witches' if he had knowledge of any of it.' I was confident in that.

'So, what? You think Agnes is responsible?' I paused. Less certain. 'Why would she?' Luna pushed.

I shook my head, and she paced from my bed, retracing the very steps she had scolded Kaspian for taking earlier. I watched her move as my brain resurfaced memory after memory of Agnes. All of the moments she was cruel, or those when she was soft. The times when she was brave, passionate, cunning, sadistic, open, warm, cold, clever, callous. Her laugh as she taught me to swing a sword and brandish a knife. Sapphire and Gaia's inability to speak caused by her spell. The way she held me as nightmares plagued my sleep after seeing my first burning. The way she held my head and forced me to watch it.

The way she spoke of revenge. The way she spoke of peace. The way witches cowered as she passed by. The respect she commanded. Earned. *Took*. Her hands running through my hair. The way she held me tight and kept me close like I was a prized possession. The way she believed *I* could be the one to unite our people. The way she didn't give me a choice.

My mind was swimming towards another blackout, until Luna stopped her pacing and breathed. 'Maybe it was just an accident?' She sat down beside me once more and took my hands in hers.

'You told me before, that one of my sisters accidentally led the army to the coven. Maybe it was just one soldier? Or an assassin, like Kaspian said? Perhaps he truly did just want to go home with her and bed her, and when she foolishly revealed herself, he . . . did what he did,' her eyes welled, bright silver burning in today's slightly-more-hazel stare. 'Just a stupid accident.'

I wanted to believe it, but it raised too many questions. 'How did one soldier kill all those witches? Did he kill himself in the process? Is that why the Bordeaux crest was found?'

'I don't know, Blaise,' she shrugged, blinking away the tears in her eyes. 'But surely that makes more sense than Agnes doing this to her own sisters!'

I bit my lip. It *didn't* make sense. But I wanted to believe it. I didn't want to think that Agnes could have murdered the Moonkeepers in cold blood. And if Luna – who had lost her mother and her entire family in the attack – didn't believe it could be Agnes, then her own daughter certainly shouldn't. Doubt screamed at me, but guilt rose to swiftly drown it out. How could I have believed Agnes to be capable of this?

'The prince is going to ask where I heard this story. He thinks Harensarra invented it to cause trouble. What do I tell him?'

'You have to tell him it *was* Harensarra. He wants to hear that, so he won't ask too many questions. He's looking for an excuse to go to war. Give him one, and take the heat off you.' I gulped. I didn't think Kaspian was aiming for war, I thought he was doing everything he could to avoid it. By doing this, I was going to cause a lot of pain.

Luna noted my hesitation. 'Even if he didn't kill my coven directly, he and his mother have caused the hatred that led that soldier to kill them. They've murdered plenty of witches before that, too. I don't care what the queen said, there's no way he's made such a name for himself by not lifting a finger of his own.'

I nodded. She had to be right.

'Luna, why were you sent here?' The question had been hovering on the end of my tongue for days and, for some reason, at that moment, the words tumbled out. It made little sense that Esmeray would risk her only heir by sending her to get close to the queen. Agnes had spares, and I was a human. I was expendable. But *Luna* . . . Ultimately, the decision had saved her life, but despite what had happened to them, the Moonkeepers would have thought the bigger risk was here, not in the coven.

Luna sighed, 'I guess I would have had to tell you eventually.'

I scowled. 'Tell me what?'

'There was talk, among the covens,' she began carefully, and then it all came out in a flood. 'Agnes had gathered the coven leaders and told them she had been training you. She told them the whole plan. But my mother, and the other coven leaders, they disagreed with her. They believed there would be repercussions. They didn't . . . they didn't have faith in you. Didn't believe that you would be able to kill another human when it came down to it, and they thought it would result in *him* using you. That you would lead him to them.'

She took a shuddering breath. 'They didn't want to be ruled over. They believed Agnes wanted the throne for herself. That she would use it, not to bring witches out of hiding, but to control the other covens and the humans alike.

'My mother, she wanted to put a stop to it.' Luna's green eyes were made glassy by tears yet to fall. 'My role here wasn't to spy on the queen. It was to protect her from Agnes. I was to get word of any potential attacks, and warn my mother so she could put a stop to it.

'When I saw you, I knew Agnes had made her move. I would have informed the queen who you were if you hadn't told me what had happened to my coven. I would have let her torture you for information on your mother. I would have let them kill *me* if it had raised suspicion on how I knew that information. Blaise, I'm so sorry! I thought I was protecting my coven, but it was too late anyway! And, for what it's worth, I'm glad I never got the chance to tell her.' Tears rolled down her freckled cheeks as she reached for my hand.

Her skin felt like ice against mine, bringing me back to reality after a moment of stunned silence. I pulled my hands out of her grip and stood, taking a few steps away from her, and Luna flinched, more tears streaming down her nose and over her pink lips.

'Blaise, I can't tell you how sorry I am! My mother was wrong! We should have listened to Agnes! We needed to attack sooner! Maybe then, my mother, and my coven, would still be alive! I want to help you now! I want to bring them all down!'

A harsh humming filled my head, pressure pushing in on all sides, and I began pacing, trying to force my thoughts to even themselves out. Agnes had never told me anything about these conversations with the other coven leaders. I squeezed my eyes shut, remembering the spell Agnes had put on Gaia and Sapphire to stop them from telling me things.

'There's something else,' Luna said slowly, and my eyes snapped to hers. They were swollen from tears, her freckled cheeks flushed, her body hitching every few moments with sobs. I wasn't sure I could take any more bad news.

'What?' I asked through gritted teeth.

Silence for one heartbeat. Two. Three.

'I've been helping witches escape from Reili.'

'You've been *what*?'

'Shhhhhh!' she hissed. 'For Mother's sake, keep it down! Unless you want me to be arrested.' I glared at her. 'Don't look at me like that! This is a good thing!' she gripped my hand.

'Of course it's a good thing! But you're risking your life, Luna!'

'I have to!' A great sob racked her body, and she dropped my hand, wrapping her arms around her torso like she was holding herself together. 'I keep asking myself why I'm the only one left! If I'd have been there, instead of *here*, would things have been different?'

Likely, only in that she would have also perished, and my heart fractured at the thought of a world without her light in it.

'I feel so much guilt, Blaise! So, when I spotted a witch in the city, disguising herself as an herb grower, I approached her, and told her I could get her out. You heard Kaspian, he's discovered some of them hiding in the city, it's not safe for them here. I had to *do* something! She agreed, and word spread. Each night I've gone into the city since, I've had another girl approach me.'

I'd thought all the witches were gone from Reili, thanks to Kaspian, but they'd just been in hiding all this time. 'I'm coming with you, when you next go.'

'No, Blaise! It's too dangerous!'

'That's not stopping you!'

'That's different.'

'How is it?'

'I'm not our future queen!' she hissed.

'Well, as your *future queen*, I order you to let me come with you!' I argued, petulantly.

'That's not how this works,' she laughed a solitary chuckle. 'Plus, you're being watched all the time.'

'I can ditch Cole.' I vowed. 'Please, Luna! I want to help.'

She eyed me carefully, considering. 'Fine. If you can lose your shadow, you can come. Don't make me regret this.'

After a moment of silence, I asked, 'was I really out for two days?'

Luna grimaced. 'It must have been shock. At first, the prince thought it was a sugar crash, after all the chocolate cake you apparently ate.' I felt a surge of disappointment as I wondered what happened to the rest of the cake. *Not important*, I scolded myself.

'After a few hours of no one being able to wake you, we started to panic. None of us had any clue what the matter was. I could have tried to heal you, but Cole and Kaspian have barely left your side.'

'Really?' I asked, embarrassed.

Luna shook her head, platinum bob bouncing with the motion. 'Kaspian carried you back himself. Wouldn't let any of the guards help, not even Cole. He's eaten in here, slept in the chair beside you. His mother is furious, by the way. He only left once, and he came back with that.'

She nodded to a small jar on the table beside my bed. Inside it was the white rose that Rosalie had gifted me at Kaspian's request. The one I had dropped before I collapsed. It's delicate petals now beginning to wilt.

He must have gone back for it.

My heart wanted to claw its way out of my rib cage, and a blush rose to my cheeks before I could stop it. Panic still sat like a weight on my chest, but something else fluttered in my stomach and wrapped itself around my heart, and it smelled like freshly cut grass and sugar.

Chapter 29

FEELING FULLY RECOVERED BY THE next evening, I pulled on a floaty, mustard-coloured dress, and donned a green cloak with a gaping hood and matching silken gloves. Nerves swooped and dived in my stomach, heart racing at a million beats a minute because, tonight, I was helping Luna smuggle a witch out of the kingdom.

We'd gone over the plan a hundred times, and Luna had spent the last day making preparations – and convincing Kaspian and Cole that I was still too sick for visitors. Kaspian had sent a doctor, who had been fooled by a high temperature that I'd created by hovering over a burning candle for a good ten minutes, causing my face to flush and forehead to feel warm.

The door joining our chambers creaked open, and Luna let herself in. She was wearing a pale purple dress of a similar nature to mine, and a dark navy cloak. To anyone who saw us, we would just look like women out for a stroll, dressed to keep out the biting winter chill that had crept over the continent. In reality, the hoods covered our faces, keeping our identities hidden, and the flowing dresses were easy to run in.

'The carriage is outside. You're sure you want to do this? I can go alone,' Luna's pale freckles sparkled in the candlelight, her brows were drawn together in an apprehensive line, and she worried her full bottom lip between her teeth as she waited for me to answer.

'I'm sure, Luna,' I took her pale hand in my gloved one and squeezed it tight. 'Let's go.'

We slipped back though the adjoining door and out of her chambers, sticking to the shadows of the wide corridors but luckily passing nobody. Until we made it to the wide entrance doors. Luna nodded politely to the guards as I kept my hood up, and I thought they would let us slip by, until one stepped forward.

'Where are you going, miss?'

Luna cringed but didn't miss a beat. 'Just for some dinner and a stroll. It's a lovely evening for star gazing,' she gestured to the cloudless sky.

'Well, be careful, it's icy out there tonight,' he smiled, broad and genuine, and we breezed past.

'Curse your good looks! He wouldn't have cared where we're going if you weren't attractive!' I hissed.

'Sorry! I'll remember to add boils to my next glamour!' she whisper-spat back. We were practically jogging across the grounds to our waiting carriage, when a figure stepped into our path. We both pulled up short as Aleera Cresthorn sneered at us, blocking our route.

'Lady Vermont! I'm *so* pleased to see you've recovered,' she snickered. How she'd recognised me under the hood I didn't know, but I pushed it back to stare her down. She clutched a hand to her chest. 'Gods! It must have been a terrible illness, you look positively ghastly.'

This bitch.

'Yes, awful! I might still be contagious, so I wouldn't get too close,' I made a show of coughing without covering my mouth.

She recoiled. 'Where are you going at such an hour when you're still so . . . disgusting.'

Luna shoved past her. 'For a walk. The fresh air will do her good. Now, if you don't mind,' Luna tried to reach for my hand and pull me past Aleera, but she had placed her small frame between us.

'I do mind, actually,' she mocked. 'You seem to have forgotten your handler, Lady Vermont.'

My teeth ground together in irritation. 'They've let me off the leash tonight,' I played into her awfulness. 'I've been a good girl, after all.'

Her shrewd eyes narrowed. 'You won't mind if *I* spend the evening with His Highness and his lacky, then, will you?'

Luna hummed, a sound that was practically a growl, at the disrespect she showed Cole, and I felt my own blood boiling as I snapped. 'Be my guest! You'll find some half-eaten pastries in my chambers, too, if you like my leftovers so much.' Her jaw dropped open, and she was about a second away from stamping her foot as I stepped around her, gripping Luna's hand and breaking for the carriage.

As the driver pushed the horses forwards, Luna breathed. 'What if she *does* go to them? I can't back out of this now! I've promised Althea I'll get her out of here!'

I shook my head. 'We won't let her down. We'll be quick. If Aleera manages to get Kaspian to pay any attention to her, they'll be chasing our tails. They've no idea where we're going, and they won't be able to prove anything.'

———— ✦ · ————

After several hours, the carriage dropped us in a quiet town on the very outskirts of Reili. Luckily, the carriage driver didn't seem remotely interested in why we had wanted to go so far. He slunk into a nearby tavern, promising not to go anywhere else until we were ready to go back to the palace.

'Mother's tits, it's cold!' Luna shivered, wrapping her arms across her chest as we waited in the darkness of a run-down wash house. Bedsheets hung on a line running from one side of the house to the other and, through the cloth, a shadowy figure appeared. 'Althea?' Luna whispered.

'Luna!' Althea came out from behind the sheets and ran to embrace Luna. Althea looked no older than twenty, but of course she was glamoured. She could have been centuries old. Her dark hair was wrapped in a lavender headscarf, and tucked into a worn violet coat that was wrapped tightly around her slender frame. Pulling away from Luna, she eyed me warily. 'Who's this?'

'Althea, this is my friend, Blaise,' Luna smiled. 'She's come to help.'

Althea sniffed the air and stumbled back a few steps. 'She's *human*.'

'Only in body. Her mind and heart, they're all witch,' Luna winked at me.

I smiled back at her. 'I promise you, Althea, I'm no threat to you.'

Althea's dark eyes narrowed, but she nodded. 'Then please, let's go.'

We crept into the night, sticking together, and trying to act as casual as possible. A few soldiers walked the streets. With the town so close to the border, and Harensarra ransacking nearby villages, their presence was completely normal, and I tried not to tense each time they walked by.

'There's an unmanned post not far from here,' Luna spoke quietly. 'Neither Harensarra nor Reili soldiers want to claim it. It's on an old minefield that's killed more soldiers than it's worth. No one is stupid enough to cross there . . . except us.'

'Mother above,' I sent up a silent prayer to keep Althea safe. 'Is there really no other way? Can't you just glamour the right paperwork and go through the border, Althea?'

Althea's gaze widened and she looked to Luna. 'You haven't told her, have you?'

I hated the sound of that. 'Haven't told me what?'

Luna grimaced. 'I kind of had Althea blow a hole in the side of the prison where they were keeping her to escape. Any minute now, soldiers are going to realise she's missing and–'

A siren blared. Shouts rung out throughout the street.

'And *that's* going to happen,' Luna grabbed Althea's hand and tugged her forwards.

'You didn't tell me she was a witch that had been *caught*!' I panted, as we ran down cobbled street after cobbled street, turning sharply as soldiers sprinted head on in our direction.

Luna cursed. 'Does it matter? You wanted to help! This is helping! In a moment, at least four other witches are going to blow more holes in the building, and they're going to bring with them another two humans that have been accused of witchcraft, too. All of these women were set to be burned tomorrow.'

'Kaspian didn't say anything about—'

Luna whirled on me, and I barely stopped running in time before slamming into her. 'Why would he say anything? This is what he *does*, Blaise! He hunts witches! The whole world knows it! He doesn't need to tell you it's happening!' She grabbed Althea's hand again and began running down another street.

I raced after her. 'But what about what his mother said?'

'She's wrong! She was just trying to manipulate him. I have the proof right here, Blaise.' She lifted Althea's hand in the air and shook it.

A boom sounded in the distance, and I guessed that was the other witches breaking out of their cells. *Fuck.* Luna was right. I'd let myself get caught up in Kaspian's charm. We needed to get these witches out.

'How will the others find us?' I asked.

Althea raised a hand, and a glowing silver trail illuminated the path we had taken. I gasped at the little bit of magic, wanting to keep it protected, as Althea dropped her hand and it vanished again. Luna tugged her forwards. I could see the unmanned posts now. Spikey metal wire blocked the path, but it had been bent upwards at the bottom, and Luna crawled underneath, Althea close behind her.

'Wait here, Blaise!' Luna ordered. 'It's too dangerous for you!'

For me. A weak and fragile human. As though *she* wouldn't also be blown up if she stepped on a sodding landmine. I sighed. 'Be careful. I'll keep guard.'

She nodded. 'Direct the others, when they get here!' Then she was off, carefully placing her feet in spots she must have marked out as safe. I didn't want to know how she'd tested that. I slipped my dagger from the sheath at my thigh and flipped it in the air a few times, trying to distract me from my fear.

A few moments later, three women were panting as they ran towards me. 'That way, under the fence,' I instructed, pointing with my dagger. 'Be careful, and follow the footprints.' Two more followed minutes later, young and frightened, clutching each other's hands, and

I gave them the same instruction. Soldiers rounded the corner, chasing the last pack of women running for freedom.

I cursed and sprang into action. As the women clambered under the fence, I slid along the ground, taking one of the soldiers out at the knees and covering my dress and cloak in dirt. He twisted on the ground, and I flicked the dagger out, watching as red bloomed on his leg where I struck. His yell of pain caused the other soldier to turn back from his pursuit of the escaped prisoners and pin his eyes on me.

He withdrew his sword and lunged, and I rolled, but the sword pinned my cloak to the ground, forcing me backwards again, hood falling back in the process. Withdrawing my dagger from the soldier's leg, I sent it spinning towards the other soldier's arm. He dodged, but not enough to avoid the dagger's enchantments, and the blade stuck in his bicep. Growling, he withdrew it with a rush of blood, and chucked it out of my reach. Now I was without a weapon.

Luckily, the first soldier was still clutching his bleeding leg, but the second was armed and poised to attack. I closed my eyes, waiting for the blow, but it never came. A squelching sound, and muffled cry, forced my eyes back open in time to see his body slump to the floor, Luna's dagger through his back. The first soldier yelled in panic, calling for back up, but Luna took the dead soldier's sword and rammed it through the other's throat. His cries warbled out as he slumped.

'Mother above! I wasn't going to kill them! Just incapacitate them,' I protested, as Luna pressed my dagger back into my hands.

'They saw your face,' she pointed to my fallen hood. 'We need to go!' She tugged me away from the scene.

'Did they all get out?' I made my heavy legs move with her.

'Yes, they're all fine. But *we* won't be, if you don't move quicker.' Shouts of more soldiers finding their fallen comrades reached us as Luna tugged me down a narrow gap between buildings. She stopped running to dust the dirt from my cloak. 'We can't look like anything other than ladies out for a walk,' she panted, and I wiped some blood spatters from her pale cheek.

'Gods, Luna! You could have warned me that was going to happen!' I gripped her arm as we walked back out onto the street, walking slow and casual, like we hadn't just murdered two of Kaspian's soldiers and aided a prison break.

'I'm sorry,' she shook her head. 'I'm sorry.'

Soldiers rushed past us, but we made it back to the carriage without being stopped. Luna dragged the drunkard driver out of the tavern, and then we were off, fleeing back to the palace.

Each time my thoughts circled back to what we had done, I could barely breathe, picturing those soldier's broken and bleeding bodies. That would have been the witches we rescued had we not helped them escape. It didn't ease my guilt. Were the other coven leaders right to doubt me? Could I kill a human when it came down to it? Could I kill *Kaspian*? I'd been trained my whole life to do exactly what Luna had and yet, I'd faltered. It couldn't happen again.

CHAPTER 30

WE STUMBLED UP THE PALACE steps and in through the large front doors, guards parting for us as we hurried inside. As the doors clunked shut behind us, I breathed a sigh of relief, but it was short-lived. For, a moment later, Kaspian's voice boomed through the corridor.

'BLAISE!'

I grimaced. *Shit.*

This was it.

I squeezed Luna's hand tight for comfort, as he stalked towards me, and my breathing hitched as his toned body, dripping with tension, got closer. Undiluted terror set in, and the colour leached from my skin, my heart suddenly in my stomach.

He knows what we've just done. He knows everything.

I released Luna's hand and pressed a palm to the dagger that was back in its sheath, ready to flee or fight – whatever was necessary to get myself and Luna out of there. I flinched as he lifted a large hand towards my face, fearing a blow. Noting my reaction, he tucked his hand back to his side, hurt in his eyes. Too late, I realised his fingers had been curled to cup my cheek.

'Areyouokay?' The syllables rushed out of him like they were all one word, and I paused. Of all the questions I had expected, that hadn't even made the top ten.

Hesitantly, he reached a hand towards me again and this time I didn't flinch. It took everything in me not to lean into his touch as he cupped the side of my face in his large hands, gently rubbing a thumb across the purple circles I knew lined my eyes, leaving a trail of fire in his finger's wake. I looked up towards his gaze, biting back a gasp at the intensity in his eyes. The now-familiar blue darkened as he scanned every inch of my face.

'Are you okay?' he asked again, slower this time, and I nodded, not trusting myself with actual words. He dropped his hand from my face and twisted to face Luna. 'Dammit, Luna! I've been going out of my mind. Cole told me to leave Blaise to rest, but you could have sent a note, or something! And taking her out of the castle? What were you thinking?'

Luna looked as taken aback as I felt. 'I-I just thought some fresh air might help,' she stammered, voice uncharacteristically small.

Kaspian ran a hand through his hair, letting it land on the back of his neck, not meeting either of our gazes. It was then that I noticed Aleera standing a few paces behind him, a flurry of emotions on her face. She was clearly torn between anger at Kaspian's reaction, but glee at us having been caught.

As if he, too, sensed her stare, Kaspian ordered, 'please, leave me alone with Lady Vermont.' Aleera glowered but slunk away, and Luna went rigid with surprise. 'Now!' he demanded, looking at her. I nodded, and she made her way up the large stairway towards her chambers.

When our gazes finally met, I sucked in a breath. The ferocity in his eyes was staggering. I made to step away, needing air, but he gripped my forearm in his strong hand and held me in place.

'Have you been avoiding me?' he asked, words so vulnerable and at odds with his tight hold on me, that I didn't know what to say. 'Why would you leave the palace? At night, with no guard? You know what Harensarra have been doing. It's dangerous out there, Blaise!'

If only he knew that the only dangerous thing out there tonight was me and Luna. I looked away, unable to face him knowing what we'd done to his soldiers.

Soldiers that were going to murder those women.

Gods, what was I supposed to feel? There had been a moment when I *thought* I knew that Kaspian hadn't been responsible for the Moonkeeper's deaths. When I thought maybe this spark between us could have been allowed to burn. But tonight was a reminder that he *had* been responsible for hunting other witches.

But the way he looked at me . . . it was so at odds with every story I'd ever heard about him. The way he interacted with his people, the way they adored him, the way he had improved their lives by inventing things . . . he wasn't the evil I'd been taught to handle. Evil didn't smell so sweet, or give you butterflies.

Yet, I'd seen it with my own eyes; the terror on the witches' faces as they fled tonight. *He'd* done that. Still, I couldn't help but take a deep inhale of his scent, couldn't help but feel safe as he gripped me so tightly.

'I'm sorry,' I said softly.

He tugged me closer, and I tilted my chin up to look at him. We were so close, our noses brushed, and an embarrassing moan slipped past my lips. His grin spread into a half-smile, dimple appearing. Mother above, he was beautiful.

'Is that an admittance to avoiding me,' his breath was hot against my lips.

I could barely think with him this close to me. 'Don't you have more important things to be doing, than worrying about me?' I asked, not really in response to his question.

I watched his face fall, as he evidently remembered where he had been going before he'd seen me. He took a step away, and I inhaled a deep breath of air that wasn't so thick now there was space between us. 'Right now, I should do. There's been another incident on the border. A couple of soldiers have been murdered.'

I didn't have to force a shocked expression onto my face. I could barely believe word had spread so fast. 'Before I go, I hate to ask, Blaise.' A shiver ran down my spine at my name on his lips, spoken so softly, so gentle, it was like he had reinvented the word. 'But do you remember who told you that our armies attacked a village in Starterra? I know it's not fair to put this pressure on you when this information could start a war. Hell, one might have already been started! But this information could give us a chance to prepare, at least.'

It felt like there was concrete between my teeth, trying to stop the lies from escaping, but I couldn't prevent what was to come. It would doom Reili to war with Harensarra, but it might give the witches their best shot at freedom. Perhaps, if I could instruct Agnes to come to the prince's aid, to fight alongside Reili and help them win the war, the people would understand that witches weren't inherently evil. They might be different, but they weren't something to fear. They could live alongside them peacefully, and aid each other when necessary. An idea formed, smashing through the walls that had been trying to stop the lies from emerging.

'I heard it in Harensarra,' I kept my voice steady. 'We stayed at an inn on the way here, and there were soldiers there. When they saw my guards' Starterra uniforms, they asked if we had heard what Reili had done to a small village in Starterra. They told us Reili soldiers burned the village to the ground, killing young children in their beds.'

The tears that came to my eyes were real as I pictured the witchlings and the suffering they must have endured, and I blinked them away to look up at Kaspian. His face was set in a cold hard line, his eyes whirlpools of dread, worry and determination. I could drown in them.

He reached for my hand, and I let him take it, his calluses scraping against my own. Both defined from years of experience in swordplay, mine softening after months without training.

'Thank you. Please don't leave the palace again without protection. I'd hate for anything to happen to you.' My knees wobbled, and guilt roared inside me. 'I have to go, but before I forget,' he reached into a back pocket, 'this came for you. I *was* going to use it as an excuse to see you when Aleera cornered me and said she'd seen you leaving.' He held out a letter and my heart dropped as I recognised the handwriting immediately.

Hesitantly, I took it from him as he brushed past me. His departing smile sent my stomach into another round of somersaults, and I couldn't pinpoint when a simple grin from him had stopped being irritating, and started raising goosebumps on my flesh.

    I sprinted up the stairs, letter branding my hand. Eager to know what Agnes had to say.

Chapter 31

'LUNA!' I BURST INTO HER chambers to find her tucked up in bed. She roused, rubbing her eyes. 'Luna! It's here! Agnes's letter!' Luna groaned and climbed out of her mountain of pillows, sleepily stumbling over to me. My chest rose and fell in deep, laboured breaths.

'Well, open it then,' she yawned.

I sliced the envelope open in one swift movement using Agnes's dagger. The enchanted parchment read:

> *Find a passageway that gets us into the palace unseen.*
>
> *We'll be ready to strike.*

Two lines. That's all there was.

'Well?' Luna looked at me expectantly. When I explained its

meagre contents she asked, incredulously, 'is that it?'

Agnes hadn't answered any of my questions about her letters to the queen. She hadn't directly addressed anything I had told her. Did she even care? Had she really sent me here to spy, or had I just been her way into the palace? A way to execute her own plan that she had been taunting Lizabeta with.

'I bet one of the passageways we've found leads outside. We'd just need to spend some more time looking, and then figure out how to get the witches through it,' Luna begun pacing.

I stared at her.

'What?' she asked.

'Since when have you started trusting Agnes so explicitly? You were sent here to betray her!' I shook my head.

'Since when did you *stop* trusting her?' Luna threw back.

'I didn't say I'd stopped,' I retorted, the words lacking bite. I hadn't even convinced myself, and Luna looked at me as if she knew it, her eyebrows shooting up towards her hair.

'Whose side are you on, anyway?' I hissed. 'This was supposed to be about peace! This isn't the plan I agreed to!'

'Isn't it?' Luna growled. 'Didn't you promise you would help get revenge for my coven's slaughter?'

'Yes! But Kaspian didn't do that!' I protested.

Luna's emerald eyes simmered. 'Did tonight show you *nothing*? You even said it yourself! Just because he didn't start the fire, doesn't mean he didn't light the match.'

'He didn't even mention the witches escaping! He was worried about *me*!'

'Of course he didn't, Blaise! He doesn't care enough to mention it! It's but a mere thorn in his side that he'll have to catch them again!' she raged. 'Do you really think if he knew who you were, he would care about you? He'd have thrown you into that prison with the rest of them! Content to burn you along with us!'

My defence of him died in my mouth. I liked to hope he would at least hesitate before he lit the match, but I couldn't be sure, and that lack of assurance meant I had no choice but to press forwards. I couldn't – I *wouldn't* – risk the future of the witches on a few kind words and a hunch. Tears welled in my eyes. How could I be so foolish as to keep falling for his charm? I was supposed to be seducing *him*, not the other way around.

Luna pulled me into a hug, and I hadn't realised how desperate I had been for comfort until my head was pressed against her shoulder and her arms were wrapped around me. It felt like I could crumble if I needed to, because she would hold me together.

'I'm on *your* side,' Luna whispered against my hair. 'You are going to be my queen. *Our* queen. I take my orders from you, not Agnes. If you don't trust her, or you simply don't agree with her, I'll help you come up with a new plan. But you have to remember who these humans are. They're not like you, Blaise.'

'What if I don't want to be queen?'

My words were barely a whisper, and I wondered whether she heard me until she said, 'I'm not sure you have a choice.'

That's what I was afraid of.

Her voice was soft when she spoke again, almost like she hoped it would ease the blow. 'Agnes will get what she wants, one way or another. I believe that more than I've ever believed anything in my life. I know I don't always sound like it, but I want peace, too. Why do you think I freed the humans from their cells? I don't *want* to spend my evenings smuggling people out of prisons, Blaise. I want to *live*! I want to be truly free, and I think you're our best shot at this working. If peace is actually achievable, it will be because *you're* the one wearing the crown. But you can't count on Kaspian and his mother changing. You'll need to be rid of them, if you want any hope of making real progress.'

Gripping my shoulders, she eased my head away from hers to look me in the eyes. 'With you, it could be different,' she squeezed her eyes shut and, when she opened them again, they were watery. 'Just look at the friendships you've built here, Blaise. Imagine what you could do with more time! You're the best sides of all of us! You have the fire, the cunning, and determination that you've inherited from the witches, but you also have the compassion, the joy, and the stubbornness of humans. You're the balance we need to truly create peace.' Her eyes turned from watery to feverish.

The passion in Luna's words ignited the beginnings of a small fire in my bones, but my own doubts doused the flames before they could burn outwards. I was terrified that the relationships I'd formed here were still too tender and fragile to withstand any real blows – let alone help me uproot an age-old hatred between peoples!

As much as I believed Cole valued our friendship, I didn't think he would hesitate to put a knife through my heart if I became a threat to Kaspian. As much as Kaspian hated the thought of being king, he had so many plans for positive change, and he wasn't going to roll over and let me take his seat. He would never allow the beings he hunted to live freely amongst his people. Luna was right, how could there be a future for the witches with him in the picture? But the thought of hurting him had started to make my stomach churn.

Even if I ignored that fact, there were all the other people who had been taught to fear and hate the witches their whole life. People like Otto, who treated me with kindness but didn't know who I was. How were they supposed to unlearn all they had been taught, just because I said so?

'What if I can't convince any of them to change? The witches *or* the humans? They both have to agree to live in peace for this to happen. Do you truly think you could forget all that humans have done to you and yours?'

Her eyes shuttered. 'Perhaps I can't ever forget but, maybe one day, I could forgive if it meant never worrying about another coven burning to the ground again. You can't give up on us now, Blaise, or we all lose!'

Her eyes were once more brimmed with tears yet to fall, and I realised abruptly that this wasn't about me. It never had been. I had to do this. Because, if I didn't, Luna was right. More covens like the Moonkeepers would be wiped from the world, taking with them the power to cure diseases that had the power to eradicate humans altogether.

I wasn't just doing this because Agnes had forced me into it anymore. I *wanted* this future for my peoples – because they were *both* my people, humans and witches, alike. I believed in this. I *wanted* this! I would never stop fighting for *this*. Because, if we didn't all learn to live together, we would all die at the hands of one another.

I swallowed hard, clearing the lump in my throat, and blinking away tears. 'I might have a plan,' I said, hesitantly. Luna beamed at me, a single, silent tear rolling down her cheek.

'What do you need me to do, *Your Highness?*'

Though the title made me cringe, it also sent shivers down my spine. I held my shoulders back and lifted my chin, picturing a delicate crown atop my head. 'First, I need you to promise me, no more breakouts, no more risk, until the crown is on my head.'

She hesitated but inclined her head in agreement. I flashed her a wicked grin. 'Let's change the world.'

CHAPTER 32

THE QUEEN HAD SENT A summons for me, and my nerves prickled as Cole escorted me through dawn-washed halls to her chambers. 'You're sure she meant to send for me?' I asked him for the fifth time.

A single nod in response.

'And she didn't say why?'

'Blaise,' my name exited Cole's lips on a sigh. 'She sent for you because you are one of her ladies-in-waiting. She has duties for you. It's certainly not for me to question what those are.'

'She's never sent for me before,' I pondered out loud, certain there must be something she had uncovered, some part of my story she had realised was folly. Cole merely grunted, and nodded to the guards at the end of the hall, who stood to the side to allow us into the queen's corridor. I took a deep breath as he knocked on the door, and a shrill, 'enter!' rung out from the other side. Cole swung the door open and held it for me.

'I'll be out here. Remember to curtsey, and for the Gods' sake, be polite,' he hissed as I hesitated in the doorway.

Throwing a scowl back at him, I ventured into the queen's quarters, finding her sat rigidly on one of her many chaise longues. Her red hair flowed around her shoulders, as opposed to its usual position pinned atop her head, but she still wore an expensive-looking gown; corset cinching her waist to a point it must've been painful for her to breathe.

'Your Majesty,' I greeted her, dipping into a low curtsey.

'Sit,' she commanded, and I obediently dropped into a deep-blue armchair, being careful to cross my ankles and sit as a lady should.

'You called for me, Your Grace?'

'Yes.' A long pause followed, and when I thought she would never expand, she finally added, with an air of distaste, 'I'm pleased to see you have recovered from your little *episode*. My son was quite beside himself with worry.'

Though I knew Kaspian had worried about me, the notion from someone else's lips brought a blush to my cheeks. The fact that it also bothered her, had me biting a lip to control my smile. 'It was kind of the prince to concern himself, but I'm quite alright now,' I answered.

She stared at me, eyes narrowed as she considered, lips pursed like she was sucking on something unpleasant. I cleared my throat, and she seemed to break out of whatever trance had held her still so long. 'I've let you get away with not fulfilling any duties for me thus far, simply because I do not enjoy your company.'

Be polite, Cole had said, so I bit down on a hundred responses and waited for whatever would come next.

'But my preferred ladies are all busy with other duties, and so it is time you pulled your weight.'

'What would you have me do for you, Your Grace?' I tried to keep the irritation from my voice but, from the way she glared, I hadn't quite managed it.

'Nothing important. Simply read me my correspondence and pen the responses,' she casually waved a hand to a mountainous stack of letters. 'I trust that, in your limited education, you were taught to read and write, yes?'

'I was, Your Majesty,' I tried not to smirk as mild disappointment soured her pale face.

'Then you may begin.'

I grabbed the first letter from the stack and began to read.

Hours later, I had barely scratched the surface of the huge pile, and my wrist ached from writing and rewriting every response. The correspondence was mind-numbingly boring. I had hoped for information I could use to share with Agnes. Secret lovers, perhaps. Information on how the kingdom hunted witches. Palace secrets, and the like. Instead, it was all tedious drivel from various lords complaining about other aristocrats, their land, or requesting audiences for their daughters to meet the prince. I carefully read around those parts, and came up with my own responses for those letters.

However, spending so long with the queen, despite its tedium, could not have come at a better time. Luna and I had spent the early hours hashing out the foundations of an idea that could get the witches into the palace, and now was as good a time as any to lay the groundwork with the queen.

'Your Majesty? I was wondering if I could run something by you?'

She glared at me, but didn't say no.

'I've had an idea,' I pressed on, 'one that I think could benefit the entire kingdom.'

The queen placed her teacup on a saucer, letting the china rattle, and raised a solitary eyebrow, which I took as permission to keep speaking.

'The kingdom is about to go to war.' She didn't react, and I could only assume that Kaspian had already informed her of the threat Harensarra posed. 'And I understand that war is something this kingdom, and its people, have been hoping to avoid. Particularly, the women.

'I think you know, as well as I do, that men go to war and never come home, and it's the women that have to pick up the pieces.' She recoiled, her eyes shuttering as she remembered the pain of losing her husband. The husband that, according to Kaspian, she truly, deeply loved.

I ploughed on, desperate to set the plan in motion before she had me removed for picking at old wounds. 'But, if Kas – His Highness – doesn't come home, then this kingdom is without an heir.' Her face paled to a shade so lucid it was almost transparent, and I understood, for the thought of anything happening to him made me feel equally uneasy. I refused to acknowledge what that meant.

'You best have a point to this,' she hissed.

'I know I am no emissary, and it was only my grandfather's title and not mine. But while here, I have picked up on a few things. I know that, without an heir, this kingdom becomes weak.' The queen looked as though she was ready to call for guards to remove me, but I hurried on. 'It's past time Kaspian chose a bride. A queen. To rule in his stead should anything happen to him. Should anything, Gods forbid, happen to *you*, Your Grace.'

She leaned forward a fraction, betraying her curiosity at where this was headed, and I could tell from her expression that this wasn't at all what she thought I would say. 'I propose we host one last ball before war befalls the kingdom. A ball to top all balls. A ball that every woman – be her lady, or pauper – is invited to. And, at the end of the event, Prince Kaspian will choose a wife. He will choose his future queen.'

It was an absurd plan, and Kaspian would throttle me if he ever found out it was my idea. But I had to do something. It needed to be spectacular, and it had to include everyone in the kingdom, because they all needed to be there to witness Agnes and the witches' arrival. Luna and I would carefully ensure that Harensarra knew that almost everyone in the kingdom was going to be in one place at one time. Then, we would antagonise them, guaranteeing an attack.

Most of the Reili army would be tasked with protecting the ball, which would give the Harensarra army a chance to get across the border and to the palace. It would also mean that most of the civilians would be protected inside the palace walls until the Sunseekers could swoop in, defeat Harensarra's army and declare themselves allies of Reili. Thus beginning the peace between our peoples.

The queen considered my idea with a slight pursing of her lips. 'How can I be sure he will choose wisely?' she asked, and my eyes flashed with victory. If that was all she was concerned about, the plan was in motion.

'I will ensure he chooses Aleera Cresthorn, Your Majesty. I will fill his head with tales of her that he will find irresistible. I'll do whatever it takes.'

The truth was, I had no such intention. Nor would I do anything to ensure he chose *me*, as had been Agnes's plan. I hadn't told Luna, I didn't plan on sticking to that plot, either. In my mind, I did not need him to choose me to sit beside him on the throne. When the Sunseekers landed, it would come to light that I was the rightful heir, anyway. My claim would be undeniable as, hopefully, when Agnes landed, Queen Lizabeta would reveal her as the witch that bedded and murdered her husband. With Agnes as my mother, and the undeniable resemblance between me and the late king, it would be only too obvious who I really was.

It occurred to me then, that I had not considered how the people would react to the witch that killed their beloved king. It truly was an awful plan. One I needed to rethink entirely.

But it was too late. Above the panicked ringing in my ears, the queen spoke. 'You are more devious than I gave you credit for, Lady Vermont. Perhaps I shall enjoy your company, after all. We will proceed with this plan. Whilst the men plan for war, we will plan for a wedding.'

Chapter 33

THE QUEEN SET A DATE for the ball – one month from the day the idea was hatched. I spent the entire week thereafter in meetings and planning sessions with the queen and the other ladies of her court, all of whom lapped up the opportunity to flaunt their wealth to the common folk. The ball was on track to be a spectacle, the likes of which Reili had never seen before.

The queen, having seen something in me she hadn't previously, released Cole from his duty of stalking my every move. Instead, he went back to being Kaspian's shadow. He had, however, found the time to have breakfast with Luna and I in my chambers each morning and, this morning, he accompanied me to the stables.

Kaspian was already there, his face bleak as he saddled Ginger, readying her for a few laps of the gardens. I did the same for Lady, and Cole offered to ready Queenie so that she could stretch her legs, too.

'I can't believe she's really making me do this! How can I choose a wife? I've never even had a steady courtship,' Kaspian complained. The queen had taken full credit for the idea, which had let me off the hook with Kas, but I still felt guilty.

'It makes sense,' Cole shrugged. 'We need to protect the future of the kingdom.'

'Just pick someone!' I chimed in. 'There are hundreds of girls dying to marry you.'

He sighed, exasperated. 'As much as you know how to flatter me, Blaise, that's not the point! I know it's probably wishful thinking, given my position, but I always wanted to marry for love. I thought, of all people, my mother would understand that!'

Cole shot him a sympathetic look, but it was somewhat undermined by his next words. 'You've always known you wouldn't rule alone. You have to choose someone.'

'He's right. Just choose. You never know, you might get lucky and die at war, and then you'll never have to go through with it!' The poorly worded joke was out before I thought it through, and Cole stared at me in complete horror.

Kaspian's mouth hung open in stunned silence. I wanted to claw the words from where they hung between us and shove them back into my mouth. Then, he started to laugh. A low chuckle at first, that grew into a deep, throaty roar as he tipped his head back and howled. Mother above. *The sound*! It turned my bones to jelly, and it was all I could do not to plead with him to choose me.

I shook the idea off. He would never choose me. Especially not if he knew the truth. *He's your enemy,* I reminded myself, for what felt like the hundredth time. He hadn't felt like my enemy, though, since he told me he wasn't responsible for the death of the Moonkeepers. And, if I'm being honest with myself, a long time before that.

He shared his chocolate cake with me, for Mother's sake! That wasn't something one's enemy did! But that was because he didn't know who I was. *You know who he is, though*. A witch-hunter. For that reason, he could never be my lover, my husband, or my king.

I suddenly felt too close to him. The sound of his laugh still reverberated through my heart, but the smell of grass and sugar clogged my nose, and I moved to the other side of Lady, putting enough distance between us that I could breathe again. Kaspian's roar of laughter died to a low chuckle, and I forced my lips into a small smile. Despite reminding myself again who he was, I regretted the joke. The thought of Kaspian dying made me want to vomit, and murder everybody responsible with my bare hands.

'Well, Blaise, I'm not sure how, but that's made me feel better!' He clutched his side like he'd given himself a stitch from laughing.

'Would it really be that awful to marry someone? To have someone by your side as you rule? Someone to share your innermost thoughts with? To ease your worries, and laugh with?' I hid behind Lady's huge body as I voiced it, scared to look at him, afraid my feelings were written on my face.

Feelings. Mother above, I shouldn't have feelings for this man!

'Of course not.' I risked a peek to find him staring at me so intensely I thought I might drown in his eyes, yet I couldn't look away. 'It's something I've wanted since I was young. But that isn't going to happen with someone I've been forced to choose. What you described is a marriage based on love.'

'Do you think you could have that with any of the women you know?' *Me*, my traitorous heart tried to offer up. He still hadn't pulled his gaze from mine for so much as a blink. 'Given time, I could have. Now I don't even have that.'

'You have a month,' Cole offered, and the spell between us dissipated as we both turned to glare at him. His cheeks flushed at the sudden attention.

'I'll try to make it count.' Kaspian swung a leg over Ginger, pulling himself up and riding out, and I followed suit on Lady, with Cole close behind on Queenie. It was a sombre ride, each of us lost in our own thoughts.

———— ✦ ————

A few hours later, I found myself tucked between Luna and Daisy Hearthorn, our heads pressed together over potential menus.

'As long as there's proper food, and none of these tiny sandwiches,' Daisy whispered to us. I liked her. If Kaspian had to choose someone other than me, I hoped it was her. Even if the thought made me murderous.

Duchess Hyacinth Caerphilly's ramblings about dress codes

brought my mind back to the room. Her idea was to enforce a minimum number of gold details, which would alienate a large proportion of the common folk, forcing them to be unable to attend.

'The point is to have them here. It's a celebration,' Daisy argued before I could, flicking her brown hair over her shoulder to make more of her face visible. The usual softness of her features was replaced with a clenched jaw; her fingers strained around her teacup. Her hazel eyes, so similar to mine, were fixed on the pruned, old duchess, who glowered back.

'What if one of them treads on my dress? Or, worse still, sees fit to touch it? They will leave their *grime* all over it! It shall be ruined! I have paid a hefty price for this new garment.' More than most of the common folk paid for their tiny houses, I would have wagered.

'Are you afraid their poorness will rub off on you, Hyacinth? It is not a disease. It is not catching,' Daisy spat.

My eyes widened in a look that imitated Cole, and I caught Luna's eye. Her mouth hung open in shock – another classic Cole impression.

'Watch your tone, girl,' Hyacinth warned. Everyone paused their conversations to watch, Aleera's face full of glee at the squabble. Mouth pressed into a thin smile, she leaned forward, eager to catch every barb.

'So, are we all agreed on fried squid to start?' Luna's forced-airy voice tried to defuse the situation.

'I will not watch my tone,' Daisy argued, as though Luna hadn't spoken. 'This ball is supposed to be inclusive. We should be welcoming the townsfolk into our home, not trying to belittle them in every hallway.'

I hadn't been aware she cared so passionately for them, and I liked that about her. Kaspian would really like that about her. Perhaps he *already* really liked her. My thoughts turned deadly in an instant. A knife was within reach, and I toyed with the idea of stabbing Daisy in the squishy part between her ribs, and . . . *oh Mother above, what had I become?* Daisy was a nice girl. A nice girl who didn't deserve to be stabbed. I repeated the sentence over and over in my head until the impulse passed.

I must have missed something vital while trying to convince myself that poor, lovely, innocent Daisy didn't deserve to be murdered with a butter knife. For Hyacinth's voice had gone up an octave, and she was yelling. Not at Daisy, but at the *queen*, requesting she remove Daisy from the palace, entirely.

Before the queen could respond, Daisy stood, chair clattering to the floor. 'There's no need. I'm leaving!' She threw her napkin onto her plate with such force that the cutlery rattled. Spinning on her heels, she strode away with her head held high.

Everyone was silent. The nervous tension lingering in the air so palpable I could have sunk my teeth into it.

'What the bloody Hell just happened?' Luna hissed in my ear.

I shrugged, not able to put any rhyme or reason to it. Daisy – shy, coy, nervous Daisy, who barely said a word, other than to Luna and I – had stormed out over an elitist comment that usually occurred ten an hour, and likely wasn't even the worst of the day.

'She could be a good ally,' Luna whispered, and I met her stare, eyes full of unspoken agreement. Anyone with the same viewpoint, who disagreed with the kingdom's elitist culture, was our friend. That loyalty could prove useful.

The conversation moved on swiftly, like what had occurred was a huge embarrassment never to be spoken about again.

'The squid, you think?' Lady Natalia was saying. 'Followed by perhaps the roast beef?'

'No. I think the brie, followed by the grilled chicken,' someone else offered.

'Oh no! The brie goes better with the lobster!'

Round and round it went, until my whole afternoon had been lost to menu debates, invitation wording, and décor ideas.

Chapter 34

THE PRINCE HAD REQUESTED WE meet, and the note, delivered by a member of the guard, said to meet him wearing clothes I could walk in.

'What does that mean?' I asked, aloud.

'I think it means you're one step closer to being his chosen bride,' Daisy offered.

I wanted to ask Luna if the note meant Kaspian had figured out who I was and wanted to push me off a cliff face somewhere, but I could hardly express that concern with Daisy present. Since *that* outburst a few days prior, Luna and I had spent a lot of time with Daisy, assuring her that we agreed with her over Hyacinth's unfair behaviour, and establishing a friendship. Despite liking Daisy, I now had to pretend *all* the time, and Luna and I had to be more careful what we discussed around her.

We had sent a letter to Agnes, informing her of the date of the ball, and our plan for the witches to swoop in and save Reili. We had also asked her to plant spies in Harensarra – all without Daisy catching on. It had meant saying goodnight and then sneaking back into one another's rooms, just to get Daisy to go to bed so we could write the damn thing.

I didn't think Daisy had ever really had friends at court. Everyone was too wary of the rumours surrounding her parentage to strike up any kind of real connection with her. I found her to be sweet and kind, and she liked to style my hair in ways that reminded me so much of Sapphire that my heart cracked each time. But her presence did nothing to help my rising anxiety.

Luna sensed my panic. 'I'm sure Daisy is right.' Her tone, at least, reassured me she didn't think I would be thrown off a cliff.

'Queen Lizabeta would hate that,' I expressed.

'All the more reason for him to choose you,' Luna grinned, and Daisy giggled.

'Oh yes, he often does things to upset her. He kissed me a few years ago, and she *hated* that.' Daisy was still giggling.

'*What?*' Luna and I shouted at the same time, and Daisy cringed.

'It wasn't a big deal! It was only a few kisses. He's a good kisser, though.'

I definitely wanted to stab her.

She'd shared *a few* kisses with Kaspian.

A few.

And she thought he was a *good* kisser.

Did he think *she* was a good kisser?

I don't care. I told myself. *I couldn't care less.*

I was going to be a queen. Queens did not fawn over boys! Not even ridiculously good-looking prince's with irritatingly adorable dimples, breathtaking eyes, and a laugh that could have been symphonised by the royal orchestra.

I shook my head. I was absolutely *not* thinking about kissing Kaspian! It wasn't happening! I couldn't think about how his soft lips would feel crashing into mine. Or about how his rough hands would scrape my cheek as he ran fingers over my face and through my hair. And I was absolutely *not* thinking about what that kiss would lead to.

Not a chance.

'What are you going to wear?' Luna's question dragged me back to reality, and the irritated edge to her voice said it wasn't the first time she'd asked.

'I don't know. I have to be able to walk in it, so probably just some leggings and a tunic,' I shrugged.

'Well, you can at least do something pretty with your hair,' Daisy grabbed me and led me to the dressing table, immediately twisting the strands into elaborate braids that sat atop my head.

On the hour, I arrived outside Kaspian's door.

'I'm surprised, you haven't kept me waiting, for once,' he grinned. I stared at him, knowing I should say something, but my tongue felt too large for my mouth. Instead, I forced out a giggle, but the sound came out strangled, like a goose being grabbed by the neck, and the prince stared at me like I'd grown an extra head. I went a shade of red even Cole had never been before.

As if summoned by another's embarrassment, Cole appeared in the doorway, and I was relieved to see he was dressed for walking, too. A Cole-shaped buffer was exactly what I needed to deflect from the stupid thoughts currently running wild in my mind. I linked arms with Cole, and the mild look of jealousy in Kaspian's eyes sent a thrill shooting through me.

'Where are we going?' I asked.

'I want to show you some of my favourite parts of Reili. You've been here for a while, now, and no one has thought to give you a proper tour,' Kaspian answered. Still looking a little jealous, he darted round to my other side and linked his arm through mine, just as I had with Cole.

The three of us walked side by side, linked together, and we looked ridiculous. Not to mention how difficult it was to actually walk! Especially for me in the middle, with no accessible use of either of my arms. Yet, despite the impracticality of it, I couldn't help but grin.

On our last visit through Reili's capital, Broozh, we had walked everywhere, but we must have been going farther this time because Kaspian had arranged a carriage. He held open the door for me, but Cole pushed his way in first.

'Thanks ever so much, the perfect gentleman,' he winked.

I stared, gobsmacked. 'Cole, did you just make a joke?'

Kaspian laughed and my toes curled in my boots. 'He's disguised it as that, yes. But really, he's pushed in first so he can check the carriage for any surprise assailants. Like they could have snuck in without our driver's notice.'

Cole scowled but didn't deny it, and I laughed all the same. I loved watching the relationship between them, their closeness fascinating me. It was clear that Cole would give his life to save Kaspian's, even if it wasn't his job. But I was also beginning to see that it wasn't a one-way loyalty. Kaspian wouldn't hesitate to protect Cole, either.

In the carriage, Cole sat on high alert on the bench opposite us, constantly checking for threats. Kaspian, on the other hand, settled into the seat next to me, and looked eagerly out of the window. When the cobbled path turned to a rough dirt track, Kaspian started pointing out landmarks and naming different towns. I tried to keep track of everything, but found myself more captivated by *him* than the scenery.

'Over there are the Hollow Hills. They're the best place to watch Reili's light festival from. Better than even the tallest tower in the palace! Over that first hill is Turtle Bay, that's a tiny beach where the Giant Turtles lay their eggs. If you're lucky, in the spring, you can see them hatch and make their way into the sea. Have you ever seen a turtle?'

I shook my head. 'Are we not stopping there?' I asked, mildly disappointed as we continued, past Hollow Hills, not even catching a glimpse of Turtle Bay.

'Not today.' There was a promise in the way he said it. A promise that he planned to take me there one day. But today was for a different adventure.

We drove for a further hour, with Kaspian pointing out his favourite taverns, a large equestrian centre where he sometimes trained Ginger, and a wooded area that he claimed was haunted by ghouls. It reminded me so much of home that I had to look away.

When we eventually stopped and exited the carriage, the sun was setting. Dusky orange hues turned to milky pinks, and a crescent-moon hung in the sky even though the sun had yet to give up its place.

'Where are we?' I asked, trying to stifle a yawn, and stretching my arms above my head. The long journey and the gentle rocking of the carriage had made me sleepy. There was nothing around us. No village, no houses, no taverns. Not a building in sight. Not even a tree. The land was barren.

'You'll see.' Kaspian and Cole shared a knowing grin.

They led me behind a cluster of boulders until we reached a cliff side, and my earlier panic started to bubble, but Kaspian offered me a hand and guided me away from the edge. When his bare skin met mine, I could have sworn sparks ignited.

'This way,' Cole gestured with his head, and I followed him into what appeared to be a cave. He held a lantern as he guided the three of us through the cave's mouth and, the deeper we got, the clearer I could hear running water. I was no longer sleepy, I was alert now, and taking in everything the glow from the lantern revealed. We were surrounded by stalagmites that formed a path for us to walk through, guiding us to something I couldn't yet see.

A bat flew overhead, and I watched as it joined several others hanging upside down from the few stalactites above. They watched as we made our way through the cave and, though I knew bats to have very poor vision, so many eyes made me uncomfortable. I remembered Gaia's bedtime stories from my childhood, several featuring tales of vampires that turned into bats, and I shifted closer to Kaspian, the warmth of his body a comfort.

'Not far now,' he whispered, which only added to my anticipation. The water noise became a roar, and I could only hear him because of how close we stood.

I barely heard Cole as he stopped and asked, 'are you ready?'

'Ready for what?' I yelled.

'This,' he held the lantern out in front of him, where it illuminated the most beautiful sight I had ever seen.

I gasped.

We were in the middle of a cave, and yet a waterfall gushed from the ceiling into a pool below, where a gentle blue light glowed from the water, making it appear shallow, though I knew it must be deeper. The light reflected on the stalactites lining the cave's roof, lighting up water droplets and making them appear like hundreds of tiny candles.

It was warm inside the cave and, as the water fell into the pool below, steam rose up, creating a mystical fog over the water. It was truly magical, and I couldn't help but wonder how some of the most enchanting things weren't magic at all, but completely natural.

'It's beautiful,' I breathed.

'I know,' Kaspian agreed. When I looked up, he wasn't looking at the waterfall, he stared right at me.

I looked away quickly and asked Cole, 'how did you find this place?'

'We stumbled upon it, really. Kas has always liked to explore.'

How did one stumble upon something like this? It was completely away from everything, in the middle of nowhere. I supposed it *was* Kaspian's duty to know his kingdom like the back of his own hand, and I guessed that meant exploring even barren wastelands for hidden gems like this.

'It's what gave me the idea for my sewage system,' Kaspian said with pride.

'Let me get this straight,' I started. 'You saw *this*, in all of its beauty, and you thought of a *sewage* system?'

Cole let out an uncharacteristic snort.

'Well, I thought about running water, which led to pipes, which led to me thinking about how we can utilise pipes to flow the unwanted waste back out to sea the same way we use them to bring water in. So yes, I guess I did,' he blinked, not seeing a problem with turning something so beautiful into an idea for waste pipes. 'You can't deny my toilet designs are a thing of beauty,' he exclaimed.

'I mean, they're better than doing your business in a hole in the ground, but I'm not sure I would call them *beautiful*.' He looked at me like I had spat in his face, and I stared back at him. Cole coughed. 'Don't get me wrong, they're genius,' I recovered. 'How did you even know how to design something so intricate?'

Kaspian's face thawed. He couldn't wait to talk about this, I realised. 'I didn't always want to be a soldier. Even when I was tiny – before I was adopted,' he said the word carefully, and it was the nicest way I could think to describe what had happened to him, 'I always wanted to be an inventor. I know it's not really a job title, but it's what I wanted to be.

'I loved taking things apart and putting them back together. Not always in the same way, but sometimes better. I would improve things.

So now, I know it's not strictly under the job description, but I think, as prince, I have a duty to improve the quality of life for those in my kingdom. And if that means spending my time working out a sewage network, I'll do it. It's just one of my many ideas for improving the city.'

I swallowed. He'd taken a step closer to me, his breath tickling the hairs on my neck. The waterfall was beautiful, but it was only the second most striking thing I'd seen today. His ocean eyes, and the way they roved up and down my body right now, they took the top spot. Cole coughed, but Kaspian didn't look away. He raised a hand to cup my cheek instead, and a shiver ran through me, despite the warmth of the cave.

'I would like to see more of your inventions,' I whispered, too scared to make too much noise in case he withdrew.

He smiled, and *shit* that dimple almost made my knees buckle. 'I would like to show you them.'

He leant forward then, but he must have felt my body tense and misread the tautness of my body, locked up with anticipation, as his trajectory changed at the last second, lips landing in my hair rather than where my lips had puckered under his stare. The heat that had pooled in my centre withered as he pulled away, leaving a sudden coldness in its place, and I wrapped an arm around myself to replace the warmth of his gaze.

Cole cleared his throat again. 'Don't set him off talking about his inventions. You won't get him to shut up about his idea for motorised carriages,' he shook his head in disbelief.

'You can't deny that it's an excellent idea! We'd have done that journey in half the time!' Kaspian, oblivious to the tension he had left in my body, animatedly discussed the idea.

'Come on, we have reservations. You can tell Blaise all about your plans for motors in the perfectly good carriage on the way to dinner.'

I cast another long look over the beautiful space, before Cole turned the lantern away and I could only see the blue glow from the pool. I turned to follow Kaspian, who was still arguing about why a motorised carriage would be better, and asked, 'are we eating at Otto's?'

'No,' Cole answered, and I felt a surge of disappointment. 'There's somewhere closer you'll love. They serve the best cheesecake in the kingdom.'

I didn't even know what a cheesecake was, but it had the word 'cake' in it, and my stomach had started to rumble, so I happily followed them out of the cave, wishing I had something other than the still-burning spot in my hair that Kaspian had pressed his lips to, to remember it by.

Chapter 35

'I AM SO FULL,' COLE sat back in his seat, clutching his stomach, and I wasn't surprised. He'd eaten a whole chicken pie to himself, with a side of creamy mash potatoes and steaming vegetables, followed by two huge slices of cheesecake, and he'd washed it all down with a glass of ale. I had opted for pink wine, my own healthy helping of pie, potatoes, and a slice of melt-in-your-mouth cheesecake.

The tavern, simply named *Billy's*, was just as busy as Otto's had been when we visited. The staff knew both Kaspian and Cole by name and were incredibly friendly, clearing out a section of the restaurant for us to sit unbothered by other patrons.

Freshly inspired by our trip to the waterfall, Kaspian had been doodling plans on a napkin for expanding his sewage system, only pausing to eat. It was fascinating, watching his mind at work. His brows furrowed in concentration, and he chewed the inside of his cheek whenever he was trying to solve something particularly tricky. I had to stop myself from staring.

'Have you got any cards?' I asked Cole.

'It's a soldier's prerogative to always carry a pack of cards,' Cole pulled a pack from a hidden pocket. 'You play?'

I nodded. 'My handlers taught me on the road.' A half-truth. I was getting good at those. I tried not to let myself feel guilty.

Cole began to shuffle the cards. 'You in?' he asked Kaspian, who looked up from his napkin, studied my face and the cards with a dimple-inducing smirk, and nodded. While Cole dealt our hands, Kaspian tucked his napkin and pencil safely into a pocket.

'Thank you for showing me the waterfall,' I picked up the cards, trying not to grin. It was already a good hand.

Kaspian's disappointment at his own hand was written all over his face when he replied, 'I wanted to show you that Reili is beautiful. It isn't all flea-infested streets or glittering palaces. It has natural beauty.'

'I was beginning to see that already,' I whispered without looking up from my cards. I could feel Kaspian's gaze on me, but I couldn't meet his eyes.

We played cards for about an hour. It turned out Kaspian's first hand had been brilliant, after all, and his disappointment had been a bluff. Once I figured that out, and sussed Cole's tell – a gentle tug on his right earlobe – I won almost every game.

'It's a good job we're not playing for money,' Cole huffed, throwing his losing hand on the table.

'Or I would have robbed you blind,' I winked at him, and Kaspian boomed a laugh that made my toes curl.

I reached to deal another round, when an ear-splitting scream sounded from outside the tavern. Cole's hand instantly went to the sword that rested on the bench beside him, and he exchanged a worried glance with Kaspian.

The bar went unnervingly silent as the huge barkeep strode across the room and wrenched the door open. A barrage of noise carried in from outside, and I strained my neck to see through the door. People were running – from *what*, I couldn't make out – and Cole was already on his feet. Kaspian wasn't far behind him.

'Stay here!' he told me, voice full of princely authority that left no room for argument. The pair of them, along with the huge barkeep, and a handful of other male patrons, disappeared out of the door, leaving the women to titter nervously among themselves.

Without warning, a huge rock shattered the front window, sending a shower of glass over the people sat in front of it. The cluster of women screamed and shielded their faces, ducking under the large wooden table they had previously occupied. The remaining men ushered their wives and companions behind them, though none were armed.

I was.

I wasn't supposed to use a weapon, but this constituted as an emergency, so I withdrew the dagger from my boot, grateful for my choice of skin-tight leggings that had forced me to put it there instead of strapping it to my thigh. Neither Cole nor Kaspian returned, but I tried not to worry about them. I needed to stay focused and defend myself, and everyone else in the tavern, if I could. I was the only one with a proper weapon.

One man had picked up a large plank of wood from behind the bar. Another had smashed a glass, and wielded the jagged edges as a weapon, but he was likely to cause more damage to himself than anyone else.

I took a deep breath and stepped forward as a handful of men swarmed through the door, brandishing swords. *Soldiers.* And not just any soldiers. They wore Harensarra uniforms.

Shit.

Women screamed and cowered under tables as the five soldiers made their way further into the room. As predicted, the man brandishing the broken glass sliced his own arm before he could attack anyone else, and a soldier's sword drove through his stomach with an awful squelching noise that I knew would echo in my nightmares forever. If I made it out.

I moved, without thinking, towards the group of soldiers, dagger ready and poised to throw. With another gruesome squelch, the soldier removed his sword from the belly of the dying man, and I launched the dagger into the air. He spun, and it pierced him right through the eye before leaving his head through the other side.

I gagged, but I couldn't stop. Jumping over stools and cowering women to retrieve the dagger, I picked it up and turned, clashing my tiny blade with a huge sword. My forearm strained with the effort of preventing the weapon from slicing through me.

The man with the wood chose that moment to whack the soldier over the head, and I took the chance to drop my arm and stick the soldier through the gut, slicing through the tough leather padding across his soft flesh. Entrails tipped out of his open stomach, and his sword clattered to the floor as he collapsed. Behind me, a woman retched as I tried to avoid slipping on his sticky insides.

Women were running through the door to escape, as two of the remaining three soldiers made grabs for their skirts, and I couldn't have been more thankful that I hadn't worn a dress today. I sliced a woman free from the soldier's grip by cutting off the back end of her skirt, and she ran away, bloomers on show. At least she had all her limbs, which was more than could be said for the soldier who had grabbed her, who now sported two less fingers thanks to my precise slashing. *That* would make grabbing women much harder.

He shrieked in pain, clutching his maimed hand as he stumbled backwards, and I whirled as another soldier let go of his own captured woman to aim straight for me. His yell of anger alerted me to his run up, and I moved so fast he didn't see the dagger hurtling towards his chest. It didn't miss its mark. He was knocked off balance, flying backwards though his arms still reached for me, as the dagger pierced him right through the heart.

A yelp of pain made me turn once more to see the man who had been defending himself with the plank of wood now cornered – the wood sliced out of his hand by the soldier's longsword. I didn't have time to retrieve my dagger, but it was no matter. I knew how to fight with all blades. Grabbing a dropped sword from the ground, I sprinted towards the pair of them. The man's wide eyes alerted the soldier to my run up and he turned just in time for our swords to clash.

He was stronger than me, and my shoulders barked in protest. I should have trained more. I should have asked Luna to practice with me. I hadn't trained since I'd been on the road, and it was only the years of practice prior that meant not all form was lost. My arms strained. If I was quick, I could dart away, but one wrong move and my foe would have the upper hand. My arms wobbled. I had to choose now, before my arms gave way and his sword sliced through me in one.

I spun, wincing as his blade clashed to the stone floor, making him curse. Turning back to face me, he picked up the sword and met me blow for blow, and then suddenly he stopped, dropping his weapon, blood pouring from his lips. I shielded my eyes from the gore as it sprayed across my face. He gurgled, then slumped to his knees, falling forward and finally going still.

My dagger protruded from his neck, and I pulled it free, meeting the brown eyes of the man who had brandished the wood. He was breathing heavily, sweat dripped from his forehead, shoulder-length, mouse-blonde hair had escaped his tie, and strands stuck to his neck, gangly limbs clearly stronger than they looked.

That was twice he had saved me. I looked around. The tavern was now empty, other than the dead bodies, me, him, and the maimed soldier.

'What's your name, sir?'

'Thomas,' he panted.

'Well, Thomas. Thank you for saving my life,' I wiped the blood from the dagger on my trouser leg.

'Right back at you! Where did you learn to fight like that?'

I grimaced. 'I'd rather not tell you, if it's all the same to you, Thomas. If we can keep this between us, I'll put your name forward for the Royal Guard. I'm good friends with the prince.'

Thomas's eyes widened and he nodded feverishly. I took in his tattered clothes, worn beyond what this fight had done to them, studied the grime on his face, which was thick, even without the addition of someone else's blood. He was poor. Poorer than most. The Guard paid alright, and it was less risky than being a frontline soldier. It was enough to buy his silence.

'Wonderful. Thomas?' He looked at me quizzically. 'Finish that one off for me, would you?' I nodded towards the maimed soldier and ran out into the evening without a look back.

A man's scream told me Thomas had done as he was asked.

———— ✦ ————

When we'd arrived in Palmira, a large town on Reili's border with Harensarra, the streets had been a buzz of activity. Now, they were deserted. Buildings had been broken into and ransacked. Fires burned in the distance. Blood spattered the pavements. The streets were empty. People had either fled to the neighbouring town, or had barricaded themselves in their homes, blowing out lanterns and hiding in the dark. Many of these people would need rehoming and, with war coming, this was a huge blow. Perhaps war was already here.

Far off yells told me the fight wasn't over and, wherever the fight was, I'd bet that was where Cole and Kaspian were, too. I groaned aloud, knowing I had to follow the danger if I wanted to find them, and I was already exhausted. I clutched the dagger tight in one hand and dragged the stolen sword loosely behind me with the other, following the cries.

Kaspian and Cole are safe, I told myself repeatedly as I moved through the streets, searching for them. The sound of steel-on-steel caught my attention, and I ran towards the noise. Cole was locked in a battle with two Harensarra soldiers, blood pouring from a wound on his temple. I fought the burning rage igniting within me, and forced myself to inhale deep lungsful of air, watching as Cole punched one soldier in the gut, leaving him bent over double, whilst he parried with the other.

I didn't move towards him. Trying to find them was a mistake. I couldn't help Cole without revealing I knew how to fight. But I couldn't stand by and watch, either. My hesitation had already cost him. The other soldier had recovered and rejoined the fight, leaving Cole on the backfoot against two.

Cole lifted his sword to meet the first's attack, but this left his back exposed to the other, and I heard his cry of pain as the soldier's sword sliced through his side. The agony in his scream brought me back to reality and, before I could talk myself out of it, I ran towards him.

Cole fell to one knee, but still managed to meet the two swords that charged him. It wouldn't be long before he made a mistake, though, and I was still more than ten feet away when I saw one soldier raise his blade as Cole met the other's attack. I didn't think, I just threw.

My dagger sped through the air with a whistle and met its target with a soft thud, landing straight between the shoulders of the soldier with his sword still raised. It clattered from his hands and Cole didn't hesitate, picking it up with his free arm and climbing back to his feet, now wielding both swords in defence. He used one to slice the man before him from chin to groin and spun to stick the other in the chest of the man who still had my dagger between his shoulder blades. Cole barely had time to take a deep breath before I launched myself into his arms, and he staggered before clinging to me.

'We told you to stay in the tavern!' he growled.

He dropped one of the swords and pushed me away from him, eyes checking me from head to toe for any injuries. When he found none, he stooped to remove my dagger from the soldier's limp body.

'We'll talk about this when we find Kas,' his nostrils flared.

Panic gripped me in a vice. I needed to get away from Cole so I could think about what excuse to give him. 'Great idea, let's split up! We'll cover more ground!' I pulled my dagger from his hand and sprinted away from him. His cries of protest faded as I ran, feeling guilty for leaving him injured and unable to catch up.

I needed to get my story straight and find Kaspian. If I did the latter, perhaps Cole would be so relieved that he'd forget all about my little throwing trick. I clutched the enchanted dagger tighter, never more grateful for magic. Without it, my friend would have been dead.

If only I could explain that to him.

CHAPTER 36

TIME TRICKLED BY, AND IT was pure luck that I hadn't run into another Harensarra soldier as I made my way through the street without any sign of Kaspian either. My feet ached, and my arms wobbled with the strain of carrying the stolen sword. I considered ditching it, but could practically hear Gaia's voice screaming how that was a terrible idea.

The town had become eerily quiet, and darkness swallowed every movement, making progress painstakingly slow. I kept my back pressed against buildings as I snuck through the city, and prayed to the Mother that Kaspian had found safety and was lying low. I shuddered, and not from the cool night air that caressed my arms and face.

I'd barely had time to process that I had taken my first life. Despite training every day to do just that, nothing had prepared me for how it would *feel*. Or how it would *smell*. That smell of death seemed to hover over the whole city now.

The sound of muffled yells stopped me in my tracks, and I listened, wishing I had the witches pointed ears to amplify every noise. A hunter's hearing. Another yell came from my left. Even if it wasn't Kaspian, someone was in trouble, and I hurried towards the noise, tired muscles protesting with every step.

Another cry of pain, this time closer, and I paused to get to grips with my surroundings. There were a few empty houses, and a small barn. I tiptoed past the double doors that were likely used for animals and peered inside a smaller side door that had been left open.

My heart sputtered.

Kaspian was on his knees, hands tied in front of him. A soldier, with several badges of honour that marked him as a commanding officer, prowled in circles around him, occasionally throwing out a boot or a fist to hit Kaspian in the gut.

I clamped a hand over my mouth to stop myself from crying out as Kaspian spat blood onto the hay-strewn floor in front of him.

Think, I commanded myself. There was only one soldier, I could take *one* down easily. Especially one with such little armour. It was a sign of Harensarra's poverty that their soldiers were only protected by thick leathers and not proper armour. I needed to time my attack just right, not giving the soldier time to get to Kaspian first.

The soldier asked Kaspian questions in hushed tones I couldn't quite make out. Had he been ordered to keep him alive? Did Kaspian have information they wanted? Whatever he had been asked, Kaspian refused to answer, which earned him another boot in the stomach. I winced, and Kaspian grunted in pain but otherwise barely moved.

As the soldier circled Kaspian once more, I edged into the barn, sticking to the shadows. Kaspian looked up once in my direction but, if he saw me, he didn't acknowledge it. Within the barn, I could hear more clearly what the soldier asked.

'Your *mother* must not value you at all. She hasn't even sent a search party for you. Although, she may not have yet realised that the wandering prince has not returned. You do not want to rule do you, Prince? Then why not give over your land and titles to *our* king? Harensarra has been trodden on between yours and Starterra's fighting for too long! The middle ground in which you both can clash! Your peace treaty didn't incite peace! It only moved your fight to *our* lands!' The man spat at Kaspian's feet.

'Well, it stops now. You are not deserving to be king! You are a lowly bastard! And that woman is not fit to be queen, either. It must end.' His accent was thick, and spittle flew with each venomous word. Kaspian didn't rise to the bait, didn't even acknowledge he had heard him.

I understood Harensarra's pain. They were a nation already on their knees, near destroyed by a Pox, who had been caught in the middle of a war they didn't want

The soldier circled Kaspian once more. Dammit, I needed him to stand still! Kaspian's gaze flicked my way, darting between my face, and the dagger in my hand. Understanding flared in his piercing eyes, and he spoke for the first time, voice ragged. 'Then let it end! Let us make peace between our nations! Do we not have a common enemy?'

Did he mean Starterra? Or the witches? It didn't matter right now. He was distracting the soldier, keeping the focus on him. He was buying me time.

But Kaspian's words hadn't calmed the soldier, they had ignited more hatred in his eyes. He paused his stalking to draw a dagger of his own, and I pulled back my shoulder, sending my blade spinning. It landed between the soldier's eyes, but not before he cut a long line down Kaspian's forearm, drawing blood. Any deeper, and the wound could have been catastrophic. The soldier fell backwards, dead in an instant, and I ran to kneel before Kaspian. I cupped his face, and he looked at me with both sorrow and pride.

'How did you find me?' His voice was hoarse.

'I followed your cries. Good job you're such a wimp,' I quipped, hot tears running down my face.

'Says the one crying,' he tried to joke, reaching for my face to brush away the tears, but his hands were still tied.

I retrieved my dagger, freeing it from the soldier's skull with a strong tug, and sliced Kaspian free from the ropes in one quick motion. Once free, he was on his feet in an instant, dragging me up with him.

Before I could address the blood that stained almost every inch of him, or find something to bind the slice along his arm, he pulled me into a fierce hug. Pushing me to arm's length, he surveyed me for any injuries – just as Cole had. Noting that the blood I was covered in wasn't mine, he pulled me back against his chest, and a sob broke loose from deep within me, so relieved I had gotten to him in time.

'Where did you learn to throw a dagger like that? Never mind. I don't care. Whoever taught you can have a spot on my Royal Guard,' he murmured against my hair.

'I've already promised a spot to one person tonight,' I grimaced against his chest.

'You have?' I could hear the smile in his voice.

'A man. Thomas. I didn't get his family name. He saved my life, twice.'

'Then I owe him double the wages.' I removed my head from his chest, needing to look at him, to check he really was okay. He smiled at me, a heartbreakingly soft smile, and wiped tears from my cheek with his thumb. He left his hand cupping my face and sighed, staring into my eyes. I couldn't look away.

'I won't tell Cole you nearly got your arse beat,' I forced out, needing to break the spell between us so I could pull myself together.

'I'm wounded,' he clutched his chest. 'You didn't think I had the situation under control?' I snorted and whacked his upper arm lightly, his answering smile so brilliant, my chest tightened to the point of pain.

'Kas, I have never been so scared in all my life,' I admitted.

His eyes flashed with pleasure at the way his nickname casually rolled off my tongue, and his stare was so unwavering that I barely remembered to breathe. His hand tightened on my face, gaze darkening as it darted from my lips to my eyes. His damp curls flopped over his forehead, and I dragged my stare down to his full lips.

My feet lifted of their own accord. On tiptoes, I stretched to meet him. He tilted his head towards me, and the scent of sugar and grass – now mixed with sweat and the copper twang of blood – enveloped me completely.

His lips brushed mine, and the touch sent an electric shiver right along my spine. I was about to pull his head closer to me for more when he pushed me behind him, snatching the dead soldier's sword up in one swift movement.

'I just saved your damn life,' I muttered. 'I don't need protecting.'

'Shhhhh,' he hissed back.

I heard what had spooked him and tensed. Heavy footsteps headed right towards us. I clutched my dagger, and Kaspian stood in a fighting stance, sword in hand, ready to swing. A shadowed figure walked into the barn and we both dove forward, my arm pulled back to throw the dagger, Kaspian's sword raised.

Cole barely met Kaspian's sword with his own, and Kas pulled back with a curse, my arm dropping at the last moment. I was going to kill Cole! We nearly *had* killed him!

'Woah!' Cole reared back. 'I thought it was you. I heard Blaise's laugh.'

'We nearly killed you!' I shrieked.

'Relax, no harm done. Are you both okay?' he asked, eyes on his prince.

Kaspian nodded. 'I look better than you, my friend.'

Cole still bled from his temple, and had a hand pressed to the deep wound in his side. 'I'll live. Which is more than can be said for this fellow,' he nodded to the fallen soldier. 'What happened here?'

'It seems Blaise has been holding out on us,' Kaspian smirked. 'She's quite the markswoman.'

Cole's grey eyes lifted from the dead body to study my face, his gaze filled with such suspicion it snapped something inside my heart. I wanted to tell him everything. I didn't want him to look at me like that ever again. But the truth would only make things worse.

'And where did you learn that?' His voice was cold, any light-heartedness between us gone. My heart skittered. I had put myself in an impossible position. Maybe I had forgotten to think of them as my enemy, but I was theirs.

'My mother, she taught me before she passed. She knew how important it was to be able to protect myself. I know it isn't ladylike to wield a sword or throw a knife, so I kept it hidden. I'm sorry, I wanted to impress everyone here, and the best way to do that was to be a proper courtier, to keep the truth hidden.' Lies mixed with truths.

Cole eyed me dubiously.

'Cole, what does it matter? Just be thankful she was here to save my life! The girl isn't on trial!' Kaspian scolded, looking at me with soft eyes. I glanced away.

'Yes, Your Highness,' Cole replied with an iciness I had never heard from him before.

Kaspian rolled his eyes, clearly used to Cole's fierce, overprotective nature. 'We should leave. There's a town out there that needs our help. I don't know if he was the last of the soldiers, but I intend to find out. Plus, you need to see a medic, Cole,' he took a step towards the door and wobbled. Cole rushed to steady him, but Kaspian batted him away. 'I'm fine. Just a little lightheaded, is all. I blame the ale.'

Cole and I exchanged a wary glance. He'd only had two pints. We both knew he could handle more than that on a bad day. Kas took another apprehensive step forward before he tumbled to the ground and Cole rushed to him. I could do nothing but stare in horror, as Kaspian's eyes closed, and his body began convulsing.

CHAPTER 37

'WHAT'S HAPPENING TO HIM?' COLE clutched his friend's body, trying to stop the violent convulsions.

'I-I don't know!' I stammered.

'*You've* been here with him! Was he injured?'

'He was cut but –' I dived for the knife the soldier had cut along Kaspian's arm with. I held it to my nose and recoiled, throwing the blade as far away as I could.

'It was poisoned!' The words fell from my lips as quickly as my heart had tumbled into my stomach at that distinctive acrid smell.

Cole's eyes were as wide as saucers. 'We need to get him to a medic!'

'There's no time! It's Foxglove!' I gulped. The venom, created from the flower that gave it its name, could slow your heart to a dangerous level once in the blood and, if not treated immediately, it could kill a grown man within an hour.

I'd spent time studying poisons in the Iron Woods, where every plant had some kind of use, whether for food, or bringing harm to others. It was a vital lesson that had to be taught to every coven member lest they accidentally poison themselves. When mixed into a poison, Foxglove had an identifiable, acidic smell. The antidote took days to brew and was useless unless administered immediately. It wasn't something someone just happened to carry on their person.

'Then what do we do?' Cole's voice was laced with panic

'We need to suck the venom out of his bloodstream!' It was the only way. Usually, the witches used leeches to suck the venom out and clean the blood, but I didn't have any of those, either.

'What?' Cole sounded horrified but I was already moving. He barred my path, that wary look of mistrust still crossing his features every time he looked at me.

'Move, Cole!'

He stood firm.

'If you don't move in the next five seconds, he is going to die! I have to do this! You have to *let me* do this!' I pleaded. It was my fault. I'd been too slow to prevent Kaspian from getting cut with a poisoned blade, and I couldn't let him die.

With a final moment of hesitation Cole stepped out of my way, and I rushed to Kaspian's now-still body. He was cold, the venom working quickly. I had to be faster. Picking up Kaspian's injured arm, I held the gash to my mouth and began to draw his poisoned blood past my lips. The foul taste forced me to gasp and pull away after only a few seconds, spitting his poisoned blood to the floor.

I took a deep breath and returned to the task as Cole watched, eyes wide with horror. I was careful not to swallow any of the blood, spitting the poisoned mouthfuls out every few seconds.

'Blaise, stop! I think something's wrong! You don't look right!' Cole was saying, but I couldn't stop. Not as each mouthful I extracted tasted less like the acidic Foxglove, and more like the usual iron of unpolluted blood. After what seemed like a lifetime, I spat out a final mouthful and dropped Kaspian's arm, the warmth returning to his body already. I huffed a sigh of relief, and slumped backwards onto my elbows beside him.

'Did it work?' Cole whispered.

'I think so,' I nodded.

'What about you?'

'I'm fine. I don't think I swallowed any. I feel fine,' I assured him.

'But Blaise, you're –' he was interrupted by a sharp intake of breath and a splutter from Kaspian, and the pair of us rushed to help him sit up.

'What happened?' he croaked, eyes still closed tight.

'You were poisoned. Blaise saved your life,' Cole answered, voice wavering.

'Again? You really need to stop doing that, Blaise, it's getting a little embarrassing for me,' Kas tried to laugh, but winced. I took his hand, squeezing it tight as he finally opened his eyes to look at me. He gasped, reaching up to cup my face. 'Well, don't you look pretty! So radiant.'

'I think he's delirious, we need to get him back to the palace,' I murmured to Cole.

'Right. You stay with him, and I'll go and find help. We need a carriage.' He squeezed Kaspian's shoulder and, after another wary glance in my direction, headed out to look for help.

Kaspian's rough hand remained on my cheek as he lowered himself back down to the ground, and I leaned into his touch, closing my eyes.

'I take back what I said before. *That's* the most scared I've ever been,' I whispered against his palm.

'Hey now, it will take more than a little bit of poison to finish the great Kaspian off,' he tried to laugh again.

'This isn't the time for jokes. You should rest. We'll get you home soon.' I removed his hand from my cheek, gripping it tightly in my own.

'We never got to finish what we started,' he murmured, voice soft, eyes already closing again. He had to be exhausted.

It took me a moment to realise he was talking about the kiss that Cole had interrupted. I was pleased his eyes were closed because I could feel my skin flushing. 'I currently taste of poison, and your blood. Believe me, you don't want to finish what you started,' I muttered back.

'Mmm, delicious.' His voice was sleepy.

I laughed. 'Get some sleep. Cole will be back with help soon.'

His breathing had already shifted, and I let myself sigh in relief as I held him, readjusting his head so that it rested on my lap, and not on the hard, blood-covered floor. I pushed his unruly hair back from his face as he slept, watching the little frown lines between his brows even out as I continued to stroke his hair back. Never taking my eyes from him, I became entranced by the way his chest dipped up and down as he heaved steady breaths, a reassurance that he was alive. I sat that way until Cole returned.

'Oh,' was all he said when he saw me still holding Kaspian. He shot me a strange look of fear and concern. It wasn't the same outright mistrust as before, but he was still suspicious.

'There's a carriage outside. I'll carry him.'

I nodded, letting the weight of the night fold over me as Cole lifted Kaspian from my arms – his own injuries forgotten though they still dripped blood – and carried his sleeping body to the waiting carriage. Slipping in behind them both, I kept a careful distance as I sat beside Cole, who laid Kaspian sprawled out across one bench.

'What will happen to all of these people now?'

'A clean-up operation has already started. Any remaining Harensarra soldiers have been caught, and will be brought to the palace dungeons for questioning. We'll have to find temporary shelter for the survivors until this area can be rebuilt.'

'I'd like to help. In any way I can,' I offered.

Cole looked at me, evaluating. Whatever he saw, he found sincere, as he nodded once before turning to watch over his friend. No one spoke again as the carriage made the journey back to the palace.

Chapter 38

THE PALACE HAD BEEN IN turmoil for the last week, the attack in Palmira unnerving even the most obnoxious of the courtiers. The halls were filled with extra members of the Royal Guard, there to protect their queen in the way they had been unable to protect their prince. Kaspian had been on bed rest since we returned, and all visitors were banned from the royal medical wing – bar his mother who, to her credit, visited him every day.

Cole was absent for the most part, too busy in the dungeons trying to obtain confessions and inside information from the captured Harensarra soldiers, their screams echoing around the palace.

Luna and Daisy had been by my side since I'd returned and gone straight to Luna's rooms in fits of tears, sobbing so hard my throat burned. I had barely been able to get the words out to tell them what had happened. Yet, despite their constant presence, I felt alone.

Kaspian's cold, lifeless body haunted me every time I shut my eyes, and nightmares of being unable to save him plagued my sleep. I could still feel his rough hand on my cheek, feel the brush of his lips on mine, and each day that went by without feeling those steadying touches once more felt like punishment for almost letting him die.

Each time I turned up to the medical wing I was told the same thing by the healers – 'We have been given orders not to let you see him.'

'That ungrateful cow,' Luna said, assuming Queen Lizabeta had given that particular order. 'You saved his life, and she won't even let you see him, let alone – oh, I don't know, *thank you!*'

Deep in my heart, I knew Cole had given the command. He hadn't come to see me once since that night. I had bumped into him one night in the dining hall and he looked weary, with deep purple bags under his eyes and an ashen face. But, when I had made to speak, he'd picked up his tray and left without a word. Despite saving Kaspian's life, he no longer trusted me.

Plans for the ball had ceased, 'until your future king makes a full recovery,' the queen had advised. Out of earshot of Daisy, Luna had whispered her concerns about our plans, and had asked whether she should delay her own intentions to spread word through Harensarra, leaving ball invitations strewn at the soldiers' barracks. The answer was no. She'd also urged me to send word to Agnes in case we needed to delay. I hadn't.

Let the witches come. Let them butcher every Harensarra soldier that dared still make their way towards the palace. A numbness had settled over me, and it contained an ethereal rage that sat like a coiled spring waiting to be released. I wanted Harensarra to burn for their part in hurting Kaspian. So yes, let the witches come, and let them rain hellfire upon all those that sought to cause him more harm.

I sat in the full yet quiet dining hall, food untouched, ignoring Luna and Daisy's worried glances, when sounds of a scuffle and a woman's pleas sounded from the hallway outside. Several of the guards on duty stood to attention, and a couple headed towards the large double doors, where raised voices carried through.

The large doors burst open, and Kaspian stormed through – in nothing but a medical gown – with Cole hot on his heels, the queen a few steps behind.

'You are not *well!*' she hissed. 'This is foolish! Return to the medical wing, at once!'

Cole looked inclined to agree, and tried to grab Kaspian's shoulder, but the prince pulled free with ease and pushed his way further into the hall. His eyes landed on mine, and he didn't falter, taking powerful strides towards me as I clambered out from the bench, not sure whether to run towards him or away from him. The look on his face unreadable.

The whole room held its breath, also uncertain of what that gleam in the prince's eye meant. I watched Luna tense and drop her cutlery, freeing her hands. To protect me. She'd freed her hands in case she needed to use magic to protect me, despite what it could cost her.

Kaspian's eyes hadn't left mine, as though he didn't see anyone else in the room full of people. Ignoring his mother's rising pleas, he didn't stop until he was directly in front of me. He paused barely an inch away, so close I could smell him, his familiar scent so thick I didn't even need to inhale to enjoy it.

'I had to know you were okay,' he breathed, surveying me. Then his confidence wavered, blue eyes filling with hurt as he whispered, so quietly only I could hear. 'You didn't visit.' My chest tightened, and I shot a glare filled with such icy rage at Cole, who now stood at Kaspian's shoulder, that he actually flinched.

'They wouldn't let me,' I whispered back, and he whirled on his mother, whose turn it was to flinch from the hurt etched on his face.

'This is not the place!' the queen urged, with a glance at Cole, who placed a firm hand on his friend's shoulder and began leading him away from the hall.

I followed, Luna in tow despite no invite being extended, and heads all around the hall whipped to us. Whispers started as we followed the queen, drowned out only as the doors swung shut behind us.

'How dare you?' Kaspian rounded on his mother as she led us down the hallway and into a small room that was being used as a storage cupboard; brooms and buckets stacked against the walls. The five of us crammed in, no one objecting to Luna's presence.

'You were unwell! And Cole and I thought it best you were able to recover in peace. Without *distractions*,' she glared at me, the word laced with venom.

Kaspian looked like he'd been slapped, and his eyes widened as he looked to Cole, pain written all over his face. Luna, too, looked shocked at Cole's part in this.

'I asked for her every day, and you told me she hadn't come.' Kaspian looked to his friend for an explanation, but Cole stayed silent, the guilt etched on his face answer enough.

'I came every day. The healers were given orders not to let me in.' My words caused Kaspian's eyes to shutter. Cole winced, and my heart clenched at the rift this would cause between them. It was bad enough when I assumed Cole was behind this, but now I knew he had partnered with the queen to keep me from Kaspian, and then *lied* to him, causing him to think I didn't want to see him . . . the betrayal stung like a physical blow.

Cole wouldn't meet my eyes. 'She isn't right for you.'

Kaspian reeled back from his friend's words and turned on his mother once more. 'How much did you pay him? What did you offer him to get him to say that? Those are your words, *Mother*!'

Cole flinched. 'I have not been bought! My loyalty remains with you,' he said at the same time the queen spoke.

'Your friend is wiser than I first thought! He has realised this girl is nothing but a distraction from your duties to this kingdom. Your duty to choose a queen!'

'I promised to choose, didn't I?' Kaspian answered, flatly.

'You cannot choose this wretch!' The queen shouted in horror.

An inhuman snarl escaped Luna, her lips pulled back in a feral growl, and everyone looked to her as though only just noticing her there. I nudged her, and she clamped her mouth shut, but anger still simmered like molten fire in her eyes. The same look was reflected in Kaspian's heated stare. My chest felt like it might crack.

Before I could do or say anything, Kaspian spoke, his voice filled with that princely command he rarely engaged. 'How dare you presume to know Blaise! How dare you treat someone who saved my life – not once, but twice – so badly! Blaise should have received the highest honours! She should not have been shunned! I may have expected this from you,' he looked to his mother before his furious eyes settled on Cole. 'But never from *you*!'

Cole had the good sense to look ashamed and threw me an apologetic glance.

'Resume your plans for the ball,' Kaspian continued. 'It goes ahead, and I will do what I feel is right for *my* kingdom before I march us into war. And Mother, if I hear of these plans being halted for any reason, I will renounce my claim to the throne and lead your army as a general but not a prince.' Queen Lizabeta's mouth hung open, but before she could protest, Kaspian spoke again. 'Luna, you will report to me every day with details of the plans for the ball, so I can make sure this is being adhered to.'

Luna's head bobbed up and down with surprise. 'Cole, you are to focus on bringing me details from those Harensarra soldiers of their king's plans. You are not to concern yourself with any other aspect of my personal life. Now, get out. All of you.'

The queen looked as though she would argue, but the look Kaspian shot her made her hold her tongue. Cole's eyes filled with regret as he looked from me to his prince and then stalked out of the door. Both the women followed, Luna still looking startled she had been tasked with keeping the queen in check. I made to leave, too, but the prince grabbed my wrist, spinning me to face him.

'Not you.'

His burning eyes softened as he drunk in the sight of me, and I stared right back at him, taking in how his skin had regained its colour since the last time I had seen him. I looked to his unruly dark hair, then to the bandaged arm that still clutched my wrist. Underneath the bandage lay the healing wound where I had extracted the poison from his body. Finally, I eyed the medical robe that finished at his knees, which he hadn't cared about when he'd marched into a room full of his soldiers, lords, and ladies, just so he could see me.

'I'm sorry,' he told me, 'that they treated you that way. Cole, especially, should know better.'

'He thinks he's protecting you. Don't be too hard on him,' I urged, because, despite my own anger at Cole, he was right to be wary of me. I swallowed my guilt, ignoring the way my tummy flipped at how right Cole really was. I *was* a threat to his prince. Even if I knew deep down that there was no way I could hurt Kas, I was still here to steal his crown, after all.

I knew it was impossible, but looking at Kaspian now, I was desperate to find a way to ensure we ruled together. I could still have him *and* protect my family. He would understand, once Agnes saved his people from Harensarra's army, how the witches could live alongside us in peace. I shut down Luna's words about him never being able to change, hoping beyond all hope that I could keep both him *and* my family safe. That I would never need to choose.

Kaspian's expression softened even further as he took a loose strand of my hair and tucked it behind my ear, then lifted my chin with his thumb and forefinger, forcing me to meet his stare. His eyes were like midnight as his voice dropped an octave.

'We have unfinished business.'

'Oh?' The word barely a sound, and rather just a shape my lips made. His own lips twitched up at my nervousness, and a familiar dimple formed, making my heart pound. My breath hitched, and the sound was Kaspian's undoing.

He bent his head towards me, his scent enough to make my head spin even before his lips crashed into mine. There was nothing light and soft about this kiss, the gentle caress he had brushed against my lips in the barn feeling like a cold handshake compared to the way he devoured me now.

His lips were firm and eager as his hands settled on my waist and in my hair, and I stumbled backwards under the pressure of his kiss until my back met the wall. Using it to steady myself, I met the pressure of his lips with my own and he groaned against me. It was my own unleashing.

I parted my lips, and he didn't hesitate for a moment before his tongue swept in to taste me. The heat of his breath melted any hesitation of my own as I ran my tongue along his bottom lip, slanting my mouth to better meet his tongue with my own until he pushed further against me, the thin fabric of the medical gown leaving nothing to the imagination.

I gasped as his considerable length pressed against my thigh through my soft dress, and I could feel heat blooming on my cheeks with a sudden awareness of how new this was to me. I had never been kissed, and certainly not like *this*. Kaspian sensed my pause and opened his eyes to meet my wide gaze. I took in how close we were, how his swollen lips hovered above mine, and how flushed his cheeks were.

His gaze turned from hungry to gentle in a heartbeat, and he removed his hand from my waist, reaching up to cup my cheek. 'You are truly the most beautiful thing I have ever seen,' he breathed against my lips. My stomach somersaulted as he planted a kiss on my lips so soft I could have imagined it. Then another on the end of my nose. Then another on my forehead. Then another in my hair. I was sure I whimpered as he held my head to his chest and breathed me in.

A knock sounded on the door and Luna called, 'Blaise, are you still in there?' Her voice poured ice water on the moment, and I groaned, a mixture of disappointment and relief washing over me. Kaspian chuckled against my hair before tilting my chin up to press his lips to mine once more. It was firm yet brief, promising so many things, saying so many unspoken words.

He pulled open the door and Luna took in the closeness of our bodies, our swollen lips, and flushed skin with a smirk on her face.

'I'll see you around, Blaise,' Kaspian promised, and then marched past Luna, his head held high, and her eyes bulging at what was clearly visible through the material of his medical gown. I linked her arm and pulled her down the hall before she could embarrass me any further.

'Well, I never,' she began with a laugh, and I smacked her arm before she could say anything else, though a smile tugged at my lips, and something else pulled at my heart.

Chapter 39

THE FOLLOWING WEEKS WERE A blur of dress fittings, theme decisions, and helping to relocate those displaced by the Harensarra attack. The ball preparations were in full swing as Kaspian had requested and, if I wasn't aiding with them, I was ensuring that the relocated villagers were settling in a city that was already full to bursting.

Luna reported to Kaspian every day, as asked, to inform him that all was going ahead, and she spent her evenings sneaking into Harensarra undetected to spread word of the event. She even went so far as to glamour herself as a Reili soldier, flaunting Reili's wealth, and bragging about the ball. The aim was to stir up as much hatred as possible, ensuring the Harensarra armies wouldn't want to miss an opportunity to attack so many in one place.

Kaspian had made a full recovery, excusing himself from the medical wing a few days after our last meet to resume his position as general. Thanks to Kaspian's agreement with his mother, more sons of nobility had been drafted into Reili's army, training from dawn until dusk, and making the troop bigger than ever. They trained and stayed close to the palace, as Kaspian wanted to remain within the grounds, which meant the dining hall was full each evening with weary soldiers, drenched in sweat and coated in dirt.

Many of the noble families had decided to no longer stay for mealtimes, only visiting the palace when required. But, where the lords and ladies turned their noses up, and retreated from the hum of the dining hall, I basked in the buzz.

The coven was always a hive of bodies coming and going. There was always a witchling who needed attending to, or a witch who required assistance, and I had missed the noise more than I realised. At first, the empty palace walls had given me time to think, to hear my own thoughts, for once. But I'd grown to realise that your own thoughts could become uncomfortably loud, and it was nice to be surrounded by the gentle chatter of others to fill the void of missing home.

The ball was the topic of conversation most nights. Soldiers were excited to see their wives again and to show them the beauty of the palace and, for those yet to couple up, the ball would be an opportunity to meet all the women Reili had to offer.

Kaspian never paused long enough to dine with us. After each day on the field training, he followed Cole into the dungeons to interrogate the Harensarra soldiers. Though, judging by the cries and shrieks that echoed through the palace walls, they were not being forthcoming with their information.

Speaking to Kas had become a rare treat. One reserved for passing each other in hallways, or on the odd occasion where we made time to ride together through the gardens. Much to my dismay, there had been no more kissing, passionate or otherwise. It seemed foolish to be insecure after the way he had devoured me, and the unspoken promises his touch had offered. However, part of me wondered whether he had finally listened to Cole and the queen, realising that he was making a huge mistake with me.

I parked that worry with all my other frets about every possible thing that could go wrong with our plan – right at the very back of my mind in a locked drawer with a broken key. Another concern, locked tightly away, was the queen. Whilst she could not forbid me from attending planning sessions or luncheons with the rest of her court, she still treated me with utter disdain.

Preferring to pretend I did not exist, she barely glanced in my direction, and she kept Lady Natalia and Lady Aleera closer than ever. It had not escaped my notice the smug looks Aleera cast at every dress fitting. Despite pretending to be from the richest family in Reili, any coin Agnes had given me had been spent on the journey here, and my fake inheritance wasn't really coming, so there wouldn't be a new gown for me. I would have to make do with wearing one of the few I had brought with me.

Luna offered to magic me up one, but magical garments were temperamental at best and, should their creator get distracted, I could just as easily end up naked in the middle of the room as I could wearing a dress that changed colour with every mood. It was one of the only areas of magic, along with the creation of living things, that didn't retain the desired effect once created. Best to stick to non-magicked clothing, no matter how plain.

Aleera had been granted the use of the queen's personal tailor. A fact she enjoyed showing off by having her fittings in the middle of the grand hall, and there could be no denying it, her gown would be spectacular. Second to only the queen's garment.

'She's deluded if she thinks a pretty dress is enough to stop him choosing you,' Daisy had scoffed, and I'd nodded in agreement, but a squirming had begun in my stomach that I hadn't been able to shift.

The excitement for everyone to show off their gowns felt like an energy you could cup and hold. The theme was a masquerade ball – Luna's careful suggestion, which had gone down a treat with the ladies of court, but was ultimately for our own devices. With masks covering faces, the witches would not need a full glamour to slip among the crowd.

It seemed easy. Perhaps *too* easy.

Betraying Kaspian made my chest ache. But, if I called the whole thing off, I would be betraying Agnes and my family. I didn't know if I even *could* call the whole thing off. The witches would be flying overnight to reach Reili in time for the ball the next day. Realising just how close I was to this unfolding, I dropped the lavish golden décor I had been holding with a clang, and everyone in the hall glared at me.

'Pull yourself together!' Luna hissed.

'Nerves,' I grimaced, and Luna studied me carefully as I retrieved the broken parts, placing them on a nearby table with shaking hands.

'Are you sure you can do this?' She spoke in hushed tones.

I swallowed the denial that wanted to burst from my lips and nodded. There was no backing out now.

After a full day of revamping the ballroom, I returned to my chambers and attempted to sleep. Instead, I tossed and turned all night long, replaying every step of the plan in my mind. Luna crept into my room halfway through the night.

'Can't sleep either?' I asked, and she shook her head as she climbed into bed with me, gripping my hand in hers as she lay beside me.

'I'm with you, no matter what happens,' she whispered, rolling to face me.

I twisted to face her, too. 'Do you think we can pull this off?'

'If anyone can, it's you, queen of two worlds,' she offered me a sleepy smile. I swallowed, the made-up title a stark reminder of the impossibility of what I was trying to do. Luna's breathing eventually evened out into the deep steady breaths of sleep, hand still clutching mine, whilst my mind refused to switch off.

Guilt chewed up my insides. No decision I made felt right anymore. No matter what I did, I would be letting someone down, and I didn't know who was more likely to forgive me, my mother, or the man I had yet to acknowledge my true feelings for.

Chapter 40

BY THE TIME THE SUN streamed through my window the next morning, I was more tired than when I had climbed into bed.

'You look like shit,' Luna commented through a yawn.

'We can't all hide behind a glamour!' I snapped back as we dressed and headed down to the dining room to break our fast.

The day was filled with last-minute decorating and finalising every detail. Whilst I would have usually hated every second, I was pleased for the distraction. My head roared with nerves; my stomach coiled with a horrid anticipation.

When I returned to my chambers after a full day's labour, I was ready to sink into a hot bath for at least an hour to rid my body of the sweat, slip into a silver gown chosen from my limited selection, and have Daisy do something fancy with my hair. A package waited on the bed, a large rectangular box made from dark stained wood, and tied with a white silk ribbon. The box alone looked fancier than the entire outfit I had planned. I picked up the surprisingly heavy package and carried it through the door linking mine and Luna's rooms.

'Did you put this in my room?'

Luna, already drawing a bath of her own, looked at me blankly. 'No. If I bought you a present, I would have bragged about it. I'm not good at surprises.'

I placed the package on her bed and stared at it.

'Well, open it!' Luna cooed.

I carefully undid the delicate ribbon and removed the lid of the oak box. Inside lay a beautiful crimson-red gown made from the softest material I had ever touched. As I lifted the dress from the box and held it against my body, Luna let out an appreciative gasp.

The gown was an intricate masterpiece, with a tulle princess skirt that cut in at the waist and plunged slightly at the bosom. Combined with off-shoulder sleeves, the garment was daring, yet sophisticated. Starting from midway up the right side of the skirt, trailing up the bodice and detailing the sleeves, were applique silver leaves that would perfectly match the mask I had already selected. I was lost for words at the sight of it, and a low whistle escaped Luna's lips as she took in the gown from top to bottom, before diving into the box and lifting a note from inside.

I placed the dress gently on her bed before plucking the note from her fingers.

> Please accept this gift and wear this gown tonight so I can find you amongst the masks.
>
> P.S. Cole made me promise no corsets.
>
> Kas.

I clutched the note tightly, reading and rereading before Luna snatched it back from me. I watched as her eyes darted across the page and she let out an excited squeal.

'There's no way he hasn't already made his choice!' she laughed, the sound cold and harsh. 'The fool has fallen hook, line, and sinker for your *fair-maiden-with-an-edge* act. It's worked better than we ever hoped! Now, we'll have a direct line to the throne!' My stomach turned to acid, bile rising in my throat, and my eyes dropped from the wicked delight on her face to the dress I didn't deserve. I needed to sit down.

'What's the matter?' Luna quizzed. 'You got what we wanted. You did it!'

I looked up at her, unable to blink away the tears that had formed in my eyes quick enough to avoid her seeing them.

'Oh. *Oh,*' Luna started, looking aghast. 'You've actually fallen for him, haven't you? Oh, Blaise!' The pity in her expression was enough to make me sink to my knees.

'I thought you knew,' I whispered. 'I thought you knew it was real.' But, of course she hadn't. She would never understand how I could have fallen for a witch-hunter.

'When?' she asked. 'When did it stop being pretend?'

'I don't know if it ever was.' The words were a scary admission. I had barely acknowledged my feelings internally, let alone out loud, and I could feel Luna's eyes bearing into me as I sobbed, still on my knees on the cold stone floor. Then, gentle arms wrapped around me, and my head was on Luna's shoulder as she rocked me gently back and forth, tears slipping down my cheeks and staining the fabric on her chest.

'Foolish girl,' she whispered against my hair. The words were soft. 'Your human heart will either save or damn us all.'

'I didn't mean to, it just happened,' I explained.

'We need to make a plan, and fast,' Luna pushed me away from the comfort of her embrace. 'If you think Agnes plans to let him live beyond tonight, you are an even greater fool than I thought.'

I recoiled.

'Oh, Blaise,' Luna said once more. 'If the people loving him wasn't enough – he hunts us! He is nothing but a threat to your reign! Not to mention, Agnes still believes he's responsible for murdering my coven! If you are to be queen, she will remove all potential threats, starting with Kaspian and Queen Lizabeta.'

'I can explain! I can tell her I don't want him harmed!' I stammered.

'Blaise, do you think she will listen? You don't even know how *Kaspian* will react! He doesn't know who you truly are, Blaise! You and he can never happen! Your only hope is to get him out of here safely before she arrives.'

'He won't ever leave his people.' The words were true and damning.

'You better hope you can convince him to, Blaise. His life depends on it.'

Chapter 41

ONE HOUR, ONE HOT BATH, and one face of makeup later, I sat in silence at my dressing room table as Daisy twisted and curled my hair into an elaborate half-up-half-down do that formed a crown made of my own hair atop my head.

My stomach churned, and I could feel sweat forming in my hair line, threatening to destroy the powder covering my face. Gods, not knowing how I could convince Kaspian to leave, or convince Agnes not to hurt a hair on his head, was making me feel ill.

Daisy didn't seem to notice my uncomfortable silence as she gushed about the dress Kaspian gifted me, and the grand gesture she thought he would make to the kingdom when showing me as his chosen bride. Daisy was a truly sweet person. How would she look at me at the end of the day, when she realised who I was, and whose hair she'd been braiding for the last month? Would I see anger or disappointment in her hazel eyes that were so like my own? Could she really be my half-sister? Would it make her understand my choices more if she was, or lead to further hatred?

THE FALSE QUEEN

Luna entered my room, and I shook my head to clear the tears that were forming. Her deep-emerald gown, and lace black mask, sparkled against her platinum hair.

'It's time, are you ready?' she asked.

'Nearly done,' Daisy replied, sticking a final pin into my hair. She clapped her hands together. 'There! Now let's get you into that dress.'

Daisy held the gown open for me to step into, and Luna pulled it up from behind me, allowing me to slip my arms into the sleeves that sat perfectly below my shoulders. The dress slid on like a silk glove. As promised, there was no corset, not even any ribbons to do up. Instead, a few delicate buttons graced the back, and Luna set about doing them up.

Each place the fabric touched my skin felt like a brand. The dress was perfect, *too* perfect, and I did not deserve it. I wanted to rip it from me. To replace the way the gentle fabric kissed my bare skin with fire. I was certain *that* would hurt less. Both Luna and Daisy stepped back to admire the dress.

'You look beautiful!' Daisy gasped, lifting her hands to her mouth.

Luna nodded in agreement and held out my matching silver mask. 'Don't forget this.' Before leaving the room, she added, 'your gown will rival even the queen's.'

Daisy squealed and followed, her pale blue gown swishing behind her, and I took a deep, steadying breath. Feeling nauseous, I took a moment to strap my dagger to my thigh and adorn the mask before chasing them both out of the room. Tonight, one way or another, everything would change.

———·✦·———

The three of us entered the ballroom together, and the heads of the entire room spun to stare as we entered. Gasps went up from all around the hall, and I clung to Daisy's hand to stop myself from falling, my head spinning already.

'Everybody's looking at you!' Daisy squealed, squeezing my hand. 'I bet they have no idea who it is. Oh, this is so exciting!'

My mouth dried up.

Is it hot in here?

It felt hot.

The nausea was coming in waves.

Luna swiped champagne flutes from a passing tray. 'Here,' she handed one to me, 'you're going to need this.'

I swallowed the bubbly liquid in one, ignoring the way the crispy sweetness made me shudder. Luna watched me carefully from behind her black mask.

'Take mine, too,' she offered, and I accepted gratefully, but this time chose to sip on the golden bubbles instead.

It was early in the evening, but the ballroom was already filling fast. The dance floor was busy, and more guests streamed through the large doors. From the windows, I could see carriage after carriage arrive at the palace gates. Almost the whole of Reili's capital would be here tonight. I swallowed. I wasn't sure the palace was big enough.

Part of our decorating had included erecting large overhead shelters in the palace grounds that would accommodate any overflow and shield them from the winter chill; autumn lost to the dropping temperatures. Luna and I had carefully chosen the location so as not to interfere with the 'landing zone' in the gardens, which was where the witches would make their way into the secret passageways, and into the palace.

With each sip of champagne, I wondered how far away they were. I probably had a few hours, at most, until the secret of who I really was – the rightful heir and daughter of witches – would be revealed. I took another heady gulp. Despite the room filling quickly, I had yet to spot Kaspian. Even with masks covering a large portion of the room's faces, I would recognise his head of hair and cocky grin anywhere.

The three of us milled at the side of the room, next to the large bay windows and drink stands. Eyes trailed me wherever I moved. I was thankful, once more for the lack of corset to the dress, as I was struggling for air as it was. My chest tightened at the thought of Cole, who had made the request. Kaspian had told him not to interfere in his personal life, but Cole had still reminded him that I would hate a corset, making the dress utterly perfect. It seemed like a Cole-shaped attempt at an apology. But what did he need to apologise for? He was right to suspect me, after all. I had built so many friendships here.

How many of them would still be standing after tonight?

It wasn't long before a tall gentleman in a smart black tuxedo and white mask asked Daisy for a dance. She beamed at the man, then at us, before disappearing onto the dance floor, and my heart twisted as I watched her spin around the floor with the grace of a swan in water.

A moment later, a tall man with close-shaven hair that I would have recognised anywhere, made his way towards us. My heart skipped a tiny beat at the sight of Cole in his royal-blue tux – the exact shade of Reili's banners – and matching mask with gold embellishments.

He paused a few inches in front of us and dipped into a low bow. Luna and I both curtsied in turn. 'Ladies,' he rose. 'You both look beautiful this evening.' We inclined our heads towards him in thanks.

'Would you mind, if I had this dance?' he offered a hand to Luna and, despite the mask hiding his cheeks, I could still see the flush creeping up the back of his neck. Luna seemed taken aback, like she hadn't noticed the looks he always cast in her direction whenever they were together.

'I'd love to,' she managed to stammer out before accepting his hand.

I watched as the dancing pairs spun round and round until it began to make me feel sick. I glanced to the throne, where the queen sat in a spectacular gown of gold silks and white lace, the corset pulling her waist so tight it was a wonder she could even sit down. The skirts ruffled in layers of golden ruching, and the colour did not compliment the fiery red hair piled atop her head, which was adorned with white and gold butterfly clips. She alone did not wear a mask to hide her face.

There was still no sign of Kaspian, and I needed some fresh air, so I made my way towards the exit. Luna broke free of her dance with Cole to catch my arm.

'I'm fine,' I told her. 'I just need some air. Go back to your dance, your partner is missing you.' Luna turned to look at Cole, and I used her distraction to slip out of the doors, down the stone corridor, and into the gardens.

There, I took some deep breaths of the crisp, evening air. The sun hadn't quite set yet, and the light was pink; the breeze gentle with a refreshing bite to it. I stared up at the glowing sky, hoping to catch sight of a witch overhead, but the skies were empty. I should have known the Sunseekers would not risk flying so close to the palace until the skies were inky black. Though they would have been stronger at the sun's highest, this way was safer.

I tried to tell myself I was excited to see them. Gaia. Sapphire. My sisters. Agnes. My family were on their way. And yet, panic flared, and it took another few minutes of deep breathing before my stomach settled enough to return to the hall.

The moment I entered I wished I hadn't. Twirling in the centre of the room, with the entire rest of the floor looking on, was Kaspian. He was dressed in a golden suit that matched his mother's dress, but, where hers looked tacky and detracting, his looked sublime, complementing his tan skin and dark hair. The golden mask, covering only his eyes, caught every glare of light. His sword, strapped to his side, was so well-polished that it rivalled even the glow of the golden mask. His dark hair bounced as he spun and twirled – with none other than Aleera Cresthorn.

My heart plummeted, and I nearly dropped the glass I held.

Aleera looked equally as stunning in the white gown the queen's tailors had made for her, the subtle dress the portrait of innocence, the white so pristine, it felt like a sin for it to brush along even the cleanest floor. The princess skirt seemed to glide as she twirled on the balls of her feet, the pearled corset so tiny, I wasn't entirely sure where she'd put her insides in order to fit into it. It wouldn't have contained even one of my breasts.

The thin sleeves were made from the purest of feathers, and her exquisite mask was all pearls and matching white down. Her yellow hair was tied back into a neat bun, adorned with a pearl comb.

The crowd watched the pair of them spin and twirl like they were the only pair in the room, and the wide grin spread across Aleera's face only widened when she caught sight of me stood hopelessly in the doorway. She twisted and dipped, tilting her head back, allowing her long white neck to point at me as the prince caught her in a bent arm.

His ocean eyes met mine for a brief moment and I couldn't take it. My heart snapped in two, and I bolted from the room, glass clattering to the floor behind me.

CHAPTER 42

HALFWAY TO THE GARDENS A voice – *his* voice – called after me.

'Blaise, wait!'

My mind screamed at me to keep running, but my traitorous heart took control of my limbs and I spun to face him as I stopped, panting. When he caught up to me, he was equally out of breath. Neither of us said a word, our heavy breathing filling the corridor, and he removed his mask so I could truly see him.

But I kept seeing the smile on his face as he had spun *her* around the dance floor. It had been the smile that showed off that irritating, stupid, infuriating dimple. My favourite smile. The one I had stupidly thought was reserved for me.

'You wore my dress,' his voice was low, and it snapped me back to reality. 'You look beautiful! More beautiful than I ever imagined!' Hurt turned to seething anger in a heartbeat.

'Why did you bother gifting me such an expensive gown? Did you want me to feel grateful while you pummelled my heart into the ground? Or was it just to get my hopes up and make me feel like even more of an idiot when I realised I meant nothing to you!' My voice rose in volume and pitch with every word, and Kaspian staggered back like I'd punched him in the gut.

'What are you talking about?' he had the gall to ask.

I huffed an exasperated laugh and spat, 'oh, forgive me! Was I not supposed to notice your little *show* with Aleera?'

'Blaise, I was just fulfilling your promise!' he winced.

'My, my what?' My anger quelled in an icy wave, replaced with utter confusion.

'You promised my mother you would get me to dance with Aleera at the next ball. I thought I would oblige and then, hopefully, she would be off our backs for the rest of the evening. At least then, you could tell my mother that you did everything you could before I made my choice!' He rubbed a large hand over his face and through his hair. 'I'm sorry, I should have told you the plan. I can see how that looked. I've never been very good at this.'

I stared at him. 'You mean you're *not* choosing Aleera?' I asked, words practically a whimper.

He rushed towards me and pulled my mask from my face to look me in the eye. 'Gods, no! Blaise, how could I? *Why* would I? I thought the gown made it obvious. Oh, bloody Hell! You're really going to make me say it, aren't you? Blaise, I choose *you*!'

I stared at him, dumbfounded, not sure what to do with the words he had laid bare between us. 'Why?' I squeaked out.

He laughed, a low chuckle that made my hairs stand on edge, and pulled me into his arms. 'Are you really trying to tell me you had no idea? You thought I would choose *Aleera Cresthorn* over everything we've shared together? Blaise, you saved my life! *Twice*! I showed you a waterfall I've only ever shared with Cole. And I don't make a habit of parading into the grand hall in a medical gown for just anyone, you know.'

'When? When did you?' I didn't know what I was asking.

'Blaise, it's been you since the moment you ate two slices of Otto's chocolate gateaux. Gods, probably even before that! It could have been the moment you raced me through the gardens, or when you called me "Your Kaspian". Maybe even when you told me you could handle yourself in that seedy tavern, before I even knew who you were. Blaise, there was never – *is* never – going to be anyone else.'

My heart skipped several beats, and I stared at him unblinking as every cell in my body sung to the tune of his confession.

'Say something,' he pleaded, bringing me back to my senses.

I *couldn't* say anything. I didn't have the words for how much his confession meant to me. I felt like I could take on anything. The plan felt like it would be a breeze, with the wind from Kaspian's declaration powering through my sails. Instead of answering with words, I reached up and pressed my lips to his. It was answer enough for Kaspian. His hands grabbed for my waist, pulling me closer to his body as his lips crashed against mine in a torrent of pressure, both greedy and loving.

My lips parted slightly as a groan escaped them and it was all he needed to dart his tongue inside, flicking gently over my own, and curling against the roof of my mouth. My hands found their way into his hair, as his began roaming my backside, pushing me flush against his body as they worked. Another gentle moan racked through me just as one escaped his own lips.

I pulled away briefly to stare up at him, taking in the way he looked at me with such softness and adoration, like he was looking at a goddess, at the Mother herself. I reached up and brushed a thumb over the dimple that had returned to his cheek as he grinned my favourite smile, and whispered, 'you're maddening.'

He winked, 'I know.'

I shook my head, a soft smile on my lips. 'It's only ever going to be you for me, too, Kas.'

His answering smile was so wide, it was a wonder it didn't split his face in two, and his lips were back against mine in an instant. They trailed a blazing line across my jaw, down my neck, and along my collar bone. I could feel him everywhere, and yet it wasn't enough, and heat pooled at my very core as I pulled his lips back to mine.

He gripped my face as he walked me backwards, never relenting the perfect pressure of his kiss. My back met a wall, and I gasped as his hip bones met mine, the friction welcome. He fumbled with a door handle, and then he was moving me backwards again. I met another wall, and he kicked the door shut behind us, his lips never leaving mine.

I couldn't get enough. I felt starved for this man, and I fisted my hands in his hair as his lips began another descent along my neck. I writhed my hips against him, and he stopped the trail of kisses along the curve of my breasts to meet my gaze. His eyes were searching, and whatever he found was answer enough as he ground against me, the friction forcing a moan from my lips. His hands were suddenly at the bottom of my skirts, hoisting them around my waist, and the way his callused hands scraped along the insides of my thighs, brushing over Agnes's dagger that was sheathed there, elicited another moan from me.

He brushed the dagger again. 'Hopefully I won't need saving tonight,' he murmured against my throat.

My heart rate sped. I was praying he wouldn't either.

Before the purpose of the evening could catch up to me and steal my focus, Kas's thumb moved aside the delicate undergarments I had on and caressed the coarse curls between my legs, and I was sure he could feel the heat there, beckoning, inviting him closer. He lifted one hand up to cup my face as the other stroked gentle circles just above the curls. 'If you want me to stop, say it,' he whispered. *Never.* There would never be any part of me that wanted this to end.

His lips found mine again as one of his fingers slipped between my thighs and into the wetness that waited. Every muscle in my body went taut, homing in on the way his finger sunk in and out of me. I was sure I whimpered as I rested my forehead against his, writhing my hips, wanting more, *needing* more contact to burn against the heat spreading through me.

His other hand cupped my breast through the dress and squeezed, and a breathy moan exited my lips. He shifted his hips against my leg. I could feel how much he wanted more, too. His want strained against his trousers, pressing into my thigh. Imagining his thickness released, coupled with the way his finger sunk into me, and how his thumb circled the sensitive bundle of nerves at my centre, pushed me over the edge, and release barrelled through me in waves.

He slipped his finger from me and sucked it into his mouth, eyes rolling back in pleasure, and it was the most erotic thing I had ever seen. Desperate for more, I began to fumble with the buttons of his trousers, but he caught my wrist, halting me.

The sting of rejection felt ridiculous given all that had just transpired between us, and he must have noticed my expression fall, because he cupped my face, pressing a gentle kiss to my lips to whisper, 'the first time I have you, it will not be in a broom cupboard.'

I looked around for the first time and, sure enough, found myself pressed against the wall of a tiny storeroom. I chuckled and let myself lean against him. He lifted my chin and bent to kiss me once more but, as he did, an almighty BOOM sounded from somewhere in the palace.

The pair of us froze in stunned silence, as another crash echoed through the stone walls.

I gulped.

The moment was over.

Harensarra were here.

Chapter 43

COURSING ADRENALINE RUSHED THROUGH me, diluted with sheer panic as I realised *this was it*.

Confused, Kas gripped my hand and dragged me from the cupboard – and headfirst into Luna, whose mask was ripped from her face, exposing wide green eyes and freckles that had paled to a ghostly hue.

'You have to get out of here!' I told Kas, voice trembling.

'What are you talking about?' He captured my face in his hands when he saw the terror in my eyes. 'Blaise, I'm a soldier! Nothing is going to happen to me! We don't even know what that noise was.'

'Men are coming through the windows!' Luna gestured towards the ballroom, and my stomach twisted with guilt.

'Kas!' I pleaded as he released my face. From the determined set of his jaw, I knew he wouldn't listen. I'd wasted any chance I had of getting him out of here on a moment of pleasure.

'Stay here!' Kaspian growled, sword already in hand. He'd gotten all but a few steps when he spun on his heel to face me once more.

Closing the gap between us, he buried a hand in my hair and lifted my face to meet his, crashing his lips against mine with hungry desire that almost made me sob.

He hitched up my skirts, and I would have flushed had he not wrenched my dagger from its sheath and handed it to me, tugging the hem back down. 'Use it if you have to.' I flipped it out of habit, watching it spin in mid-air and catching it by the ruby-decorated hilt.

Kaspian grinned. 'That's my girl. Stay together,' he nodded at Luna. 'And stay safe!' Then, he turned once more and ran towards the cries echoing through the palace.

'Mother above! That made even *my* knees go wobbly!' Luna teased. She sniffed the air. 'You smell like sex.' I silently cursed the heightened senses of witches.

'Come on! We have to move, and fast!'

———— ·✦· ————

Harensarra soldiers had infiltrated the walls quicker than expected, and chaos had spread across the lower levels of the palace. Screams of terror filled the air, and dresses of all colours zoomed past us as women desperately fled the scene, screaming for their loved ones who had joined the fight.

Grunts of pain and clashing metal were ringing out from the ballroom, but Luna and I couldn't assist there. We had to get to the gardens. I begged whatever Gods were listening to keep Daisy, Cole and Kaspian safe until I could find them and ensure it for myself. I gripped my dagger so hard the ruby hilt left indents in my palm, and Luna lifted a sword, that had been glamoured to fit in her bag, as we pushed through the fray.

Harensarra soldiers streamed by, and we slunk against the walls. It seemed impossible there were this many of them! The unmistakable squelch of a sword tearing through skin and guts came from nearby, and another wave of nausea nearly toppled me.

A soldier in Reili's royal-blue guarded a gaggle of finely-dressed nobles, directing them towards the open front doors. Outside, carriages tried to load as many people in as possible before heading back out towards various towns and villages – anywhere away from the palace.

This ball had been *my* idea. These innocent people were fleeing for their lives because of *my* plan. We had drawn Harensarra here, and the ball had made the Reili people sitting ducks. The people's trip to the palace had been a once in a lifetime opportunity that had ended in fear and panic.

Because of me.

Another flow of townsfolk rounded the corner, a Harensarra soldier hot on their heels. With a cruel laugh, he reached for a woman and dragged her backwards by her skirts, delighting in her terrified shrieks.

Cursing, I launched my dagger at the disappearing purple uniform, and a grunt told me it had met its target, allowing the group to disappear out of the large double doors and sprint towards the nearest carriage.

With a mighty creak, the ballroom doors almost tore from their hinges, as both common folk, and soldiers from both sides, rushed into the corridor. I strained my neck for any sign of Cole or Daisy, who had been inside when the attack started, but it was difficult to pinpoint anyone in the sea of masked faces.

Luna didn't hesitate, striking down anyone in purple that headed in our direction. Groaning, I realised my dagger, and only weapon, was still lodged in the back of a soldier's head.

I whirled, desperately looking for another weapon. I caught sight of a fallen soldier still clutching his sword. It was all I needed. As weapons clashed behind me, and shouts rang from every direction, I sprinted towards the dead man, noting the blue uniform and gold crest that marked him as a member of the Royal Guard. When I saw his face, my knees buckled.

Thomas.

The man who had saved me in the tavern all those weeks ago.

His brown eyes stared up at me, unseeing. Mousey hair was plastered to his head, slick with sweat. His face eternally frozen in a painful grimace, due to a deep wound in his stomach still pumping enormous amounts of blood, as if unaware it had already rendered Thomas dead.

With nothing to go off but his hometown and his first name,

Kaspian had found the man that had saved my life twice and rewarded him, as promised, with a spot on the Royal Guard.

I had gotten him killed.

I might as well have swung the blade myself.

My breaths came hard and fast. Hyperventilating and unable to tear my eyes from Thomas's own blank gaze, only Luna's voice, yelling at me to duck, brought me back to the present.

I crouched just in time, as a sword swiped above my head. I couldn't hesitate a moment longer. I swiped Thomas's steel – ignoring the way his already-stiffening fingers held on a little too tight – and spun to face my attacker.

He could have been handsome, if not for a large purple scar that ran the full length of his face, like someone had run a stained penny perfectly down the centre. His fair hair stuck to his forehead from damp sweat, and his uniform looked several sizes too small. Undeterred by the strain his shirt had on his biceps, he swiped at me again, but I was smaller and faster. I barely felt my sharp blade slice through the man's torso, a spray of blood splashing my face.

I moved. Each face a blur, as I looked for purple and attacked, vaguely aware of Luna doing the same beside me. We were alongside around twenty soldiers in blue, who didn't at all seem to question two women in ball gowns fighting alongside them. Every move Agnes and Gaia had taught me came naturally, and I was thankful for the hours I had spent training in dresses, for I knew exactly how to spin out of reach without getting tangled. It felt weirdly exhilarating to finally put my skills to use without restraint.

We were being herded towards the rear end of the palace, and the more purple bodies we chopped down, the more filed through the open ballroom doors and into the corridor. Corpses littered the floor, making it virtually impossible to place a foot down without the sickening crunch of bones, or the squelch of bloodied limbs.

My sword met another, and my arm screamed in protest. There was no way I could keep this up for much longer. How much time had passed? It could have been minutes or hours since the fight began. Everything blurred into moments of attacking, blocking, and retreating.

'Where are they?' Luna hissed, between the clangs her sword made against her attacker's.

'They'll be here,' I promised.

They had to come.

Agnes had promised.

Even if we didn't make it to the gardens to meet them, the witches knew the plan. Knew to get themselves into the castle and join Reili's troops.

A loud crash was followed by reinforcements in blue uniforms bursting into the corridor, and I heard Luna breathe a sigh of relief as a long arm swung over the top of our heads, downing the soldiers both she and I had been fending off.

I spun to thank our saviour and came face-to-face with Cole. I could have hugged him, but Luna beat me to it, throwing her arms around his middle.

'You beautiful great lug!' she laughed, as the last of the Harensarra soldiers in the corridor fell. Cole had also found Daisy, and Aleera Cresthorn, who were so close to him they practically hung from his legs. Tears tracked down Aleera's cheeks, but Daisy's jaw was set in a firm line, eyes determined. A crimson flush was already taking hold of Cole's neck and cheeks as he pulled himself free of Luna's grip.

'Come on, there's more of them. We need to get out of here!' he gripped her pale hand and pulled her along the hallway. I grabbed Daisy's arm before she could run after him, pressing Thomas's sword into her hands. Her eyes widened in panic.

'Quick, in here!' I shoved her and Aleera into the nearest room. 'I'm going to lock the door behind me.' I plucked the key from the inside, thanking the Gods it had been left there. 'Stay here until this is over, and if anyone breaks through the door, stick the sharp end somewhere soft!'

Aleera whimpered, but Daisy nodded, gripping the sword and raising it, ready to jab it through flesh if she had to. Wishing I had time to hug her, and that I wasn't leaving her with only Aleera and her terror for company, I locked them both in the room and ran to catch up with Cole and Luna. I snatched another discarded sword as I weaved through a few of the braver townsfolk, who had also picked up fallen weapons and joined the fight.

'Where's Kaspian?' I asked.

'With the queen,' Cole responded.

'Well, where is the queen?' I tried again.

'Safe. For now.' His words were clipped as he led us out of the back door and into the palace gardens. He cast a look back at me as we made our way outside, the night air cool against the sweat on my forehead, and whatever he saw on my face made his expression soften.

'They're safe,' he vowed. 'Kaspian will join us as soon as reinforcements arrive to protect the queen.'

'Reinforcements from where?' Luna asked.

'Anyone that survived the initial attack on our borders has been called back to the palace. There's no point them defending something that has already been infiltrated.'

'But that could take hours?' I questioned.

Cole nodded.

Where in the Mother's name was Agnes?

A quick look around the gardens told me the witches hadn't arrived yet. No forms lingered in the shadows. No discarded brooms littered the grounds. A mild panic that they weren't coming coursed through my veins.

'It's cold,' Luna complained, as if the chill was the worst thing she'd faced this evening. Neither me nor Cole could answer before a swarm of Harensarra soldiers ran from the palace and chased us further into the gardens.

Cole pushed us behind him as the fighting began anew, but we jumped out from the limited protection of his large body, tearing through the soldiers aiming right for him. He blinked at Luna in surprise, his eyes narrowing towards me. I rolled my eyes, and stuck my sword into the gut of an approaching soldier for emphasis. Cole grunted once in mild approval before launching himself completely into battle.

'Seriously, where are they?' Luna asked again. 'They should be right where we are now!'

I didn't have the answer, so I said nothing. Luna grunted as she brought her sword down to clash with an attacking soldier. I darted around the other side of her attacker and pushed my sword through his back, wincing at the now-familiar sound of pierced organs.

Sweat dripped from my forehead, and my hands were beginning to cramp around the sword. It should have been over by now. With each passing minute, more innocent people died.

Distracted, years of training went out of the window, and I tripped over my twisted skirts, landing on my backside. I looked up into the brown eyes of my attacker, who looked as exhausted as I felt as he lifted his sword once more to bring it down on top of me. I was forced to roll sideways, and his almost lethal blow caught in my skirt, tearing a large chunk from the bottom. I silently mourned the beautiful dress, before realising my new advantage.

I jumped back to my feet. 'Many thanks, you've done me a favour,' I mumbled, my legs free to move more easily with the bottom layer of skirt removed. My gratitude ended with a blade through his side. He collapsed beside me as a commotion from the palace caught my attention.

People were running out of the doors in every direction, some pointing towards the sky. I tried to look up but was tackled to the ground. I dropped the sword in surprise, as all the air in my lungs escaped in one painful whoosh. Despite not being able to breathe, I tried to raise my arms, ready to defend any potential blows with my fists, but when I looked up at my assailant, a familiar ocean gaze found mine.

Kaspian hovered above me, shielding me with his body, quick apologies tumbling from his lips. Cole was at his back, defending the pair of us as a feral-looking Harensarra soldier swung wildly. Cole parried and spun, finally besting him with a punch to the ribs and a sword through the lungs.

'I'm so sorry!' Kaspian babbled again. 'You weren't looking! You almost got butchered right in front of me and I didn't think! I'm so sorry!' Before I got enough air down to tell him it was okay, a series of almighty thuds crashed around us, and screams of horror pierced the night as the ground shook.

The witches had landed.

Chapter 44

BROOMS LAY DISCARDED AS THE witches threw themselves into the attack, tearing down soldier after soldier in purple with no effort at all. I heaved a sigh of relief, half sobbing, half laughing, as an army of witches tore towards the castle leaving Reili's soldiers untouched. Kaspian leapt to his feet, pulling me up with him. He stared dumbfounded at the events unfurling in front of him. Cole rubbed at his eyes, like he couldn't believe what he was seeing.

'Y-your orders, Sire?' he stammered, looking to Kaspian.

I held my breath.

'Go and help them, dammit!' Kas called to his soldiers. 'Until every last one of those Harensarra bastards is either killed or captured, assume they are on our side!' He turned to Cole. 'We decide what to do about them after. Spread the word!'

I released a gush of air, and Luna did the same beside me. The witches weren't safe, by any means, but Kaspian's order had bought them time. Time to prove they were here to help. Every soldier in the gardens, including Cole and Kaspian, launched themselves towards the bulk of the fighting now making its way back inside the palace walls. Spells bounced everywhere as the witches battled on, now in harmony with the Reili soldiers.

I made to follow when I was nearly tackled again by Ophelia launching herself at me, and throwing her arms around me in a hug so fierce I had to double-check it was really her. She had never hugged me in all our nineteen years, and was she . . . crying?

Not far behind her was Marbella, who didn't scoop me up in the same fashion as Ophelia, but shot me an uncharacteristically bashful smile, tears welling in her own eyes, before she took my hand and linked her fingers through mine.

'You need to get out of here, Blaise! This isn't what you think it is! She isn't here to –'

'Phe!' Marbella snapped, stopping Ophelia midsentence. 'You can't! She'll know it was you. She'll kill you!'

Ophelia paled, her violet eyes filling with terror. She looked over my shoulder to find Luna watching us in silence. My heart cracked as Luna's eyes filled with unshed tears. She wouldn't get her own family reunions.

'You!' Ophelia addressed Luna. 'You have to get her out of here! She isn't safe! None of you are safe!'

'What do you mean? Agnes came! You all came!' It didn't matter that they were late. They'd come. I beamed at her.

'No, it's all wrong! It's all wrong!' Ophelia clutched the sides of her head, rocking slightly. Panic gripped me in its vice. I looked to Marbella for reassurance, but her onyx eyes were fixed on her favourite sister, laced with concern.

'It's too loud for her. There are too many thoughts. I need to get her somewhere quiet.' Marbella tried to pull Ophelia away from me, but she removed her hands from her head in a flash and dug sharp nails into my shoulders.

'No! I have to help! You must listen to me, *please*! You need to leave!' Ophelia begged. 'She'll ruin everything!'

'Ophelia, you have to tell me what you mean!' I tried prying her nails from where they had embedded in my flesh, drawing blood, but she clung tighter, eyes wide in panic.

I gritted my teeth against the pain. 'Marbella, what is she talking about?'

'I can't tell you! She'll kill her if she knows it was us! And she'll know! She *always* knows!' Her eyes shuttered as if reliving past horrors. Ophelia screamed, tearing her nails from my skin, clutching her head once more. Blood ran down my shoulders from the puncture wounds.

There had to be thousands of people in the palace grounds, and Ophelia could hear every one of their minds. I could only imagine the sheer terror she was experiencing through others right now. How loud everything must be in her head. She sunk to the ground, sobs racking her body.

'Phe,' Marbella coaxed, dropping to the ground beside her. 'Phe, it's going to be okay! Blaise is going to be okay! She's leaving now. Aren't you?' She shot me a pointed glare that said I didn't have to leave the grounds, I just needed to not be *here*.

I nodded, understanding. 'Yes, we're leaving now!' I backed away, gripping Luna's wrist, dragging her with me as we retreated from a sobbing Ophelia and a stone-faced Marbella.

We were headed back towards the palace when the fighting burst through the doors towards us. This time, it was Harensarra soldiers who had been forced out into the dark night, with witches and the Reili army surrounding them, forcing them further into the open.

My heart leapt as I caught sight of Sapphire and Gaia, with Kaspian and Cole alongside them. It was a vision made true, of the future I dreamed of. A future where everyone, regardless of power, worked alongside one another. This plan was going to work! The humans were seeing what a help the witches could be.

Humans and witches alike were tending to the fallen Reili soldiers. Humans were coming to the aid of witches when Harensarra soldiers tried to sneak up from behind, and witches were casting protective spells over the remaining Reili army. They were becoming a team, better than I could have ever hoped for.

There were only a few Harensarra soldiers remaining, and they were surrendering, swords dropping to the ground and arms raised in a sign of peace. A group of Reili soldiers rounded up those who had given up the fight and led them inside the palace, likely to the dungeons.

I stared open-mouthed as the fighting finally ceased, and witches extended hands to fallen humans. The humans took them – without recoiling at the elongated fingers – allowing the witches to help them to their feet. I'd all but forgotten what would come next. It didn't seem important anymore. Kaspian had chosen me. We would rule together. Agnes would see her plan work after all.

Cole noticed Luna and I, and made his way over, eyes roving us both up and down, determining we were okay. Most of the blood I was covered in was not my own, apart from the already-scabbing holes that Ophelia had left in my shoulders and a few scratches.

Luna rushed to him and threw her arms around his neck, pulling him tightly against her. He hesitated at first, then hugged her back, dipping his head low as to rest on her forehead. I was only looking at an embrace, but it somehow felt more intimate, and I looked away, trying to find Kaspian's face in the crowd. I spotted him making his way towards me and grinned.

'KASPIAN!'

I grimaced as the queen came flying out of the palace doors, eyes on her son.

'How dare you let these *things* into my home!' she gestured to the witches. Wisely, none of them reacted.

Kaspian spun to face her. 'Mother, they have come to our aid! Perhaps you could show a little more gratitude!' My heart skittered. Something inside me knew then that he couldn't be the monstrous witch hunter the world had accused him of. Not when he had given them a chance to help.

'You are a fool! Look around you! See how easily they tore these soldiers down! You think they won't turn on you, too? We're *all* human to them! And *they* . . . they are abominations! Guards! Seize them all! Burn them all!' The queen's red hair tumbled from its pins, her dress dirty and torn, voice hoarse from screaming.

Nobody moved.

'I gave you an order!' she shrieked.

The army turned as one and looked to Kaspian. My heart swelled. They did not answer to her. They answered to their king.

'Stand down, Mother,' Kaspian commanded, voice full of authority, as the queen picked up an abandoned dagger and made her way towards the nearest witch. The witch laughed, whipping the dagger away on a gust of wind.

Queen Lizabeta howled in fury and retrieved a fallen sword, swinging at the witch, who leaped out of the way just in time. She placed a protective spell around herself, the bubble of magic reflecting in the moonlight.

'Someone grab her before she hurts herself!' Kaspian ordered.

A lone guard glided towards her, and I looked to Luna to see if she had seen what I had – the unmistakeable sheen of a glamour surrounding the man as he moved – but she still hadn't dragged her gaze from Cole. The guard clutched the queen's wrists, holding them behind her.

'Unhand me! Unhand me at once!' she raged. 'I am your *queen*!'

'You are no queen of mine,' the guard said, before taking his sword and driving it deep into her belly.

Chapter 45

'*NO!* I SCREAMED, AS QUEEN Lizabeta fell to her knees, blood gushing from the wound in her stomach and pouring from her mouth.

The guard's glamour dropped to reveal flowing golden hair, and a striking face I would recognise from a mile away. A hiss went up from the crowd as Agnes's unnatural silver eyes, pointed ears and extra knuckles made her unmistakeable as a predator. Kaspian stared in disbelief as his mother crumpled to the floor and Agnes withdrew the sword, driving it once more right through the queen's heart.

'I've waited nineteen long years to do that!' she spat.

For a heartbeat, the world stopped spinning. Then, chaos erupted, the easy atmosphere between peoples vanishing in a split second. Soldiers picked up their swords. Witches took defensive stances, hands poised ready to protect and attack.

No.

It was all falling apart.

So quickly, everything I had envisioned for my peoples was crumbling. My knees threatened to buckle.

'*You!*' Lizabeta's voice was garbled, a death rattle.

'Me,' Agnes beamed. 'I told you I'd come for you! That not even your precious *prince* would save you!' She cackled, and it was the most awful sound I'd ever heard.

Lizabeta's eyes were drifting away. She was dying, but smiled like she found the whole thing poetic. She reached out a hand, and it was as though she could see something the rest of us couldn't.

'My love, you waited for me,' she forced out, and then the light left her eyes completely.

Agnes's rage was palpable. Even in her last moments, Lizabeta's love for her husband – the fallen king, *my father* – was unrivalled. Kaspian ran towards his fallen mother, and I ran after him, certain of what was coming next. Luna's and Cole's footsteps pounded behind me.

'Kas, don't!' I bellowed as he tried to run past Agnes to his mother. In one fluid movement, Agnes dropped her sword and grabbed Kaspian's wrist. Spinning him into her body, she summoned a dropped knife, the hilt flying into her hand, and she pressed it to his throat.

'Please!' I begged, coming to a halt in front of them. 'Please don't!'

I tried to reach for Kaspian, but drew short as a protective bubble was cast around them, shielding them both. Several soldiers tried to rush the bubble and found themselves flung backwards, howling as their limbs were severed by the steaming spell. It was magic I'd read about, but never seen. Dark magic. I spat the bile that rose in my throat onto the ground.

Not deterred, more soldiers tried to pierce the protection, desperate to save their king. They, too, were flung backwards, until it was clear that no one was getting through Agnes's charm. They could only watch in horror as she pushed the knife deeper against Kaspian's throat. For the first time, Agnes's eyes landed on me, and she smiled. A twisted thing that I couldn't return.

'This wasn't the plan!' I whimpered, each word laced with both icy rage and undeniable pain. 'There could have been peace between our peoples! You have destroyed everything!'

'*Peace*? There could never be peace between us, naïve, insolent child! These people have burned us alive for centuries, and you thought we could ever live in peace?' She cackled, cold and bitter. 'No, my sweet child! This was always about revenge!'

I looked around to the other witches who filled the gardens, some of them nodding in agreement, anger and a cold excitement in their eyes. But many shook their heads. This was a clear betrayal of why they had come. Relief flooded me when I saw both Gaia and Sapphire among those with shame in their eyes.

'Then why did you send me here? I will not rule this way!' I didn't dare look at Kaspian. I couldn't stomach his reaction to the words that were a confession of the real reason I was here. An admission of my betrayal.

Agnes's golden hair bounced as she tipped her head back and laughed. 'Your gullibility is becoming tiresome, child. As if I ever intended to give you the crown! No, darling, you were simply my way in. My spy. My weapon!'

'But I am the rightful heir! I am King Kaspian's daughter!'

A gasp went up from around the gardens. A nervous, tangible energy, enunciated by shocked whispers. Cole stiffened beside me, and I risked a glance at Kaspian, as the realisation of exactly who I was settled into his face.

'How could you?' He spoke through gritted teeth, each word scraping the blade along his throat, drawing blood. The sight started a scorching fury in my blood that ran along my veins, making it hard to concentrate on anything else.

'What's that, boy?' Agnes ran the flat edge of the blade along his jaw. The way she looked at him only made the fire that crawled through my insides burn hotter. 'Disappointed in my dear daughter, here? Mother above, aren't we all. I thought by now she would see the truth. How all of *this*,' she gestured around her with one hand, keeping the knife in her other pressed to Kaspian's throat, 'has been in motion since before she was born.'

She addressed me as she said, 'I, too, wanted peace once, child. I did everything I could to give us a life where we didn't have to hide. I even enchanted the king of Starterra to surrender the war to Reili, giving your *father* everything he ever wanted – even the babes he craved with that wretch! Children she could never give him!' her neck cricked towards Lizabeta's lifeless body. 'And *still*, it wasn't enough for him to love me as I was!'

Her eyes shuttered, grip on the dagger loosening slightly, and I realised then, that this had always been about love. Agnes had loved King Kaspian, in her own twisted way. She had denied it ever since, but there was no denying that look on her face – like her heart had been torn from her chest.

I was sure I wore the same expression.

'I showed him who I really was, trusting his love was true, hoping that we would find sanctuary and peace in Reili. But . . . well . . . you know the rest. He betrayed me and I was forced to kill him.' Her eyes snapped from grief to anger in a heartbeat.

'So, do not lecture me about peace child! I tried to have it, and humans denied me it! And now, I will offer them the same courtesy!'

Chapter 46

'MOTHER MINE,' I STARTED, PUSHING as close as I could to her protective bubble. 'It doesn't have to be this way! Look at the way we all worked together today. Kaspian chose me! We can rule together! Our sisters will be safe here!'

'Fool!' Agnes huffed a laugh. 'He chose you, did he? He did not know who you are! It is the same tale, repeated.'

I dared a look at Kaspian. His anguished eyes were pinned on me. 'I do not think so. His love is true.'

Gods, I believed it.

The hurt in his expression wouldn't be there if he didn't love me. Whether it would be enough to forgive me, was another matter. Agnes tipped her head back and cackled, her long slender throat exposed to the moonlight. The sound set fire to my veins once more.

'Oh, is that so? Does he know that all of this,' she gestured to the battle scene around us, 'was your plan? Does he know that countless innocent people died today because *you* commanded it? Let's ask him, shall we? Boy, did you know? And do you love her still?'

Kaspian's ocean gaze grew stormy. Anger contorted his jaw, muscles ticking as he gritted his teeth together. Looking at me with such intense disappointment, I wished I could look away, but I knew I deserved it. Deserved much more than the cold and bitter fury in his eyes. I forced myself to hold his gaze and endure it. Staring back, I hoped he could read the fierce, unyielding love in my eyes. He looked away, saying nothing.

'I'll put this right!' I vowed to him.

'Don't.' He spat, still not looking at me. My heart tore in two with an audible shredding so deafening I was surprised no one else reacted to it.

'You see, child! We are nothing to them.'

'I am not the same as you!' I tried to shout, but my throat felt ravaged by the fire still smouldering along the entire length of my body. 'I'm not a witch! I'm human! And I will *not* kill him just because he doesn't return my love!' My voice caught, and tears filled my eyes.

Agnes eyed me with disappointment, before her gaze drifted and landed on Luna behind me. 'Oh look. I missed one,' she snarled as she looked at Luna, whose glamour had fallen to reveal her true self.

Her platinum bobbed hair had become moon-kissed white curls that flowed down her back, and her eyes were pools of fury, blacker than the night sky. Her skin was as soft and pale as the moon's glow, and her once honeyed freckles were now specks of silver stardust dusted across her nose and cheeks. She was one of the most beautiful witches I had ever seen.

Luna paused, letting Agnes's words sink in. Fury lit her features, the moonlight washing her in its glow like it shone just to fuel her rage. 'You'll pay for this!' she growled.

My head snapped between them until it clicked.

I missed one.

I felt like the air had been knocked from me. I'd been right before. 'It *was* you! You killed the Moonkeepers!' I stared in horror at Agnes, barely recognising the woman who raised me, protected me, loved me.

'And the penny drops,' she laughed.

Luna extended her arms, fists balled together above her head, ready to try any spell to blast Agnes from her protective bubble. Having seen what happened to the soldiers that attempted to penetrate that space,

Cole reached out and grabbed her wrists, forcing her hands apart.

I watched as he reached for the girl he had spent a year building a friendship with – perhaps something more – and saw as hurt, anger, and disgust flitted across his face as he beheld the thing she had transformed into. The thing he feared the most. But still, he reached for her. Tugging her out of harm's way. He held her firm but gently as she fought to escape his grip. If that action alone wasn't proof that they could change, I didn't know what was.

My heart couldn't take much more tearing, and the fire inside scorched along the underside of my skin, every inch of me burning as I raged.

It was too much.

Agnes's betrayal didn't only extend to me. She had murdered an entire coven in cold blood, to set things in motion. She had used it to convince me that the witches could be offered a chance at peace. A peace she had never sought in the first place! So many people had died because of her scheming!

'I grow tired of this, Blaise!' my mother tightened her grip on Kaspian, barely casting a second glance at Luna, who was still trying to remove herself from Cole's grip in an almost feral rage. 'Say goodbye to your lover, daughter mine.'

I couldn't breathe.

Fire seared my lungs.

Heat coursed up my throat and behind my retinas.

Luna had stopped struggling. I felt her eyes upon me. Panic was written on Cole's face. Luna's mouth opened and closed as though talking. She could have been calling my name, I didn't know. I couldn't hear beyond the roaring in my ears.

Searing pain burned up my spine.

I twisted and met Kaspian's terrified gaze. The dagger no longer rested at his throat. Agnes was running the blade along it, opening a thin strip of skin at his neck. Terror held me in a chokehold. Unable to move, pressure built behind my eyes, as Kaspian's hands clutched at his throat and came away bloody.

My stomach hollowed, and pain like nothing I had ever felt erupted from my very core at the sight of his blood.

I exploded outwards, the pressure within me erupting.

CHAPTER 47

THE WORLD WAS ON FIRE.

The gardens were no longer full of greens. Instead, they were licked in orange as the flames roared to life, engulfing everything in sight. The blaze crept towards the palace walls, thick smoke billowing in its wake.

The fire that had been burning up my entire body like a horrible fever had flung itself from within me, erupting into the world around me. I must have blacked out, because I hadn't seen it happen, and yet the burning sensation was gone.

Agnes had been flung backwards, releasing her grip on Kaspian, who had fallen to the floor still clutching his throat. She recovered quickly, clambering to her feet, and I thought I registered a momentary glimpse of shock, and perhaps some fear in her eyes, before her mouth spread into a frenzied smile of uncontained glee.

The burning was gone, only to be replaced with pain like I had never felt before, and it speared through my entire body as I tried to claw my way towards Kaspian. My spine seemed to snap, and I could feel – and *hear* – bones clicking and shifting throughout my entire body. I screamed in agony, as the sound around me returned at such an intense volume it was almost unbearable.

Fighting broke out as soldiers tried to get to their king, whose blood was still dripping from his open wound. Agnes danced away, as other witches leapt in to defend her. Her cackle pierced through my skull, and I slapped my hands over my ears.

Ears that were . . . *pointed*.

I pulled my hands away in shock, staring down at them in horror. Long fingers replaced my familiar delicate hands, an extra knuckle on each formed and shifted into place with sickening crunches.

It was excruciating.

Luna dropped to her knees beside me and held me as I screamed. 'What is she doing to me?' I repeated between agonised sobs. Luna placed my head on her shoulder and held me to her, rubbing soothing circles on my back. A strand of sweat-drenched golden hair fell in front of my eyes.

That wasn't right.

My hair wasn't golden, it was brown.

I looked up at Luna, her face so striking in its new beauty that I almost had to shield my eyes. Searching behind her, Cole defended our backs from soldier after soldier getting to us. He didn't strike to kill, just to deter, as fellow members of the Guard – his *friends* – launched themselves at us. I couldn't fathom why he hadn't joined them. Or why he wasn't already at Kaspian's side.

Colours and shapes sprang to life in front of me, allowing me to see further and in more detail than I ever had before. It was as though someone had been holding a thin cloth over my eyes my entire life. I'd been able to see through it, but it had been blocking my true vision.

Throat ravaged from screaming, I gulped down air. Even breathing felt strange. 'What is happening to me?' I sobbed.

Agnes appeared in front of me, as quickly as she had danced away, the glee on her face at odds with everything else going on around us. With a flick of her wrist, Kaspian's body jolted and flew to land roughly on his knees in front of me.

'Take a good look, boy,' she commanded. 'I want you to know what she really is before you take your last breath!'

The terror on Kaspian's face only ramped up when he looked at me.

'You see, daughter mine! They are not capable of loving *us*!' she growled. Flicking her wrists again, Kaspian's body crumpled to the floor, and I ripped myself from Luna's arms to crawl to him.

Agnes howled with laughter. 'Pathetic!'

'What did you do to her?' Luna bellowed, as Cole fell to the ground beside me, reaching for his king.

'What did *I* do to her? I have done *nothing*! She has become her true self! She has broken free from my magic, and she did that all by herself! She's powerful, too! I did not know they served human blood here as a delicacy, Blaise, but somehow you have gotten your hands on some. Only the Rite could have given you this much power!' She gestured towards the world, still on fire around us, soldiers and witches alike were now fleeing from the blaze.

The blood. *Kaspian's* blood. When I had sucked the venom from his arm, had it caused this?

My brain rebuffed her confession. 'This is a glamour. Drop it! I am no witch!'

She barked a laugh as Sapphire approached from behind her, eyes full of sorrow. 'Oh, the irony! Blaise, I have had a glamour on you from the moment I conceived you. A glamour so powerful it was undetectable, even to other witches! Your whole life, you have grown up believing you were human. But *this*,' she closed in and brushed a rough hand over my face, 'this is your true self. And what a beauty you are! A powerful beauty! Do not waste what you have been given. This plan has been in motion for nineteen years, do not undo all my hard work for a *boy*!'

I flinched away, dragging Kaspian's body with me. He had stopped moving. That couldn't be a good sign. Bile rose in my already-ravaged throat.

It couldn't be true.

She couldn't have lied to me for my entire life.

Was that kind of magic even possible? Had I really been born just to be a tool? A *weapon*, in her games?

How many had known what Agnes hid from me? I looked to Sapphire, who moved her head in an almost imperceptible nod. Was this what she had been trying to tell me that day when Agnes's magic had seized hers and Gaia's voices?

'That is enough, Agnes!' Gaia knelt beside me and placed a steadying hand on my back. 'This has gone too far! You promised us peace! She is just a child!'

'Do not even begin to lecture me, Gaia! You have been in on this since she was a girl!' Agnes snarled.

'We should have never been so foolish!' Sapphire drew Agnes's attention.

'Help him!' I begged Gaia, using the momentary distraction. 'If you truly knew about this, you owe me that much!'

She hesitated. Then, she put her hands on Kaspian's throat. Cole tried to pull his body away, but Luna grabbed his arms, letting Gaia heal the wound with her magic. I watched as his skin knitted back together, but he didn't wake. It could be too late. Even magic couldn't bring someone back from the dead. Panic clogged my throat as I felt for a pulse.

There. Weak. But there.

Agnes's hiss brought my attention back to her. She had thrown Sapphire to the ground.

'I will not ask you again, Blaise! Side with me and we can rule together along with your sisters. Ophelia's gifts, Marbella's beauty, and your raw, untrained power, will make us an unstoppable force! We will be free!

'Humans are weak! They possess nothing but hatred! Let us rule as we should. Let us embrace the powerful beings that we are! We should not have to hide, and we will not run from their stakes and matches anymore! Come with me, Blaise, and we can rule the whole world if we want to!'

She was wrong.

Humans weren't weak. They were strong and intelligent and creative. They weren't hateful. They were kind and empathetic and interesting.

I thought of every time a stranger had shown me kindness while I'd been in Reili. I pictured the faces of those I had met, from little Ruthie constantly exploring and running off from her mother – a type of inquisitiveness that would lead to brilliant discoveries. To Otto, who loved to cook and to bake and who had been so overjoyed that I'd eaten two slices of his cake that he'd gifted me the whole thing. To Cole, who had shown me friendship, even in times I didn't deserve it. And to Thomas, who had risked his life to save a stranger, and ultimately given everything for his country. I had to believe they would still do those things, regardless of *what* I was, because they would recognise *who* I was on the inside.

I could still be the bridge between our peoples.

I stood, Luna clutching my hand, helping me to rise on unsteady feet. I thought of her family, murdered in cold blood by Agnes's own hands. Agnes had lost herself so desperately in her revenge for a love that had burned her, that she had turned on those she claimed to protect.

'Look around you, mother mine!' I interrupted her monologue of self-righteousness. 'Look at the peace you destroyed here today! These people, they were our road to freedom. Now, because of you, we are at war once more!'

Scrabbling to my feet, unsteady on my knew limbs, I stood facing her. Everything hurt. But *there*, under all the pain, I felt something new, yet seemingly ancient, lurking in my blood. *Magic*. There had been times I had begged the Mother for this. Now I prayed she would help me use it.

'You made a mistake, not telling me sooner who I was. Because, even though I have the body of a witch, I have the heart of a human, and it is full of love and of wonder. It has not yet been painted black by your poison. And it is fierce!'

Reaching inside myself, desperately clinging to the well of power that had opened like a pit inside me, I threw my hands up in the air like I'd seen the witches do, and poured my new magic into a spell so powerful that Agnes was blown off her feet.

Just as Kaspian took a deep gulp of breath and bolted upright.

Chapter 48

'RUN!' I BEGGED KASPIAN, AS Agnes scrambled to her feet, lips pulled back in a feral snarl.

He stared at me like I had a tail and horns, which, given the circumstances, could have been a real possibility. I gave him a gentle shove and he came to life, picking up a fallen sword and turning his sights on Agnes.

I cursed.

That was the opposite of what I wanted.

'You can't win this fight! You just almost died!' I pleaded with him.

'I won't leave you!' I couldn't read the emotions in his dirt-covered face.

'Touching,' Agnes spat. Her hands poised to defend, not attack, eyes filled with an emotion I had rarely seen flit across her face.

Fear.

'I can't let you die for me! Your people need you!' I told him, ignoring Agnes.

'Then don't get me killed,' he smirked, though the attempt at humour didn't reach his eyes. Eyes that had almost never opened again until seconds ago. I gulped, raising my hands, completely unsure of myself.

Agnes called across the few feet that separated us. 'She has more chance of hurting herself than she does me! She is completely untrained!' To me, she added, 'give this up, Blaise! Join me, and I will train you myself. Help you harness that power to become unstoppable!'

Fires still blazed all around us. Evidence that I couldn't control my power . . . and yet she hadn't attacked again, her silver eyes uncertain. I had an advantage, I realised. My magic had just been born, similar to when a witch performed the Rite and was given her powers for the first time.

That was the most powerful a witch could ever be. Even battle-trained witches wouldn't pick a fight with a newly gifted witch on her Rite Day. Wars had once been waged with newly fledged witches at the front lines, ready to blast enemies apart. I didn't need Agnes's help to become unstoppable. Right now, I already was.

My power had been given life. This was *my* Rite, and I could stop her! Though I'd blasted through a lot of that initial power when my magic exploded out of me, I could still feel it, writhing through my new body, begging me to use it.

'Stand back!' My words were an order to Kaspian, not a request. Despite my new confidence, Agnes was right. I had no training, and I could just as easily hurt myself, or someone I loved, as I tried to take her down. Kas heeded my warning and took several shaky steps behind me, though his weapon remained raised.

Agnes hissed, her anger summoning several other witches to flank her. I gulped. Stopping Agnes would have been hard enough. Then I felt a gentle squeeze on my shoulder, and I looked to my left. Luna stood by my side, looking as fierce as she was beautiful, and I grimaced at my friend, squeezing her hand tight. To my right, appeared Gaia and Sapphire. My mother sneered at their betrayal, but they didn't cower. Cole stood beside Luna, in front of his king. Whether he was there for her, him, or both – didn't matter. He was there, and my heart swelled at the sight.

'We don't have to do this!' I gave her one final chance. 'This can end right now! You can leave, go back home. I will ensure that no humans give chase!'

She laughed as though it was the funniest thing she had ever heard. 'If you really think they will let us walk from this battlefield alive, you are very much mistaken! If you think you have any power over what happens after that, you are even more a fool! And, if you somehow survive this, daughter mine, your *lover* will have you burned at the stake as his first act of king!'

A pause.

I hoped Kas would fill it with a denial, but none came. I put that hurt to one side as Agnes ploughed on, trying once more to get me to join her. 'But it's not too late! I can forgive your betrayal, as it is in part my own fault for keeping you disguised as human for so long. It will take some adjusting for you to get used to who you really are. Join me now, and we can wipe the stain of this race from the world, leaving us to thrive as we should!'

Her sharp canines flashed in a twisted smile that made my blood run cold. I understood then, why humans thought witches to be monsters. I wouldn't be like that. Agnes was right, it *was* her fault that I was human at heart, and no extra knuckles, pointed ears, or golden hair would change that. I stood defiant, still clutching Luna's hand. She squeezed it tight.

'So be it!' Agnes spat, and the world erupted into anarchy once more.

Chapter 49

'RAISE YOUR HANDS! SWOOP YOUR left down! Arc your right arm!'

Gaia yelled instructions at me as we fought, the on-the-fly training better than helplessly waving my arms about and hoping for something to happen. But soon, Gaia became locked in her own battle, unable to offer any aid. Luna fiercely fought two of my mother's minions, and I recognised them from the coven – Hazel and Morganne. If I had to bet, I'd say they'd been on the side that wanted to eat me when they thought I was a human babe.

Sapphire had three witches at her back, and Cole and Kas were also locked in a sword fight with one particularly psychotic witch who seemed to be enjoying toying with them both. Kas's movements were too sluggish to be considered threatening, leaving Cole doing most of the work. Which left one more witch, besides Agnes, who set her sights on me. Agnes watched from behind her, content to let the others get their hands dirty before she intervened.

Taking Gaia's basic instructions, I got a few hits on target, and, thanks to my new power, they were strong enough to send the witch sprawling. But she soon recovered, snarling and baring her teeth.

My magic felt heavy under my skin, like it begged for release, like what I'd already expelled hadn't even taken the edge off.

I don't know how to use you, I silently told it.

Let me help you, it whispered back.

The witch started towards me again and I didn't think. I just moved my arms and magic flung from me. One second the witch was there, the next she was gone.

Someone screamed.

The erratic witch, who had been fighting Kas and Cole, pointed to a mound on the floor in front of me. It took a second for me to understand what I was seeing and, once I did, I wanted to vomit. Before me, were the shredded remains of the witch I had cast a spell at.

Agnes's eyes bulged, and there was no denying the genuine fear on her face. Gaia blinked at the flesh pile, and Sapphire looked as nauseous as I felt. Cole used the distraction to stick his sword through his foe's gut and the witch coughed once, blood spilling out of her mouth as she fell lifeless to the ground.

Two of the witches Sapphire fought had summoned their brooms, taking to the skies without looking back. Around me, the fighting continued. Cole rushed to assist Luna as one of her opponents briefly got the upper hand, and Gaia and Sapphire's remaining enemies continued to wage war.

I looked down at my hands. Hands that had shredded skin and guts until it was just a mound of flesh. Agnes took a step toward me.

'Daughter mine, you harness dark, dark magic, the likes of which has not been seen for centuries! First fire – our greatest enemy – spills from your body. And now *this*! You must reconsider your choice! You must join me! You were born to be my heir, to achieve great things with me! I should have never kept you trapped in that weak body. I see that now! Come to me.' She took another tentative step towards me, arms outstretched like she wanted me to fall into them.

'Stop! Don't come any closer!' My voice wobbled but she stopped, fear radiating from her as I still stared at my hands.

'The humans will never allow you to live among them! Not now they know the power you possess!' Agnes tried a different angle, desperate for me to come with her. I winced. Had this power been gifted to Agnes instead, the world would have already been torn apart. Was the Mother punishing her, or me? For me, it didn't feel like a gift.

I glanced away from my hands, towards Kaspian, who remained fighting alongside Cole and Luna, and my heart strained against my chest. Why had I fallen so hopelessly for someone the world would never allow me to experience a life with? My heart fractured. As it ripped, my magic seemed to thrive under my pain, its goal becoming clear as it whispered to me, *destroy, destroy, destroy.*

Agnes took my hesitation as a sign to step closer. 'Daughter mine,' her voice was softer, more caring than before. It would have been easy to forget everything and see her as the woman who raised me, if my magic hadn't continued to hum with the need to destroy her as she approached. 'I have pushed too far. Forgive me. I have much explaining to do. Come with me. We can go home. Back to the Iron Woods. You miss the woods, don't you?'

My eyes squeezed shut as I pictured the way the willows blew in a gentle spring breeze, the way animals skittered through the camp, and how the witchlings chased them for fun, making adorable squeals of delight. I knew she was playing me, but I longed to return to that simple life. Back before I knew who I was, where I was surrounded by a mother that loved me, and friends that hadn't lied to me my whole life.

Before I met a prince and dreamed of something more.

But no matter how much I missed the forest, it would never be home anymore. There was no going back to a life where I didn't know I was a witch. Where my heart didn't belong entirely to someone else. I opened my eyes once more, and my gaze found Kaspian's. He, Cole, and Luna, had pinned the two witches to the ground, and Gaia held them there with a spell.

Kaspian's sea-blue eyes bore into mine. *He* was my home. Regardless of whether I was welcome.

'Come, sweet child. Come home with me.' Agnes took another step, hand outstretched, a plaintive smile on her face.

Destroy, destroy, destroy, the dark magic hummed louder the closer she neared.

'No!' I screamed. At Agnes, the magic, the world. 'Enough!' I flung my shaky hands out but, this time, Agnes was ready for the burst of magic. She countered, and I could see the wave of power coming for me, unable to move from its path.

I fell backwards, a heavy weight landing on top of me with a grunt, and it took a moment to register that Kaspian had jumped over me, shielding my body with his, taking the brunt of the hit.

'You saved my life,' I was stunned.

'I had to repay the favour at some point,' he tried to smile, but it faltered as he took in my changed appearance. It was a strange time to feel self-conscious, but I panicked under his scrutiny, realising that I had no idea what my new face looked like.

From under Kas's body, I watched as a snarling Luna rounded on Agnes, spell after spell colliding in the air. Kas rose, offering me a hand, and I took it tentatively, expecting him to recoil from my elongated fingers. He held on for a moment, staring at them, no doubt seeing the blood they were stained with, then let go. I winced, but there was no time for the hurt to truly register as I quickly joined Luna.

'That one is for my Mamma!' she yelled, as she landed a blow to Agnes's side, who gasped in pain. 'That one is for my sisters!' Luna cried, as she struck Agnes's back when she tried to dance out of the way. 'And that one, is for Blaise!' she sobbed as she dealt an angry spell to Agnes's chest. Agnes growled with surprise and anger. It wasn't often she was bested in a duel, and her hands moved quickly as Luna tried to wipe the tears from her eyes.

'No!' Cole shouted, grabbing Luna around the waist and hauling her out of harm's way. A spell scorched the ground where Luna had been stood, and she blinked at it, falling back against Cole's chest, clutching the arms still wrapped around her middle for support.

'My patience is wearing thin, child!' Agnes hissed at me. 'Come with me by choice, or by force. Either way, you *will* follow me! Those left alive when you do is determined by how quietly you–'

She trailed off, clutching her stomach, a gaping wound blasted through her middle. Agnes opened her mouth to say something, but blood poured out instead, and she fell to her knees, offering a clear view of her attackers.

Marbella and Ophelia stood, with one of their hands wrapped tightly in the other's, the other outstretched, combining their magic in a blow that had toppled the mighty Agnes. Ophelia looked more composed than the last time I had seen her. The humans had long since retreated to the palace, no doubt allowing her some reprieve from the thousands of thoughts. Marbella wore an expression of thunder, anger rolling across her body in waves.

'My girls,' Agnes sputtered, confused as she too saw who had come for her. 'What is the meaning of this?'

'It's over, Mother,' Ophelia's words were a soft whisper that my newly pointed ears heard clear as though they had been spoken directly into them. 'You kept our sister from us all these years. You made us wary of her human form, even fearful of her. But you will no longer separate us.'

Icy rage spread through my veins. I had believed they hated me, I hadn't realised they *feared* me. That Agnes had been dripping poison in their ears, wanting them to feel that way, wanting to separate us. Ophelia's soft violet eyes met mine, an apology held in her gaze, and Marbella's stony expression softened some as she looked at me.

Agnes laughed a shrill cackle, her teeth stained with her own blood as she tentatively rose to her feet, clutching her entrails to keep them inside her body, using magic to slowly knit the wound together.

I rushed to my sisters, standing in front of them with my arms spread wide to shield them from the onslaught I knew was coming. But they came to stand beside me, shaking their heads. Marbella took my hand first, skin cold against mine.

'We stand together, Sister.'

Ophelia took my other hand. 'Until the end.'

Tears clouded my vision. My whole life, I had longed to be their sister – their *true* sister, not an extra they hadn't ordered. Agnes had taken that from all of us.

I blinked the tears away and looked to my mother, who was weakened, but not destroyed, having stitched herself together enough to move freely. Wiping blood from her mouth on the back of her hand, she attacked. But Ophelia was there, reading every move in her thoughts. Blocking, and blocking again. Marbella's cold fury, and fierce need to protect the other half of her – perhaps one third now, I supposed – drove her forward to attack.

I watched as the two of them moved in sync. Across the grass, Luna was helping Gaia and Sapphire to put an end to the remaining witches, who were feral in their desire to protect their coven leader. Cole and Kaspian had their swords ready in case anything went awry.

My magic hummed, but I ignored the darkest parts of it, focusing instead on the softer strands. I didn't want my mother obliterated into nothing, I just wanted her gone from here. From my home.

When I moved into battle, I was once more reminded that I didn't know what I was doing, but it didn't matter. The fearless Agnes was scared of something, and that something was my power. I didn't land a single hit, Ophelia and Marbella doing everything that I couldn't, but it was *me* she eyed with caution. *Me* she spun away from into the path of a blast from Marbella that forced her once more to her knees.

'Enough!' she spat more blood. 'I surrender!' Her words were short and clipped, her silver eyes filled with rage. Marbella pinned her arms above her head with magic, and Agnes rolled her eyes. 'That is hardly necessary, I have surrendered.'

Marbella smirked. 'You can't be too careful.'

'What do you want to do with her?' Ophelia asked me.

Blood dripped from Agnes's temple and mouth. My fires still raged on behind her. My magic thrummed against my skull.

Destroy, destroy, destroy.

'Agnes Sunseeker, you are banished from this kingdom!' I started. 'Should you ever step foot within its borders again, you will be burned. Now go! And don't come back!'

Agnes smirked.

Ophelia and Marbella looked stunned.

Luna snarled with rage.

Gaia and Sapphire stood unnaturally still.

I looked to Kaspian, and my mercy almost snapped as I eyed the fresh scar on his throat. He evaluated me coolly. The final decision would be his, after all. He was now king. And this was *his* kingdom. After a nod from him, Marbella released Agnes from the spell.

Her silver eyes flashed with something I couldn't read and, before anyone could move, she held out a hand, broom zooming through the air to land in it, and fled into the night sky without so much as a glance back at us.

'Sire!' Cole protested.

'It's too late, Cole. She's gone,' Kaspian sighed. 'Find someone to put these fires out.'

'And the rest of them?' Cole's wariness was etched in every line on his face.

'Find them rooms. And not the dungeons, Cole,' he added. 'Get them a hot meal, and have a healer check them over.'

Cole bowed his head. 'Yes, Your Grace.'

'And Cole,' Kas added, 'ask the guards to retrieve my mother's body.'

CHAPTER 50

THE DAYS THAT FOLLOWED WERE a tired blur. Cole had done as he was asked, and found rooms for Gaia, Sapphire, Marbella, and Ophelia. Kaspian had met with them all privately and asked them, for their own safety, to keep a human glamour on when they were within the grounds.

They weren't allowed to leave the palace for now, until Kaspian could guarantee they weren't a threat to the townsfolk, but they weren't prisoners. And, though they didn't like it, they all agreed, and even thanked Kaspian for his hospitality, offering to help where they could with the clean-up. Kaspian accepted their help on the condition they didn't use magic.

Luna and I had been allowed to return to our old chambers. She had resumed her glamoured appearance and attempted to fix mine, but my magic refused to be bound by another again, parts of my true self breaking through every attempt. In the end, she'd given up.

Kaspian kept his distance, remaining busy dealing with the surviving Harensarra soldiers, and negotiating with their king for some semblance of peace. The other humans avoided me, as well. Cole, in particular, and I couldn't blame them. There was no hiding what I was when the glamour wouldn't sit in place.

But today, a summons had arrived from Kaspian, asking me to meet him in his chambers. My stomach had been in knots ever since the note arrived, and it took every ounce of willpower not to run in the opposite direction as I dragged my feet towards his door. I raised my fist to knock but paused, hearing voices inside.

'You can't be serious about this! She's a witch! She lied to all of us!' Cole was saying.

'She had no idea what she was,' Kas sounded exhausted, as though they had gone over this before.

'You don't know that! This could all still be part of their plan!' Cole protested.

'They had us at their mercy, Cole. It wouldn't make sense to banish Agnes if Blaise were in on it. Plus, I could see it in her eyes that she had no idea.'

'Eyes you don't even recognise. She is a threat. A monster!' Cole's voice grew more frantic.

'That's enough, Cole! She is no threat to me.' Kas's voice carried an air of authority I had never heard him use before.

'That's not how the people will see it. She *is* a witch. And, even if she wasn't one, she was raised by them. Trained to infiltrate this palace and pick us off one by one. You expect your people to overlook that?' Cole's anger burned through the door. 'Your mother built her whole reign on her hatred of them. Hatred *you* shared!'

'I expect the people to trust my judgment as their king. As I am expecting you to do, too.' Kaspian's words were clipped. He didn't enjoy pulling rank on his oldest friend. 'That hatred was taught. It can be unlearned.'

I imagined Cole recoiling at the notion. 'I can't just forget what I saw! She set the whole place on fire! She turned a witch to nothing but a mound of flesh! And that's *without* training!'

'That wasn't a request, Cole!' The words left no room for argument. 'You are to respect my decision, or leave!'

Cole hesitated, words dripping with venom when he finally answered. 'Yes, *Your Grace.*'

He wrenched open the door, startling as he saw me. Barging past me, he left me stood in the doorway, staring dumbfounded at a wary-looking Kas, who sat at his desk, head slumped in his hands.

I glanced around his office, this being the first time I had ever stepped inside Kaspian's private quarters. It was bare, and nothing like the lavish quarters his mother had resided in. Yet, despite the lack of eccentric furniture or trinkets, the space oozed Kaspian. From the worn desk he sat at, which was strewn with paperwork, to the bookcases spread along the walls, littered with books on strategies and training drills. Above the desk, hung the framed piece of glass Cole had told me about, and the reminder of the story brought a small smile to my lips.

'I suppose you heard all that?' Kaspian let his hands fall away from his face, finally looking at me, eyes betraying the full level of his exhaustion.

'Most of it,' I muttered, ignoring my urge to go to him.

'Mm.' Kas grunted. 'Not how I wanted you to hear it.'

'When was the last time you slept?' I asked.

His eyes crinkled in a half smile. 'That's the only question you have?'

'It seems like the most important one.' I took a hesitant step towards him. When he didn't balk, I took another. 'You've been avoiding me,' I stated.

He sighed. 'I know, and I am sorry. I needed some time to think. To process everything I saw that day. To grieve.'

I winced, wishing I could have been a comfort to him in his grief, instead of another form of turmoil. 'I'm sorry,' I offered, not knowing what else to say.

He shook his head. 'I know.'

Silence hung between us.

'What did you decide?' I finally asked.

'Well, you just heard it, didn't you.'

'That's ridiculous!'

'What is?' he asked, startled by my outburst.

'You can't still be choosing me, Kas!' It hurt to acknowledge what he had said, and it hurt more to acknowledge its preposterousness. Even in my wildest dreams about what would happen next, I hadn't even considered being with him as an option. Being allowed to leave with our lives, and find Agnes before she did any more damage, had been the best outcome I had dared hope for.

'Why not? Or have I been a fool, and it really was all a lie? You really do feel nothing for me?' His eyes were a stormy ocean.

'Of course it wasn't a lie!' I took another step towards him, and he rose from his chair.

'Then how am I being ridiculous?' he asked, moving around the desk to stand in front of me. My eyes dipped to the stark white scar at his throat that stood out against his tan skin, and I forced the power that lurked within my blood, down, down, down.

'Because you can't possibly still have feelings for me!' The rage I felt, at seeing the reminder of how close I had come to losing him, made its way into my voice.

He looked dumbfounded. 'Why can't I?'

I laughed without humour. 'Kas, you can't be serious! I'm a witch!'

'That changes nothing.'

'It changes *everything*!'

'Only if we let it!' He took another step towards me, until our noses touched, and our breath mingled. 'I *wanted* to hate you! Wanted to want to banish you, to force you out of my life. I spent the first day after everything happened trying to convince myself that I *did* hate you! But, as time went on, I could barely stand being apart from you. I missed your humour, and the way you challenge me. You make me a better person! It wasn't your hair or your eyes that I fell for, it was your heart! That hasn't changed, I assume. And now you're in front of me, it feels like I can breathe normally again.' He took a deep breath, emphasising his point, and his eyes were crazed as they met mine.

'You've hunted my kind,' I pointed out. His face filled with remorse, but before he could say anything, I added, 'And yet, I couldn't hate you either. Believe me, I tried.'

His eyes crinkled with slight amusement before shuttering against emotions I couldn't decipher. 'I'll spend my life making up for my part to play in what I have done to your people, if you would let me.'

'The people won't allow it, Kas.' Not his. And not mine

'Ah, you see, there's a little benefit in being king, and that's that they have to do what I say,' he smirked.

'You're not that kind of king,' I shook my head.

'I will be anything I have to be if it means I get to have you.' The words fell thick between us.

'Don't make me hope for this, Kas. It's not possible.' I dipped my head, scared to look at him, but he held my chin up, forcing me to meet his eyes, the touch of his fingers like an electric shock through my body.

He didn't recoil from my silver eyes or acknowledge the golden hair he didn't know. He just slowly pressed his lips to mine, and I squeezed my eyes shut against the exquisite taste of him. He groaned against me as I gave in and kissed him back.

After a moment, he pulled away, a little breathless. 'There is no one in this kingdom, on this *continent*, that can tell me it is wrong to be with you when it feels this good. If the people cannot trust me to choose a wife, then they cannot trust me to be their king. It's me, and my queen. Or nothing.'

My heart damn-near exploded out of my chest. Cole had been right, I *was* a stranger, not only to them, but to myself. I didn't recognise my eyes, my hair, my hands. None of it felt like me. But my heart . . . *that* felt human. Because only human hearts could *feel* this much. And Kas saw me for my heart, damning the rest of it. It was all I needed. Yet I still couldn't believe it.

The way he had looked at me on the battlefield. The things I had done to put us there. How could he ever forgive me?

'Gods, Kas. You don't know how many times I've dreamed of you saying this. I never thought it was possible.' A tear slipped down my face and he pressed a kiss to the cheek where it landed.

'If it's wrong to love you, I don't ever want to be right, Blaise Sunseeker.' I stilled at the words, but Kaspian's entire face lit up with a smile, the one with the dimple. 'I love you, Blaise. Choose this. Choose me. Choose *us*. Because I'll never stop choosing you.'

Another tear slipped free, even as I giggled. 'I love you too, Kas. I'll always choose you.'

Chapter 51

THE FUNERAL WAS AS GRAND and extravagant as anyone would expect a queen's funeral to be. Four pale-white stallions pulled a glass carriage containing a golden casket through the streets of Broozh, and the people threw white roses at it as it went by, a tear in their eyes for their fallen queen.

'Hypocrites. They bloody hated her!' Luna hissed in my ear.

I shushed her by stepping hard on her foot. Though she may have been right, thousands came to show their respects to the monarch, as the carriage made its way through the streets towards the palace. There, her body would be buried in the royal cemetery, laid to rest next to the husband that she loved. *My father*. Of all the things we had discussed in the days since Kas had told me he loved me, the matter of who my father was had not been one of them.

I wasn't sure whether it was he or I that wasn't ready for that conversation, or the acknowledgement that, strictly speaking, I had more claim to Reili's throne than him. I didn't want it without him, anyway. We would speak about it in time. We had a life ahead of us now, and I couldn't help but marvel at that prospect. I would spend my life with Kaspian. He had chosen me, in spite of everything.

He was yet to tell his people of his decision. He planned to do so after his coronation in a few days' time. That way, it would be more difficult for anyone to contest his choice. His ruling as king would be final. There would need to be a lot more scheming required to obstruct him, which was something I had no doubt they would attempt, but we would cross that bridge when the time came. Together. Winged creatures dove in circles in my stomach.

'Come on, we should head back to the palace. Kas will want to see you when it's over,' Daisy Hearthorn tugged on my hand.

After the battle, Cole had found Daisy still locked in the room I had left her in, sword gripped so tightly it had cut into her palms. I had been so relieved she was okay – less so relieved that Aleera, who was discovered in a pile of her own vomit, was also unharmed – that, without thinking how she might perceive me, I had run to her room and pulled her into a tight embrace.

She had hugged me back and, when we'd broken apart, she'd looked up at me through wet lashes and said, 'you really *are* a witch? You best use that power to summon some snacks, I want to hear everything!' I had laughed through my sobs. I could only hope that the rest of Reili's people would welcome me so, though it seemed more likely they would react as Cole had.

The topic of Cole was strictly forbidden from conversation with Luna, who growled each time anyone mentioned his name, and spent any time she was required to be in a room with him giving him a death stare. He ignored her entirely, as he did me. But I had seen the way he fought to protect her, even after she had revealed her true self, and the way he had wrapped a protective arm around her to pull her out of harm's way. I had to hope he would come around eventually.

I let Daisy tug me through the crowd back toward the palace. I couldn't be by Kas's side while he laid his mother to rest, not whilst my glamour still wouldn't take hold and the grounds would be full of nobles, but I would be there for him when he needed to get away from it all.

'She would have loved that,' Kas sighed, as we took a private stroll around the gardens – many areas still damaged from my magic's eruption. 'Everyone talking about how much they loved her, and what a good queen she was. It was all lies, of course. Those people don't care about anyone but themselves, but she would have loved it all the same.' He spoke of the lords and ladies who were present at the final burial. 'I can't wait until they're all gone.'

'Kas!' I lightly smacked his shoulder, and he smiled. I would never get used to it, him smiling at me like that, despite knowing what I was.

'I wish you could have been there,' he sighed once more.

'I know. If only the damn glamour would hold.' I let out a frustrated groan.

'I wouldn't want you there as anyone but you,' his expression turned serious. 'After the coronation, when I announce you as my queen, I don't want you to feel you have to hide behind a glamour.'

I stared at him. 'You make the others wear a glamour.'

'Only for their own safety. After we join as one, they won't need to. They will be protected under my rule. *Our* rule.'

'How are you so okay with this?' I asked, bewildered.

'You have my heart,' he said, as if that answered everything.

'And you mine, but if it turned out you were a goblin with three heads, I'm not sure I would handle it as well as you.'

He laughed, and the sound sung to every part of me. 'There are going to be people who try and tear us apart. I'm not fool enough to deny that.'

Destroy, destroy, destroy.

My magic hummed through my body at the mention of a threat to us, but I pushed it down, down, down, locking that dark power away like I had done so many times in the past week.

'But if we can forgive each other for our evils, I have to believe that our peoples can too.' Kas added, running a hand through his rich brown curls.

'I thank the Mother every single day for you,' I told him.

'Well, thank her from me, too,' he winked, and flashed my favourite smile, the one with the dimple, before pressing a kiss to my

forehead. 'Now come, I have a coronation speech to prepare, and I need your opinion.' I groaned and he swatted me playfully.
I could do this forever.
With any luck, I would get to.

Chapter 52

CORONATION DAY ARRIVED, AND MY stomach flipped uncomfortably as Daisy helped me into a gown, and pushed me into a chair so she could control the nest I called my hair.

'May I?' I glanced up as Sapphire appeared, and Daisy nodded pleasantly, excusing herself. Sapphire's long fingers ran through my hair, human glamour gone now we were alone. Her nails scraped my skin, but not in an unpleasant way. Oh, how I had missed this! Sitting still while her deft fingers twisted my hair this way and that. My hair had changed, *I* had changed, but this somehow felt the same.

'I'm proud of you, for showing your mother mercy.' Her words were unexpected, and I sat even stiller, pushing that dark magic further down inside me. 'She would not have shown you the same compassion, and that is why I am here, being forced to wear the skin of my enemy, under their rule, instead of with her.'

I frowned, and she caught the expression in the mirror, letting out a small, breathy, laugh. 'My dear girl, the forest calls. I miss my home, but I stay for you. For the world I know you're going to build. I followed Agnes into battle many times, and I thought I would follow her until the end of my days. But I realised that, what I would *not* do, was follow her to the end of the world. Which is what she would accomplish if she got her way. Your way will bring peace,' she pinned the finished braid atop my head in a crown made from hair.

Once she was done, she placed a gentle kiss on the top of my head and left, leaving me to stare at my reflection. It was hard not to see Agnes staring back at me. My silver eyes were exactly her shade, my hair hers too. But Agnes had never once looked so lost as I did. For all her faults, I had always admired her confidence.

It was hard to align my memories of Agnes with the truth of who she really was. My mind warred between wanting to be comforted by the mother I had loved my whole life, and wanting to run far away from the witch who sought so much power she would turn sister on sister and wage a war with innocents.

I looked away from the reflection I still didn't recognise, and stood. With deep breaths, I made my way towards the throne room to watch Kaspian take the first step in the rest of our lives.

'People are staring!' I hissed at Luna.

She shrugged, a wicked glint in her glamoured green eyes. 'You look sublime. Of course they're staring.'

I rolled my eyes. 'Oh yeah! It's got *nothing* to do with the fact that I'm a witch! None whatsoever.'

'Count yourself lucky you don't have to hide,' she chastised. 'My glamour is starting to itch.'

'Are they supposed to do that?'

It was her turn to roll her eyes. 'You're ridiculous.'

'You said it!'

'Will you two be quiet,' Gaia shushed, as ceremonial music began to bounce around the packed throne room. My stomach took a nervous dive, and I craned my head to try and get the first glimpse of the about-to-be king.

I saw Cole first, dressed in his royal-blue guard's uniform, a sword strapped to his side, the handle polished so fiercely his face reflected in it. He walked with his chin high, a smile barely contained. He was proud of his friend. Despite everything currently unravelling between them, he couldn't be happier that Kaspian would be crowned.

Luna made a gagging sound as she caught sight of him. I stamped on her foot as he looked in our direction, and his smile fell away to be replaced with a frown, eyes showing more fear than anger.

'Would you *stop* doing that!' Luna spat through clenched teeth.

'*Shhhh!*' Gaia hissed.

More guards piled through the doors, though, even Luna would have to admit, not one of them was as handsome or well-presented as Cole. Then, *he* entered through the large oak doors, and the entire room seemed to fall away.

Kas looked more regal than I had ever seen him. His hair, usually ruffled with boyish charm, had been combed away from his face, with just one or two waves escaping the carefully styled quiff to fall across his forehead. His midnight-blue eyes were made ever brighter by the deep azure shirt he wore, and the collar stretched towards his chiselled chin that had been shaved for the occasion. Over his shoulders draped a royal-blue cloak lined with stained gold fur. But the most endearing thing of all, was the grimace on his face. Like he would do anything to be anywhere else right now.

I put my fingers to my lips to stifle a giggle, just as his eyes found mine in the crowd. His grimace was immediately replaced with my favourite smile, and I heard several women swoon. I could have rolled my eyes, but I didn't want to look away from his for even one second. He held my gaze until he passed, and a shiver rolled all the way down my spine as I turned to watch him ascend the steps to the dais.

A man, who represented the Gods, stood atop the podium, dressed in all-white robes, holy book in hand. Kas greeted him with a smile, and the man dipped his head ever so slightly in response, before reciting passages in a holy tongue. Cole's sharp gaze was trained on us, as though concerned the holy words spoken would make us burst into flames.

'Oh, please,' Luna whispered, having had the same thought. 'We believe in the same Gods as you do.' She wasn't wrong. We all believed in the Gods, the witches believing that they created the Mother. But humans preferred to believe that she was Hell's offering, or simply that she didn't exist at all. Luna glared at Cole until he looked back to his friend, a hint of shame in his eyes.

The man recited passage after passage, words I didn't care to recall, and I watched Kas take a deep breath, preparing for what was coming. His gaze found mine again.

'Do you swear to protect this realm, and all those who reside within it?' the holy speaker asked Kaspian, his old voice shaky.

Kas swallowed and answered, never once taking his eyes off me, 'I swear it.'

'Do you swear to always choose that which betters the kingdom of Reili and keeps it from harm?'

My palms began to sweat as Kaspian answered, 'I swear it.'

'Will you vow to honour your forebearers, and the name of Bordeaux?'

Kas hesitated, considering the question, before answering, 'I swear it.'

The whole room held its breath, or maybe it was just me. But then, the holy man dipped his head again, and a royal-blue velvet cushion was brought forward. A simple golden crown, no jewels, no fuss, sat upon it. It had been designed especially for Kaspian, and Mother above did it suit him! The priest's old hands shakily lifted the crown from the pillow as Kas knelt before him and the room exhaled as one.

'Declare your vows,' he ordered.

Kaspian cleared his throat, 'I, Kaspian Warwick-Bordeaux, vow to defend, honour and reinvent Reili, from this day until my last.'

The world stilled as he spoke the names – one of the woman who birthed him, and the other of her who raised him – and promised that Reili would never be the same. After a beat in which my heart hammered violently, the holy speaker placed the crown gently on Kas's head, and his voice carried across the throne room.

'Long live the king.'

A chorus of cheers swept through the room as Kas stood, chin held high as he looked out upon his subjects, and I joined in as the crowd echoed the chant until our throats were dry.

Chapter 53

KAS PRESSED HIS LIPS TO my temple and whispered into my hair. 'You look radiant.'

I couldn't stop the blush that crept into my cheeks. 'Your Majesty,' I dipped into a curtsy, letting my backside press against him and savouring the gentle hiss that parted his lips.

'Call me that again, and my first ruling as king will be to have you locked in the dungeons.' His tone was playful as he hauled me back to my full height by my arm.

I turned to face him as he looked out across the sea of dancers. Lords, ladies, and common folk alike had been invited to celebrate the coronation, making the room more packed than ever, and allowing me to hide in the shadows. Not from him – he had found me anyway – but from the whispers of *'witch'* that followed me everywhere I went. The whole of the kingdom knew who I was, and they didn't understand why their king had invited me rather than burn me at the stake.

'But it's who you are now,' I told him as I watched him watching his people. 'I do not mock you with it. It suits you.'

'You only *know* how to mock,' he grinned, eyes drawn back to me. 'To you I am just Kaspian.'

'Your Kaspian,' I curtsied again, and he smiled my favourite smile, shaking his head at the reminder.

'I can't wait a second longer. Come.' He pulled my hand and, for a heart-stopping moment, I thought he would take me to bed. Instead, he pulled me atop the dais in front of his people, which was infinitely more terrifying.

The music came to an abrupt halt and the dancers stopped, looking for the source of the interruption. Some glared – namely Aleera Cresthorn – when they saw the king's hand holding mine. Others watched with curiosity. I found friendly faces in the crowd.

Daisy, who was beaming up at me. Luna, who watched the room with an expression that said she would fight for me if she had to. My sisters watched in matching gowns from the side of the room. Ophelia, with her face scrunched in concentration, as she tried to keep the hundreds of thoughts that were barraging her from ruining her evening. And Marbella, who smirked, not needing to read minds to know what was about to happen. Sapphire and Gaia, who were near the exit, should things go sideways. And Cole, who had one hand on his sword, moving slowly towards Luna, looking like he would fight *for* her, not against her. I looked to each of them, over and over, until Kas started speaking and my eyes lifted to his.

'My mother was a great woman, a strong woman, and I mourn her passing. But her prejudice has cost us all something,' he started, squeezing my hand. 'I am not blameless. I blindly followed her hatred into dark places,' he continued. 'But today, I swore a vow that I would reinvent Reili, and I will start by righting my wrongs, and following my heart. I have chosen to marry, as my mother wished. And, if she chooses to accept, I will take Blaise Sunseeker as my bride, and she will rule beside me as your queen.' His azure eyes slid to mine, and they held so much feeling in them that I felt pinned under their weight.

A moment of silence followed, where it was just me and Kas and no one else in the world, and then the pin dropped. The bubble burst, and the cries sounded out.

'But she's a witch!'

'Witch lover!'

'Burn the demon!'

'The king's gone mad!'

I squeezed my eyes shut, but a gentle hand cupped my face and forced me to meet his gaze. 'Look at me, not them,' he whispered. 'I choose you. I choose us. And I will keep choosing you for as long as I breathe. Be my queen?' he asked, a crooked smile on his face, crown already a little lopsided to match, and not a slither of doubt in his stormy eyes.

'Only if you call me Your Blaise,' I giggled, the sound at odds with the tears running down my face. Kas laughed, and I would never tire of the sound, or the way he pressed a soft kiss to my lips.

The crowd roared angrily.

'Silence!' Kas commanded, loud enough to carry to the back of the room, and stern enough that they obeyed. 'This kingdom has been held back by its fear for too long! The hate in our hearts has caused endless pain. To these glorious beings, and our own kind! We will join our peoples, and we will watch this nation thrive with possibilities. With opportunities for *all* beings!'

I couldn't take my eyes off him, and my heart squeezed painfully. In that moment, he had become a king. One who would uphold his vows in his own way, giving his people the opportunity to become more than what they were now. In that instant, it didn't matter that there were people who would fight to tear us apart. That, out there somewhere, Agnes was recovering and regaining strength, and would most likely return hell-bent on not just revenge but obliteration. It didn't matter that I had a dark power I didn't understand lurking beneath the surface, or that I didn't know how to use my magic at all. It didn't matter that the war with Harensarra was far from over.

All that mattered was here.

Right now.

The way his ocean gaze held mine, his dimple appearing in a way that made my knees weak.

He was my king. And I, his queen. And nothing in this world would tear me from him.

Chapter 54

Agnes

THE IRON WOODS SANG ITS usual symphony of noises but, in amongst it, was a cacophony of screaming.

My screaming.

Screams of rage.

The ache of betrayal I felt deep in my gut, fuelling my ragged cries of anguish.

'Your Majesty,' Hazel approached my destroyed tent, my belongings littering the forest floor in the aftermath of my outburst.

'Do not call me that!' I snapped.

I had failed.

There was no crown upon my head and, worst of all, my most precious belongings had been taken from me. All three of my daughters had turned on me. How had I not seen this coming? How had I not better leashed them?

I thought I'd given Blaise enough hatred in her heart to shut out the wiles of men. The boy had been attractive, I'd give her that, but worth a kingdom? Worth selling her family down the river? And the other two . . . it must have been the cursed blood of their human father that had turned them all soft.

It's your fault, my mind screamed.

I knew how poisonous these creatures could be, and I'd sent her anyway. Of course, I didn't know how powerful she would become. She'd been glamoured since she was a foetus, with dark magic. Magic that had drained me. When she'd erupted with all that fire, she'd taken a part of my power down with her. It was the only reason her untrained attempts, and her sisters' feeble powers, had bested me.

And that other power.

I shuddered.

The likes of it hadn't been seen for centuries. I knew. I'd researched it. Hunted it down. Stained my soul black trying to attain it – all to kill that bitch queen! In the end, a blade had done the job just as well.

But that magic had emerged again. In Blaise. The soft-hearted, human-loving, failed experiment. The Mother was cruel in her humour.

'Agnes,' Hazel said instead, and I snapped my gaze to hers. She was no Gaia, no Sapphire, but at least she hadn't deserted me. *As if they are any better than me.* Blaise would soon find out the extent of their own evils.

'What is it?'

'She is awoken.' Her black eyes glittered like onyx.

My lips curled back in a laugh, my own eyes twinkling with tormented humour. I swept over the floor, looking for a book of dark magic; tossed to the floor in my rage.

There.

I flipped quickly through the pages until I found the incantation. 'Quickly,' I ordered. 'Take me to her.'

———— ✦ ————

'You've seen better days,' I said coolly as I approached my prisoner. Chained to a tree, she looked so small and pathetic.

Her head snapped up, long white hair hanging limply over her face. Her black eyes were nearly lifeless, skin pallid and bruised. I gripped her chin in between my fingers, being sure to make it hurt. This wouldn't do. She needed her strength if she were to be of any use to me.

'What do you want, Agnes?' she asked, voice raspy.

No, this wouldn't do at all.

'I want what belongs to me.'

She laughed, the sound like nails on a chalkboard. If I'd had hackles, they'd have raised. 'I'll never help you get that bloody crown, Agnes!'

'Ah, you see, that's where you're wrong,' I sneered. 'You will, if you want to see your daughter again, Esmeray.'

Her eyes bulged. 'Luna . . . Luna's alive?'

'For now.' I revelled in the pain that twisted her features, the single tear that raced down the Moonkeeper's face.

'W-What do you want from me?' she stammered.

'Oh, not much really.' I released her face and picked some invisible lint from my blood red cloak. 'Just your power, and a sprinkle of revenge.'

She flinched and tried to recoil backwards, but the tree stood firm, not giving her an inch. 'Now, be a good girl and sit still. This *will* hurt.' I flicked a dagger from my pocket and drove it into her heart, before twisting it and turning it on myself right through my own chest. 'Read the spell, Hazel!' I commanded.

Hazel took the book I had handed her and began to chant.

Yes. Yes!

I could feel the magic working.

My heart was slowing, stopping, breaking. . . gone.

Esmeray screamed and rattled against her chains as her power of the moon began to fuse with my sun-kissed magic – and Mother above it burned! I writhed against it, shutting my eyes, letting the Moonkeeper's screams ground me. As Hazel's incantations came to an abrupt halt, the wound over my chest began to knit shut and, as Esmeray whimpered, I knew hers had healed too.

When I opened my eyes, Hazel was cowering on the floor, and Esmeray looked even paler; skin almost glassy as she panted for air.

But my body – my *power* – it was glowing like on my Rite Day. My heart was gone. No longer was I weighted by its uselessness. No longer burdened by its *feelings*. With it gone, my magic had been reborn. I had harnessed the power of another's for my own. I closed my eyes and pictured my daughter's true face, so like my own.

'Prepare the coven,' I ordered a quivering Hazel. 'Let us remind my sweet daughter who her mother is.'

ACKNOWLEDGEMENTS

Well, here we are. The acknowledgements. There was a point I never thought I would get here. The False Queen has been a real labour of love and I'm so happy it's out in the world, for you to (hopefully) enjoy. And it wouldn't have been possible without everyone I'm about to mention and many more who I won't.

Char and Mollie-Eve, you each read countless drafts of this book, and your enthusiasm and support of me never wavered. I can't thank you enough for the belief, the laughs, and the friendship you have given me over the years. I love you both more than you'll ever know.

Paige and Emma, my girl gang. I wouldn't be the person I am without the laughter and the complete lack of judgement you have always so kindly granted me.

My editor, and cover designer, Lauren at Wonderporium Ink. Your talent knows no bounds. Truly. Working with you has been nothing but a delight and this story is infinitely better for you having laid your caring hands on it. I shall treasure your Taylor Swift references throughout this manuscript forever and always.

My family and in laws, for always offering support, cooking me countless meals and listening to me rant about things you don't understand. I sincerely hope you skipped chapter 42 as asked, otherwise, maybe let's not speak for a while.

Sphere and Ri, your unconditional love and support is something I will never take for granted. I'll cherish you always.

Hayley and April, I simply wouldn't have been able to work full time and publish this book if it weren't for both of you being an endless source of light and laughter during the workday. Thank you for always being shoulders to cry on, listening to me bang on about characters you hadn't met yet, and always helping me come up with new marketing ideas for this book. I'm secretly dreading doing this again, knowing I'm not going to be working with you two.

Loki, Nox & Eddie, the best furry friends a girl could ask for. Your purrs and boops have gotten me through so much.

To anyone that shared a post on bookstagram, left a review, read an arc or helped support this little indie author in any way, a million times thank you.

And for my husband, who has supported this dream of mine in more ways than one. I don't know what I did to deserve a man like you, but I'd do it a thousand times over. Thank you for not letting me give up, and for giving me the time and space to write, even when there was a house to run! I love you more than I could ever write down.

Finally, to you, the reader. If you've made it this far, you've made this author's dreams come true. A million times thank you.

ABOUT THE AUTHOR

Meg Humble is a marketeer by day, writer by night. If you can't find her hunkered down in front of her laptop writing, you'll find her cosied up under a blanket reading, or cat-trapped by one of her beloved floofs.

Website: www.meghumbleauthor.co.uk
Email: meg@meghumbleauthor.co.uk
Instagram: @meghumble.author

To be the first to know about upcoming releases, sign up to Meg's newsletter here: https://meghumbleauthor.co.uk/#newsletter

THANK YOU FOR READING!

If you enjoyed this book, please support the author by leaving a review and spreading the word about The False Queen.

WANT MORE IN THE CURSED QUEEN SERIES?

Blaise & Kaspian will return in the next Cursed Queen novel in 2025.

Printed in Great Britain
by Amazon